Dangerous Waters

Dangerous Waters

Book 1
Sisters in Blood

by

CM Michaels

Dangerous Waters: Sisters in Blood (book 1)

Copyright © 2013 by CM Michaels

ISBN: 978-1-942212-69-0

All rights reserved. No part of this book may be reproduced or transmitted in any form without written permission from the publisher, except by a reviewer who may quote brief passages for review purposes.

This book is a work of fiction and any resemblance to any person, living or dead, any place, events or occurrences, is purely coincidental. The characters and story lines are created from the author's imagination or are used fictitiously.

Warning:

This book may contain graphic sexual material and/or profanity and is not meant to be read by any person under the age of 18.

Hydra Publications
Goshen, Kentucky 40026
www.hydrapublications.com

Printed in The United States of America

Acknowledgements

As the first book in the *Sisters in Blood* series, *Dangerous Waters* is only the beginning of the adventures that await Brooke, her coven and her multiple love interests. But bringing this novel to fruition has been a journey of its own. First and foremost, thank you to my loving wife, Teresa, who after three years of my almost constant nagging probably hears me cry out "editor" in her sleep. Your creative ideas helped take the story in entirely new directions. To my four-legged daughter, Sophie, you brighten my days and make it impossible not to smile.

Thank you to my beta readers: Jenn, Craig, Kevin, Christy, Brit and Claudia. Your constructive feedback on those initial rough drafts was invaluable. And let's not forget the talented cast who posed for the cover and brought scenes from the book to life in the trailer: Jocelyn Elyssa, Zachera Wollenberg, Chris Coy, Samantha Roman, Britney Brown, Danielle Mcpherson, Katie Robison, Maryrose Jakeway, Blair Pitcairn, Hunter Lee Eagle, Jenn Campbell and Sara Anne Ostrowski. You will always be part of the *Dangerous Waters* family.

A huge hug and thank you goes out to Leslie Karen Lutz, my incredibly talented and patient editor. You didn't shy away from asking for major revisions where needed, and the book is much better for it. I owe the largest debt of all to Marci and the rest of the Freya's Bower staff. Thank you for believing in my novel, and for making my dream of becoming a published author a reality.

Mom and Dad, thank you for raising such a tight knit family and always encouraging me to try new things. Your belief that your kids could accomplish anything they set their minds to was contagious. I wouldn't trade my childhood for anything.

Prologue

The ornately carved golden doors of the global court swung open, and the raucous crowd settled into their seats. Soldiers outfitted in full battle gear streamed in, marching down the long marble aisle to the raised gallery that formed a half circle behind the five vampire containment chairs. They each carried a debilitating knockout stick and a shoulder-fired laser rifle. The electromagnetic waves generated by the RF frequency systems in their helmets shielded their thoughts and ensured that not even the strongest of their enemy could hijack their minds.

Once they were positioned, the bailiff typed a code into the touch pad on the wall, and a steel panel slid open. Four hooded figures emerged, surrounded by several more guards who forcefully escorted them to their chairs. Their shackled ankles and wrists were smeared with conductive jelly and attached to electrical leads. As soon as they were seated, thick metal bands extended around their shins, thighs, chests, biceps and forearms, firmly securing them in place.

None of the prisoners made a sound, knowing that even a whimper would be met with another punishing jolt of current from the collars fastened around their necks, but that did little to lessen the deafening noise in the room. Every seat of the three-story grand hall was occupied for this momentous event, with another 750,000 people crammed into Central Park outside. Reporters from around the globe scrambled to get their last pretrial clips recorded before the court was called to order.

"Some are questioning the tactics of the global court this morning," an Austrian reporter stated in her native German, "using vampires and humans as bait in an effort to lure what most people consider to be the Vampire Queen out of hiding. So far their plan doesn't seem to have worked, as there have been no sensor reports of vampire activity in or around New York, but with the executions moving forward today, things are expected to intensify."

"All rise!" the bailiff bellowed out through the hall. "This court is now in session. The honorable global court inquisitor O'Callaghan presiding."

An imposing figure with short, golden locks entered from behind the bailiff, motioning for people to take their seats. He gathered his floor-length white and purple robes in his left hand, made his way over to the furthest prisoner and yanked the hood from her head.

"So this is the all-powerful Sienna," the inquisitor mocked, squeezing the bound woman's cheeks with his hand.

"How disappointing."

Her once beautiful face was disfigured by several charred-black electrical burns. Blood and pus oozed out of the open wounds. The pungent salve packed into her broken nose made her eyes tear up and prevented her from smelling anything.

"Do you have anything you wish to say in your defense before I render my verdict?" the inquisitor asked, deactivating the device around her throat so she could speak.

"This will never work– she knows her life is far more important than mine."

"It's possible she'd let you die," he acknowledged. "But both of her parents, her mate and her best friend? No, I think that's far too much to expect her to endure. Sooner or later she'll come, and the world will celebrate her execution."

Sienna snapped to attention, her green eyes widening in horror at the news of who else had been captured.

"You have no idea what you've done– everyone in this building's going to die."

The crowd erupted at her outburst, and the inquisitor held up his hand to silence them. "And how exactly is your precious queen going to manage that? She'll be welcomed to our fair city by twenty thousand volts from the first alarm she trips. Not enough to kill your kind, but plenty to leave her unconscious until– "

"Sir, a perimeter alarm's been triggered just outside the north gate," a soldier interrupted from the gallery.

He wheeled on the man in a fit of anger. "Interrupt me again, and I'll disembowel you! People have been jumping the fence all day– contact the guards at the gate and have them check it out."

"We tried sir. Calls have been placed to the guard desk, the three closest perimeter sweep teams and the north tactical unit– they're not responding."

"Who's not responding, you imbecile!"

"Any of them."

"It's too late," Sienna said, gazing at his panic-stricken face. "She's here."

"Clear the courtroom and take the prisoners back into custody!" he commanded.

Dangerous Waters

Before anyone could move, a massive explosion rocked the third-floor balcony, raining debris and body parts down on the crowd below. The auditorium filled with a choking white smoke. The crowd flooded for the exits, which were soon hopelessly jammed. They started to push and trample each other in a desperate attempt to escape.

The lone set of stairs to the balcony was located outside the courtroom, so the soldiers had no choice but to yield the high ground to their unseen enemy. Several of them panicked and fired blindly into the smoke, only adding to the chaos. The commanding officer who'd been talking with the inquisitor raised his rifle– his body no longer under his control– and sent a chest high laser beam though the entire gallery, cutting several of his fellow soldiers in half. The ones who survived were turned to dust by an energy burst that blew out the entire back of the building.

Moments later, a woman dressed in skin-tight black leather swooped down onto the marble floor, drawing two broadswords from the sheaths on her back. Her vengeful glare bore into the inquisitor, who took three running steps and dove for a knockout stick that had come to rest a few feet in front of him. His body was suspended mid leap. The inquisitor glanced down in total disbelief at the marble tile he was now hovering over before being catapulted sideways into the solid steel outer wall of the holding cells.

The vampire advanced but had to break off her attack when a laser tore through the floor inches in front of her black leather boots. In a move too fast to be seen, she coiled and launched herself across the courtroom, landing amongst the small group of soldiers who had fought their way through the crowd. A bright red mist filled the air as she executed her elegant dance of death, moving with the grace and agility of a jungle cat.

By the time she returned to the inquisitor, he'd managed to pull his body up into a sitting position and was taking short, labored breaths. She raised his chin with the tip of her blood-covered blade, wanting him to see who was delivering him to hell.

He let out something between a choking sound and a chuckle, spitting blood from his mouth. "Releasing the locks requires an order from me, and the code can only be entered remotely by central command. They're all going to burn."

"Don't flatter yourself– there's nothing I need from you." She fixed her gaze on the restraints binding Sienna to the chair. Within seconds they started to rattle, shaking more and more violently until they broke free and dropped to the floor.

His lower lip trembled in fear. "Wh– what are you?"

"The last thing your wife and three kids are ever going to see." She flicked her wrist, and his severed head fell into his lap.

Fire was rapidly engulfing the courtroom, and waves of torrid heat washed over her face. She scanned the hall in search of any additional threats. Most of the remaining people had succumbed to the noxious gas that was making her gag. Those who were left were sprawled out on the floor, clinging to the last threads of life. Assured that they weren't in any imminent danger, she sheathed her weapons and turned toward Sienna.

"Hi, Mom."

"I told you not to come."

She laughed, wiping some of the blood from her face. "You can ground me when we get home. Can you walk?"

Sienna took a tentative step forward before gripping her side and doubling over in pain. "Not far. Your father's in worse shape, though. Brooke, his heart –"

"I know– I can hear it." Brooke reached behind her back, pulled a sports bottle out of the top of her pants and tossed it to Sienna. "You'll need your strength."

"Thanks." Using both hands, she reset the bones in her nose, and then popped the top, poured about a quarter of the bottle over her face and chugged down the rest. Within a few seconds the wounds healed over. They both jumped when one of the rafters crashed to the floor behind them. "I think that's our cue. Let's get out of here."

Brooke concentrated on her father's restraints. As soon as they broke free, his hunched-over body pitched forward into Sienna's waiting arms, and she eased him onto his back. "Hang in there, David," she whispered, removing his hood. "We'll get you to a hospital soon."

The whirling noise from dozens of approaching helicopters sent them scrambling to free the others. Countless soldiers– an entire brigade at least– charged into the mouth of the blown-out opening just as the last of the restraints fell.

"My God," Sienna gasped. "There's too many, sweetheart, even for you."

"I'm what they want," Brooke said with a resigned nod. "Take my father and head north. Stick to the rooftops until you get outside the city so you don't trip any alarms."

Dangerous Waters

Sienna was appalled. "We're not leaving you here to die."

"No fucking way!" Her quirky, endlessly compassionate soul mate grabbed her by the shoulders, glaring at her. "You're my wife– I'm not going anywhere without you."

Stepping forward to flank her mate, her goddess of a best friend– still looking runway ready in spite of her ordeal– flashed a warm but determined smile. "Neither am I. Like it or not, we're in this together."

Tears pricked the corners of her eyes. Part of her wanted to say yes, to have them all fight together to the end, but she knew how selfish that was. Three vampires with too weak of a trance ability to penetrate the RF jamming would be all but useless against an army this size, and if she fled with them, any chance they had of escaping vanished. She'd resisted the stupid "Queen" title from the moment it'd been forced upon her– the first and only order she'd ever given her family was that they never bow to her– but invoking that authority was the only way she'd get them to leave. Using her telekinetic ability, Brooke pushed them away, knocking her mate to the floor.

"As your queen I command it! Move!"

They all shot her stunned looks laced with an edge of betrayal. Without another word, Sienna hoisted David into her arms and disappeared into what remained of the third floor balcony, the other two vampires close behind.

The exchange had cost her precious seconds she could have used to move to a far more defensible position. As it was, she was now surrounded, with the only gap coming from the roaring wall of flames at her back. All of the soldiers had their knockout sticks in hand. Apparently they were intent on taking her alive. Brooke arched her hands out in front of her, and a glimmering light began to radiate between them. Once it had fully materialized, she thrust her arms forward, hurling a ball of plasma into the advancing troops that obliterated the entire first wave. The hundreds behind them closed in, driving her back toward the flames. There was no escape. She defiantly drew her swords before the first blow from a knockout stick sent her tumbling to her knees. The second incapacitated her completely.

When she came to, she was in the cargo hold of a Blackhawk helicopter, and a soldier was fitting a voice restraint collar around her neck. Her boots had been removed, and her wrists and ankles were bound together with the latest alloy composite, stronger than even she could break with sheer force alone.

"Sir? We've got her," the commanding officer called over his satellite phone. He listened for a few moments, and then handed the phone back to his first lieutenant. "Bring me the laser shears."

"Yes, colonel." The first lieutenant relayed the order and soon had them in his hand. "Here you go, sir."

"Prop her up."

Two soldiers stepped forward and raised Brooke into a sitting position. The colonel flipped on the shears, took hold of her chin and shaved off all of her milk chocolate-colored hair.

"This cap is packed with lorazepam," he said, sliding a black swim cap onto her now bald head. "It's a potent tranquilizer that's absorbed through your skin. In a couple minutes you won't be able to remember your name, let alone trance anyone."

He started to walk away, and then stopped and turned back toward her. "And this is a gift from me, for killing over three hundred of my men." The colonel removed the guard from the shears and stuck the tip of his combat knife into the beam, heating it to a molten red. The other soldiers moved aside as he bent down over her and burned a large V deep into her forehead. Brooke screamed in agony, and five thousand volts fired into her throat. Her eyes rolled back in her head, and her jaw fell slack.

Chapter One
A New Beginning

There should be a support group for people who are thinking about making a monumental change in their lives, some kind of twelve-step program for the logically impaired. *My name is Emily Waters, and I'm an idiot. Catchy.*

My mind began to race as I merged onto 93-North, heading toward Boston University– my home for the next four years. Reminding myself that I'd begged, pleaded and all but sold my soul for this *opportunity* since the end of my junior year made me want to slam my forehead into the steering wheel. It had taken a sustained and creative campaign to convert my father from the no-way-in-hell camp to the begrudgingly supportive agreement we had now. The thought of me living in such a big city so far from home still terrified him. Even broken up over two days, the nine hundred-mile trek from Traverse City, Michigan, wasn't one I wanted to repeat anytime soon, and there wouldn't be a flight home until at least Thanksgiving.

It was almost midnight by the time I slipped my Camry into a vacant orange permit spot, over five blocks from my dorm. Not that I had any right to complain. As one of the only non-commuting freshman to have a car– most middle-class parents would never think about shelling out $1,200 a year for an overnight permit when there were far less expensive alternatives– I considered myself beyond lucky. Picturing my dad's ashen face when our orientation tour guide mentioned the BU shuttle, zip car and rideshare programs made me snort. She might as well have suggested I become a pole dancer or star in porn. He filled out the parking application on the spot.

I threw the door open, and a pleasant fall breeze swept in, rousing me from my dreary-eyed stupor. After climbing out, I stretched my arms up above my head, let out a big yawn and gazed back into my Camry. Except for the tiny cubby hole I'd somehow squeezed myself into, every inch was packed– there was no way I was lugging all this stuff up to my room tonight. I had serious doubts that it would still be here in the morning, but I didn't care. Several hours of unconsciousness would give me the escape I needed from the remorse and fear that had been overwhelming me all day.

Shelton Hall resembled a typical mid- to low-end apartment building, far more concerned with function than style. It had eight stories and a sandy-brown brick exterior accented with white trim. My seventh-floor room overlooked the Charles River and was setup with two bedrooms connected to a central living room and bathroom.

When I opened the door, a tall, athletic girl hopped up off the couch and came over to greet me. Her dirty-blonde hair was still wet and pulled up into a clip.

"Hi, you must be Emily. I'm Angela."

"Hey Angela, nice to meet you. Are you the only one here?"

She grinned. "I think the rest of them are in bed already– it's kinda late."

"Yeah, it's a longer drive than I thought."

"Um, we're in the room on the right," she said, nodding her head in that direction. "Our roommates are Wendy and Stacey."

"Have you met them yet?" My eyes focused on her oversized Linkin Park t-shirt. At least she had good taste in music.

"I met Stacey earlier today– she's really nice. I haven't seen Wendy." Angela rubbed her eyes with the palm of her hand. "Well, I'm off to bed. Nice to meet you."

"You too."

It only took a couple minutes for me to unpack my tote bag into the little bit of space that was left in the cramped bathroom– the only bathroom. If my new roommates spent half as long getting ready in the morning as I did, I'd be waiting for hours. A new wave of panic set in as I finished brushing my teeth, washed my face and headed for my room. Angela was already in bed, so I eased the door closed and flopped down on my bare mattress, kicking myself for not bringing my pillow up from the car.

"I've got an extra pillow if you need one," she offered, apparently having noticed that I hadn't carried one up with me during our brief introduction.

"Thanks." I felt it land on my face a half-second later. Pretty impressive aim in the dark. As soon as I laid my head down, I was asleep.

* * * *

I'd heard Angela get up at some ungodly hour, grumbling something about practice. She was back now, and I knew I had to get going. My late arrival on Sunday meant that I only had today to get settled in. I rolled out of bed and ventured out into the main room.

Dangerous Waters

"Morning Emily." Angela was plopped on the couch holding a tall glass of orange juice and a plate of Pop-Tarts in her lap.

I tried to cover my coveting of her pastries with an exaggerated stretch. "Hey Angela, how long have you been up?"

"Since five," she said, licking the sticky blueberry filling from her fingertips. "We have volleyball practice at six for the next two weeks. Sorry if I woke you."

"Oh…no, that's okay. I just can't picture getting up that early. Thanks for letting me borrow your pillow."

The door to the bedroom across from ours was open, but there was no sign of Stacey or Wendy. Still half asleep, I lumbered off toward the bathroom, not realizing until just before I reached for the handle that it was occupied. The door swung open and a petite girl draped in a towel stepped out, almost running into me.

"Oh!" She stumbled backward and braced herself on the vanity. Once she recovered, her face came alight with an eager smile. "Hi Emily. I'm Stacey!"

"Hey Stacey. Sorry for scaring you."

She waved my apology away like I was being silly and wrapped an arm around my side, surprising me with a rather tight hug. "Don't worry about it, roomie."

Stacey was a tiny little thing, but her charismatic personality and curvy, toned body ensured she would never be lost in a crowd. Even in a towel and with no makeup, she was beautiful. She looked like she could be doing a Neutrogena ad.

I wondered what she was thinking as she glanced over my body. I was about five feet five, skinny but still fairly athletic, with long legs for my height. My hazel eyes and somewhat pronounced cheek bones gave me a bit of an exotic look, which is a good thing given my depressingly lifeless, chocolate-brown hair. If it wasn't for my recently added blonde highlights, I'd have spent the next four years with my hair tucked under a Tigers hat.

After a long, soothing shower, I threw on my clothes from the night before, gave my dad a quick call to let him know I made it okay and went to bring up the first of many loads from my car.

"Where are you headed?" Angela asked.

I extended my lower lip and blew out a puff of air in an exaggerated sigh. "I've got a lot of unpacking to do."

She sat her juice down and jumped to her feet. "Let me give you a hand."

"Thanks." I wouldn't have been comfortable asking for her help yet, but I wasn't about to turn her down.

"Give me a minute and I'll be down to help too," Stacey chimed in, ducking into her bedroom to get dressed.

"Take your time… We'll be at this a while," I groaned.

What I thought would be an all-day task ended up only taking a few minutes. There were parking spaces right in front of the dorm for unloading, and by the end of our second trip, several guys had joined in the effort. They all knew Stacey, of course. I don't think half of them had any idea whose stuff they were carrying. Not that they would care as long as it was Stacey doing the asking. When we finished, I thanked everyone and went to work unpacking the mountain of crap that now filled most of our bedroom.

The sun had almost set when I heard a faint knock on my half-shut door. Stacey peeked her head through the doorway.

"Hey, we're going to get something to eat and thought you could use a break. You must be hungry."

Actually I was starving, as evidenced by my Pop-Tart drooling earlier. The last meal I had was somewhere near Buffalo. "Um, yeah. That sounds good. Where are we going?"

"A little Italian place not far from here. You'll love it!"

When we left the dorm, Stacey motioned toward a small silver car parked in the unloading zone, one I recognized instantly– a Prius. I was really beginning to like this girl. "I'll drive. Hop in."

The restaurant was on the bottom floor of an old brick apartment building that was mostly vacant. It had oversized glass windows all along the front and one side and "Antonio's" scrolled across the black canopy covering the doorway. The place was empty except for a family of four near the back. The waitress sat us at a table with a prime view of the Grampy's Best Buy gas station across the street and brought out some homemade bread.

I had just taken a huge bite when Angela spoke. "So, where are you from, Emily?"

"A small town in northern Michigan called Traverse City," I muttered, covering my mouth. "How about you?"

"San Jose– and you thought you were far from home!" she joked.

"How did you end up here?" I asked, surprised that a California girl would come so far north.

"I got a volleyball scholarship, and they have a great business school. I'm a management information systems major."

"Ahh. How about you Stacey?"

"Born and raised," she said with a smirk. "I grew up a few blocks from here. I'm not sure what I want to go into yet, something in medicine. What are you studying?"

"Conservation biology and global warming." I paused and gazed out the window at her car. "Nice Prius, by the way." Her face beamed.

My mind wandered when Stacey and Angela started talking about a party they were going to later tonight. Stacey was definitely right about the restaurant – the food was amazing. It probably helped that I was starving, but I was pretty sure this was the best chicken parmesan I'd ever had. There's no way I would have ever found this place, in spite of it being less than five miles from our dorm, as it would have required far more exploration of the streets of Boston than I felt comfortable with. Up until now I'd been planning on a steady diet of campus cafeteria food. Maybe BU wouldn't be so bad after all.

I suddenly noticed that Stacey was waving her hand in front of me. "Earth to Emily," she said in a robot voice.

"Sorry. Guess I kinda spaced out. What did I miss?"

Angela giggled and thonked me on the nose with her breadstick. "We wanted to know if you would come to our party tonight."

I tried to slap it away on her second attempt but she was too quick, so I settled for wiping my face. "Sure. Where is it?"

"It's kind of campus wide," Stacey explained, looking on in disgust as Angela bit off the end of the breadstick she'd hit me with and swallowed it. "People go from one room to the other. It won't really get going until ten-thirty or eleven."

"Count me in." My inner geek cried out that I should be in bed by then– especially since I had an early class in the morning– but after eighteen years of always being the good little girl, it was time to let myself live a little.

Stacey raised her arms over her head. "Yay!"

* * * *

As soon as we returned to the dorm, I got back to work. With great relief, and after what felt like an eternity, I pulled open the bottom drawer of my dresser, stuffed my pile of jeans into it and tossed the last of my bags into the bottom of the closet.

When I heard music in the living room, I spun around and glanced at the clock– it was already past 9:00. Even though I was sure they knew what I'd been up to, I didn't want Angela and Stacey to think I was hiding in here, so after taking a quick peek in the mirror, I hurried out to join them.

Stacey was dancing around the room arranging snacks on the coffee table and both end tables. Two guys who'd helped me unpack earlier walked in carrying oversized duffel bags, dropping them on the floor with obvious relief before sprawling out on our couch. Angela unzipped the one closest to her, tossed aside some clothes and pulled out two bags of ice. I could see a case of Bud light and some liquor bottles in the bottom. No wonder they were straining.

"Emily! You're alive!" Stacey held her hands over her heart as if she'd been truly worried about me.

I laughed. "Sorry I've been such a hermit today. It's almost party time!"

"You know it! EVERYONE is going to be here!"

I didn't doubt that, given who was throwing our party. I peered down at the faded out jeans and gray and pink Yellowstone National Park t-shirt I was wearing– not exactly high fashion, but good enough for a college dorm party. Or at least that's what I thought until I took in what Stacey had on. Her black, long sleeve, square neck dress was accented with red pumps and a gorgeous jeweled chain belt. My eyes darted to Angela, hoping that Ms. Fashion Queen was just strutting her stuff, only to find her decked out in a red, cowl neck, X-back dress and red stiletto heels. *What kind of party is this?*

Feeling more than a little self-conscious, I pictured the dresses I'd brought with me. There was nothing that came close to what they were wearing. Who was I kidding? I didn't *own* anything that resembled what they had on.

Stacey picked up on my apprehension and hurried over to comfort me. "What's wrong?"

"You and Angela are dressed so– formal," I whispered, not wanting anyone else to overhear. "I don't have anything like that."

Her eyes lit up like Christmas morning as she eagerly took hold of my hands and dragged me off behind her. "Come with me!"

When we reached her closet, Stacey began to rifle through her dresses while I took off my clothes. She pulled one out and turned toward me, holding it up against my chest. It was navy blue, sleeveless, with white trim across the top and a bow in the small of the back. The material felt like silk. After helping me step into it, she reached around my waist and zipped up the back. Since I was a good three inches taller than she was, what was meant to be an above-the-knee dress only came down to about the middle of my thighs. I took a seat on the end of her bed and waited while she fumbled through the pile of shoes in her closet.

"What size are you?" she hollered.

"Six or seven, depending on the shoes."

"Perfect!" She presented me with a pair of blue three-inch heels that had a really cute decorative strap around the ankle. When I fumbled trying to get the tiny pins through the microscopic holes, she bent down and affixed the straps herself, and then motioned to the chair by her dresser. "Have a seat, Ms. Waters."

I could certainly apply my own makeup, but Stacey seemed to be having a good time, so I did as instructed and closed my eyes. After a couple minutes she paused to admire her work, made one last touch up to my eyeliner and stepped aside so I could see the full length mirror behind her.

"Wow!" I gasped, taken aback by my reflection. Realizing how conceited that sounded, I tried to continue. "I mean you did– "

"No, wow is right," she interrupted. "Guys are going to be crawling over each other to get to you."

"What kind of party is this exactly?"

Stacey tilted her head and arched her brows. "What do you mean?"

I motioned to what we were wearing. "Isn't this a bit much for a dorm party?"

She let out a good natured laugh as she went to work with her curling iron, twisting my long, layered bangs before setting them so they were transformed into playful ringlets. "Well, this isn't just any dorm party. It's also kind of an informal pledge drive for the sororities on campus. The actual recruitment isn't until January, but making a good impression during the fall party makes it a thousand times easier to get in. I'm planning to pledge with Alpha Phi. My mom and older sister are Alpha Phi, so it's kind of a family tradition. Even if you don't want to pledge, it's still a great party though. It gets bigger every year."

"Thanks for doing this. I owe you big time." I turned back and forth, admiring myself in the mirror.

She gave me a quick hug. "Let's go have some fun!"

Our living room was already filling up with people. All of the women were dressed very elegantly, and even most of the guys were wearing suits or tuxes. The breakfast nook had been transformed into a makeshift bar. Two guys were standing behind it, mixing drinks and grabbing beers from the ice-filled sink. I recognized one of them from this morning and made my way over to him.

"Mike, right?" I shouted over the music.

"Emily? Wow! You look– hot!"

I could feel my cheeks blushing. "Thanks."

"Can I get you something to drink?" he said, doing his best to maintain eye contact after his rather lengthy initial assessment.

Dorm party or not, I couldn't stand the taste of beer. Even the smell of it made me want to vomit. "Do you have anything fruity?"

He flashed me a crooked, conspiring smile. "How about a strawberry margarita?"

At best I'd hoped they might have a couple wine coolers tucked away. All I'd seen them serve so far were straight shots, rum and Coke, and screwdrivers. "Is that really an option?"

Mike grabbed a pitcher from underneath the counter and poured me a tall glass. "We keep the good stuff hidden away for friends. Enjoy the party!"

"You too," I said, giving his forearm an appreciate squeeze as I took the glass.

After stepping away from the bar, I sipped my drink and glanced around the room. Stacey was talking with three girls who were arranged in a semicircle facing her– no doubt from one of the sororities. They were all laughing and appeared to be as taken by her as I was. Angela was dancing with one of the guys who had helped her carry the ice bags and alcohol for the party. He'd changed into a stylish white tux with a cummerbund that matched her dress, and looked very handsome, even if he was a little stocky for my taste. Not that it would matter if he was my type. Judging by how well they moved together, they'd been dating for quite some time.

I felt someone brush up against my shoulder and turned to find a tall, rugged guy smiling at me. His wavy hair was tossed about in that intentionally unkempt style, his face covered by at least a week's worth of stubble. He was comparatively underdressed, wearing an untucked button down shirt and khaki pants, but it was a look he wore well. His captivating, deep blue eyes seemed to draw me into them. I was breathless.

"How's it going? I'm Tyler," he said in a sexy-as-hell southern accent.

My heart raced faster. "Hey Tyler. I'm Emily."

He took my hand and held me at arm's length. "You're lookin' fine woman. Damn!"

"Thank you." His eyes lingered on my chest longer than I would have liked, but at least he was into me.

"Would you like to dance?"

"Sure." I sat my drink down on the coffee table and bounced to the music while we made our way toward the center of the room. I'd always loved to dance, especially to up tempo techno music like this. DJ Wag's "The Day the Earth Caught Fire" thundered through the crowd.

Tyler placed his hands on my hips and swung his body in perfect rhythm with mine. His moves were somewhat unorthodox, but his impeccable timing more than made up for it. When Darude's "Sandstorm" began to play, I reached my arms up over my head and let myself loose. He pulled me closer, locking his wrists behind my back, and I felt his muscles press against my sides. The song transitioned again, and I spotted Angela dancing nearby. I leaned away and turned toward her, expecting Tyler to release me, but he yanked me back hard against his chest instead.

"Not so tight, Tyler," I kept my voice firm but calm.

He grinned and started to grind his body into me.

"Stop it! I don't like that!"

I thought he was easing up when he took his hands off my back, until he slid them into my hair and pushed my head forward, smashing his lips into mine. My knee shot up into his groin with all of my strength, and he grunted and crumpled to the floor.

The whole room dissolved into a hazy, surreal fog. I don't know how long I'd been standing there shaking before I noticed that Angela was talking to me. "Emily? Emily? Are you okay?"

I couldn't answer. When I burst into tears she grabbed my hand, pulled me into our room and slammed the door. I collapsed on my mattress and buried my head under my pillow to drown out my crying.

"I can't believe he did that to you. What an asshole!"

"I let things go too far," I mumbled between sobs. "I shouldn't have encouraged him."

"Bullshit. You didn't do anything wrong. He deserved what you did and a lot more– some of which I'd bet he's getting right now from Doug and Mike. They're *escorting* him out."

After a quick knock Stacey opened the door and ducked into our room. Without any hesitation, she climbed onto my bed and took me in her arms. "I'm so sorry. Are you okay?"

As I hugged Stacey, I remembered how important this party was to her, how much time she and Angela had spent setting it up. Now they were both in here with me. I took a deep breath, sat up and wiped my eyes. "I'm not going to ruin your party."

"This isn't your fault. You're not ruining anything," Stacey said, sweeping the hair back from my face.

"Okay. *He* won't ruin your party," I clarified. "Look, nothing really happened. So he forced me to kiss him– it's not like he hurt me." I tried to keep my voice flat to convince them, but I could tell they weren't buying it, so I stood up and took a step toward the door.

Stacey reached out to stop me. "Emme, at least let me clean you up first."

I couldn't help but smile at the sound of a familiar nickname. "What'd you call me?"

"Um, Emme. Is that okay?"

I snorted. "Sure. It was my nickname all through high school."

"While we're on nicknames, my friends call me Angie," Angela chimed in.

"Hey Angie!" Stacey and I yelled together. We all giggled.

By the time we rejoined the party, people were back dancing again, and the room was even more crowded than before. Doug greeted Angela like they'd been apart for hours, twirling her around in the air and planting a kiss on her lips. She let out a playful shriek, gripped his lapel and held him close, lengthening the embrace. It didn't look like he was any worse for wear.

Mike seemed fine as well and was back behind the bar. When I walked by, he hollered my name, holding up another margarita.

"Thanks, Mike," I said, taking the glass from him.

"You gotta tell me where that came from." Seeing my confused expression, he continued. "Tyler's a big guy, and you put him down hard. Where'd you learn to do that?"

"Oh that. My dad made me take a self-defense class in order to come here."

"Ahh." He made a couple karate moves with his arms, mocking me. I punched his shoulder before we both started to laugh.

"So what happened to him after I left?" I wondered.

"Doug and I picked him up and dragged him into the courtyard. When we let him go, he took a swing at Doug– bad move. He was still lying on the ground when I left."

Mike glanced at the bar, where there were a ton of people waiting for drinks. "Duty calls, ugh."

I wanted to ask him to dance, but all I managed to get out before he left was a sheepish little giggle. After mouthing some obscenities to myself, I sucked down half my drink and walked into the living room.

There was a girl standing by herself in the far corner with an unnaturally large space around her, given how crowded the room was. Intrigued, I nudged my way past several people to get a better view. She was wearing a powder blue lace dress that came down well past her knees and clung to her slender, curvy body. I tried not to be too conspicuous, taking another sip and pretending to dance, but when I peeked in her direction again, she was smiling at me. I froze for a moment, and then awkwardly smiled back and walked up to her.

"Hi. I'm Emily!" I sang out, anxious to make up for the staring.

"What a pretty name to go with such a pretty face." She regarded me with comforting brown eyes as she took my chin between her thumb and forefinger. "My name is Raven."

I was curious about her unusual name, but decided not to comment since she'd just complimented mine. "Nice to meet you. I love your dress."

"Thanks– it's one of my favorites." She motioned down my body with her hand. "Is that new?"

"It's my roommate's. She gave me kind of a mercy makeover so I'd fit in."

Raven's more defined facial features gave her the look of an upperclassman, maybe a junior. Long tresses of golden, natural blonde hair draped alluringly across her cheeks. As I stood next to her, I detected a scent that I couldn't place. I was sure I'd never smelled anything like it before. It was kind of pleasant, but overpoweringly so, like someone had bathed in a very weak perfume.

"Would you like to get some air?"

How did she know that? Did I make a face at the smell? Shit. First I stare at her, and then I act like an obnoxious five-year-old. Raven just smiled and motioned toward the door. She didn't seem offended, at least not that I could tell. "That sounds good."

We worked our way through the crowd and went down the steps into the courtyard. It was a cool night, and the slight breeze blowing across my cheeks felt very refreshing.

Raven swept the wayward hair from her eyes and placed her hand on my shoulder. "So Emily, what are you studying?"

"Conservation biology and global warming. The environment is really important to me."

"Out to save the world are ya," she teased, keeping step with me as we headed along Bay State road toward campus. "Actually, that's a very interesting field. The earth has changed a lot in the last few decades."

"How about you?" I asked.

"Cell biology, molecular biology and genetics, with an emphasis on research. The human body fascinates me."

Watching her effortlessly glide across the pavement in spite of her formfitting dress and stiletto heels was mesmerizing. I'd already stumbled twice on the weathered sidewalk. "That sounds cool. Where are you from?"

"Quebec originally. I've lived all over since then. Based on your accent I'd guess you're from somewhere in the upper Midwest. Am I close?"

"Very. I'm from northern Michigan." As I turned my head to grin at her my right heel caught in a particularly nasty crack, sending me careening forward. My hands shot out to break my fall, only to find a moment later that I was safely back on my feet.

Raven made sure I was steady before she released me. "Careful. This sidewalk is a deathtrap."

We couldn't have been walking closer together, but it was still amazing that she'd had time to catch me given how suddenly I'd tripped. And in that dress no less. The girl moved like a ninja.

"Um, thanks. That could have been kinda ugly."

"You were well on your way to at least an eight. The Russian judge would have screwed you, of course." She playfully nudged my shoulder as we both laughed. "How did you end up at Boston University?"

"A combination of things really. I was impressed with their conservation biology program and the school, but that's only part of it. I felt like I needed to get out on my own, far enough away so that I couldn't just run home whenever I needed something."

I let out a deep sigh and continued. "My mom died in a car accident when I was five, so my dad and I pretty much did everything together growing up. He's always been there for me, and I've tried to make life as easy as I can for him. I got almost straight A's in school, I've never had a serious boyfriend, I've never been drunk, never smoked or cut class, never really got into any trouble. Not that I came here to get into trouble– it's just that I feel like I don't really know who I am. Geesh, I bet you're sorry you asked. Get a couple drinks in me and I can't shut up."

"Living on your own for the first time teaches everyone a lot about themselves. I'm sorry about your mom. Losing her at such a young age must have been hard on both of you."

Dangerous Waters

I nodded, and we continued to stroll along in a somewhat somber but comfortable silence. When we reached Deerfield Street, we rounded the corner and walked the short distance to Storrow Drive, passing by the condo-style office building adjacent to our dorm. You could just catch a glimpse of the ink-black river through the thick row of maple trees that lined the bank on the far side of the divided highway.

"I know we just met, but could I make a rather personal observation?" Raven asked, turning to read my face.

"Ah… Sure, I guess."

"I was impressed with how you handled yourself at the party tonight. Not just that you defended yourself, which was very brave, but that you recovered so quickly emotionally. Most girls would still be in their beds crying if that had happened to them."

"You wouldn't say that if you had seen me when I was in my bedroom," I said, trying to deflect the undeserved compliment.

"Yes, I would," she countered. "You were in your room for less than fifteen minutes after a guy twice your size forced himself on you, making you physically fight him off. Very impressive." She paused for a long moment, as if debating what she wanted to say. "Emily– "

"Emme," I interrupted, reflexively taking her hand like we'd been friends for years. I immediately tried to let go– horrified that I'd crossed all kinds of personal space boundaries– but she held my hand firm. How could I feel so comfortable with her already? Even earlier at the party, it hadn't bothered me at all when she'd held my chin in a strangely intimate and old-fashioned gesture.

She let out a little laugh. "Emme, I don't usually go to parties, since large crowds tend to make me uncomfortable. Most people pick up on that somehow and avoid me. But when you saw that I was alone, you introduced yourself and made me feel welcome. That was very sweet. I'd be honored to have you as a friend."

"Thanks. I'm so glad I met you tonight."

Raven gave my hand an affectionate squeeze. "Me too. Well, I'd better get home– I have physics at eight-thirty tomorrow."

My eyebrows shot up in surprise. "You do? With Mr. Lautner?"

"Yeah, I think so."

I couldn't contain my overjoyed smile. Having a class together meant we'd get to hang out at least twice a week. "Sweet! I'll see ya in the morning then!"

Raven had parked in a small lot further down Deerfield Street, so when we reached the corner of Bay State Road, we exchanged a quick hug and said goodbye. I spent the rest of the walk back to Shelton Hall reflecting. There's no doubt Tyler's assault would stick with me a while, but Raven and I had bonded instantly, and my roommates were super cool. Mike and Doug would likely become good friends as well. I'd even managed to venture into the city without getting myself killed, as shocked as that would make my father. After five months of almost constant worry, my new life in Boston was off to a promising start.

Chapter Two
School Daze

I scrambled into an open seat moments before Mr. Lautner began to go over the syllabus that his assistant was still passing out. I was a mess— same t-shirt and jeans as yesterday. By the time I'd gotten back from my walk with Raven, our dorm room had been abandoned. I assumed the party had just migrated to another location, since I'd only been gone thirty minutes. All I wanted to do was take some aspirin and go to bed, but when I turned the handle on my bedroom door, it didn't budge. Inside I heard the unmistakable sounds that told me Doug and Angie were having a more intimate party of their own. After everything they'd done for me earlier, letting them have some time together seemed like the least I could do.

So here I was— no pen, no paper and no physics book. Not exactly how I planned to start my first college class.

I took a copy of the syllabus from the stack being passed down my row. Mid-term ten percent, final exam thirty percent, attendance ten percent, project twenty percent, quizzes ten percent— pretty typical. Having had physics my senior year in high school, I was sure this was going to be the easiest of my four classes.

Mr. Lautner was in his mid- to late forties and heavyset, something he was obviously self-conscious about. Every couple of steps he would slide his khakis back up, grab the bottom of his navy blue sweater-vest and pull it down over his pants. I tried not to stare, but the repetitive motion kept pulling my eyes right back to his gut. As if that wasn't annoying enough, he spoke much louder than was necessary for the small room, which wasn't helping my headache. I didn't see Raven anywhere, but it was difficult to get a good look without being too conspicuous. Hopefully today's class would be a short one since it was the first day.

The thought had barely left my mind when Mr. Lautner said, "Have chapters one through three read for Thursday. Have a good day."

I bolted for the door.

As I exited Brown hall, I heard a familiar voice. "Emme!" Raven hollered, waving her hand in the air.

I half bounded up to her. "Hi Raven. Sorry I couldn't find you in there."

"You didn't overlook me. I had some things to take care of. Did I miss anything?"

"Not really, he just went over the syllabus. I grabbed an extra copy for you on the way out."

"Thanks." She quickly glanced over my body, the corners of her mouth rising up in a cute little smile. "You're traveling light this morning."

"Yeah, I kinda had to improvise. I slept in Stacey's room last night since my room was– occupied."

"Your roommate and her boyfriend?"

"Yep, Angela and Doug," I added, realizing she never met them. We walked over to a nearby bench and took a seat.

Raven lifted her oversized purse into her lap and started digging through it. "I was hoping I would catch you. What are you doing tomorrow?"

"Not much– just catching up on some homework. I don't have any classes or anything."

"Wonderful" She handed me a Boston whale adventures pamphlet. "How would you like to go whale watching with me?"

"Are you kidding! I've only wanted to do that since I was, like, seven! What time?"

"The cruise leaves at ten a.m., but we should get to Long Wharf by nine-fifteen at the latest. It's about thirty minutes from here, so I'll pick you up at eight-thirty if that's okay."

I was about to tell her that it was beyond okay– that I would be lucky if I could even sleep tonight– when I noticed the prices. *Shit.* The boarding ticket alone was more than I had on me, and it didn't include drinks or food. "Sorry Raven, but I'll have to save up for a while. Can we do it in a couple weeks?"

"It's my treat."

"Are you sure?" I said, my eyes studying hers. I hated feeling like a leech, but I couldn't make myself turn down her offer. To me, this was like back stage passes to a Ke$ha concert.

She patted the knee of my jeans. "Definitely. It's been a few years since I went. I'm looking forward to this as much as you are."

"I seriously doubt that!"

Raven laughed. "Okay, maybe not quite as much as you are. Don't forget your sunglasses and wear plenty of sunscreen– the glare off the water can be pretty intense."

Dangerous Waters

I was about to ask if she wanted to grab breakfast when she sprung to her feet. "Sorry to run off so quick, but I've got to move my car before it gets towed. See ya tomorrow, Emme."

"Thanks Raven," I called after her. She glanced back over her shoulder and waved as she galloped off toward the faculty parking lot.

* * * *

My expectations for the cafeteria food couldn't have been much lower, given the crudtastic selection offered up in high school, so when I walked in and saw people actually cooking on a grill, my jaw just about hit the floor. They were even using real eggs, rather than that liquid stuff from a carton that tastes like snot.

I stuffed myself with blueberry pancakes, fresh fruit and an oversized cinnamon roll, and then plodded half-way across campus to my advanced calculus class. Within minutes I was nodding off, causing me to miss the homework assignment and the attendance sheet, which apparently had been circulated during one of my naps. Getting up at 6:00 was hard enough for me on a good day. After an all-you-can-eat buffet and less than four hours sleep, I was dead on my feet.

When I got up to leave, the professor motioned me toward the front of the room and asked for my name. I was tempted to lie, but unless I was going to drop the class, she was bound to figure out who I was eventually. She jotted a note down on the attendance sheet then tore into me about how she would not tolerate such blatant disrespect in her classroom. It took ten minutes of assuring her it would never happen again before she finally dismissed me with a flick of her fingers. Being shooed away like a gnat was almost more than I could take, even if I did deserve it. I clamped my teeth down on my tongue and hurried out into the hall, knowing full well that if I let out so much as a peep, my next stop would be the Dean's office.

I spent almost the entire walk back to the dorm trying to come to terms with what happened. My teachers always liked me. Hell, they *loved* me. Even on those rare days when I committed some minor transgression, they hardly noticed. Not here. I wasn't even through my first day and I already had a professor who would volunteer to lead my public flogging if given the chance.

Anxious to get back on the right track, I crashed for a couple hours then checked the course description for my 6:00 p.m. English lit class, making double sure I'd bought all the right books. Hopefully we'd start off with *Macbeth*, since I'd read it several times and had even played Lady Macbeth during my brief and disastrous stint in drama club. After spending over three weeks rehearsing, I got to perform in front of an audience all of one time before being reassigned to the stage crew. The best my dad could manage was, "You got your lines right," which pretty much summed up my stellar performance to a T.

Out of all of my classes, this was the only one that wasn't within walking distance, so I hopped in my Camry and took off almost an hour early. Seeing that the tiny surface lot directly across the street from the annexes was full, I continued on to the six-level parking garage about a quarter mile down the street. Even after a mini-concert in my car, blasting Imagine Dragon's "Radioactive" and Fall Out Boy's "Light 'Em Up" so loud that the glass shook, I still walked in with twenty-five minutes to spare.

The hall had tiered seating like a theater with three aisles dissecting the massive room into thirds. The threadbare fabric on the seats suggested it'd been a while since the last refurbishing, as did the circa 1990 red carpeting. Since I had nothing else to do, I pulled out *Macbeth* and started to read. I'd just finished the second scene of the first act when Angie plopped down in the seat beside me.

"How now, my lord! Why do you keep alone, of sorriest fancies your companions making, using those thoughts which should indeed have died with them they think on? Things without all remedy should be without regard. What's done is done," she said, quoting the second scene of the third act perfectly.

"Out, damned spot! Out, I say!– One, two. Why, then, 'tis time to do 't. Hell is murky!– Fie, my lord, fie! A soldier, and afeard? What need we fear who knows it, when none can call our power to account?– Yet who would have thought the old man to have had so much blood in him," I countered. We both laughed.

"Spoken verbatim, but what does it mean?" A husky voice asked from behind us. We both wheeled around to see a thirty-something professor sprawled out on the steps. His flip-flop clad feet and long pony tail clashed with his sport coat and slacks, but somehow he pulled it off.

I confidently met his gaze. "Lady Macbeth's guilt is eating away at her. She's sleepwalking in the scene, mumbling jumbled thoughts about not being able to get the blood off her hands and not understanding Macbeth's reluctance to act. She's telling her husband that they don't need to be scared, since no one can prove that they killed the King."

"You'll need to learn to make your answers less literal, but you definitely grasp the material," he said, walking down the steps to join us. "What are your names?"

"I'm Emily Waters. This is my friend, Angela Stevens."

"Who delivered a spot-on quote of her own. Nice to meet both of you. I'm Dr. Wesley Clark." He reached out and shook our hands. "I have to admit, I'm impressed. And that doesn't happen very often. I'll be expecting great things from you two this semester."

He gave us a polite nod and then went to the blackboard and wrote his name. Having the bar set so high could seriously come back to bite us in the ass, but I'd take high expectations over threats of expulsion any day.

"Drama club?" Angie guessed.

I just nodded, hoping I wouldn't have to admit that memorizing my lines was the only part I'd been good at.

"What character?

"Lady Macbeth. How about you?"

"Ursula– it was kind of cool playing a witch."

I giggled. "I bet. You'd look good in a pointy hat."

She rolled her eyes at me. "Actually, I wore a hooded black cloak with a green glow-stick inside to light up my face. We all got three inch acrylic nails and painted them florescent green so they glowed in the dark. It was a kick-ass costume."

"Sounds a hell of a lot better than mine," I agreed. "My gown must have weighed ten pounds, and they made me wear a corset underneath."

"Like the old-fashioned kind that squished your guts?"

"Exactly– I could barely breathe in the stupid thing."

"Damn." She briefly glanced at my mid-section, as if I was still wearing it, before focusing her attention on my overstuffed backpack. "How are your classes going so far?"

Seeing me cringe, Angie burst into laughter. "That well, huh? What happened?"

"I kinda slept through calculus then got my ass chewed out by the professor afterwards. I'm seriously considering dropping it."

"Okay, not the best first impression," she conceded. "You don't need to do anything right away though– drop and add doesn't end for almost three weeks. If she's still being a bitch after some major brown-nosing on your part, you can always drop then."

"I really don't want to carry less than sixteen credits though. How would I catch up in another class if I wait that long?"

"My 12:30 political science course was, like, half empty. I'm sure you could get into it if you end up wanting to switch. We don't have any tests until midterms, and I'd have all the notes for you to copy."

Political science wouldn't be my first choice, but it would satisfy a general elective, and having another class with Angie would be cool. "Sounds like a plan. Thanks."

Dr. Clark glanced up at us and smiled before starting his lecture, diving right into a scene from the second act. His spirited performance quickly captured the attention of even the back row, I'm-only-here-because-the-rest-of-the-pre-req-classes-were-full crowd. I was really going to like this class.

Chapter Three
Thar She Blows!

"We're on the top deck," Raven said, motioning toward the stairway to my left.

A thick metal chain marked with a florescent yellow "reserved" sign was draped across the bottom, blocking my path.

Seeing me hesitate, Raven reached past me and unclasped the chain, ushering me in like a maître d'. "Waters, party of two."

"Seriously? What if we get caught? I really don't want to miss this."

"Never been caught yet," she said with a wry smile.

I stared at her for a few seconds, sure that she was joking. When she didn't crack I reluctantly started up the steps.

A leathery voice bellowed out from above. "Can't you read? This area is private!"

I froze in my tracks, as if standing still would somehow prevent the codgy, Captain Ahab old geezer from noticing me.

"Raven? Is that you? I'll be damned! Come up and give an old man a hug!"

I followed behind her as she sprung up the stairs and into his outstretched arms. "It's good to see you again, Cecil."

"What's it been? Two years?"

"Almost three," she said, giving him a couple heartfelt pats on the back before pulling away. "I hope it wasn't too much trouble getting the things I requested."

He let out a lighthearted chuckle. "Well, the message I got from Mason was 'Some chick called and asked for this crap,' but we got it taken care of. I swear there's something wrong with that kid."

Raven stepped aside and gestured toward me. "This is my friend Emily."

"Pleased to meet you," Cecil said, greeting me with a polite nod. His gray, unkempt goatee did little to soften his weathered face.

"Nice to meet you too." I couldn't keep from giggling when I read his "I'm out of chum, are there any Republicans onboard?" t-shirt. "Big tea party supporter, I see."

He snorted. "Yeah, me and Sarah are tight."

"Cecil, you know– " Raven began before being cut off.

"I know, I know. No campaigning on deck. I've actually gotten a lot better about it."

The frustrated look on her face told me she didn't believe that for a second, but I could also see a hint of a smile playing at her lips.

Raven and I toured the giant, three-deck catamaran and met the rest of the crew while the ship slowly made its way out past Deer Island Park and into Massachusetts Bay. When we returned to the private upper level, we settled into luxuriously padded chairs next to the rail.

"Please tell me you don't own your own cruise ship." I couldn't think of any other explanation for the crew taking orders from her– not to mention her admonishing the captain.

"It's my family's. We bought it a few years ago as an investment after going on one of the tours. And I wouldn't exactly call it a cruise ship– it only seats three hundred."

All I could do is shake my head. *Only* three hundred. "You could have told me. I must have looked like an idiot trying to sneak up the steps."

She cast me a wicked grin. "No… You didn't reach full idiot status until you pretended to be invisible."

I took a swing at her left shoulder, which was only about a foot from me, but she leaned out of the way before I could connect. "Bitch."

"And proud of it!" We both laughed.

It was early September and not even noon, but the temperature was already in the seventies. Taking the Banana Boat sunscreen out of my purse, I pushed my cargo Bermuda shorts further up my thighs and coated my legs and arms. After sliding the straps of my tank top down over my shoulders, I did my neck and chest, being careful not to get any on my necklace.

"That's cute. Where did you get it?" Raven asked, lifting my necklace up toward her. It had a thin silver chain and a pendant with two dolphins jumping.

"It was my mom's. My dad gave it to her for their first anniversary. They had dolphins swim with them while they were snorkeling in the Bahamas on their honeymoon. My mom was a research biologist, so that must have been like a dream for her. When she died my dad gave it to me– I've never taken it off since."

Raven lightly stroked my hair. "That's really sweet. I'm glad you have something special to remember her by."

"So am I." I could feel tears stinging at my eyes behind my sunglasses, and tried to blink them away.

We sat in silence, listening to the soothing hum of the engines and the crashing sound of the waves breaking against the hull while she continued to fidget with my windswept hair. "God, your hair is a mess."

"I wonder why? Couldn't have anything to do with driving all the way over here with the windows down."

"You've got a point. Don't you love how it feels though?"

Maybe if I was a golden retriever. Having all four windows all the way down when we were going seventy was definitely not my idea of fun– my hair had left whip marks across my cheeks. "I guess."

In an instant Raven was on her feet and pointing out over the water. "Over there! Off the port side…about sixteen-hundred meters!"

I leapt up and leaned my head over her shoulder, staring in the direction she was pointing, but all I could see were white-capped waves stretching out to the horizon.

"What you got, Raven?" Cecil asked, stepping out of the wheelhouse to take a look.

"I think it's Cardhu. No wait… It's Coral! He just submerged. Take us about forty degrees to port."

"I'm on it." Cecil flew back into the wheelhouse and began to change course.

"What is it? I can't see anything!"

Raven handed me a pair of high definition 7 X 50 marine binoculars. "Try these. Look just off to your left way out where that big wave just broke. Coral is a twenty-two-year-old male humpback whale. He got his name from the flukes on his tail that look like coral."

Almost as soon as I had adjusted the binoculars, Coral's spiky head broke the surface, sending air and water spewing out of his blow hole. "Oh my God! Look! He's huge!"

"About thirty-seven tons. I wish he was feeding so you could see him leap out of the water. Maybe he'll sing for us instead."

"How would we hear it? Do you have audio equipment?"

She laughed. "Wouldn't be much of a whale watching boat without it. Let me know if you hear anything."

I could feel Raven place headphones over my ears, but I was too excited to take my eyes off of Coral for even a second to thank her. After dipping just under the surface a couple more times, he arched his back, brought his tail completely out of the water and drove down into the depths. "I see what you mean about his tail. What causes the different coloring?"

"All those black lines you see are from killer whale teeth."

I was shocked. "Really?"

"Yep. Mostly when they are calves, although pods of killer whales have been known to kill adults occasionally."

By the time Coral surfaced, the boat was right alongside him. Instead of diving again, he sat almost motionless with his head under the water. I was just about to ask what was wrong when beautiful, high pitched cries filled my ears. "He's singing, Raven! You've gotta hear this!"

"Pretty incredible, isn't it?"

"It's friggin amazing! How long will he keep it up?"

"Anywhere from a couple minutes to half an hour. We record it all digitally, so I can make you a CD or load it on your iPod if you want."

"Definitely!" The rest of the world fell away as I watched, Coral's siren-like song enchanting me. The waves breaking against the hull bathed my face in a salty mist, almost as if I was swimming alongside him.

* * * *

We followed Coral for another hour before turning back toward the Stellwagon Bank National Marine Sanctuary, hoping to spot more humpbacks and a few other species. I was still peering through my binoculars when Raven tapped my shoulder. "How about some lunch?"

I turned to see a small table draped with a white table cloth. Two wrought iron chairs sat across from each other, but there was only one place setting. "You're not eating?"

She placed a hand over her belly and blew out a deep breath. "My stomach gets a little queasy with the waves. Dramamine helps, but it's still enough to kill my appetite."

"I can wait until we get to shore. I don't want to make you watch me eat."

Raven held my chair, seating me like we were at a fine restaurant rather than sitting atop the boat deck, and then glided around the table to ease into her own chair. She moved with the controlled grace of an accomplished dancer, making me even more curious about her. "It's okay– really. Besides, I want to see what you think of our specialties."

As bad as I felt stuffing my face while she sat there sipping a bottled water, the food was to die for– homemade clam chowder, fresh caught, lightly battered cod fillets, steamed shrimp and cheddar-baked biscuits. They even had diet Mt. Dew. When I couldn't take another bite, I pushed my plate away and leaned back in my chair.

She gave me an expectant look. "Well?"

"Are you kidding? That's only the best seafood I've ever had. I haven't eaten that much in my life. How do you make any money serving that to everyone?"

"When I said *our* specialties I meant Boston's," she explained with a smirk. "The fanciest thing on our menu is a double-cheeseburger."

"I can't believe you did all this just for me. You're awesome Raven. Thanks." With the exception of my dad and Brittney– my best friend since I was twelve – no one had ever gone to half this much trouble even for my birthday, including my grandparents. Maybe she was trying a little too hard, but was that really a bad thing? She was funny, easy to talk to, and was one of the most intriguing people I'd ever met. My dad always told me you could judge a lot about a person's character by seeing how they treat people that work for them. Even grumpy old Cecil adored her.

Raven raised her sunglasses up onto her forehead and flashed a quick smile, running the back of her fingers tenderly across my cheek. "There's no need to thank me, Emme. I haven't had this much fun in a long time."

* * * *

The rest of the afternoon flew by. While we didn't spot any more large whales, Minkes and white-sided Dolphins swam around us constantly, and I maxed out the memory card on my digital camera long before we started back. When we reached shore I stopped flipping through the images just long enough to climb into Raven's SUV. Even with my hair whipping across my face– apparently that conversation had fallen on deaf ears– I was so engrossed in what I was doing that I didn't even see the flashing lights behind us until we were pulling over.

"Shit. Shit. Shit," Raven grumbled, smacking her fist against the wheel to accentuate each word.

"What's wrong? Were we speeding?"

"You could say that– about thirty-five over." She paused and shook her head. "They're going to take my license away for sure this time. My mom will kill me."

I'd never done anything close to illegal, but there was no way I was letting today end like this. My heart leapt into overdrive as I took a quick glance behind us, making sure that the police officer was still in the car. "Switch with me."

"Emme, this is major. They could charg– "

"Come on, hurry up," I interrupted, already sliding behind her.

She had barely gotten into the passenger seat before the female officer was at my window. "License, registration and proof of insurance."

Raven retrieved the registration and insurance cards from the visor above my head but could only watch while I tried to fish my license out of my wallet.

Seeing how badly my hands were shaking, the officer finally just reached in and took it from me. "It's going to be okay, miss. Do you have any idea how fast you were going?"

"I'm– I'm sorry," I mumbled.

She studied my face for a moment, and then glanced down at my license. "I see you're from Michigan. What brings you to Boston?"

"Boston University. Student– I'm a student."

"This car is registered to a Stephanie Jennings. Is that you?" she asked, looking at Raven.

"No Ma'am," Raven replied, sliding her own ID out of her purse and handing it to her. "Stephanie is my cousin. She's living with us while she goes to school. We're sharing a car to cut down on costs."

"Why aren't you driving?"

"Emily and I went on a whale watching tour today. I had a couple of wine coolers on the boat, so I thought it would be best if she drove. I should have warned her that the speed limit dropped back there. I'm sorry."

She peered intently into my eyes. "Have you been drinking?"

"I'm um…only eighteen."

The corners of her mouth rose up in a reluctant grin. "That doesn't exactly stop everyone. You look sober enough though, and I don't smell anything on your breath. Sit tight– I'll be back in a minute."

I closed my eyes and took a couple deep breaths, trying to calm myself. "Jesus, I think I'm going to puke."

"You're doing great, Emme. You have no idea how much this means to me. I'll pay for whatever tickets you get, along with the increase in your insurance premiums."

Since my dad paid my insurance pulling that off would be quite the trick, but it wasn't like he was going to disown me for getting a speeding ticket. "That's what friends are for, right?"

She tucked a few stray locks behind my ear and gazed deep into my eyes, as if she were trying to evaluate my soul. "Friends that are worth having."

I'd just started to lean in for a hug when the officer returned. "Emily, since you're new in town and were not driving recklessly, I'm letting you off with a warning for your speeding. Not wearing your seat belt is another matter. I've seen too many teenagers scraped off these roads to let anyone slide on that."

She turned her attention to Raven. "It was very responsible of you to hand over your keys after consuming alcohol. I spoke with Stephanie and confirmed your arrangement with the car. She wasn't too pleased to find out that someone else had been driving it, but I'll let you two work that out. I'm citing you for not wearing your seatbelt as well. You're free to go. Please drive safely." She handed me two pink slips of paper along with our IDs then headed back to her cruiser.

Raven reached out and took them from me. "Two twenty-five dollar tickets and no points on your license. Sweet."

"So my insurance won't go up?"

"Nope– not unless you switch companies."

"Cool. So do we just hang out until she leaves then switch back?" Beads of sweat were streaming down my temples, and my heart was thundering against my ribs like I'd just run a marathon. Would she have arrested us if we'd been caught? Hauled us off in handcuffs in the back of the cruiser? My dad may not have cared about a speeding ticket, but racking up a criminal record my first week in Boston? Yeah, that would have gotten my ass recalled to Traverse City faster than a salmonella-filled jar of peanut butter. It was an unbelievably stupid and reckless thing to do, but I'd never felt so alive.

"It'd be safer if you just drive. I'll tell ya where to go."

Chapter Four
Exposure

"Emme," Raven whispered, tapping me on the shoulder.

I glanced up from the whale pictures I had hidden inside my physics book to see Mr. Lautner leaning against his desk with his eyes focused on me. "Did you complete the reading assignment?"

"Yes." It was almost the truth– I'd skimmed the first three chapters.

"Then what's the answer?"

"Um…answer to what?" The room filled with snorts and giggles. I knew I had about five seconds to do something before I was permanently added to yet another professor's shit list. "I'm sorry Mr. Lautner. I was reading ahead and missed your question."

He grunted, pulling his pants up again. "I said, what are the three main differences between mass and weight?"

"Oh that's easy. Weight is a measurement of the pull of gravity on an object. It's measured on a scale and changes with location. Mass is a measurement of the matter in an object. The location has no impact on it, and it's measured on a balance against a known amount."

"Very good Ms. Waters. Maybe next time you can respond without bringing my class to a grinding halt."

I had to bite my lip to suppress a smirk. "Yes sir."

When class ended I slung my backpack over my shoulder and turned toward Raven. "Would you like to get some breakfast?"

"I already ate," she said, jotting the homework assignment down in her notebook. "I'd be happy to keep you company though."

We headed across the sparsely populated courtyard toward the cafeteria. It was a gorgeous morning with barely a cloud in the sky. The leaves of the massive, mature trees scattered throughout the lengthy but fairly narrow open space hadn't started to turn yet. I couldn't wait to see the peak colors in a month or so. Still gliding forward along the straight path, I leaned my head back and took in the warmth of the sun as it beamed down on my face. I could tell by Raven's pensive look that she wanted to ask me something, but every time I thought she was about to speak, her eyes would dart away again. I finally put my hand on her shoulder and brought us to a stop. "What's wrong?"

"You're going to think I'm weird." Was she crying? Jesus, she looked scared out of her mind, like she was about to confess she performed ritualistic cat sacrifices, and she was sure I'd bolt for good.

"I would never think that," I assured her, wiping a stray tear from her cheek. "You're my friend."

A tentative, cautiously hopeful smile crossed her lips. "I got you something. I thought these would go great with your necklace."

Raven pulled a sterling silver jewelry box out of her pocket and handed it to me. Inside the case was a gorgeous pair of silver earrings, dangling down to diamond-encrusted hoops with a dolphin jumping backward through them.

"Holy crap!" Stupefied beyond words, I took a couple of minutes to compose my thoughts. Then I asked the obvious question– even though I was pretty sure I already knew the answer. "Are those…diamonds?"

"Please take them," Raven begged. "I just– we had such a good time yesterday. Then I saw these at the mall and thought of you. God, I sound like a stalker. Shit." Dejected, she wiped her eyes with her palms and reached for the box, already gathering herself for a hasty retreat.

I closed my hand over the top before she could get a hold of it. Refusing her obscenely expensive present might be the right thing to do, but it would also crush her. "They're so beautiful."

Her arms coiled around my back in a vertebrae realigning hug that made my eyes bug out of my head. Holy fuck, she was strong. By the time I forced air back into my lungs she'd taken the earrings out of the case and placed them in my ears. She took a step back, admiring them.

"Well?" I asked, turning my head from side to side like a model.

Her face beamed. "They look amazing on you!"

"Thanks, Raven. Besides my mom's necklace, this is the nicest gift anyone's ever given me. I don't know what to get you yet, but I'll think of something." Talk about a hopeless shopping trip. Whatever little trinket I could afford to buy her would seem like something straight out of a supermarket gumball machine by comparison.

"I know something I would really like– a gift only you could give me."

Rather than responding to my dumbfounded expression, she led me into the cafeteria, thru the dining area and down a side hall to a small banquet room. As soon as I reached the hall, I began to detect the same unfamiliar scent from the party, the one I'd noticed when I was near her for the first time. Raven took a seat in a booth in the far corner that had walls on three sides. I slid in across from her, totally confused. The scent was strong– stronger than at the party– and it was obviously coming from her.

"I'm ready for my gift."

Here? What's she expecting me to give her? "Um…what would you like?"

She took in a slow breath, her features contorting into a vulnerable semi-frown. "What do you smell?"

"Smell? I don't know, cinnamon, syrup– "

"You know what I mean. Please, tell me exactly what *it* smells like."

So much for playing stupid. Fuck. Could there be a more awkward topic to talk about with someone you liked? I'd rather do the whole foot-in-stirrup routine and let her play gynecologist for the day. "It's not repulsive or anything. It's kind of a floral scent, like lilac but really unique. In open areas I can hardly even smell it. It's pretty strong here though."

"How strong? Please be honest."

Given how unconvincing my attempts at being deceitful typically were, I decided to just go with the truth. All I'd succeed in doing by lying was make her regret opening up to me. "In this tiny, enclosed space, it's making me a little nauseous."

"Thank you," Raven muttered.

"Is it your perfume? What's the scent coming from?"

She sighed. "Me. Some kind of birth defect– no one knows exactly."

Quickly changing sides, I sat down next to her, close enough so our faces were almost touching. I took a deep breath and kissed her on the cheek. "I think you smell great."

We shared a long, emotional embrace as she buried her head in the crease of my shoulder. Finally, she leaned back and wiped her eyes on a napkin. "Would you like to see a cool trick I can do?"

"Sure!" I said, happy for the long overdue change in topic.

She motioned across the booth to where I'd been seated before. "I need you to sit directly across from me."

I dutifully shuffled back to the other side of the booth and scooted down until I was in front of her. "This good?"

She placed her hand on top of mine, giving them a little pat. "Perfect. Now, have you ever been hypnotized?"

"Nope. I've seen it on TV though. Can you do that?" My voice rose up at the end in hopeful awe. If Raven could go all yours-eyes-are-feeling-sleepy on me that would be seriously cool.

"Kind of. Would you mind if I tried it on you?"

"Sounds like fun. What do I do? Count back from a hundred or something?"

"Just be still, focus on me and don't talk."

My eyes locked on hers. *What now?* I intended to say, only to find that I couldn't make my lips move. Even when I tried to smile, my face remained frozen in a vacant stare. It was like I was in REM sleep, and my thoughts were being cut off from my body. Then I was back. I blinked a couple times and tried to gather myself. "Whoa! That was intense. How'd you do that?"

She grinned. "My mom taught me. Pretty cool huh."

"Very! So the next time the phone rings, am I going to bark like a dog?"

Raven flashed me a shrewd smile. "Even better. What do you smell now?"

I took a deep breath. "Oh my God. How did… Wow. I can't smell your scent at all." I'd always figured people that were hypnotized were in on the act, or were just falling victim to the power of suggestion, like someone telling you not to think about a giant white elephant. But this was no parlor trick. What had been an overwhelming scent just seconds before was just…gone. Raven had some kind of extra sensory ability to manipulate my mind. I wasn't sure if I should be impressed or terrified by that. I guess I was a little of both.

"It won't last– I'm just suppressing that particular smell. Well, your ability to process it, anyway."

I swept her golden blonde hair back from her eyes and took hold of her slightly lowered chin, raising it until she met my gaze. "You don't need to keep your scent from me, you know, but it's pretty badass that you can."

As we made our way back toward the dining room I finally realized what she had wanted, what in the end I had given her…my acceptance.

* * * *

After breakfast I had just enough time to grab a jumbo-sized cafe mocha before beginning the long trek to advanced calculus. Coffee wasn't really my thing, not even super-sugary-flavored stuff like this, but it jolted my body more than Diet Dew.

Taking Angie's advice, I grabbed a seat in the front row, raised my hand for every question and even volunteered to hand out the quizzes. If Professor Alzera noticed my blatant ass-kissing, she never let it show. She only called on me once, and seemed almost disappointed when I supplied the correct answer. Political science was looking better all the time.

When we were finally dismissed, I headed back to the dorm. My next class wasn't until 6:00 p.m., and I was hoping Angie or Stacey would be up for doing something. My hopes faded when I noticed we had company. Stacey was sitting on the couch next to a woman in a tan suit, and Angie was leaning against the bedroom doorway, speaking to an older man dressed in a blue sport coat.

I walked toward who I assumed was Angie's father. "Hi, I'm Emily," I said.

"Ms. Emily Waters?"

Being addressed so formally set me on edge. I could feel the tiny hair on the back of my neck start to tingle. "Yeah."

"Agent O'Connell, FBI. I have a few questions for you regarding Wendy Taylor."

I was so not tracking this conversation. What the hell was the FBI doing here? "Who?"

He gave me a suffering eye roll, like he'd rather hand in his badge than speak with another dimwitted teenager. "Wendy Taylor, your roommate."

"Oh, I haven't met her yet."

"So you've never seen this woman?" He held a picture up in front of me.

I briefly glanced at it. "Nope."

After jotting far too long of a note given my four letter response, he flipped to the front pocket of the three ring binder and tucked the picture away. "How long have you been on campus?"

"I got here late Sunday night, around midnight."

"And you are staying in the bedroom with Angela Stevens, correct?"

Was he going anywhere with this? "Yes."

"Have you at any time entered the bedroom assigned to Stacey Andrews and Wendy Taylor?"

The way his eyes bored into mine unnerved me. I was afraid telling him "yes" would be all but confessing to whatever crimes had been committed. "Stacey helped me get ready for a party Monday night, and I slept in Wendy's bed afterwards."

"Why didn't you sleep in your own bed?" he questioned, shooting me a sideways glance while he continued to scribble in his pad.

Oh, this wasn't awkward at all. Now I got to tell my roommate that I listened to her bumping uglies with her boy toy. In front of the FBI, no less. "I went for a walk late that night to get some air. When I got back my door was closed. I could hear Angie and Doug in there, so I went into the other room to sleep."

"And by Angie you are referring to Angela Stevens?"

No. I'm referring to Angelina Jolie, because that would make so much sense in this conversation. What was with this guy? "Yes."

"Ms. Stevens, did someone sleep with you in your room Monday night?"

Angie's cheeks had gone crimson. Apparently talking about her sex life in front of the FBI wasn't a great thrill for her, either. "Yes. My boyfriend, Doug Morris."

"We'll need to speak with him. Do you have a number we can reach him at?" Angie got out her cell phone and read out his number.

"Emily, we'll need DNA samples from you to match up with the forensic evidence gathered from Wendy's room, so that we can eliminate known DNA. We can gather this now, or you can come downtown to the FBI office or police station. You're not a suspect, but you are entitled to consult an attorney before providing these samples."

That would be more comforting if I had any idea what I *wasn't* a suspect for. I thought about calling my dad before I did something really stupid, but telling him I was being questioned by the FBI would be strikes one and two against this place, regardless of what they were questioning me about. Besides, it's not like we had some fancy ass lawyer on retainer. "No, that's okay. I would prefer to do it here."

Agent O'Connell put on latex gloves then took a pair of tweezers out of a sealed container. After he pulled out a couple strands of my hair, he put them in a numbered plastic bag then took a cotton swab out and rubbed it on the inside of my cheek.

"Thank you," he said, placing the swab into a small bottle.

Stacey walked over to stand next to Angie as Agent O'Connell's partner joined him at his side. "Agent Higgins, FBI," she said, holding up her badge. "We know most everyone on campus was at the party, but if you all could write down the names and contact information for anyone you know of who may have been in Wendy Taylor's bedroom, we would appreciate it."

"Sure," Stacey agreed, her head bobbing up and down like one of those plastic figurines with a spring for a neck. Her hands were shaking so badly she tucked them back into her jeans. Angie and I nodded as well.

"What happened to her?" I braced myself for the worst. If they were taking DNA samples, she had to be either missing or dead.

"As we explained to your roommates, Wendy was reported missing by her mother Tuesday morning," Agent Higgins said. "She talked to her mom Friday evening, but didn't meet her for lunch on Sunday. She never picked up her books and has been absent from all of her classes. The Boston Police Department referred the case to us since it's the third missing person case they've received in the area this month. The cases may be completely unrelated, but I would be extra vigilant until we know for sure."

I felt like I'd been kicked in the stomach by a Clydesdale. And judging by Angie and Stacey's sickly white faces, they weren't taking the news any better. Our roommate was missing. Christ, she wasn't even the only one. Agent O'Connell began to grill Stacey about her lack of a boyfriend, challenging her claim that she hadn't been intimate with anyone since arriving at school like she was a prostitute. Maybe if Barney Fife spent half as much time researching leads as he did prying into the sex lives of college co-eds, we wouldn't have to rely on being *extra vigilant.*

After the agents left, we collapsed on the couch in complete shock.

"God, I hope she's okay," Angie muttered.

Stacey shook her head in disbelief. "Three people missing in the last month."

"Scary," I said, feeling almost numb.

Angie turned her attention to me. "I'm sorry about Monday night– I didn't mean to take over our room."

I waved her concern away. Given what had just happened that was the least of my worries. "No problem. I thought you guys could use some privacy."

"Oh my God!" Stacey shouted out of the blue, making Angie and I jump about three feet in the air. Christ, if she kept that up, she'd be the death of me long before my sophomore year. She lifted up one of my earrings. "Where'd you get these? They're beautiful!"

"Thanks. Raven gave them to me this morning. I told her it was way too much, but she insisted."

Stacey tilted her head to the side and furrowed her brows. "Why'd she get you a gift? Is it your birthday?"

"No. I think she was just happy to have a new friend."

"I can't wait to meet her," Angie said. It sounded like a token response, but there was sincerity in her eyes. She wasn't just saying what I wanted to hear.

"Me too," Stacey agreed. "And not just because she owns her own cruise ship and buys five thousand dollar earrings for people she's known less than a week. Honest." We all giggled.

I was excited at the thought of Raven becoming friends with them. I'd have to find a way to explain her scent before they met, so Raven wouldn't have to worry about it.

The brief moment of levity passed, and my mind shifted back to Wendy, picturing what would happen if news about a missing BU freshman girl went national before my dad heard from me. "I've gotta call my dad!" I blurted out, jumping to my feet. Angie and Stacey both stared at me for a second, and then scrambled for their own phones.

I lay down on my bed and selected his number. We spent a few minutes chatting about how my classes were going, what I thought of my roommates, and the whale watching trip with Raven.

I would have liked to keep the pleasant conversation going, but I knew it wasn't going to be easy to bring up the main reason for my call regardless of how long I waited. "Dad, I need to let you know about something you may see on the news. Don't freak out, okay?"

"That depends," he said hesitantly.

"My other roommate, Wendy, hasn't shown up for any of her classes yet, and her mom reported her missing on Tuesday. A couple agents from the FBI were over here asking us some questions today. They said it'd likely turn out to be nothing, but they were being overly thorough since they've had a couple other reports this month. I'm sure she's just on her way home or something."

I waited for him to reply, but there was only silence. "Dad?"

"I knew better than to let you go to such a big city. What was I thinking? Just pack up your stuff– we can take care of everything else when you get home."

"I'm not coming home. I love it here!"

"Emily, please be reasonable. Your roommate is missing. You're getting questioned by the FBI. You can't expect me to just sit back and let something happen to you."

"I'm sure Wendy is fine," I argued. "She's only been gone for a few days. And it's not like three missing people in a city this size is anything unusual. Even if something bad did happen to all of them, I would have better odds of getting run over by a truck than being kidnapped or whatever."

"I know you think you like it there, but it's too big of a risk to take. Please, for me, come home where I can keep you safe." The vulnerability in his voice tore me up inside. He could lecture me all he wanted without much effect, but if he made me feel like I was hurting him? Game over. That was my kryptonite.

"Dad, I love you. You mean everything to me. But you have to let me grow up and get out on my own. You know how badly I want to go into conservation biology, and as much as I wish it were true, there's nowhere that you can guarantee I'd be safe. Remember last summer when I got hit by a car on my bike? That happened less than a mile from our house and would have killed me if I'd gotten to the intersection a second earlier. I can't live my life in a bubble. Not even for you."

I could hear him sobbing quietly and I began to cry. Ever since my mom died I'd occasionally caught muffled whimpers from his room or outside in the garage, but he never cried in front of me. How far was I willing to take this to get my way? And at what cost?

"You're my whole life. All I want in this world is for you to be safe and happy."

"I know," I choked out through my tears.

"Promise me this, okay?" he pleaded.

"What?"

"If your roommate was taken from the school, or the police say anything about the students on campus being in danger, then you'll come home, at least until they catch whoever is doing this."

"I promise." The selfish part of me was reluctant to agree to anything, but his compromise sounded reasonable, and it wasn't like I was immune to fear. If someone was going Freddie Krueger on college co-eds, I'd be more than happy to get the hell out of here.

"I love you. Please be careful."

"I will, Dad. I love you too. I'll give you a call Saturday and let you know how the rest of the week goes."

"Okay. Bye sweetheart."

I walked back into the living room, wiping my cheeks. Angie was sitting in the corner of the room, still on the phone.

"I see your call went about as well as mine," Stacey joked. She was lying flat on her back with her legs strung uncomfortably over the raised end of the couch, mindlessly texting on her Samsung Galaxy.

"My dad's terrified– he all but demanded that I come home."

"My mom saw the story on the local news this morning, but she was shocked to hear that Wendy was our roommate. The guy that's missing was last seen at a Laundromat less than a mile from our house." I had forgotten that her family lived nearby. At least I didn't have to worry about my dad.

Angie finished her call and walked over to us. "Glad that's over– my dad wanted to hop on the first plane out here." She let out a long sigh and gnawed on her lip. "I was going to go down to the rec center before all this happened."

"Volleyball practice?" I guessed.

"No, just wanted to work up a sweat. I was hoping there'd be a pick-up basketball game going on, or someone would want to play tennis."

If I spent any more time imagining the gruesome things that might have happened to Wendy, I'd never be able to walk to class tonight. Nothing got my mind off things better than going all out on the court. "I played tennis in high school. Are you still up for it?"

Angela was hesitant. "I don't know how much fun it would be for you. I'm not very good."

"Want to join us?" I asked, glancing at Stacey. "We could play one on two." Leaving her here alone after what we'd just been through seemed wrong. Besides, if Angie really was just learning, having Stacey tag along would make it more fun for all of us.

She did a little bouncy step thing that made her chin length hair flap up above her ears. Was anybody really this…chipper? "Definitely! Not that I'll be able to help much."

Angie and I went into our room to change. There were a couple tennis dresses in my closet, but I thought that would be a bit much for a casual game, so I threw on black spandex capri leggings and a pink tennis tank and grabbed my bag.

"Do you have a racquet, Angie?" I didn't see a bag or anything, and it looked like she was ready to go.

"No. They have some at the rec center we can use. Nothing fancy, but good enough for my game."

"I've got two with me, so we'll just need one."

When we walked out to meet Stacey my jaw fell open. She was wearing a pink Nike tennis dress with black trim, and had an Adidas tennis bag in her hand.

"Not much help, huh!" I grumbled with mock accusation.

She grinned mischievously. "I've played a few times."

The rec center was gigantic and fairly new. It had three basketball courts inside a running track, an Olympic-size swimming pool with diving platforms, four volleyball courts and six tennis courts. I handed my extra racquet to Angie and began to stretch while they headed for the other end of the court. It felt good to be on a tennis court again after not playing for a couple months. I was pretty sure I'd been snowed by Stacey, but it'd make it more fun if it was competitive.

We hit a few balls easily back and forth to warm up. Stacey was very graceful. I could tell from her footwork, grip and swing that she'd received formal instruction at some point. Angie looked like a soccer player in a basketball game, trying to make up for her lack of skill with pure athleticism.

"Ready when you are. Your serve!" Stacey shouted.

I picked up a ball and moved to the right side of center so I could serve to her. She clearly wasn't a novice, but I wouldn't know how good she was until I saw her at full speed. I decided to go easy until then so I didn't embarrass her.

Tossing the ball over my head, I took about half a swing and sent a serve to her forehand. Stacey quickly slid her feet into position and sent her return screaming down the line to my left, leaving me no chance of getting to it.

"Fifteen – Love!" she called out with a wide smile before bounding over to the other side of the court. Technically, if this was doubles I'd be serving to Angie now, but letting Stacey field my serves made more sense given our skill level, and Angie would get plenty of chances to play during the rallies.

Okay, so half speed was out. My heart started to pound with adrenaline as my competitiveness kicked in. I went through the usual pre-serve routine I'd do in a match. Stacey was playing fairly deep and off wide to the side, trying to keep as much to her forehand as possible. It was time to find out just how good she was. I hit a slice serve that landed just inside the center line with a lot of spin to make it skid and curve to the left on impact. Stacey took a couple running steps to her right and flailed her racquet out in desperation as the ball sailed by her.

"Fifteen – All!" I yelled, earning me a glare and a loud huff.

I went on to win the game in straight points. While Stacey had obviously had some coaching over the years and was quite talented, I could tell that she'd never played competitively. I eased up and let them exchange long rallies with me. Angie's face lit up whenever she managed to get her return over the net. Stacey had the endless patience of a kindergarten teacher, continuously giving her pointers on her stance, how to shuffle her feet into the proper position and the importance of following through with her swing. Angie caught on remarkably fast.

Playing with uneven teams served as a constant reminder of our missing roommate, not to mention my now rather precarious future as a BU student, a future that hinged upon what happened to her and the others. But as the games grew more spirited, they became a better distraction. By the last set I had to play almost full out just to hold my own against them.

We made our way to a soda machine, got some energy drinks and plopped down on the ground, exhausted.

"You're really good," Angie praised, looking up almost in awe at me. "Why don't you go out for tennis here?"

I wiped my forehead with a towel, more to hide my face than anything. I never knew how to act when people complimented me. "Thanks. Unfortunately I'm only average compared to other people who've played competitively. I could probably make the team but I'd have to walk on. Without a scholarship I couldn't afford the time, since I'll have to start working part-time soon."

"Did you see how quick Angie picked things up out there? My partner is coming on strong. We're gonna take you down next time!" Stacey pointed the end of her racquet at my face like she was calling me out.

I laughed. "I did actually. You're quite the athlete, Angie. You were even returning some of my full speed serves by the end."

Angie wrapped her arm around Stacey's shoulders and gave her a squeeze. "Thanks to my awesome coach."

"Same time next week?" I hoped they'd be willing to make this a regular thing. I hadn't realized how much I'd missed playing.

"You're on!" Stacey hollered. Angie enthusiastically slapped her hand.

Chapter Five
No Good Deed...

I'd set up my schedule to have all of my classes on Tuesday and Thursday, so that I could work during the weekend and have Monday and Wednesday off to catch up on homework, laundry and the other weekly chores. That meant that Tuesdays and Thursdays were going to be long, with eight hours of classes both days.

Backpack in tow, I selected the Ke$ha playlist on my iPod and headed off to Biology, allowing some extra time to search for the room in the sprawling arts and sciences building. As if being ginormous wasn't bad enough, it had twisting, maze-like corridors that caused even upperclassmen to get turned around.

By sheer luck the third lab I came across was mine, located just around the corner from the main entrance. The handful of guys who'd arrived before me were scattered, one to a table, across the back half of the room. A couple of them weren't hard to look at, especially the blonde-haired lean pile of muscles who was tapping his fingers to the rhythm of whatever song he was listening to, but I didn't want the drama that would come with choosing a partner before it was mathematically necessary. I made my way to an empty table near the front and took a seat. The black countertops had sinks in the center and microscopes in front of each seat. Since I had time to kill, I tucked my iPod into my backpack, pulled out my book and flipped through the first chapter.

The low hum of noise grew louder, and I heard the distinct sound of chalk being pressed against a blackboard. *Welcome to Intro to Biology 108. Dr. Jessica Hailey.* The professor was in her late thirties to early forties and was fairly tall, with mousy brown shoulder length hair. She was wearing a red blouse and a below-the-knee skirt with very comfortable looking flats.

I glanced to my right and was disappointed to find that the seat next to me was still vacant. Not having a partner for labs wouldn't make this class any easier.

As Dr. Hailey worked her way toward the back of the room, greeting each student and personally handing them a syllabus, something grabbed my attention. A unique scent I was coming to love. It was fairly weak in such a large room, but there was no mistaking it. I spun around and spotted Raven walking toward me with a wide grin on her face.

Dangerous Waters

"Hey there," she said, sliding into the empty chair. Her eyes lit up when she noticed that I was still wearing the earrings she'd given me.

"Hi, Raven!" I all but shouted. It wasn't too surprising that we had a couple of the same foundation courses, given that our majors were in similar fields, but I still felt extremely lucky. When I tried to sneak a quick hug, I heard a woman clear her throat behind me.

"Looks like you two are hitting it off," Dr. Hailey teased. "I'm Dr. Jessica Hailey. You can call me Dr. Hailey or Jessica, whichever you prefer."

I gave her an embarrassed half-smile. "Nice to meet you Dr. Hailey, Emily Waters."

"Welcome, Emily." She placed a syllabus in front of me, and took a couple steps over to Raven.

Raven greeted her with a somewhat formal handshake that Dr. Hailey awkwardly returned. "Raven…Williams," she added as an afterthought. There was something off about the way Raven said her name. More than just the pause, it lacked the practiced delivery of something that had been uttered thousands of times. I thought that maybe she'd recently married and was still getting used to her new name, but I didn't see a ring on her finger.

"What an unusual name. Nice to meet you, Raven." She handed her a syllabus and moved on to the next row.

Raven peeked at it, set it aside and leaned in close to me. "So how was the rest of your day?"

"Great. I played tennis this afternoon with Stacey and Angie. How about you?"

"Pretty uneventful, did some laundry and paid a few bills. How long have you played tennis?"

"Ever since I was nine. I was on the tennis team in high school. It felt great to play again."

She scrunched her eyebrows at me. "How'd you play with three of you?"

"I played against both of them. It worked out well. Stacey is pretty good, and Angie got a lot better by the time we were done. Do you play?"

"I used to– I was pretty serious about it for a while."

I couldn't contain my almost childlike smile. "Sweet! We can play doubles. We're playing again next Thursday if you're free." In an instant her entire expression changed. The disappointed look in her eyes had me backpedaling. "If that doesn't work– "

Raven gestured toward the front of the room, cutting me off. "Later."

Dr. Hailey was starting her lecture on basic cell biology: the anatomy of cells, different abilities of cells, types of simple organisms, etc. After about an hour and a half of lecturing she passed out slides containing Amoebas and Paramecium to each of the tables. Raven and I laughed a couple times while we worked through the questions on our first lab, but I could tell that she was still upset. I couldn't wait for class to be over so we could talk.

When the lecture ended, she practically jumped out of her seat and bolted for the door. I stuffed my books into my bag as fast as I could and followed her into the courtyard. We sat on a bench next to the large fountain in the center in total silence for a couple of minutes, watching the water tumble down over the cascading leaf-shaped ledges and back into the pool below.

Raven absently picked at the seam of her wool pencil skirt. "They don't know me, Emme. Do you remember this morning in the booth?"

"Yeah."

Her eyes met mine. "When I sweat it's a lot stronger than that. Even in an open area like the rec center, it'd be noticeable."

"I was thinking about that earlier today. I was going to ask you if I could talk to them about it. I'm sure they'd understand– they're both really nice."

"I don't exactly share that with everyone." She stared at me, letting her words sink in. "If rumors spread across campus, I'd be humiliated. Are you sure you can trust that they wouldn't tell anyone? Sure enough to risk our friendship?"

I realized instantly how selfish I was being, wanting to spread her deepest secrets just to make life more convenient for me. "I don't know what I was thinking. I'm sorry Raven– I promise I won't tell them."

She stroked the hair along my cheek, twisting it between her fingers before tucking it behind my ear. "There's nothing to be sorry about. You didn't tell anyone, not even your closest friends. Of course you'd like us all to be able to hang out together. I'm the one who should be apologizing."

What did she have to apologize for? Making the mistake of ever trusting me in the first place? "For what?"

"For making you choose who to spend your time with, and lie to your friends to cover for me. I had no right to put you in this situation."

"You aren't forcing me to choose– there's plenty of time to do stuff with all you guys." I paused, my eyes darting to the ground. "And they're not my closest friends here, you are."

Raven wrapped her arm around my shoulders and held me tight. "You're the only real friend I've got."

How was that even possible? Were people really that close-minded? She was amazing. I grinned as I recalled how well I knew her scent now, how I could tell she was close by even before I could see her.

"What are you thinking about?" she wondered, noticing my abrupt change in mood.

I rested my head against her neck and returned her embrace. "Just how I knew you were coming into Biology class before I saw you– I'm getting really good at detecting your scent."

Raven started to giggle, and then abruptly stopped, her body stiffening under my hands.

"What's wrong?"

Silence.

It seemed crazy that she'd take what I said as an insult, but she was clearly pissed about something. "I didn't mean that in a bad way," I tried to explain. "I just meant that it's exciting, like we have our own secret language."

"I know exactly what you meant," she snapped.

My eyes welled up and my lower lip began to tremble. "Please don't be angry. Damn it! I'm so stupid!"

"It's not you." Raven said, patting my shoulder to comfort me. "It's just that what you said made me realize that I've put you in danger, and I don't know how to get you out of it."

"In…danger?"

Raven kissed the top of my head then pulled away so she could meet my gaze. "I thought I could open up to you over time without causing any harm. I should have seen what it would lead you to think, what it could lead you to do."

"I don't understand," I muttered. How could knowing what she smells like put me in danger? Was it some kind of secret? Maybe her mom didn't want anyone to know about the whole mind-scrambling thing, and the scent was somehow tied into that. But even if that was the case, there's no way Raven would let her mom hurt me.

"There's still a lot that you don't know about me. Things I hadn't planned on telling you for quite a while, if ever. I've decided that you need to know all of it. It's the only way to keep you safe."

I wiped my cheeks and managed a faint smile. "There's nothing you could tell me that'd make me not want to be your friend."

"I really hope that's true," she said with a heavy sigh. I'd seen people on death row look more optimistic. Damn. "Could you meet me for lunch at my house tomorrow?"

"Sure. Oh, I guess I need an address."

She laughed. "Trust me. It'd be *easier* if we ride together. I'll meet you outside your dorm at noon."

Okay... what was that supposed to mean? Her inflection didn't sound like she was referring to tricky driving directions. And it wasn't like she was from the hood– she owned a cruise ship, for god sakes. What's the worst that could happen? The butler pegging me as poor white trash and blocking the door? Maybe she was just worried her family wouldn't like me. As long as *she* did, that's all I cared about. "What should I bring?"

"You don't need to bring anything– other than an open mind."

"You can count on that." I assured her. Her family may have run off the rest of her would-be friends– or made her feel so self-conscious about being different that she didn't even try to make friends anymore– but I'll be damned if they'd intimidate me. The last five days had been a whirlwind of adventure, shared secrets and bizarre experiences. I couldn't wait to see what tomorrow and the years that followed would bring.

"Have a good night," Raven whispered, disappearing into the darkness like a shadow.

* * * *

The second the alarm sounded, I kicked off the covers and sprang out of bed. I'd spent most of the night lying wide-eyed on my back, mulling over all the things Raven might tell me, but I had way too much to do to even think about hitting the snooze. In spite of what she'd said, I wasn't about to show up for lunch with her family empty handed. I had no idea what to bring though. If I knew what we were having, or at least what kind of food they liked, it would have given me something to go off of. Hell, I didn't even know who *they* were. With the exception of her cousin, Stephanie, she'd never mentioned anyone specific.

I debated ideas while I showered. Didn't everyone always bring a bottle of wine? I was still underage though. And even if I could get someone to buy it for me, an eighteen-year-old showing up with alcohol probably wouldn't make the best impression. If I had access to a kitchen, I could at least make brownies or chocolate chip cookies, not that I was Betty Crocker or anything. Picking up a dessert sounded promising, but what? From where? Then I remembered the lunch we'd eaten at Antonio's– all of us had raved about their cheesecake.

Now that I'd figured out what to bring, I needed to find something to wear. It only took a few seconds to flip through the dresses I'd brought with me and select my favorite. It was navy blue with three quarter length sleeves and pleats starting near the waist that made the bottom look like a skirt. I slipped it on along with my nicest pumps, and then pulled my hair up into a French braid to show off the earrings Raven had given me. Once I'd fastened the bottom with an elastic band, I flipped open my laptop and googled Antonio's. The clerk agreed to take my order, but told me that they didn't open until 11:00.

I had almost two hours to kill, so I pulled out my physics book and started on our assignment for Tuesday. The questions on the handout followed right along with the assigned chapters, but my mind wandered constantly, forcing me to re-read sections multiple times. I'd barely finished the first page when it was time to go. Since getting lost was a distinct possibility, even with the directions I'd printed out, I tore a blank page out of my notebook and scribbled a quick note.

Raven,
Went to Antonio's to pick up dessert for lunch.
Should be back before noon.
      Emme

The traffic was surprisingly heavy for a mid-Friday morning. The stop-and-go, bumper-to-bumper driving along Storrow Drive made it difficult to steal glances at the map, let alone enjoy the picturesque view of the Charles River. A baseball stadium sat just across the river along with a football field and several tennis courts, all part of MIT's recreational facilities. Brownstone apartment buildings as high as fifteen stories dominated the skyline all along Storrow drive, but when I reached Cambridge Street, the city took on a more industrial feel. In spite of the traffic and my efforts to take in the sights, I managed to make it to Antonio's in less than fifteen minutes. Seeing that all of the parking spaces in front of the restaurant were full, mostly with delivery trucks, I turned left into the alley and parked in a spot along the curb.

It was a dreary morning, cool and quite windy. Dark gray overcast blocked out the sun, and there was a slight drizzle coming down. I hoped that it would rain harder, since my Camry was in desperate need of a wash. While it still ran fine, it was nothing to look at, thanks to several Michigan winters and a couple accidents. Not exactly the type of car you run through ten dollar car washes. I couldn't wait to get a hybrid, but there was no way I'd be able to afford a new car until after I graduated and got a real job.

My umbrella was still buried somewhere in my closet, so I hopped onto the weed infested, crumbling sidewalk and hurried up the alley to the restaurant, doing my best to cover my head with my purse. Most of the tables still had chairs flipped upside down on top of them, and with the exception of a couple of employees, the place was deserted. A frazzled looking bus boy was hustling around, trying to get ready for the lunch crowd, while three waitresses huddled in the back discussing table assignments. Not wanting to bother them, I made my way up to the counter. An older man stepped out of the kitchen, wearing a plain white t-shirt, black trousers and a white apron covered with fresh stains.

"What can I help ya with?"

"Take out order for Waters. I called a couple hours ago."

He disappeared into the back for a moment, and returned with a large white box. "That'll be $37.10."

I anxiously pulled my wallet out of my purse, wishing I'd asked how much it was ahead of time, and handed him my last two twenty dollar bills. It wasn't like I was going to starve or anything– a cafeteria meal plan was included in my room and board– but doing laundry was going to be tight for the next couple weeks. The fact that I'd blown through my entire monthly allowance in less than a week also meant I had a hell of a lot to learn about managing money. I'd felt guilty about taking the hundred bucks from my dad in the first place, knowing that he had a stack of past-due bills on the table. There was no way I was going to hit him up for more the first week I was here. After tucking my change away, I picked up the cheesecake and headed out the door.

The sun was just starting to break through the clouds when I rounded the corner into the alley. The dessert smelled delicious, and my stomach growled in anticipation, reminding me that I hadn't eaten breakfast. I'd almost reached my car when a far better scent captured my attention– Raven. I eagerly spun around, expecting to find her there, but she was nowhere in sight. The three people I could see were standing on the curb across the alley. Only one was a woman, and there was almost no resemblance to Raven other than the color of her hair. I took another deep breath– I definitely smelled her. *Where is she?* Since the scent was coming from their direction, I walked past my car and out into the alley to get a better view. One of the men motioned toward me, muttering something to the woman.

The man on the left was wearing jeans and an untucked, button down shirt. Everything about him was unremarkable, the kind of person who could walk through a crowd of a thousand people without anyone remembering him. The man on the right was a good four inches taller, probably six feet five, with a stocky build and wavy blonde hair that spilled over his collar in the back. He was dressed in black jeans and a long sleeve Polo shirt. The shorter man gazed further up the alley, while the taller of the two walked back to the corner and looked out into the street.

The hair on the back of my neck stood straight up when it dawned on me what they were doing– checking if anyone else was around. As if she could hear the sudden change in my heartbeat, the woman whirled and glared at me. I watched in a kind of suspended disbelief as my arms fell limp at my sides, sending the cheesecake tumbling to the street below. *Help me!! Help!!* I screamed. But my lips didn't move– I was frozen. With a confident, almost whore-like strut, I sauntered toward the woman, entirely against my will. The men let out a boisterous round of approving cat calls and whistles before turning to walk further up the alley. *Oh, fuck! No, no, no! Oh, Jesus, this isn't happening. Just force yourself to look away from her and stop walking!*

My body continued to glide forward until I stood directly in front of her– it was hopeless. She was wearing a skimpy black tank under an unbuttoned jacket that left her pierced naval exposed, and worn, comfortable looking jeans. Her long, curly blonde hair was blowing up behind her like a golden cape. "Let me guess… You'd like me to kill you, stuff your body into a barrel and light it on fire."

I eagerly nodded my head.

"Oh, come on, you can do better than that. Where's the enthusiasm? Do you want to die or not?"

"Please kill me!" I wailed. "I'm such a worthless, pathetic little bitch. Don't make me live any longer. Please!" Hearing myself speak the words was horrifying. My dad had begged for me to come home yesterday. Now he was going to lose his only child. It would destroy him.

"All right, all right. If you insist." She flashed an evil grin before heading off to join the men, who were waiting for her at the end of the alley. I followed close behind.

The alley dead-ended behind a three-story abandoned warehouse. All of the windows had been busted out and were covered by sheets of plywood that were tagged with several layers of graffiti. We made our way to the one closest to the far end of the building. The larger guy slid the plywood off to the side and held it while the other two climbed through. I got down on all fours, placing my hands and knees in the grime that covered the street, and crawled through the opening, dropping into a basement with a thud.

After I got back to my feet, we continued down a long, shadowy hallway that emptied into a small room with a metal table in the center. It smelled noxious, like a mixture of kerosene, decaying flesh and sewer water laced with what I'd thought was Raven's scent. Our conversation from the night before made sense to me now. This was the danger she'd put me in— I'd assumed that the unique scent I'd come to love was hers alone.

The woman turned her back to me and pulled her hair off to the side. I reached behind my head and unclasped my mother's necklace— my most cherished possession— and placed it around her neck. *No! No! Oh, please, God, please, no!* I was crying inside, even if tears wouldn't come out of my frozen eyes.

She removed the diamond-hoop earrings Raven had given me and slipped them on, then turned back toward me to model them. "They look much better on me, don't you agree?"

"Definitely!"

She let out a sickening laugh. "So you don't mind if I keep them?"

"Not at all— I'd be honored."

"Give it a rest, Terr," the guy in the button down shirt said. "The whole parrot thing stopped being funny about a hundred people ago."

She flipped him off. "Bite me, douche-bag. I'll play with her as long as I want to."

"No, you won't," the bigger guy cut in. "If I hear another word out of her mouth, you're going to be watching us feed. Got me? Grow up, for Christ sakes."

She looked beyond pissed, but she bit back whatever smart-ass retort she'd thought of and focused on me. I wrapped my fingers around the bottom of my dress and lifted it up over my head. The woman took the elastic band out of my hair and unbraided it with her fingers, letting it fall loose around my face. Her hands moved on to my bra, unclasping it from the front and sliding it off the back of my arms. All that was left were my blue boy-short panties, which I removed without the slightest bit of hesitation. My body was perfectly calm— not even my heart raced as it should. Only my mind was reacting properly to the horror that was happening to me.

Dangerous Waters

Four foot flames shot up out of a barrel in the hallway, sending warmth and light flooding into the small room. The woman standing next to me picked up my clothes and tossed them carelessly into the flames. Somehow watching them burn made everything seem final. I was going to die, and no one was ever going to find me.

At some command only my body could hear, I got up onto the metal table and lay on my back. The woman walked up to my right side while the man with the button down shirt made his way to my left. The stocky guy with the black jeans stood facing me at my feet. She lifted my right arm up off the table and slid the nails of her left hand across my wrist, cutting through my flesh like a scalpel. I could feel the warm blood flowing across my skin, but there wasn't any pain. She lifted my wrist up to her mouth and thirstily drank from it, letting the excess run down her chin.

After a couple of minutes my head was turned to the left. The man standing there took my left hand and held it up against his chest. He ran his fingertips along the side of my body, across my breast and down the length of my arm before gracefully stroking my wrist. His cut went much deeper, causing blood to spurt into the air before he covered the gash with his mouth. With both of them siphoning blood from my veins, my body was growing colder by the second. I knew I'd be dead soon.

Suddenly both of my arms dropped off the sides of the table as a gust of air washed over my body. The room was a blur in motion. I realized that I was no longer tranced, but I was too weak to move. With a great deal of effort, I managed to lift my head up just far enough to see what was going on.

The two men were standing shoulder to shoulder across the entrance to the room with their arms held in fighting position at their chins. The woman had fled to the back corner and crouched in a defensive posture. Something was moving behind the men, but I couldn't make it out. Then I heard her.

"Let her go," Raven demanded.

"I don't want to hurt you," the larger man said. "Our families have known each other a very long time. But you have no right to interfere with our feeding. Please leave before this turns into something everyone will regret."

"Alexander, you know me. You know I'd never do this under normal circumstances. Please listen to me before you react."

"Leave now or die!" the smaller man yelled.

"Keep your mouth shut, Travis," Alexander ordered, cuffing the back of his head. "Let's go with the CliffsNotes version. What's left of the girl's blood is going to waste, and we don't want to have to make another kill."

Raven focused on the growing pool of blood beneath my dangling right wrist. Seeing me shattered whatever hold she'd maintained on her emotions up to now, and she dropped her head to her palm in tears. "Can I bandage her wrists while we talk?" she forced out through quivering lips. "I need some time to explain, and she'll be dead soon if I don't."

His shoulders raised in an indifferent shrug. "I think that ships sailed, but what the hell… Knock yourself out."

Raven nodded and raced to my side. After removing her shirt, she tore it up into long, narrow strips, tying them around my wrists and at the pressure points near my elbows and the tops of my arms. She worked so fast that it hurt my head to watch her. At least I wasn't cold anymore. Come to think of it, I couldn't feel much of anything anymore. *Why does it seem like I'm floating? Am I still breathing? Am I—dead?*

Pungent, ice cold water splashed across my face, startling me back to consciousness. "Stay with me, Emme!" Raven cried out, still shaking my shoulders. "Please!" Staring up at her mascara streaked cheeks and watery brown eyes made me wish I could comfort her. Hopefully the fact that she somehow knew these freaks would keep her from getting killed.

"Get on with it," Alexander grumbled.

She turned to confront him. "Emily and I have grown extremely close. Look at me… I haven't cried for a human since my parents died. She was going to meet me for lunch at our house today, where I was planning to tell her everything. You know how lonely this life can be, how monotonous it can get. I haven't felt this alive in decades. To you she's just another meal, easily replaced. I'd be happy to bring you a replacement."

"So you're making friends with your food now? What's gotten into you?"

"I don't know," she said with a sigh. "There's something special about her. She's been kinder to me than anyone outside of my family has ever been, even when I was human."

His face softened a bit as his eyes met mine. "It's not like I really care whose blood I drink. There's a problem though."

"Which is?"

"She knows what we look like. Where we feed. You know I can't expose my coven like that– Stefan would end me."

Raven glanced at me, her face full of despair. "That only matters if she's human."

Dangerous Waters

"So you plan to infect her?" Alexander arched his brows and dismissively shook his head, like that was the stupidest idea he'd ever heard. "Does Sienna know this?"

"Not yet. You know how my coven works. Emily will only be allowed to join us if Sienna accepts her, and if she chooses this life."

"And if either of them doesn't?"

She closed her eyes as she mouthed the words. "She'll be killed."

He nodded his approval. "I can't let this drag out. Every day that goes by with her human puts my family at risk."

"Be reasonable. You know she needs to heal first. Given the extent of her injuries, that could take months."

Alexander paced while he thought, stopping twice to look back at me. "Out of respect for Sienna and your coven, I'll let you take her with you. You have until Thanksgiving to bring this to a conclusion and provide confirmation either way. If you can agree to those terms, take her and leave."

Raven let out a deep sigh as she trailed her fingers gently along my cheek. "Thank you, Alexander. Stefan was right to put his trust in you. I accept your terms. There is one other thing."

"What else can I do for you today?" he shot back sarcastically.

"Could Teresa return Emily's jewelry to her? The necklace was her mother's and is really important to her. The earrings were a gift from me."

Teresa screamed in protest.

"It sounds like she's pretty attached to them," Alexander said. "I won't make her give them back. Now take your friend and leave while you still can."

"Alexander– "

"Damn it! Enough!" Alexander lunged forward as he spoke, causing Raven to recoil in fear. "Get out of here. Now!"

Raven lifted my limp, blood-stained body into her arms, and I drifted into nothingness.

Chapter Six
Sienna's Coven

"Here we have a white seventeen- to twenty-year-old female with deep lacerations to both wrists. She was found just outside the front of the hospital at one p.m. this afternoon, naked and unconscious with her wrists wrapped in strips of clothing. She was in surgery for almost three hours while the surgeons repaired the damaged muscular tissue, tendons and blood vessels. Each wrist required over twenty stitches. Since we couldn't type and cross her, she received four units of O negative before and during the surgery. The officer standing guard needs to be notified as soon as she's conscious. Questions?"

"Why is she strapped to the bed?"

"Given the possible suicide attempt, we need to take every precaution to ensure that she doesn't try to harm herself. Once she's stable we'll send her for a psych consult. Other questions? Okay, moving on...."

I cracked my eyes open, checking to make sure they'd left. I'd caught enough of their conversation to guess that they were doctors making rounds, along with the part about a cop wanting to talk with me. A quick glance around the room confirmed I was in a hospital. There was an IV pole and heart monitor to my left, and two chairs propped in the corner, both empty. A white, half mesh curtain was drawn most of the way around my bed, but not in front of the windows, and the afternoon sunlight was blinding me. Thick leather straps tethered my arms to the metal side rails of the bed, preventing me from shielding my face.

So Raven had dumped me here, lying naked in the street for the world to see, and didn't even stick around to find out if I survived. How could I have been so wrong about her? She was a monster, just like them— whatever they were. Not human, that's for sure. Birth condition, cool trick my mom taught me... Everything I thought she'd confided in me was nothing but lies. She was even worse than they were. At least they didn't pretend to be my friend.

My eyelids were heavy with an unnatural sleepiness, but I could still feel a throbbing pain in my wrists in spite of the drugs. I tried to recall what happened before I passed out. Most of it was a blur, except for small fragments of the conversation between Raven and Alexander, bartering over me like a piece of meat. Not that those made any sense. *That's only a problem if she's still human— what's that mean? She's going to infect me? With what?*

Then I remembered what Raven had agreed to, that I'd either be turned into whatever she was by Thanksgiving or she'd kill me. Nice. On top of everything else, my mom's necklace was now around that evil bitch Teresa's neck. Even though they were wrong about the cause of my current condition, the hospital was right to restrain me– I wanted nothing more than to die.

Still, I was alive. Wasn't there some good in that? My dad hadn't lost his daughter. Yet, anyway. I realized that was the problem. Maybe in several years, and with lots of therapy, I could recover enough to resume some small piece of my former life, but I wasn't being given that option. Instead I'd be killed two months from now, probably in some equally gruesome fashion. It was like being on some kind of demonic death row. I fell back into a deep sleep, overtaken by the drugs.

When I finally woke, the faint light of the moon was casting shadows across my bed. Their unmistakable scent filled the room. My eyes darted to the chairs, where Raven sat watching me.

Surprisingly, I was far more angry than afraid. I wanted to rip into her for her betrayal, for making me care for her when she'd done nothing but lie from the beginning, but her pleading, remorseful look was disarming. If the mountain of tissues on the coffee table was any indication, she'd been crying for a while. "I can't begin to tell you how sorry I am."

"So sorry you're going to kill me yourself in two months," I shot back with an icy glare. *Yeah, I remember, bitch.*

She started to move toward the bed but stopped cold when I reached for the nurse call button, raising her hands in mock surrender like I was a jumper she was trying to talk off the ledge. "You have to let me explain– there's so much you don't understand."

"What don't I understand? How you're going to kill me? I could probably guess after today."

"Would you stop with that?" she said with a rather annoyed looking shake of her head. "I don't have any intention of killing you."

"Really? I seem to recall something about Thanksgiving and having to prove to them that I'm dead."

Raven studied my face for what felt like an hour, and then glanced away and bit down on her lip. "That wasn't the only option."

I actually laughed. "Oh, you're right. I could become a monster like you, whatever you are, and go around torturing and murdering people."

Raven's whole demeanor changed as she took two predatory steps toward the bed. I frantically tried to press the button, but my thumb was frozen along with the rest of my body. "If you're that confident you'd choose death over an immortal life you don't even understand, then I guess there's no reason to wait."

I wanted to be brave. To stay strong to my conviction that I would never want to become like her, but when she slid the pillow out from under my head and smothered my face, my imminent death became all too real. *Oh God, stop! I don't want to die! Please!*

The pillow disappeared as Raven pulled me into a hug. "I'm so sorry, Emme. That's the only way I could think of to get through to you. I just need you to give me a chance, and let me show you how incredible your new life can be." Seeing my tears, she swept my hair away and kissed my forehead. "This is all my fault. If I wouldn't have confided in you, none of this would have happened. At least I could have told you everything sooner, so you would've known to run from my scent rather than follow it. How could I have done this to you? I love you!" Still holding me tight, she pressed her head against my chest and bawled.

When our tears were cried out, Raven sat next to me with her arm draped across my waist. I wanted to hate her, to see nothing but some vile beast sitting in front of me. That would've been so much easier than admitting the truth. In spite of being outnumbered three to one, she'd risked her life to save me and had taken me to a hospital without any assurances that I wouldn't talk. Raven had accepted an ultimatum that I was sure put her family in danger. And while her timing left something to be desired, it wasn't like she hadn't intended to tell me the truth. Human or not, she was the same person who made me light up whenever she entered the room. Regardless of what had happened to me, she was still my friend. When my lips rose in an affectionate smile Raven engulfed me in a bone-crunching embrace, knowing forgiveness was behind it.

"Could you untie me?" I asked, lifting my arms against the straps.

She inspected the leather restraints for a minute, and then took my right arm and carefully ran her fingernails underneath my wrist. The strap fell to the floor.

"Like built in Ginsu knives," I teased.

She laughed, freeing my other arm. "You up for getting out of here?"

"Absolutely!" I wanted no part of talking with the police, or having anyone find out who I was. Raven slid the IV out of my arm, taping a piece of cotton over the wound to stop the bleeding, then went back to her chair and returned carrying a small duffel bag.

"Some clothes," she said, answering my unspoken question. She helped me get to my feet and braced my body while I slid my gown off. In a couple of minutes I was dressed in jeans and a red turtleneck sweater. The shoes were a little loose, but I could manage.

"How are we breaking out of here?" I motioned toward the door. "I heard them say something about a cop guarding me."

She grinned. "That wouldn't be a problem even if he was still out there, but he left a few hours ago. It's almost three a.m., and they think you're tethered to your bed." Raven opened the window, ripped out the screen and peeked back over her shoulder. "Follow me."

In one smooth motion she launched herself through the window. After scrambling to the edge I peered down and saw her standing safely on the ground, encouraging me to jump. It was hard to gauge the height in the darkness, but it looked like at least the fourth floor. Way too high to fall safely– even if she did catch me. My mind went to work on the calculations, trying to convince myself of the stupidity of this idea. If I was forty feet up, I'd be falling at over twenty miles per hour when I hit the ground, which would happen in just over two seconds.

All of my reluctance vanished when someone tried to open the jammed outer door to my room. I threw my legs out the window, slid my butt to the edge, closed my eyes and pushed. I was weightless in free fall for only a split second before I was cradled in her arms. It wasn't until we landed that I realized she'd jumped to catch me, halving the distance of the fall. We raced through the darkness to the hospital parking lot where my navy blue Camry was waiting.

"Mind if I drive?" she asked, jingling my keys.

"Not at all." When I climbed into the passenger seat, I felt something poke me in the butt. I reached behind me and pulled out my purse. "Where'd you find this?"

"In the alley next to what was left of the cheesecake you bought. I don't think anything was taken. There's still a couple dollars in your wallet along with your credit card. Your cell phone and iPod are in there too."

"Cool– at least I don't have that to deal with."

She slipped her cell phone out of her jeans and selected a number while she exited the hospital parking lot. I heard a woman answer after several rings. "Hey

Sienna, we're on our way. Please let everyone know we're coming." Raven paused, listening to Sienna's response. "I'll tell her. Thanks."

"What'd she say?" The car was fairly quiet, but I could still only make out about every fifth word.

"She's really looking forward to meeting you. She asked me to explain a few things on the way so you'd have a little better idea what to expect. " Raven pulled into the left turn lane and coasted to a stop at a four way intersection. The newfound rebellious side of me wondered why she was bothering to wait for a green light. There wasn't another car for miles. Even the gas station was deserted. "They'll all be waiting for us in the living room, where they'll each put you under their trance. As a show of trust you need to be submissive, like you were with me in the cafeteria. Humans can't prevent our trance, but we can detect how much someone is fighting us. It's kind of like how a wolf trying to join a new pack submits to the existing pack members. They'll also be able to read your thoughts to varying degrees, so it's important that you're conscious of what you're thinking."

A wave of panic raced through me. There was no way I wouldn't be afraid after what I'd just been through. If that was going to be interpreted as a sign of mistrust, I was screwed. "Raven, I can't."

"It's okay. They know what happened and understand that you'll be afraid. That'll make your submissiveness that much more impressive."

"I can do submissive," I said with a nervous laugh. "Who will I be meeting?"

Raven stepped on the accelerator as she took the onramp onto I-93, and my beat up old Camry bucked in protest. Whatever passing gear it had once possessed gave up the ghost about 60,000 miles ago. She blew out a slow breath and impatiently tapped her fingers on the steering wheel. "Sienna is the matriarch of our family– she brought each of us into this life. She was nineteen when she was infected in 1107. I was the first of our current family to join her, in 1814, when I was twenty. I have two sisters, Ruby and Sandy. Ruby is the oldest in terms of natural age. She was twenty-six when she joined us in 1937. Sandy was twenty-two in 1971. I had a brother, Colt, but he died in 1860. Sienna and I miss him terribly."

My jaw hung open in shocked silence. 1107? Holy shit. Sienna had been alive long before the first American colonies. Even Raven was almost two hundred years old. "What…are you?" I asked, not at all sure I was ready to hear the answer.

Dangerous Waters

She gnawed her lip in thought for a moment while she switched lanes. "That's not as easy of a question as it sounds. Genetically I'm as human as you are, but a virus has permanently altered my body. I guess you could call me a vampire, since the disease I'm inflicted with is the root of the myths."

"But you're not pale and cold, the sun doesn't bother you, you don't have fangs, your heart beats– it doesn't fit."

"Exactly. We still use the term to identify our kind, but the true meaning was lost to the public centuries ago."

Vampires. Even after having my body hijacked and drained of blood, I couldn't get my head around it. I felt like I'd been sucked into one of the urban fantasy novels that were piled in my closet. Next she'd be telling me I was actually a werewolf…or maybe a witch. Casting spells would be pretty cool. Of course with my luck I'd turn dark and destroy the world or something. There was also the very real possibility that I'd snapped after my mom died, and I was lying in a padded room somewhere imagining this crazy-ass nightmare. But the pain in my stitched together wrists felt all too real.

I guess I needed to find out what kind of life I was in for, starting with the most obvious. I gave Raven a squeamish look. "Do all vampires drink human blood?"

She nodded. "We'll get into the specifics as to why later, but for now it suffices to say that we haven't found a way to sustain ourselves without it."

"Where do you get it? Like blood banks and stuff? Your family doesn't kill people, right?"

She met my eyes with a contrite gaze. "We don't have a choice. The blood needs to be fresh, and we can't zap people's brains like on TV and make them forget that we just sucked a pint out of them. If we let even our most cooperative victims go, it wouldn't be long before we were exposed. The only way for us to survive is to stay hidden in the shadows of society."

So much for them being the *good* vampires who popped open a protein shake when they were hungry. But as difficult as that was to hear, what she was saying made sense. I could only imagine the fear and chaos that would erupt if humans found out that they were no longer at the top of the food chain.

"It would be all out war," Raven responded.

"God, you really can read my mind– that's pretty wild. Can you fly or climb walls like in the movies?"

"It's not like we have magic powers or anything," she said with an amused smile. "There are a lot of things we can do that appear to be superhuman, but they're just byproducts of the disease."

I glanced up at her youthful face. An eternal twenty-year-old. If news ever did get out about vampirism, Hollywood actresses would be lining up in droves. "Do you live forever? Will you always look like you're twenty?"

Raven slowed as she exited the highway and merged onto a two lane road I'd missed the name of. From what little I could see from her headlights, we were surrounded by a dense forest with no houses or businesses of any kind. "We don't age, and we'd never die of natural causes, but we can be killed."

"How?" If the cause of vampirism really was a virus, then there was nothing demonic about them, which ruled out the *traditional* methods.

She snorted. "Yeah, crosses and holy water haven't killed many vampires. The most common cause of death is others of our kind. It takes an incredible amount of force to injure us. More than humans can inflict, even with handheld weapons. I couldn't take a tank round to the chest or anything, but combined with our other physical and mental gifts, we don't have much to fear from individual humans."

"So what else will I have to deal with if I do this, besides having to drink human blood I mean." Not that killing people wasn't bad enough. But if there were other drawbacks I'd rather find out now than after I'd committed myself to going through with it.

"You know of our scent of course– that can be difficult to manage. The changes that prevent us from aging have negative side effects as well, like having no ability to heal."

"I remember you saying something about having to wait until I was healed before I could be infected. Is that why?"

"Exactly. Any injuries that weren't fully healed before the transformation would never heal. There are quite a few things we'll need to do to prepare you physically."

"Raven," I whispered, picking nervously at a loose thread on my sweater. "I know you were just trying to get my attention in the hospital, but are you really going to kill me if I decide I can't do this?"

My words cut through her. We rode in silence for a couple of miles with her choking back tears before she'd recovered enough to respond. "Agreeing to Alexander's terms was the only way I could save your life. If we backed out, they'd come after us, which would force my family to step in. I'm sorry, but I won't risk having any of them get killed for a promise that I made. Some friend, huh." She shook her head in disgust.

Dangerous Waters

"Hey, I'd be ashes in a trash barrel right now if it wasn't for you. And I get what you're saying– risking your own life is a hell of a lot different than risking your family. I hope you know I would never put you in that situation. I promise I won't try to escape or anything."

"I know you won't," she said, patting me on the knee. "If I had even the slightest doubt you wouldn't be here right now."

"How can you be so sure? I mean, I'm glad you trust me, but you've only known me for– " Memories of the ride home from our whale watching trip stopped me cold. "The ticket. That's it, isn't it? You were testing me."

A smirk appeared on her lips for just an instant before she turned serious. "After we spent the day together, I knew I wanted you to be my sister, but being a part of our coven requires a degree of selflessness that isn't at all common, especially with your generation. Before I could even think of exposing myself, I had to see if you had that in you."

"So telling me about your scent and trancing me after physics was just the next step?"

"Kind of– it's not like I've done this before, at least not on my own. I thought if I opened up to you gradually, it'd be less of a shock. Until last night anyway, when I realized just how dangerous that could be."

It dawned on me that I had no idea what would happen in the coming days and weeks. I didn't know if I'd be allowed to talk to my dad, to go to school or to see my roommates again. Maybe the plan was to make everyone think that I'd died, so that regardless of what I chose, my old life would be behind me. In some ways pretending would be worse than actual death, knowing all the pain I was causing and being around to witness it. If Angie and Stacey hadn't reporting me missing by now, they wouldn't wait much longer, not after hearing about Wendy yesterday.

"What do we do about school and my friends and family? I really don't want them to think something happened to me."

I could tell from her expression that she was prepared for this. "We'll call the registrar's office on Monday and delay your admission to the summer. I know you planned on working part-time, but there's no need while you're in school– our family is set financially.

"Angie and Stacey think that you're sleeping over at my house tonight, so we're okay for now. You'll need to tell them you had a death in the family or something, some excuse to explain being away for several months. As for your dad, you need to continue to call him like you usually would so he doesn't get concerned. Your physical appearance won't change, so there's no reason you can't visit him for a while as well."

I wasn't sure what *a while* meant, but however long that equated to, it was better than never seeing him again. Assuming I chose to become a vampire, of course, and that I was even given that choice in the first place. Up until now, I'd been so preoccupied with the decision I had to make that I hadn't even considered the possibility that Sienna could say no. "Do you think Sienna will like me?"

"It's not just a matter of her liking you," Raven clarified. "She needs to be assured that you'll fit in with her family, and that this is a life you truly want to live. It's equally important that Ruby and Sandy accept you as a sister. If any of us doesn't want to take you into our family, Sienna will not allow it to happen."

The car slowed and she turned onto a small drive. I'd been so engulfed in our conversation that I had no idea where Raven had taken us. The drive wound its way up a small hillside through thick hardwood trees and pines. The outline of a brightly lit house finally came into view, nestled amongst the surrounding forest. Raven pulled up in front and parked alongside her SUV. My heart shot into overdrive, pounding like a hummingbird's wings. I was about to walk into a house full of vampires, all of them holding my fate in their hands.

Raven pulled my now shaking body into her arms and kissing my forehead. "Everyone is going to love you, Emme. Just be yourself and try to relax."

After a long embrace, I hopped out of the car and followed her up a creek stone walkway to the front porch. The house resembled a luxury cabin, with split log siding and a full-length porch accented by four pine rocking chairs. The front door opened as we approached, and a young woman with reddish-blonde shoulder length hair, a lightly freckled face and a wide smile gazed at me. She was roughly my height and had a very similar build, maybe a couple pounds lighter.

"Welcome to our home, Emily. My name is Sienna," she said in a thick Irish accent. Her arms stretched toward me, and I hurried forward to hug her.

"Nice to meet you. I love your accent," I added awkwardly, not knowing what else to say."

Her eyes warmed as she glided her fingers along the length of my jaw line. "That's very kind. I believe I have something that belongs to you." When Sienna opened her left hand, my mother's necklace was inside.

I could feel my lower lip started to quiver. "How? How did– "

"I had a few words with my dear friend Stefan," she interrupted, clasping it around my neck. "He was not at all pleased to hear about how you were treated."

I wondered if she'd also gotten my earrings back. It seemed logical, but I didn't see them. Sienna grinned and motioned behind me.

"May I?" Raven offered.

I held my hair up while she placed them back in my ears. Tears trailed down my cheeks the entire time. I'd lost all control of my life, and I wasn't even sure I had much of a future to look forward to, but this still mattered– even if I died tonight.

Sienna took my arm and led me into the house. As we entered the living room, we crossed over a section of bare hardwood floor before reaching the luxurious white area rug in the center. The massive carpet occupied the entire space between the chocolate-brown leather couches and the creek stone fireplace in the corner. The walls were covered in lightly stained knotty pine. To the left I could see the entrance to the dining room and kitchen, along with a long, darkened hallway. A second story extended over the room, with a grand staircase and an intricately carved wood railing.

Raven's sisters stood behind the couches, waiting for me. The older woman was a couple inches shorter than I was and very thin. Shiny black hair flowed down to the small of her back, with long layers starting around her cheeks, and she had mysterious dark brown eyes.

"Hi. You must be– Ruby?" I said, walking up to her.

"Very good. Nice to meet you, Emme." She took my hands and shot me a compassionate look. In an instant I was frozen.

My right hand reached up and held my pendant. *It was my mom's*, I thought, figuring that she was asking me about the significance of it. *My dad gave it to her on their first anniversary. They went snorkeling on their honeymoon and had dolphins swim with them. They never forgot that moment, especially not my mom—she always loved wildlife and nature. He gave it to me when I was five, after she died in a car accident, and I've worn it ever since. I know it's just a necklace, but it feels like a small part of her is still with me.*

Ruby released me from her control and pulled me into her arms, sniffling back tears as we hugged. "I'm so sorry. Thank God Sienna was able to get it back for you."

"Thanks, Ruby. And I agree– I owe her big time."

As I headed toward Sandy I noticed that she was wiping her cheeks as well. Did she *hear* my story about the necklace? I had no idea how the whole mind reading thing worked, what the limitations were.

Her light-blonde hair was styled in a more modern pixie cut, with layers at her eyes and the middle of her ears. It had a subtle part on the left side, with wispy bangs touching the tops of her eyebrows. She was wearing pink and white layered t-shirts with light tan cargo pants, which accentuated her lean, fit body. "Hey Sandy."

"Emily." She placed her fingers under my chin and raised it until I was peering straight into her pale blue eyes.

I felt my body being taken from me again. A jolt of fear shot through me as my head bent to the left to lean against my shoulder. My hands swept the hair away from the right side of my neck, grabbed the top of my sweater and stretched it down over my shoulder.

Please don't, I begged. How could Raven not have mentioned that they might feed on me? Maybe she was just as surprised as I was, but I didn't see her rushing in to stop Sandy. I guess I was on my own. *I'm totally exhausted and I feel like shit—I don't think my body could take it.*

"Then you'll let me feed tomorrow? After you've eaten and gotten some rest?"

You won't even have to trance me. If becoming a walking blood bag was what it would take to stay alive, I'd do it, at least until I had a chance to make up my mind.

When she opened her mouth and placed her lips against my exposed throat, I thought her hunger had won out. I braced for the pain– and felt my cheeks scrunch up in a wince instead. "I'm sorry I had to do that, especially after what you've been through, but by letting you live with us we're all placing our lives in your hands. Before I could give that kind of trust, I needed to know that you were willing to place your life in ours."

Another test. I'd passed apparently, in spite of my groveling. "I know it'd be a lot easier and safer for you just to kill me. Thank you for giving me a chance. I promise I won't be any trouble."

I wasn't sure what to do next. I'd already met Sienna, but I hadn't submitted to her yet. And what about Raven? Would she be expecting a turn as well? I glanced in her direction and saw her nod toward Sienna. Taking my cue, I walked over to where she stood near the entrance to the dining room. "You have a wonderful family. Thank you so much for allowing me to meet them."

"Raven was right about you." Her mouth widened into a radiant smile that made her tranquil green eyes even more beautiful. "You have remarkable mental strength and a loving, tolerant heart." Sienna raised my hands up above my head so she could closely inspect my bandaged wrists. "I'm familiar with the agreement she made with Alexander, and I truly hope you choose to become my daughter. You'll need to understand everything there is to know about this life– good and bad– before you can make a decision. I can only accept a fully informed choice. Over the next few weeks we'll educate you and physically prepare you while your body heals. It's late, and I know you're exhausted. Raven will show you to your room." Sienna glided her fingers through my hair as she leaned in and kissed me on the cheek. "Have a good night, my child."

"Thank you, for everything," I said, holding my necklace. "I could never repay you for what you've already done for me."

Raven led me down the hallway past several closed doors before stopping in front of the last door on the left side of the hall. She flipped it open and turned on the light. "Welcome home."

In the center of the enormous room sat a beautiful Queen Victoria canopy bed. The hardwood floors were covered in lush white rugs, and a fire was burning in a creek stone fireplace in the far right corner. There was a mahogany desk against the wall to my left with a laptop, printer and widescreen monitor on top of it. The far left corner contained an oversized brown leather chair, which matched the love seat on the opposite wall. Raven led me across the room to the master bath, which had a Jacuzzi tub and a separate shower. The white marble countertops held a double sink with gold plated faucets. She playfully spun me around and took me to the walk-in closet, enjoying the tour.

All of my clothes from the dorm were neatly hung, taking up a small fraction of the space. There were two built-in oak dressers across the back and a large, mostly empty shoe rack along the right wall.

"How did you get my stuff from the dorm?" She'd obviously made up a much more permanent cover story than having me sleep over.

"I told Angie that your dad suffered a mild heart attack, and that you were taking some time off of school to be with him. You were planning to return this summer and couldn't wait to see her and Stacey again. I said that you were very sorry you couldn't stop by to say good bye in person, but you had to catch a plane and that you would call them soon. I was gathering your things to ship back to you in Traverse City, since you didn't have time to pack. Angie and Doug helped me load everything into my SUV. Sorry I wasn't totally honest on the way over here. I didn't want to freak you out by telling you that I'd already moved you in."

There's no way I would have come up with anything half that convincing. "That's okay. Thanks for taking care of it." It bothered me that I had to lie to them, but I knew I didn't have a choice. Regardless of what I decided, I wouldn't be able to see them for a while. My dad didn't even have the number to my dorm room, so there wasn't much risk of them talking to him– not as long as they could get a hold of me. And if they could no longer reach me, it would mean that he was in for far worse news than finding out that his daughter had left school.

I absently flipped through the blouses and dresses in front of me, shivering as I passed over the padded hanger that my favorite blue dress had rested on. God, was this really all I owned? Granted, skinny jeans, leggings and yoga pants were the staples of my athletic, semi-tomboyish look, and I had a closet full of seldom-worn crap at home that I hadn't brought with me, but still. This was kind of pathetic.

"We've got a lot of shopping to do!" Raven said, interpreting my thoughts.

I turned back toward the bedroom and surveyed the massive space. "This is too much. This room's bigger than my parent's house. I don't deserve all this."

She rolled her eyes at me. "This is actually one of the smaller bedrooms– wait until you see mine. I know it may seem extravagant, but Sienna provides all of us with a very comfortable life."

"I need to thank her– "

"In the morning. Right now you need to get some sleep. There are pain pills in the medicine cabinet." Raven kissed me on the forehead and left.

I threw on a pair of jersey knit pajamas and headed to the bathroom. The drawers were stocked with everything I could possibly need, but all I was interested in at the moment were the pills. The medication from the hospital had worn off, and my wrists were killing me. I opened the medicine cabinet and spotted a prescription bottle on the lower shelf. It was made out to Raven– Tylenol 4 with codeine. After swallowing one of the pills I brushed my teeth, pulled back the Egyptian cotton sheets and crawled into bed. The dwindling light from the fire danced across the walls and ceiling, lulling me to sleep.

Chapter Seven
Vampire 101

I awoke to a light tapping noise on my door. "Come in," I mumbled through my covers. "What time is it, Raven? How long did I sleep?"

"Sorry to wake you," Sienna replied. "It's almost one p.m.– I wanted to see how you were doing." She sat on the edge of my bed and draped her arm over my side.

I quickly pulled back the covers and sat up. "That's okay. I slept great. This room is unbelievable! Thank you so much for letting me stay here."

She slid her bangle bracelets up further on her forearm so they rested just below the sleeve of her red, ballet neck tee. "No need to thank me. Please, think of this house as your home. How's the pain?"

"The pills really helped– it's not too bad right now." I remembered getting up at some point in the night and taking another one.

"I'm glad. You'll have to sponge bathe for the next few days in order to keep the incisions dry. Please let me know if there's anything that you need."

Having Sienna care for me made me realize how much I missed my mom. It felt good to have maternal affection again, even if she was just being a gracious host.

"My sweet child, you can't imagine how wonderful that makes me feel," she said, patting my hand.

My cheeks heated up as my fingers nervously worked over the seam of the comforter. When was I going to learn to reign in my thoughts? "If you can't tell already, I have almost zero control over what goes through my head. How can I keep from hurting someone by thinking something I'd never say to them?"

"We're very good at reading not just the words people think, but also their underlying thoughts and opinions, including things from their past. We can even determine if they intend to act on them."

I half rolled my eyes. This sounded like something straight out of a Star Trek episode. All that was missing was the Vulcan mind meld.

"Let me demonstrate," she said, picking up on my skepticism. "Think about a real event from your life, but try to mislead me with your thoughts to conceal the truth about what happened."

I answered her challenge with narrowed eyes, like we both had our hands over the grip of a six-shooter and were about to draw. After thinking the answer to a couple potential questions before I determined how to disguise it, I realized it would have to be something spur of the moment. *My best friend in high school was Amanda Fisher. We met in sixth grade at a tennis camp. She is going to the University of Michigan now.* "Okay." I started reciting one of my favorite poems in my head in an effort to occupy my mind.

Sienna laughed at my playfulness. "Let me give this a try. You actually despised Amanda *Carter* whom you met in fourth grade. Your best friend is Brittney Mills, who you did meet at tennis camp in sixth grade. Neither of them is going to U of M, although Brittney did apply there."

"How did… I never even thought about most of that!" I said in disbelief. "Can you read my whole mind?"

"No, the person has to think about something for us to access it," she explained. "But your mind suppresses dozens of thoughts for every conscious one it processes. If the brain couldn't do this, people would go mad from the noise in their heads. As you continued on with your story about when you met Amanda, you simultaneously thought about how much you disliked her and who your best friend really was."

"That's too cool! Will I be able to do that?" I was surprised that I didn't feel the need to qualify my question with a "if I choose to be infected" comment. Was I already that confident I was going to choose this life?

Sienna paused, like she didn't know which question to answer first. "You do seem fairly certain of your choice, but that could change as you learn more. Remember, the only choice that matters is the one you make after you're fully informed. As for what mental abilities you'd have, all of our kind can read minds and take control of them, although the strength of these abilities varies from person to person. There are some other things that only a few of us can do. It all depends on your genealogy. Very weak forms of hypnotism and telepathy are still common abilities among modern humans. At some point in our distant past, all humans needed to be able to harness the power of a much stronger form of these gifts just to survive. The transformation process revives these dormant abilities." Sienna stood up and moved toward the door, stretching the bottom of her capri leggings back down below her knees. "Raven will get into more detail with you later. I'd better let you get cleaned up."

After struggling to wash what I could without getting my bandages wet, I threw on my pink rugby striped hoodie and gray lounge pants, grabbed my cell phone and plopped on my bed. I'd promised to call my dad today, and I couldn't risk having him get worried and start calling around. He picked up after the first ring.

"Hi, Dad."

"Hi, honey, I thought you forgot all about me."

I knew he was joking, but his words still pulled at my heart. It took every ounce of strength I had to keep from bursting into tears. "Never."

"So how are things going?"

"Pretty good. I got caught up on most of my homework yesterday, so I should be able to have some fun this weekend. I think it's going to work out well having all my classes on Tuesday and Thursday."

"Good. Are you and your roommates still getting along okay?"

"They're awesome. We played tennis on Thursday. Stacey's pretty good." I wasn't sure if he was referring to Wendy or not, but I wasn't going to mention that unless he made me.

"Do you still have your killer serve?" he asked with a chuckle.

"You know it! I played against both of them. It was a good workout."

"That's my girl! How's Raven doing?"

"She's so cool, Dad. She's in my biology class too. We've been hanging out quite a bit together. I've even gotten to know a few of her friends."

"That's great, Emily. You've always been so good at meeting new people." After a long pause he continued. "What's going on with your other roommate? Have they found her yet?"

"I haven't heard anything new. Nothing's happened around town that I know of either." I nervously bit my lip— my dad could always tell when I wasn't being truthful with him.

"Promise me you'll tell me if you hear anything, okay?" I could hear the anxiety and doubt in his voice.

"I will, Dad. Please try not to worry. I'm really happy."

"I'm so glad to hear that. Hey, I hate to cut this short, but John and I are heading out to play golf. Can I give you a call later?"

"Sure. You'd better hit a few in the trees to make sure he wins." John was at least ten years younger than my dad, but he'd been his boss at the gear manufacturing plant for the last five years.

He snorted. "Oh, I don't have to let him win. I wish I were half as good at golf as you are at tennis."

"Love ya, Dad."

"Love you too. I'll talk to ya soon."

It felt so good to hear his voice again. There were a lot of things I'd never be able to talk to him about, and it killed me to have to lie so much, but our brief conversation reminded me just how badly I needed him. I'd have to make this work somehow.

It was after 3:00 when I finally made my way into the kitchen. I'd decided to give Stacey and Angie a call, and spent most of the conversation adding inane details to Raven's story about my dad. There were so many things I needed to tell them: what happened to me yesterday, what vampires smelled like, where *not* to go for Italian food ever again. But telling other people was exactly what Alexander was afraid I'd do— the reason behind his ultimatum. If vampire rumors started up around campus, our deal would be off, and Raven and I'd both be killed.

I teetered next to the fridge, wondering what I'd find inside. Would they keep blood around for snacks? What about food? Did they eat anything besides blood? Could they? I laughed when I found myself comparing theories from the books and movies I'd seen, like they were the authority on the subject. When I swung open the stainless steel doors, my jaw all but hit the floor. The industrial-size fridge was packed with almost every food imaginable, like a mini-grocery store.

"I tried to tell Sienna she was going overboard," Raven said, leaning back against the counter next to me. "She wanted to make sure you had all your favorites, and since we didn't know what those were yet– "

"You figured you'd just buy everything," I finished for her. "Thanks."

Not wanting to make a huge mess in the spotless kitchen, I poured myself a bowl of Apple Jacks and started munching on them while I waited for my toast to pop up. Raven watched me with amusement.

"Something funny?"

She grinned. "It's been over a hundred and ninety years since I ate anything. Food was a lot simpler back then. What's that taste like?"

"Um, it's really sweet with a little bit of apple flavoring. It's mostly sugar. Would you like to try?" I held my spoon up to her mouth.

"We can't, Emme."

I should have figured that since she hadn't eaten in so long, but I didn't understand what would stop her. "Why? What would happen if you ate?"

"I'd start to feel nauseous and bloated within a few minutes, kind of like food poisoning. It'd continue to get worse until I vomited. Even then I wouldn't feel better right away. I tried to eat eggs once right after I was changed– it was brutal."

I sat in silence for a moment, her words sinking in. No more lasagna, seafood or chocolate. Only blood, forever.

"What's wrong?"

"I was just thinking about all the stuff I'll never be able to eat again. How do you deal with that?"

"It's really hard at first," Raven admitted. "I still miss some of my favorites. Over time you'll learn to view eating as something you need to do to sustain yourself, and detach it from the emotional pleasure it used to bring. I don't even think about it much anymore. There usually isn't any food around to tempt us."

"What do you miss the most?"

"Hmm," she said, tapping her fingernails on the counter. "I'd have to say homemade apple pie and ice cream."

"Good choice!"

Raven's brows lifted in curiosity as her gaze met mine. "How about you? What do you think you'll miss the most?"

I curled my lips in thought. I was a self-confessed pasta addict, especially my grandma's lasagna. But my dad's fresh caught Walleye was a huge summer favorite. Then there was Tony's. What didn't I like there? I'd all but grown up on their shrimp baskets and banana splits. And I'd never met a pizza I didn't like, or variety of chocolate, for that matter. God help the poor soul that was trapped in a chocolate-free house with me. As much as I loved food, I was surprised I didn't weigh six hundred pounds. "It's a toss-up between my grandma's lasagna and chocolate."

Raven draped her arm around my shoulders and gave me a quick hug. "This conversation reminds me of all the things I still need to explain. Are you up for getting out of the house today?"

"Definitely! Where are we going?"

"I thought we could go for a walk in the back yard."

"Sounds like fun." What little I'd seen of the yard last night was beautiful. I couldn't wait to see it in the daylight.

After scarfing down the rest of my cereal, I followed her out the back door. There were at least forty acres of open land behind the house that sloped down to a large pond on the edge of the woods. A small creek wound its way across the valley and emptied into the pond. The land was overgrown with natural grasses like a meadow, and there were several ridges of undisturbed forest lying beyond the creek. The morning air was crisp and had a heavy pine scent to it. We slowly made our way toward the far west side of the pond, following one of several well-worn paths.

"I hope you don't mind if I lecture a bit. Given your interest in science, I think you'll find a lot of this fascinating."

I stepped up alongside her, walking along the grassy edge of the trail, so I could see better and didn't have to speak into her back. "The more detail the better– it's not like I consider changing species every day."

"True," Raven agreed, flashing me a smile. "I thought I'd start by describing the virus's effects at the cellular level. It causes your cell membranes to harden, forming a cell wall like plants, but infinitely stronger and more flexible. It remains selectively permeable, which allows us to utilize the nutrients and energy from our blood while blocking all viruses and bacteria.

"The hardening of the cell walls prevents cells from dividing, so the body can no longer make new cells. That's why we can't heal if we're injured. The virus also changes the intracellular fluid from the usual liquid to a type of preservative substance that keeps our cells from wearing out. This substance gives off a distinct odor, which is the source of our unique scent."

"Where did the virus come from? I mean, I'm assuming it's passed through your blood, since being fed on didn't turn me, but how would the first people have been infected?"

She shrugged her shoulders. "No one knows for sure. It dates back well beyond any formal records. We do know that it's a symbiotic virus that goes to great lengths to preserve its host. Our guess is that it first inhabited some sort of primitive bacteria that early humans ingested. Once inside the body, the virus would have adapted to spread to human cells.

"We're not a perfect host for it, since it interferes with our ability to sustain ourselves. The first human victims would have almost certainly starved to death. People infected with the virus probably figured out that drinking other people's blood kept them alive through some sort of primitive blood ritual. Humans lived in small bands of nomadic clans in our early days, so it's unlikely that the virus would have spread beyond a handful of people for thousands of years."

I had to drop back behind her as the trail narrowed and we descended down a fairly steep knoll that was overgrown with wild rose bushes. "Why can't vampires eat food?" I asked, recalling our earlier conversation. "What is it that makes you get sick?"

Raven picked up a loose stone the size of a flattened muskmelon before I could trip on it. With a casual flick of her wrist she sent it sailing hundreds of yards, landing dead center in the pond with an impressive splash. Okay then. If there were any ill-advised, last-ditch escape plans dancing around inside my head, knowing that she could decapitate me from a quarter mile away certainly put the kibosh on them. "The virus affects the mechanical and chemical digestive processes of the stomach and small intestine," she said nonchalantly, like she'd done nothing more impressive than skip a stone. "The only process that functions is absorption, so the proteins, fats, sugars and other nutrients our bodies require need to already be broken down into a form that can be absorbed directly into our blood."

Something about her explanation didn't make sense. I got the digestive part, but what she was describing as far as base nutrients sounded like what you could get in any number of modern nutritional drinks. I wasn't stupid enough to think I'd stumbled onto some great epiphany they'd never thought of– there were GNC stores everywhere, after all– but I was still curious.

"There are tons of liquid supplements that have amino acids, glucose and other nutrients in them. Isn't that basically what you get from blood? Why can't you just drink those?"

Raven gathered a fistful of her long blonde hair and slowly exhaled as her shoulders slumped. "Sienna and I spent years trying to answer that question. We even created several compounds of our own. All of them either made us sick or passed through us without any absorption. We finally concluded that the virus itself has evolved over thousands of years so that it can only extract nutrients from ingested blood. Since blood was the only viable food source available until the recent health craze, it makes sense that natural selection would have favored the strains of the virus that were specialists. Our best hope at this point is to manipulate the virus genetically– or get it to mutate on its own through controlled experiments– so that it can process non-blood alternatives."

"So that's why you're studying cell biology and genetics," I said, moving up beside her again as the trail wound through a thin set of pines. "Should I change my major?" The prospect of abandoning my lifelong dream struck me like a vicious punch to the gut, but rising temperatures and melting ice caps seemed kind of insignificant at the moment.

Raven placed her hand on my shoulder and brought us to a stop, turning me to look at her. "Absolutely not. Your longevity will allow you to study global warming's progression over time and guide our efforts to combat it. Our very survival– at least for the foreseeable future– depends on a stable earth capable of sustaining human life." Her eyes brightened in a devious, none too innocent grin. "Consider it our plan B."

Plan B as in, if they couldn't find an alternate food source, it was my job to ensure the *cattle* continued to thrive. Not exactly altruistic, but she was at least partially kidding. I hoped. I gave her a what-am-I-going-to-do-with-you huff. "Nice, Raven. Way to sleaze up my dream."

"I aim to please."

I shot my shoulder into her, which I instantly regretted. It was like smashing into iron. After giving it a few rubs we resumed walking again. "So what about animals? Why couldn't we feed on them instead?"

"Very few animals eat anything close to the balanced diet that we require, and their bodies only produce some of the essential enzymes, acids and other chemical compounds that don't come from food. We can feed on them in a pinch, but we couldn't survive on a pure animal diet for very long. And before you ask, raiding blood banks or hospitals isn't an option either, since blood that's been processed and stored loses its nutritional value. We need to drink fresh human blood every seven to ten days. If we don't, we become lethargic and would eventually die of starvation."

Raven took my hand to steady me as we shimmied down a rocky side hill and popped out of the trees. The crystal clear pond was less than twenty yards away, and was home to several families of ducks. The sound of frogs croaking away the afternoon was super relaxing, and made me feel like I was back in Northern Michigan.

"Can we drink anything besides blood?" I asked, watching the smallest of the baby ducks paddle his little legs off trying to catch up to his mama. The thought of drinking blood as food was disgusting enough. I couldn't imagine having to quench my thirst with it too.

"Drinking water is as important to us as it is to humans. We can drink most other semi-clear liquids as well. We don't get anything out of them, but they still taste good." Raven turned and peered back into the forest. I tried to follow her gaze, but I couldn't spot what had captured her attention. "Shh," she whispered.

We stood and watched as a doe and her yearling fawn emerged from the woods at the edge of the clearing. The doe gracefully leaped over the creek and paused while the clumsy fawn splashed his way through it. After he rejoined his mom, they slowly meandered out of sight. I knew from our whale watching trip that Raven loved nature, but I was still thrilled to see the look of pure fascination in her eyes.

She took my hand, and we started walking again, following the creek bed toward a distant pine ridge. "Sienna mentioned that the transformation process revives dormant mental abilities. How does it do that? Where did our abilities come from?"

"When the dormant cells in our brains are transformed by the virus, they start to serve whatever function they had originally– our minds basically become aware of them again. Humans only use about five percent of their brains today. That's mainly because our needs have changed over time, as we continue to adapt to a changing environment."

When we rounded the first corner, the creek forked to the left, cutting off our path. It was only about eight feet across the tiny tributary, and I was tempted to jump it, but I really didn't feel like coming up short and tumbling backward into the shallow water. Seeing my hesitation, Raven opened her arms, and I hopped into them with a giggle. With no more effort than a regular stride she sprang across the gap, landing a good ten feet down the trail.

"There was a small group of vampires in London that did extensive research on the origin of our mental powers back in the beginning of the twentieth century," she continued after setting me back on my feet. "They theorized that our trance ability stemmed from the last ice age, when primitive humans, a pathetically weak animal with minimal intelligence, managed to drive all of the great beasts to extinction in a very short period. Only those with a natural ability to calm their prey long enough for their clan members to spear it survived to have offspring. Over time natural selection strengthened this latent calming ability into a more forceful hypnotic trance, allowing them to control the minds of the beasts completely. As we moved our way up the food chain, we no longer required this ability to survive, and it was bred out of us. Similarly, the need to read each other's minds was diminished with the development of complex oral and written communication skills. The abilities we receive and the strength of them depends on our genealogy. We only regain powers that our bloodline once had, and that are still dormant in our minds."

When we reached the top of the ridge Raven led me through some thick underbrush to a small clearing with a picturesque view of miles of untamed forest. "I come up here whenever I need to get away from things for a while," she said as she gazed almost reverently over the land. "I know it was probably more of a hike getting here than you bargained for, but I wanted you to see it."

I laced my fingers through hers and squeezed her hand. "It's beautiful,

Raven. Thank you for bringing me here." Neither of us felt the need to say anything more. I lost myself in the scents and sounds unique to the deep woods, from the endless chatter of a nearby fox squirrel to the cawing of a crow, and the thick, earthy pine scent of the needle rich soil.

As we headed down the fairly steep pine ridge toward home I couldn't resist asking a couple more questions. "You said that I'd look the same after I'm changed. Can our bodies change at all once we're vampires?"

"Not really," she said, holding back a pine bow so it didn't whiplash me in the face. "Your appearance is basically locked in by the transformation. Your weight will remain constant, since your body can't create or break down cells, and your skin tone will never change regardless of how much sun you're exposed to. Also, your hair and nails will no longer grow, so you need to have them how you want them before you're changed. As you've seen, our nails play a vital role in our lives for feeding and defense."

"So to prepare myself, I'll need to grow my nails out, heal completely and make sure my hair is how I want it. Am I missing anything?"

The almost maniacal grin on her face made me wish I'd never asked. "Your strength will be determined by how much muscle tissue you have when you're changed, so it would be wise for us to make you as strong as possible before then. We setup a room for you with nautilus and cardio equipment along with some free weights. We can do aerobics and Pilates together too!"

I started to imagine my superhuman best friend running me ragged in our home gym and was suddenly grateful that we only had until Thanksgiving to change me.

Chapter Eight
Twenty Questions

Seeing a small flash of movement, I glanced up from the ancient copy of *The Maltese Falcon* I was reading to find a decked out Sienna and Raven standing in my bedroom doorway. Sienna's sheer top revealed a skimpy black tank underneath that went well with her jet-black designer jeans and three-inch heels. Raven's red sleeveless dress covered leather knee boots, and was accented by a three-quarter length black leather coat. "Where are you going?"

"We thought we'd catch a movie," Raven replied, fastening the two buttons at her waist.

I gave her a hopeful look. "Can I come? I could be ready in like five minutes."

Raven shared a look with Sienna as they both smiled. "That would kinda defeat the purpose."

"So you're sick of me already?" I joked.

Sienna snorted. "Not quite– we thought it'd be good for you to spend some time with Sandy and Ruby."

"Oh." It dawned on me that I hadn't seen either of them since we met. It's not like I was avoiding them or anything. I'd just slept most of the day, and then spent the rest of the time walking with Raven. Okay, that wasn't entirely true. Judging by my bookmark, I'd spent at least the last four hours curled up on my bed reading. *Shit.* "I didn't realize it had gotten so late."

"That's certainly understandable." Sienna took a seat on the bed next to me and picked up the book. "Hammett was a true master of the hard-boiled detective genre. I've read this countless times, and it still mesmerizes me."

"But Sandy and Ruby must think– "

"What? That your whole life's been turned upside down and you're doing your best to cope?" Raven countered. "Trust me. They get it."

Sienna patted my knee, and then stood up, walking over to join Raven. "We won't be too late. Our numbers are in the contact list on your phone, so give us a call if you need anything."

"I'm fine– I'm sure we'll find something fun to do." I was pretty sure that "something fun" would end up being a couple hours of awkwardly watching TV together, but even that would be a huge step forward from where we were now.

After following them to the door, I went into the kitchen and made a grilled cheese sandwich, grabbed a bag of cool ranch Doritos and a diet Mountain Dew and took a seat at the table.

Sandy and Ruby were sprawled out on the living room floor, playing some kind of Xbox 360 military game. They had the volume cranked up so high that it sounded like we were being invaded. I was tempted to join them, but figured eating on the couch might be frowned upon. *Hell... Eating's frowned upon.*

"Good one, Emme!" Ruby hollered.

"Um– thanks." Damn. I was really going to have to get used to this whole mind reading thing.

I didn't want to seem like I'd just traded hiding in my bedroom for hiding in the dining room, so I ate as fast as I could, washed the dishes and took a seat on the couch behind Sandy. From what I could tell they were fighting against each other, but I had no idea who was winning.

"There's another controller over there," Sandy said, motioning toward the coffee table with her head. "Just hit the start button and use the left stick to scroll through the menus."

"Okay." My eyes widened when I picked it up. There were buttons, triggers and control sticks all over the friggin' thing. Granted, I'd never been much of a gamer, but that didn't keep me from feeling like a complete dork. When the TV went silent, I glanced up and saw Ruby and Sandy smiling at me.

"We could watch a movie," Ruby suggested.

Before I could respond, Sandy grabbed the remote and turned off the TV. "I've got a better idea. Let's play *ask Emme*."

Oh God. "Ask me what?"

"Whatever we want– kind of like twenty questions."

I fought back the urge to let out a huge yawn, claim how tired I was from the pain killers and bolt for my bedroom. Being questioned by people you couldn't hold anything back from sounded more like an interrogation than a game, but they had to get to know me somehow. "Can I pass if I don't like a question?"

Sandy grinned as she mulled over my request. "We'll do it like truth or dare. If you don't like the question, you can choose the challenge instead. Sound fair?"

"I can live with that. Fire away."

To my surprise, Ruby was the first to jump in, tossing her long dark hair over her shoulder as she leaned back against the opposite couch. "I know you're into tennis and the whole nature thing, but what else do you like to do? What do you and your friend Brittney do for fun?"

I felt a huge rush of relief. Hopefully the rest of the questions would be this easy. "We both love to dance. Even if we go to a movie or bowling or whatever, we almost always end up at the club. In the winter we go snowboarding. Most of the time though we just hang out at each other's house, or do stuff with my dad."

"Not a lot of teenagers would hang out with their friend's parents. Sounds like she's pretty down to earth."

"She is," I agreed. "But our families are really close too."

Sandy got up and took a seat next to me on the couch, tucking her black nylon-clad legs beneath her. The neckline of her thin pink sweater hung at the edge of her shoulders, showcasing a lacy black cami that didn't quite reach the top of her leather skirt. I'd never be bold enough to wear dark maroon lipstick or eye shadow, let alone the black leather choker she had on, but I had to admit the semi-goth look worked for her. Given her club-worthy outfit, I was guessing she'd either rearranged her plans to spend time with me, or was still planning to head out later on. She scrunched her lips around for a few seconds before her brows shot up. "Oh, this is a good one! What are you the most ashamed of in your life?"

So much for the softball questions. Fuck. Nice to meet you too. I peered down at the floor while I considered some of the many options I had to choose from. Getting annihilated in the state championship singles final was right up there. So was cheating on a chemistry exam my junior year. And not making much of an effort to get to know my grandparents had to be in my top five for sure. But while all of those bothered me, I didn't beat myself up over them– not every day anyway. There was only one thing that ever made me cry myself to sleep. "I'd say it's that I remember so little about my mom. I know I was young when she died, but it's not like I was a baby. How could I totally forget her? I can't even remember what her voice sounded like anymore."

Sandy leaned in and gave me a hug. "God, I'm so sorry. I swear I'm not usually such an insensitive bitch. This was a really stupid idea."

"No, it's okay. Let's keep going."

I could see the concern and doubt in her eyes. "Are you sure?"

"Two down, eighteen to go." I tucked a chunk of hair behind my ear and forced a smile. If I wanted us to be close, I would have to let them in.

"What's your favorite vampire movie?" Ruby asked, obviously trying to lighten the mood.

"The first *Underworld* by far— Selene really kicks ass. I dressed up like her for a Halloween party my junior year, but most people thought I was either Lara Croft or Trinity."

Sandy arched her eyebrows. "Leather top and everything?"

"Yep. I even dyed my hair jet black with that temp color stuff. My dad thought I was nuts."

"I'm surprised he let you out of the house," Ruby cut in. "A seventeen-year-old going to a party dressed head-to-toe in skin-tight leather— how'd you pull that off?"

I could feel my cheeks blushing. "I got dressed at Britt's house."

"Ahh." They both laughed.

"Okay, back to the real questions," Sandy insisted. "Out of everything you've accomplished so far, what are you the most proud of?"

I curled my lip in thought. "God, that's hard...getting accepted to BU, I guess. That or the project I did for my gold award in girl scouts."

"What was your project?"

"I organized a bunch of volunteers to repaint the wolf exhibit at our zoo. We also planted trees to give them some shade and put in a little enclosure like a den. They only have two wolves, but it always made me so sad to see them just lying there in a little dirt area without anything to do. We ended up having a really good time."

"This one's more philosophical," Ruby said, crossing her maroon legging-clad legs Indian style so she was sitting more upright. "If I handed you ten million dollars right now, no strings attached, what would you do with it?"

Given what I knew about their finances, this was hardly some far-fetched "what if" scenario, and my response might determine whether they were willing to accept me as a sister. *Not that there's any pressure or anything… Jesus.* "I've never had more than a thousand dollars in my life, so if I'm being totally honest, I don't know what the hell I'd do. I'd like to think that I'd pay off my dad's house, make sure he had enough money to retire, and spend the rest buying land around Yellowstone for the buffalo to graze on in the winter."

"You left out solving world hunger, Miss Michigan," Sandy teased, holding her hand up to my face like a microphone.

I laughed and slapped it away. "Shut up! Let's see you do any better. At least I was honest."

"Don't let her fool you– she's just as impressed as I am. You didn't have a single thought about spending a dollar of it on yourself."

Sandy huffed and gave us both an exaggerated eye roll. "We'll anoint her for sainthood later. Right now it's time to get down and dirty."

Oh crap.

My dread only made her smile widen further. "So, let's have it. Who was the lucky guy who deflowered our fine young princess? Did he rock your world?"

"Dare!" I all but screamed at her. The not-so-sordid details of my pathetic sex life weren't anything I wanted to talk about. The closest I'd come to getting laid was after my senior prom, when Logan, my boyfriend for all of two months, climbed into bed with me and slid his hand between my legs while we made out. Things got pretty steamy with both of us naked, and before long I found myself going down on him. Any chance he had of taking it further ended– along with our relationship– when he held my head down on top of him and came in my mouth. Of course telling me to "swallow it baby, like a good little whore" probably didn't help his cause any.

"Dare? Seriously? Shit! Why'd I agree to that?" Sandy complained.

"Oh, screw you– like you didn't already read my mind." Her poker face wasn't that good.

"Men can be real assholes sometimes," Ruby muttered. "I'm glad you didn't let him treat you that way."

"Me too," Sandy added. "But you should have played along with the prick until he kissed you, and then spit it back in his mouth."

Ruby and I both burst out laughing. "Damn it! That would've been perfect!" I said. "Where were you five months ago!"

Sandy slid her arm around my side and pulled me close to her. "I think you'll fit right in around here, roomie."

"Thanks– I'm really glad we did this." Figuring I had nothing to lose, I picked up the joystick that had intimidated me earlier. "You up for training a new recruit?"

"Hell ya!" Sandy said, scrambling off the couch to reclaim her spot on the floor.

We spent most of the night battling our way through incredibly complex missions, laughing our asses off as I died one horrid death after another. Whatever genes were responsible for video game proficiency, I sure as hell didn't inherit them. But regardless of how many times they had to tell me which button did what, or replay missions that they could have won on their own with their eyes closed, they never lost their patience. I even got yelled at by Sienna for the first time when I left my icy glass of diet Mt. Dew on the coffee table without using a coaster. My life was still a mess. And I had impossible decisions to make. But this was starting to feel like a home.

Chapter Nine
The Choice

I cast the shower a yearning glance and finished wiping myself down with a damp washcloth. Missing one day hadn't been much of an inconvenience, but now I felt sticky and gross all over, and I still had five days of sponge baths to go. I could only hope that the funky smell I was picking up was coming from my pajamas.

"Emme?" Sienna called through the door.

"Yeah, be right out." At least I'd have clean bandages soon– the yellowish drainage stains were disgusting.

"Would you like me to wash your back?" she offered.

"Ah, sure. If you wouldn't mind."

"Not at all."

Holding my towel across my chest, I spun around so my back was facing the door.

Sienna picked up the washcloth I'd been using, rinsed it out in the sink and began to gently slide it across my shoulders. "Is that too hot?"

"No– that feels good." She was even combining the bath with a light massage.

Once she'd finished with my shoulders, she continued down my back, toweled me dry and helped me into my bathrobe. I followed her out of the bathroom and sat on my bed facing her with my right arm raised toward her chest so she could brace it while she removed the bandages. She didn't take hold of it, and it looked like she was a million miles away. "What's wrong?"

"I'm just worried," she said, letting out a strained sigh. "It's far too soon. I would never have timed it like this if I'd known."

"Sorry Sienna, you lost me. Timed what?"

"It's been over a week since we fed."

"Oh." I could feel a nervous shudder tingle up my spine. "So you're going to be, um…going out today?"

"Unfortunately we have to feed here. I thought about dropping you off somewhere, but I think it'd be best if you just stayed in your room. You're going to know what we're doing whether you're here or not, and I'd rather be with you to help you through it."

As weird as it would be to know that they were killing someone just outside my door, her logic made sense. It'd be even worse if I was alone. "I won't have to do anything, right?"

She cupped my cheek with her hand, caressing it lightly with her thumb. "Nothing at all. We can watch TV or do whatever you like."

"And you'll be with me the whole time?"

"Well, one of us will be, yes."

Oh right, she'd have to feed at some point. I gazed into her eyes and nodded my head. "Okay."

Sienna leaned forward and kissed me on the forehead. "Thank you for being so brave, sweetheart. I know this is going to be difficult, but we'll get through it together."

Her simple term of endearment warmed me inside like a cozy fire, one that reached all the way to my soul. The sudden and intense attachment I felt was inexplicable. I wanted to have a mother again. I wanted her to *love* me.

"I'd be truly blessed to have such a splendid daughter," Sienna said, sweeping my bangs away from my eyes with her fingers. "And as my child you'd be loved until the very last beat of my heart. Unfortunately, that's not a decision you're ready to make."

My head drooped as I slumped back away from her. I felt like one of those puppies at the pet store that was good enough to pet for a few minutes but not quite worth taking home. "I know what I'm choosing– Raven spent hours talking with me yesterday."

She tilted my chin up with her fingers and smiled. "You'd be the first puppy out of the cage. But you'll need to feed alongside me before I can accept your choice."

The thought of drinking blood alone made my stomach curl, and it wasn't like I'd be grabbing a sports bottle of O negative out of the fridge. Could I really take part in killing someone? Hundreds of people? I wouldn't even let my dad go deer hunting. Now I was just supposed to snap my fingers and become a serial killer? Not that anyone in my adoptive family fit that mold. They were some of the most kindhearted, compassionate people I'd ever met. God, this was confusing. "I hope I can do it someday."

"So do I baby, but that's nothing you need to worry about today."

I pulled back and wiped my tear-stained cheeks on the sleeve of my robe. "Speaking of today, how much time do I have to get ready?"

Dangerous Waters

"They should be back in an hour or so. We'd better get started."

Sienna removed the old bandages then inspected my wounds, pressing lightly around the edges of the cuts to check for pain. Thankfully, they appeared to be healthy. The edges of my skin were stitched together in long, jagged lines. It'd be quite a while before they scarred over. After replacing the pads, she wrapped my wrists in gauze and put a layer of bright pink vet wrap over the top for protection.

"Any numbness? Did I wrap them too tight?"

I flexed and gripped my hands a couple times. "No– they feel pretty good."

Sienna gave my shoulder a pat. "I'll step out so you can get dressed." Don't worry. I'll be back before they arrive."

* * * *

I figured that if I was confined to my room, I might as well be comfortable, so I threw on my favorite sweatpants and an oversized t-shirt, grabbed the remote and flopped on the bed. Nothing held my interest for more than a few seconds. When I grew tired of switching channels, I gave up and pulled out my laptop.

The people I cared about staying in touch with usually texted me, posted on my wall or called, so I never received much email that wasn't junk, pretty much just distant relatives and pseudo friends. I declined an offer to visit my cousin over spring break, citing my lack of cash. He was a senior at the University of Montana and, compared to the rest of my mom's relatives, was actually pretty cool. Unfortunately his mom was a complete bitch who treated my dad like shit.

Thinking about my dad wasn't helping. What would he think of me after today? At the very least I was going to end up being an accomplice to murder. And if he ever saw me again, it would mean that I'd killed people myself. I was so not ready to deal with any of that, so I hopped on the internet and went to Facebook. I was still flipping through Britt's latest photo album when Sienna walked in, closing the door behind her.

"*Friends* or *Everybody loves Raymond*?" she asked, holding up two box sets.

"Definitely *Friends*." The last thing I wanted to do was think more about families, even goofy, fictional ones.

Sienna inserted a disc then curled up next to me on the bed. By the end of the first scene my uneasiness was gone, and we were both laughing and recalling our favorite episodes. I was having such a good time that I managed to forget *why* we were in here— until Raven took Sienna's place.

There were no outward signs that she'd done anything, but just seeing her was enough to snap me back into reality. Somewhere in this house somebody's loved one was being slowly drained of their life, and I was just sitting here. I wasn't stupid enough to think I could actually stop them, but what did it say about me that I wasn't at least begging and pleading for them not to go through with it? Hell, I wasn't even crying.

Maybe it was just too abstract to seem real. After all, I hadn't actually seen anyone or heard anything. For all I knew they'd changed their mind and were just watching TV out in the living room. It was like trying to make yourself care about a faceless victim you heard about on the news— just white noise.

But what if that wasn't the case? What if seeing someone die didn't totally freak me out like it should? If I could stand to be in the same room when they fed, I'd be one step closer to feeding myself— and one step closer to living beyond Thanksgiving.

Raven swept my hair back and tucked it behind my ear. "I totally get your logic, but trying to push yourself could also backfire. You're handling this better than any of us would have ever dreamed. Let's not ruin it by rushing you into something you're not ready for."

"Please. I need to do this."

She sat in silence, gnawing at her lip, and then let out an exasperated groan. "If this doesn't go well, Sienna's going to kill me."

* * * *

My heart took on an almost spastic rhythm as I crept down the hall behind her, stopping at the first door on the right side of the hall. Raven turned the handle, pushed it open, and then stepped aside and motioned me forward. I could see Sandy standing near the back of the room, her surprise fading into an amused smile. I'd almost reached her before I glanced to my left and froze in my tracks. A middle-aged white female dressed in worn, tattered clothes was lying on a hospital gurney with her arms stretched out to her sides. Ruby and Sienna had a hold of them, and were feasting on her blood.

Raven tried to comfort me, but rather than being repulsed by the sight of them feeding, I saw the naturalness of it— they looked like a lion pride on a kill.

Dangerous Waters

There wasn't any taunting or torture, they weren't making the woman watch, and she was still fully clothed. Her eyes were closed and she seemed at peace.

When Sienna finished, Raven led me to her side. I couldn't get a good read on her expression, somewhere between fear and concern, but at least she didn't look angry. Using the top of her shirt, she wiped the blood off her lips, and then just sat there, studying my face.

I'm okay, I assured her. *Really. It looked very natural, like you were a lioness.*

I could tell that she wanted to believe me, but she just kept staring, sure that I'd break down at any second and run screaming from the room. When she realized that she still had a hold of the woman's arm, she snapped out of her trance and laid it down by her side.

I continued to watch as blood seeped out onto the gurney, wondering what it would taste like and if I'd ever be able to make myself drink it. I still had ten weeks, but what difference would that really make? What would change between now and then that would make this any easier? At some point I was going to have to do this, or accept that I couldn't and forfeit my life. In spite of what everyone had said about me having plenty of time, I knew I was facing my decision. If I couldn't do this, I couldn't join them, and I would never see my dad again.

"Emme, come on, this is crazy," Raven pleaded. "You're putting way too much pressure on yourself. No one expected you to even be able to leave your bedroom tonight. The fact that you could watch us so calmly is a great sign that you'll be able to feed in time."

"I have to try," I muttered, lifting the woman's arm up to my mouth. Dark red blood was still bubbling out of her severed vein, running across her skin and down onto the floor. I touched it with my tongue. It tasted hot and salty, like when I had a nosebleed and had to swallow some of it.

My eyes drifted shut as I wrapped my lips around her wrist and began to suck, awkwardly at first, and then settling into a rhythmic motion. Blood started to pump into my mouth, and I eagerly swallowed it down. It was as if my body sensed that I needed to drink to sustain my life. My need was dictated by circumstances rather than hunger, but her blood was no less essential to my survival. After taking several gulps, I placed her arm back by her side, wiped my mouth and glanced up at everyone. For the first time, they resembled the pale creatures of myth, their faces bleached white by shock.

Four shocked vampires watching a human drink blood—this has got to be a first.

Sienna cupped my face with her hands and gave me a serene smile. "That was incredibly brave of you, and I accept your choice. But the choice is not yours alone. Go with Raven now, so she can prepare you for your naming ceremony. If all of my daughters take you as their sister, you will become my child. Either way, your human life will end tonight."

* * * *

Raven knocked on my door then poked her head in. I hadn't moved since collapsing on my bed in shock. I'd thought making myself drink had freed me from my pending death sentence. Instead it'd just expedited the sentencing phase of my trial. I hadn't given them a chance to get to know me at all. Now they had to accept me as a sister– tonight. Fuck, how did I get myself into these things? "I'm kinda freaking out here."

She plopped down next to me on the bed and patted my knee. "Relax, Emme. I've already talked with Sandy and Ruby. They would have liked some more time to get to know you, but you must have made a pretty good impression last night. They're both on board."

"What about Sienna? Did you hear her in there? I thought she'd be happy." Recalling the indifference in Sienna's voice as she'd told me I might die tonight made me hug my knees against my chest.

Raven pulled my trembling body into her arms. "Are you serious? Have you seen the way she looks at you? If she's a lioness, you're her prized new cub. She loves you."

I let out a breath I hadn't even realized I'd been holding. So maybe I wasn't going to die tonight. Yay me. "What did she mean by my naming ceremony? Is it like a religious thing?"

"The names you know us by are not our birth names," Raven began. "They were given to each of us when we joined this family. We've found that it's safer to use names that don't have a past, especially with the advent of the internet. If someone that met you in 2040 searched for an Emily Waters from Traverse City, it wouldn't take much digging to figure out when you graduated, or to find pictures to compare you to. Not all covens take this precaution, but Sienna always has."

So her name wasn't actually Raven. That threw me a bit. I couldn't imagine her as anything else. "What's your real name?"

"Elizabeth Black."

Certainly not that. Although Beth Black was kind of catchy. "Pretty…but I like Raven better."

"So do I," she said with a grin. "Ruby's name was Mary Jewel, Sandy's was Maria Glass and Colt's was Nicholaus De Marre. Are you detecting a pattern?" Her face filled with anticipation, waiting for me to catch on.

I ran them through my head again. *Elizabeth Black… Raven, Mary Jewel… Ruby, Maria Glass… Sandy, Nicholaus De Marre… Colt.* I may not have been Mensa material, but even I didn't have much trouble with that encryption. "They're all a play on your last names. Is Sienna's last name Brown?"

"Well, that one kinda breaks the pattern. She came up with her naming scheme when she named Colt, but she chose her name based on her favorite color. Probably because she couldn't make much out of her real name, Aillenn Inghean Domnall."

"So my new name will be something off of Waters. Any hints?" I gave her the most pathetic, puppy dog look I could muster. I was never any good at waiting for surprises. My dad had got so fed up with my snooping at Christmas that he started keeping everything locked in his office at work.

She just laughed. "I honestly don't know, ya goof. She hasn't told any of us. There are a lot of possibilities."

"What do we do for last names? Will mine be Williams too?"

"We assume new public identities with our own surnames each time we move. Sienna will probably use your coven name on your first license, just to make things less confusing for you, but that will be the only time it's used."

"Wait a minute," I said, my brow furrowing. "Aren't you going by Raven right now?"

"I'm not supposed to be. I had to create a second ID when we started spending time together, since you already knew me as Raven." She tilted her head and a warm smile lit her mouth. "I was so impressed with your bravery and kindness that night at the party. When I told you my real name and invited you to go outside for a walk, I was already beginning to hope you might become my sister."

Suddenly our run in with the police made a lot more sense. "So the car was registered to you. But if you're Stephanie, who'd the cop talk to when she called?"

"Sienna and I list each other's cell phones as our contact numbers, just as Sandy and Ruby do. If we ever get a call we don't recognize, we answer generically and figure out what needs to be said."

"I wondered why you stumbled so much with your last name in biology."

She laughed. "Yeah, you'd think it'd become second nature after a while, but it always takes me a few weeks when we move. And switching names twice was even worse. I was just starting to get used to Jennings. "

"But what if they check? How did you register?"

"Our ability to read minds makes it very easy to get passwords. After that it's just a matter of some late night data entry and voila! Raven Williams is registered. Makes it easy to get the classes you want too."

"How sneaky! I like it!"

Raven leaned her shoulder into me and smiled. "I've got a surprise for you – wait right here." She disappeared into my closet then returned holding a large white box. "To make up for the dress you lost."

The memory of watching my dress burn made my whole body cringe, but I quickly brushed it aside. "You didn't have to do that."

"Open it."

After pulling the top off I peeled back the tissue paper, revealing a beautiful maroon halter dress. I sprang to my feet so Raven could hold it up to me. It came down to my knee and had a plunging neckline that went well below my breasts. With almost reckless abandon, I ripped off my clothes and slid it on.

"I knew it was perfect for you!" Raven hurried me to a mirror so I could see.

I wasn't used to showing so much cleavage, but it looked incredible. I slipped into my favorite gladiator sandals, which matched my dress to a T, and took a seat in front of the vanity mirror while she meticulously applied my makeup.

"So what all's involved with the ceremony?" I asked as she switched over to French braiding my hair.

"We'll each ask for the gift of your blood, and after we've tasted it, we'll make a pledge to you. Once we finish, you'll repeat the pledge back to us."

"Okay. I think I can handle that."

She took a step back, admiring her work. "You look amazing. I've gotta run and get ready now– I'll come get you in a couple of minutes."

I stared at myself in the mirror while I thought of potential names. I'd never looked so mature or so beautiful. Raven returned wearing a stunning white strapless satin dress and escorted me from the room.

When we entered the living room, Ruby and Sandy took my hands and led me toward Sienna, who stood near the back with a glowing smile on her face.

Dangerous Waters

The room was lit with soft candlelight, and I could hear classical music playing in the background. The entire experience felt magical.

Sandy and Ruby released me and lined up to Sienna's left. Raven joined them, standing next to Ruby, and motioned for me to come to her. She lifted my right hand, palm side up, and ran a nail across the tip of my index finger. I felt a sharp sting, and blood began to ooze from the wound.

"Emme, would you give me the gift of life, the gift of your blood?"

"Yes," I responded, reaching my hand toward Raven's mouth. I could feel the pressure as she began to suck.

After a moment she stopped and kneeled down on the floor. "I pledge to defend you with my life, and to always place the needs of the coven and my sisters above my own." Her face beamed as she sprung to her feet.

I kneeled before her. "Raven, I pledge to defend you with my life, and to always place the needs of the coven and my sisters above my own." Raven helped me stand, and then wrapped her arms around me in a heartfelt embrace. I repeated the ritual with Ruby, Sandy and Sienna.

"We welcome a new member to our family tonight, my loved ones," Sienna proclaimed. "Her physical transformation will not happen for a couple months, but she's made her choice to join us for eternity, and we have all accepted her. Emily's life has now come to an end. While she will assume many identities for the outside world, from this moment forward she will be known to our coven as Brooke."

I hadn't felt any sort of connection to the potential names that had crossed my mind earlier, but hearing Brooke for the first time made my skin tingle. There was some sort of unexplainable rightness to it, like finding the perfect house to call home.

Chapter Ten
On The Prowl

Raven and I strolled along a wide, well groomed trail toward a small wooden bridge that crossed over the creek just east of the pond. The Black-eyed Susan, evening primrose and goldenrod were in full bloom, framing the path in a variety of vivid yellow shades. It had been almost a week since the last time we walked together. I was finally off the pain pills and had fallen into a pretty normal routine, if you could ever call living in a house full of vampires as a vampire-in-training normal.

Starting the day off with a steaming hot shower had me in a great mood, and feeling the warmth of the sun on my face was only adding to it. But my mind was also flooded with questions. Raven had explained what the virus would do to the cells in my body, but I had no idea what it would feel like as I was being changed. Or how long the transition would take. Would I just pass out after drinking the blood and wake up when it was over? Okay… That was probably wishful thinking, but hey, a girl could dream.

"So what's the transformation like?" I asked, turning my head to glance at her. She had her spun gold hair braided down the side, and was absently running her fingers through the end of her pony tail, which stopped just short of her waist. "Does it hurt? How long will it take?"

Raven stopped walking and blankly stared at the ground. Her eyes drifted closed as she let out a deep sigh.

"That bad?" Shit. So not the reaction I was hoping for.

"There aren't words to describe how much pain you'll be in. Every cell in your body will hurt while it's being mutated, but your vital organs are by far the worst. You'll have a massive heart attack– strong enough to kill anyone that wasn't being transformed– and your lungs will feel totally useless, like they've been crushed. Once the virus reaches your brain, you'll lose all control of your mind, and you'll have the mother of all headaches. As for how long it'll last, you'll be writhing in pain for at least twenty-four hours." Raven lifted my hand and squeezed it against her chest. "I wish there was some way I could keep you from having to go through this. I'm so sorry."

"Hey, I'd already be dead if it wasn't for you," I said, trying to cheer her up.

"Instead I get to find out what it's like to have sisters, and feel at least a little like I have a mom again. Not to mention the whole living for eternity thing. I can handle one day of agony in exchange for that."

Raven cupped my face and kissed me on the forehead. "Thank you, my sister. Your bravery never ceases to amaze me. I'll do everything I can to help you through it."

"I know you will. Could I accidentally hurt any of you? What if I trance someone and make you do something to yourselves before I even know what I'm doing?"

"No need to worry about going postal on your new family," she said, the corners of her mouth crinkling in amusement. "Our hardened brain cells are impenetrable to even the most gifted amongst us."

I was stunned. "Wait. You can't read each other's minds?"

"Nope, our thoughts are our own. I'm glad that we can't really. Everyone gets pissed at the people they live with sometimes. If all of those thoughts were known, it would be far more difficult to get along."

Raven's eyes shifted to my hair. After peering at it for a couple seconds she reached up and ran her fingers through the blonde highlights. "Chemically processed hair doesn't take well to the transformation. The damaged cells often break apart, causing the treated portion to fall off. It'd be best if we cut the highlights out ahead of time while we can still use scissors. It looks like most of your layers are on the top, so that shouldn't be too bad. I'm sure Sandy will come up with something pretty for you– she used to be a professional hair stylist."

"My natural hair color is so boring, though. I just got all of these highlights put in a month ago. I'll lose half my hair!" I pulled on my highlights for emphasis, and Raven roared with laughter.

"What's so funny?" I demanded. When she kept up the hee-haw routine, I huffed and stomped off toward the house. She quickly caught up with me.

"I'm sorry for laughing," she choked out before snorting and turning away.

"Sounds like it. I'm glad you find me being bald for eternity so fucking hilarious."

Raven stepped in front of me, blocking my path. "You're not going to be bald. You have tons of hair that isn't colored. And I promise Sandy will come up with something really cute. You like her hair don't you? Not that yours will need to be anywhere near that short."

I pictured Sandy's short blonde pixie cut in my mind. It was cute. I'd wondered how it'd look on me when I first met her. Having her cut my hair would also be a nice bonding experience. But that didn't mean I wasn't still angry. "Yes I do, and I'm sure she'll come up with something decent for me, but I don't think that having to lose even some of my hair is anything to laugh about."

"I really am sorry. It's just that you've handled all of the other life altering changes so well. I was surprised to see you have such a strong reaction to getting a haircut, of all things. Do you forgive me?"

Raven's sad puppy dog expression was irresistible. I swear she could hack off both of my legs with a switch blade, and then make me feel sorry for dulling her knife with my flesh. "Like I could ever stay mad at you when you look at me like that."

"Good to know," she said with a smile. I rolled my eyes, and she gave my shoulder a squeeze.

When we reached the hand-crafted mahogany bridge, we stopped in the middle and leaned against the rail, enjoying the view of the east end of the dog-leg shaped pond. From this angle I could just see the edge of the pines we had walked through before. As I stared at the picturesque landscape, a revelation of sorts came to me. If vampires couldn't create new cells, I wouldn't be able to shed and reform my uterine lining each month– I'd never have another period. I liked the sound of that, but it also meant I'd never have kids. As an only child without any close nieces or nephews, my opportunities to babysit or do other nurturing type stuff had been limited. Brittney's younger sister Rachel was cool, but I was almost sixteen before I really got to know her. Motherhood had seldom crossed my mind. Still, it was a little disheartening to know that was no longer an option.

At least I wouldn't have to worry about getting knocked up unintentionally, not that there'd been any real chance of that happening so far in my life. When I met Tyler at the dorm party, I was so into him. If he wouldn't have turned out to be such an asshole, who knows what might have developed between us? Who would I be able to meet now? I didn't even want to think about the only male vampires I knew.

"I don't mean to eavesdrop on your thoughts," Raven said, lacing her fingers through mine. "But not being able to bear children is a huge sacrifice. It was the hardest thing for me to accept when I chose to join Sienna. I know it's a little different in your case, given the ultimatum you were under. As for what guys you'll meet, our family travels extensively, and we have close friends all over the world. Believe me– you'll have tons of guys to choose from. There is something else we need to do before you're changed though."

"What?" I finally prodded after an awkward silence.

Raven's cheeks went from a soft pink to a deep scarlet. "I don't know how to say this. I didn't know you were…that you had never had sex."

"Yeah right, like Sandy and Ruby didn't tell you." It's not like we'd sworn an oath of secrecy or anything, and even if we had, I was pretty sure hot gossip like that would have spread like wildfire.

"You told them? When?"

The hurt look in her eyes removed all doubt that she was telling the truth – and gave me a newfound respect for Sandy and Ruby– but it also filled me with guilt. As my close friend, and the one who brought me into this family, I'm sure hearing that I'd chosen to share something so personal with her sisters instead of her felt like a slap in the face. "The night you and Sienna left us alone. Sandy turned asking me questions into kind of a game, and it just came out. I wasn't trying to hold anything back from you. I just assumed that they told you guys everything."

"I can't blame you for doing exactly what Sienna and I asked you to do," Raven reassured me. "And I'm not surprised they didn't say anything. Spreading something that intimate without your permission would not only undermine their attempt to bond with you, it would also have gotten them in hot water with Sienna."

"So what did you mean before about there being something else I had to do? And how exactly did we jump from that to me being a virgin?"

"Actually they're kind of related. If you want to be able to have sex as a vampire, you'll need to break your hymen before you're changed so it can heal. It'd be almost impossible to break afterwards, and even if you could, you'd never stop bleeding."

"So I need to get laid!" I blurted out in disbelief.

She grinned. "Well, that would be the most fun of the alternatives. You could also take matters into your own hands, so to speak."

"Eeww!" There was no way I was losing my virginity to a piece of plastic.

Raven burst out laughing at my thoughts. "I hear ya– not exactly what every girl dreams about."

"How would I meet somebody? I'm not going to school or anything, and it's not like I have a lot of time."

Her eyes lit up with excitement. "We'll all go clubbing tonight!"

Now I was the one blushing. My new family was taking me out to get laid. I sure didn't see this coming.

* * * *

"Sienna, Ruby, Sandy!" Raven yelled, storming into the house like a commando. I staggered in behind her, gasping for breath from trying to match her easy stride. Sienna leaped off the couch in a blur and landed in a fighting stance facing the doorway.

"It's okay, Sienna," I said, trying to calm her.

She studied me more intently for a moment, and then bounded over to us with a wide grin on her face. "I know just the dress I'm going to wear!"

As if music was already playing, Sienna started rhythmically swinging her hips. Raven joined in, dancing close to her. They both looked like typical teenage girls goofing around with their friends. Given Sienna's role as head of the family, it was easy to forget that physically she was only nineteen. Ruby and Sandy appeared at the wooden railing overlooking the living room, leaped over it in tandem and landed gracefully on the balls of their feet.

Techno music shook the room like a crack of thunder, making me jump about two feet in the air. Raven was still standing next to the stereo, wildly swaying to the thumping beat. No longer content to watch, I let myself drift into the hazy, surreal world that always encompassed me when I danced. By the third song Sandy and I had paired off together. She took my hands in hers and raised them up over our heads, swinging them in synch with our bodies. Our faces were now only inches apart. Her short blonde hair framed the dainty features of her beautiful face perfectly. Pale rose eye shadow accented her compelling blue eyes, and her full, cherry red lips shined with gloss. I felt her sweet breath on my face, and wondered what she'd do if I kissed her.

My cheeks burned with embarrassment, realizing what my entire family had just heard me think. Sandy seemed surprised, but made no effort to move away from me. "I'm so sorry San– "

"Thank you for your kind thoughts," she interrupted, placing her finger on my lips. "You're just a curious teenager, Brooke. It's perfectly normal. And I think you're beautiful too."

Sandy closed her eyes and pressed her soft lips gently against mine. My lower lip separated hers as her fingers slid into my hair. After several tender kisses, her mouth opened wider and our tongues met. A passionate moan erupted from my throat.

Sandy leaned away from me with a smirk on her face. "Someone's horny!"

I gave her a sheepish laugh– she didn't know just how right she was. In a few hours I was going to be throwing myself at every decent looking guy I came across until someone slept with me. My only guide for what it might feel like was Britt's experience with her annoying boyfriend Kyle her sophomore year. Her first time was so uncomfortable that they didn't repeat the performance for over a week. Then again, Kyle always made me uncomfortable, so who knows what that meant. God, would I have to bring rubbers with me? It's not like I was on the pill or anything, and I sure as hell didn't want to get pregnant.

In an instant the room was deathly quiet. Everyone had stopped dancing and stood facing me, all of them smiling. *Crap.* I couldn't wait until I was a vampire– having all of my thoughts broadcast to the world was getting really old. And the more comfortable I got around my new family the more freely my mind wandered. I realized now that all Sienna had picked up on before was the plan to go out to clubs. Now everyone knew the purpose.

Sienna put her arm around my shoulders and guided me to the couch. "If you're comfortable talking about it with me or one of your sisters, I'm sure we could answer some of your questions."

I'm not sure comfortable would be the word I'd choose, given that talking about your sex life was awkward with pretty much anyone, but there were some things I needed to know if I was going to do this. "I know how important it is for me not to get pregnant, but I don't have a diaphragm and I'm not on the pill. What precautions do I need to take?"

"We'll make a stop on the way into town to get a few things," Sienna said, pausing to give my hand a reassuring pat. "In addition to having him wear a condom, you'll want to use spermicidal cream and make sure he pulls out before he has an orgasm. When was your last period?"

"It ended four days ago." I looked at her for some indication as to whether that was a good thing or not.

She answered with a warm smile. "That will help– that's one of the least fertile times of the month. With the other precautions you should be fine."

"How much will it hurt? Will I be able to enjoy it at all?"

"You'll feel kind of a ripping sensation when your hymen is broken. After that happens, you should be able to enjoy the rest. You'll bleed a little as well, so don't be alarmed."

"How long will it take me to heal?"

"A week or so at most." Sienna cast Raven a meaningful glance. "I'm so thankful we didn't overlook this."

I chewed on my lip while I tried to think of some way to ask my next question without making myself sound like a skanky whore. "Normally I'd never do anything like this, but I don't want this to drag out– there are so many other things I need to focus on. What can I do to make sure I find someone who will sleep with me tonight?"

"We wouldn't be having this conversation if you made a habit of this sort of thing," Sienna pointed out with a playful grin. "Assuming you don't want us to kill your first partner, we won't be able to expose ourselves to him. There are other things we can do to help though. As you meet people you're interested in, we can read their minds and let you know if they're willing. We can also warn you if they think of anything you'd want to stay away from, like hurting you, or that they have a disease."

"Where would we go if I do meet someone?" I figured bringing him back here was out, and I wasn't crazy about the idea of going somewhere alone with some guy I didn't even know.

Sienna's face hardened, responding to the mere mention of me putting myself in danger as if it were an imminent threat. "I would never let that happen. We'll get a couple of hotel rooms. When you're ready, we'll follow you back to the hotel and be in the next room in case you need us."

"Thanks," I muttered, leaning my upper body against her chest. Sienna folded her arms around me like a protective blanket and kissed my head. As much as I missed my mom, I couldn't imagine having this intimate of a conversation with her about sex, let alone asking her to take me bar hunting and provide the accommodations for the hook up. Sienna was like the perfect hybrid between a doting parent and an enabling best friend.

* * * *

Since we had some time to kill, I figured I might as well get another task checked off my list. I got up and turned toward Sandy, who was leaning over the back of the couch, resting on her forearms. Her cap sleeve, black-and-white contrast top had an angled bottom that blended perfectly into her super clingy Ponte knit leggings. But what made the outfit was her three inch heel, black suede ankle boots. I'd trade my car and everything else I owned for a pair. Seeing how fashion conscious my new sister was further bolstered my confidence. My eternal hairstyle was in good hands. "Sandy, Raven told me that my highlights have to go. Would you be willing to give me a haircut?"

Her face lit up with a broad smile that made her eyes sparkle. "Are you kidding? I can't wait to get my hands on that hair. Come with me." Before I could respond, she grabbed my hand and carted me off toward my room.

After depositing me in front of my vanity mirror, she raced up the stairs to get her supplies. Turning my head a few times to get a good look, I surveyed what all would have to be cut. It appeared that I'd lose almost all of the longer layers of my bangs, along with fairly large chunks scattered around the sides and back. Hopefully Sandy would have some way of making it look decent. She returned carrying scissors, some clips, a spray bottle and a comb.

"Did you have anything particular in mind?" she asked, setting her supplies down next to me.

"What are my options?"

Sandy played with my hair while she thought. "Hmm... We could do a short bob, a pixie cut or long and short."

"What's long and short?" It sounded obvious, but I'd never heard of it before.

"It has long layers in the back, is choppy all around and has heavy, uneven bangs that you could tuck behind your ears or leave in front of your face," she explained.

"What would a short bob look like?"

"The longest part of your hair would be about an inch above your chin, and it would pretty tightly hug your face."

Trying to picture how I'd look with either of them was impossible. I'd been wearing my hair the same way since I was eight. I decided I'd be far better off letting her decide. "What do you think would look best on me?"

She didn't hesitate at all. "The long and short– the short layers you'll need to have in the front will blend in better."

Here goes nothing. "Let's do it."

Sandy shielded my eyes while she wet down my hair, and then gently worked the comb through it, removing the snarls. She began to separate and cut away the long highlights framing the right side of my face. Ten-inch strands of blonde hair tumbled into my lap.

"Sorry about earlier," I said, gazing at her reflection in the mirror.

She grinned. "I'm not. That's the best kiss I've had in a long time."

I could feel my cheeks burning again. "I don't know what came over me.

God, I'm weird sometimes."

Sandy stopped cutting and put her hand on my shoulder. "Hey, all you did was think about it. I kissed you, remember?"

"I wouldn't exactly say I fought you off."

She let out a cute little giggle. "True."

After removing the last of my bleached bangs, Sandy gathered my longer hair together, twirled it and clipped it to the top of my head. She took down one thin layer at a time, weeding out the remaining highlights along the right side of my head. I knew she was just getting started— she hadn't even begun to actually style it yet— but right now it looked like I'd been the victim of a tragic shredder incident.

Anxious to get my mind off what she was doing, I blurted out the first question that popped into my head. "How do we choose our— prey?" I was going to say *victims*, but that sounded too criminal.

She paused for a moment as she considered the question. The way she wrinkled her nose and sucked on her bottom lip was adorable. "Well, we have to travel to different cities so that there aren't too many missing person cases in one area. We only go to large cities, where those things happen often enough to not raise too much suspicion. This area is nice, as there are a lot of cities within a day's drive. As for the actual hunting, it's mostly about waiting for a good opportunity to present itself then taking advantage of it. Obviously we'd never take kids or celebrities, or anyone who wasn't alone, but we really don't evaluate them beyond that. If we tried to justify our choices, we'd never feed."

A chill ran down my spine. Alexander, Travis and Teresa had done exactly what she was describing— take advantage of an opportunity. How could I hate them for doing the same thing I'd be doing with my own family soon? Unless I wanted to be a total hypocrite, I'd have to forgive them. Besides, Sienna had mentioned that she was old friends with Stefan. I was sure she wouldn't want there to be bad blood between our covens. Once I was a vampire, I'd have to reach out to them. Maybe I could get them to leave Angie and Stacey alone as a favor to me.

Sandy wrapped her arm around my chest, hugging me from behind. "Sienna will be so happy to hear that. She was worried that you'd hold a grudge against them— not that anyone would blame you. Making you strip naked, give away your precious belongings and watch as they fed on you was completely unnecessary and inexcusable. Not to mention Travis's groping, or Teresa treating you like some kind of talking Barbie. Stefan should have taught them better than that. I think he would be very impressed with your gesture and would be happy to instruct his coven to steer clear of your friends."

"I hope so."

She started working her way across the back, cutting several thick layers into my hair, with the longest layer ending near the nape of my neck. By the time she'd finished I could feel air flowing across exposed skin above my shoulders.

"Do we always feed together?" I'd stopped looking in the mirror entirely, and was doing my best to avoid a full-out panic attack at the sizeable mound of brown and blonde hair that had formed on the floor.

Sandy laughed as she kicked some of it further under the chair. "No judging until I'm finished! And to answer your question, we do for the most part. There's enough blood in one person to feed all of us, so it'd be wasteful not to. Sometimes we feed alone or with other friends when we travel separately, but that's rare."

"What do we do with the bodies afterwards?" I hadn't been in the room where we'd fed since Sunday, but I was sure the woman wasn't in there anymore. After almost a week, even I'd smell it by now.

"They're cremated along with the sheets and anything else that gets contaminated. All of the homes we rotate between have incinerators, which were purchased and installed very discretely."

"Raven told me how long Sienna's been alive. You guys must have homes all over the world." Even if she took thirty years to pay off a traditional mortgage each time, they'd have thirty by now, and from what I'd heard they were far more likely to own banks than borrow from them. "

"We own quite a few," Sandy admitted. "So far I've lived in England, Ireland, Canada and Brazil, along with five different states. They're all kept in move-in condition, complete with clothing and everything else we need. All of our properties are owned by a private corporation, so our names can change without having to go through the legal hassles of trying to will everything to ourselves. Homes are torn down and rebuilt when they get too dated. If we don't think we'd want to return to an area, the property is sold, and we replace it with a new location. We have to move every four or five years to keep people from noticing that we aren't aging, and we never go back to a place we've lived for at least a hundred years."

Sandy began to cut choppy layers into the front and sides, forming heavy, uneven bangs that hung down along my cheeks, and left my ears totally exposed. She spent a few minutes adding some finishing touches, and then moved out from in front of the mirror so I could see. I slowly turned my head from side to side.

"Do you like it?" she asked, her face growing concerned.

It was drastically different, far shorter than I'd ever worn my hair, but I loved it. It looked playful and modern, and went well with my face. "Oh Sandy, you're awesome! I love it! Thank you so much!"

She blew out a deep breath as the nervous lines above her brows disappeared. "Anytime, sis. We'll give it a final touch up just before you're changed." Sandy stepped back and appraised my outfit, taking in my sweatshirt and jeans. "What are you going to wear tonight?"

"Um, hmm… I'm not sure. Would you help me pick something out?" Given her own edgy style, I knew I could trust her to make me look like I belonged at the clubs we'd be hitting.

"Of course– let's see what we have to work with." Sandy headed for my closet with me close behind.

She made comments as she flipped through the few dresses that I had hanging. "Very pretty but too formal, too boring, yawn, yawn, yawn, orange– really? Oh God!"

"Tell me what you really think," I grumbled. Only the maroon halter dress had been spared from her wrath.

Sandy ignored me and headed for my built-in dressers, rapidly rifling through my drawers. "My God woman, don't you own anything sexy?"

I just looked at her with an I-guess-not expression on my face.

She let out an exasperated groan. "This is hopeless. Let's go to my room."

* * * *

We stopped in the living room to show off her handy work, and then continued on up the stairs. Even though I'd been here a week, this was the first time I'd stepped foot on the second floor. There was a large family room at the top of the stairway with Victorian furniture, beautiful hardwood floors and built-in shelves overflowing with books. A hallway led to a guest bath and two large bedrooms.

"That's Ruby's room," Sandy said as we walked past the first one. Sandy's room was set up almost identical to mine. I assumed that they had hired professional decorators when they moved in and changed very little since then.

Given what she'd said about the houses being in move-in condition, that made sense. Any desire you had to personalize them would probably fade after the third or fourth move in fifteen years.

"Exactly," Sandy replied, already halfway to her closet. "Get undressed and have a seat."

I kicked off my tennis shoes, slid out of my jeans, folded up my light blue BU sweatshirt and made a pile next to the bed. "Don't forget about my wrists," I reminded her. Looking like I'd attempted suicide recently probably wasn't the best way to pick someone up.

"Oh, good point. Thanks." Sandy returned holding only lingerie. She handed me a black lace embroidered teddy with garter belts and black thigh high stockings, and then darted off for her closet again.

The one-piece teddy unzipped in the back and had a thong bottom with snaps in the crotch. Just looking at it made my cheeks blush– it was pretty much the standard outfit for a playboy bunny. After unclasping my bra, I removed my panties and pulled on the teddy. The underwire lifted my breasts, filling out the lace cups nicely. Rather than trying to balance myself, I took a seat on the bed to slide the stockings on, and then stood up and attached them to the garters. My hands glided over my thighs and along my waist as my breathing quickened.

Sandy snorted.

"Damn it!" I was beyond embarrassed to be caught in a sexual daydream for the second time in less than a day.

"You look hot! God help the poor boy that sees you in that." After zipping up my teddy, she held up a black, cotton-spandex, U-neck, long sleeve dress. I slid my arms into the sleeves as she pulled it down over my body. The dress came to mid-thigh, barely covering the tops of my stockings, and clung tightly to every curve.

Sandy held my hands at arm's length and surveyed my body. Her eyes lingered. "Stunning," she whispered. "Do you have any red pumps?"

"Ah… Yeah. Toward the ba– " I quit talking when I realized she'd already left the room. She returned seconds later and slid them on my feet.

"Now for the finishing touches," she called out, leading me back to her closet. Sandy wrapped a loose fitting red belt around my waist and grabbed a red Louis Vuitton handbag off the bottom shelf.

She stepped back and peered into my eyes. "This is one night you probably don't want to be thinking about your mom."

It took me a second, but when I realized what she meant I unclasped my necklace and handed it to her. She laid it on top of her jewelry box, and then placed a black velvet choker around my neck, like one I'd imagine a femme vampire wearing in some B rate flick.

"To remind you why you are doing this."

I hadn't thought about it, but she was right. At some point tonight I was bound to come to my senses and try to back out of this. Right now I was just having fun playing dress up. While I understood why I had to do it, that didn't change that I was a mostly innocent, somewhat naïve teenager who'd be trying to act like a trashy bar slut. Maybe plastic wouldn't be so bad after all.

"Are you nervous?" she asked, even though I was sure she'd already read my thoughts.

"Very, but I'm excited too. It'll be a lot of fun going out with everyone." That much was true. I couldn't wait to dance with them.

"You know it!" Sandy shook her hips in front of me.

I laughed and pulled her into a long embrace. "Thanks for all of your help today. I'm really lucky to have you as a sister."

"Thank you for making me truly feel like your sister. Now get downstairs, Sienna needs to see you before we go."

Sienna was waiting for me in the living room. Her eyes widened as she watched me walk down the steps. "You look…naughty."

I giggled. "That's kinda the idea."

"You'll need this," she said, holding up a Massachusetts driver's license.

"Brooke Davis." I knew the last name meant nothing, but I was still curious about what made her choose it. Then I noticed the age. "Eighteen! Are you kidding me? What's the point of a fake ID if I still can't drink!"

"You'll be using that ID for the next five years," Sienna explained. "And I'm sorry, but I doubt if anyone would believe that you were twenty-five. Twenty-two is pushing it."

I huffed defiantly and stuffed it into my wallet.

"Could I see that for a minute?"

"My wallet? Sure."

Sienna searched both inner pockets, removing my Michigan driver's license, credit cards and everything else that had ties back to my former life. "Put this stuff in your desk drawer. You'll need it when you start classes this summer, and when you visit your father."

Food was the last thing on my mind, but I figured I'd better eat something in case my sisters did hook me up with some drinks. Being unconscious would put a serious cramp in the whole "getting laid" plan. After picking at a turkey sandwich and salad like it was five day old spinach, I brushed my teeth and carefully touched up my makeup. There were several voices in the living room now, and I knew they were waiting for me. I took a couple deep breaths to calm my nerves and went to join them.

Chapter Eleven
The End of Innocence

In spite of the deafening music, our awful singing and constant laughing and giggling, I managed to pay attention while Raven drove into Boston. Not having any idea where I'd been living for the last week made me feel more like a detainee than a family member. Then again, I wasn't exactly free to tell them I was taking a pass on the whole vamp thing and roam about the country as I saw fit. The "Hotel California" lyrics danced through my mind.

The private drive that led to our house was off of Randolph Avenue, which cut straight though the Blue Hills reservation, home to thousands of acres of undisturbed forest. Raven headed south on Randolph Avenue and merged onto I-93, continuing on for several miles until we stopped at a drug store near the edge of town. I let out a sigh of relief when Sienna hopped out without asking me to join her.

After a couple minutes she returned, handing me a small plastic bag. "Put these in your purse."

Without so much as a glance, I fished out what I assumed were the condoms and cream, undid the clasp and stuffed them in.

"Put it on him yourself," Sandy instructed, leaning in close to me. "Guys are all thumbs when they know they're about to get laid, and it has to be done right. Once he's hard, place it over the tip and roll it all the way to the base. If he's able to go more than once, you'll need to use a new one each time. The applicator for the cream is just like a yeast infection plunger. You need to wait to put it in until just before you have sex, though."

"Um, thanks." I couldn't believe how nonchalantly she was talking about this stuff. She didn't even seem to be embarrassed.

I thought about my dad's attempt at having "the talk" with me when I turned fourteen. Fortunately, he was even more terrified than I was. After mumbling a couple of comments about waiting for someone I loved and being careful, he stared at the ground and asked if I understood. I jumped on the chance to end the conversation of course, even though he really hadn't said anything.

At least he'd tried to talk with me that time. When I had my first period I came home from school and found tampons and maxi-pads on my dresser, along with an article talking about puberty. I guess he'd seen blood in my panties when he was doing the laundry. I would've given anything to speak to my mom about the way boys were looking at me, the thoughts I was starting to have about them and what was happening to me physically. (As an added bonus, my breasts developed sooner than any of my friends.)

When Raven pulled into the Sheraton parking lot, I peered up at the hotel in disbelief. It had to be twenty stories tall. A fifth floor was unusual for the places I was used to staying in. Raven swung around next to the lobby and walked inside with Sienna.

"So, where are we headed?" I asked, turning toward Sandy and Ruby.

"We'll probably start out at Venu," Sandy replied. "You'll like it– the club is really high energy, and they play awesome techno music along with hip-hop and some rap. If we strike out there, we'll head to The Liquor Store. It's a complete dive, but it's a great place to hook up."

Sienna slid back into her seat, reached behind her and handed me a card key. "You're in 1726. We're right next door in 1727."

"Thanks," I said, tucking it into my purse.

"Oh, in case you need to get a cab or anything."

I looked up just in time to see a wad of cash land in my lap. I didn't stop to count it, but it had to be at least a couple hundred. "Sienna, this is too much."

She just grinned.

I knew there was no way she was going to take it back, so I stuffed it into my wallet and shouted, "First rounds on me!" The car broke out in cheers.

* * * *

It was almost 11:30 when we walked up to the Venu entrance. People were lined up half way down the block, but Sienna led us right to the front steps. My heart felt like an out of control jackhammer. I'd never tried to get into a popular club like this, let alone cut the line. Sienna, Ruby, Sandy and Raven were all so beautiful that I had no doubt they'd get in– I couldn't say the same for me. Even with what I was wearing, I was still just a typical college freshman. They probably saw hundreds of women every night who were more attractive.

The bouncer was gigantic and dressed in solid black, his arms and chest bulging out through his skin-tight shirt. His neck had to be as wide as my waist. A long jagged scar ran above his right eye, across his cheek and off toward his right ear. I shivered, picturing the fights he'd been in.

He took one glance at Sienna in her red, open-backed jersey dress with criss-cross spaghetti straps and motioned her inside. His mouth fell open when Raven followed, looking truly stunning in a black, racer-back tank dress with a crochet skirt and a white ribbon belt. Sandy confidently reached out and took his hand, strolling by in her taupe, V-neck babydoll dress. I could feel Ruby nudge me to follow, and I timidly stepped forward, trying to steady my breathing. His eyes slowly made their way down my body before he smiled and motioned for me to pass.

"He totally wants you!" Ruby said as she entered the club behind me. "He's still staring at your ass." I snorted and wrapped my arm around her shoulders.

The club was enormous and was already packed. It had two dance floors on the first level surrounded by small tables and bars along each wall. Techno music blared through the room. Ruby took my hand as we fought our way through the crowd toward the closest bar. Before we were half way there, Sienna stood up and flagged us down. Somehow she'd already managed to grab a table.

"Where's Raven and Sandy?" I yelled over the music, sitting down next to her. She motioned toward the line at the bar.

After a couple minutes they returned carrying several drinks. Raven handed Sienna a glass of white wine and set a strawberry margarita down in front of me. "How did– "

She flashed me an impish smile. "From the party."

It was hard to believe that was less than two weeks ago. I remembered how beautiful Raven looked that night and how easy it was for me to open up to her. We'd become almost instant best friends.

I'd just finished my drink when Mikesh's "Sounds of the Club" came on. "Let's go!" I hollered, hopping off my chair.

They all followed behind me, and we twisted our way through the mass of people toward the closest dance floor. In no time I was swallowed up by the crowd. I could feel someone dancing up against my back, placing his hands on my waist as we shook our hips together. We soon drifted apart and several others joined in.

The DJ had transitioned into another song before I finally spotted Sienna and Raven near the other end of the floor. I was almost half way to them when someone took my right arm and spun me around. A wave of pure elation raced through me when I found myself face to face with Sandy. She moved with such agility and grace that I was mesmerized. I let out a playful shriek and frantically moved my body with hers. After a couple of minutes I caught a glimpse of Ruby nearby, the strobe lights reflecting off of her silky black hair. Sandy and I spread apart so she could join us.

When Firewall's "Sincere" began to play, I launched into one of my rehearsed routines. My sisters moved in perfect harmony with me, obviously reading my mind, and the crowd around us moved further away and started to cheer.

Suddenly a spotlight was shining on the three of us, and the DJ called out, "Check out the babes on floor two, lookin' fine." It was surreal. I'd never been "showcased" in my life. I didn't even know clubs did that anymore. While the added attention was a little unnerving, I was having too much fun to care.

After the song ended, the light shifted off of us, and everyone returned to dancing. We made our way back to a table.

"You're amazing, Brooke!" Sienna said, placing her hand on my shoulder. "Where did you learn to dance like that?"

I shot Sandy and Ruby a smile. They really hadn't shared *anything*. "Pretty much all Britt and I did through high school. We'd work on little routines for some of our favorite songs– just goofing around really. You guys are unbelievable. So graceful. I feel like a klutz compared to you."

Raven sipped at what was left of her drink, as if getting the last drop out of the bottom was a matter of life and death, before finally giving up and setting the very empty glass on the table. "Our improved sense of balance, hearing and agility makes us far better dancers than we ever were as humans. In spite of our gifts, you outshine all of us. I can't wait to watch you move once you're changed."

I blushed at her compliments. The music was loud enough that I didn't need to worry about people overhearing us. "How do you keep up with the latest dance styles?"

"If you think about it, we really have an advantage over teens of any given generation," Sienna said, her shoulders swaying to the music. "We're in our prime as new dances start to emerge, and remain in our prime when they become popular. It's very important that we constantly update the way we talk, dress and act so that people believe we're from the current time. That's why we make a point of doing things like this, in addition to just having fun, of course."

A cute waitress in a black tank dress approached our table and handed me a strawberry margarita. "From the gentlemen at the bar."

We all glanced to our right as the waitress placed the rest of the drinks on the table. A twenty-something guy with a rounded chin, pronounced cheek bones and a broad nose tipped his drink toward me. His long black hair came almost to his shoulder and was tossed messily about.

My heart jumped into my throat when I heard Sienna whisper, "That's Stefan."

When she motioned him to our table, he walked straight to me, took my hand and kissed it like a gentleman. "Emily, my beautiful lady, I am Stefan."

"It's nice to meet you, Stefan. Actually, my name is Brooke now."

Stefan gazed at Sienna with a puzzled expression on his face. "My dear Sienna, she has been with you for less than a week. I've never known you to act so hastily. Does she truly know what she has chosen?"

The corners of her mouth rose in a friendly but assertive smile. "Stefan, Brooke is quite special. She's taken to this life like no other I have seen. I assure you she is fully informed– I would never have accepted her choice otherwise. She has already fed with my family."

His eyes shot back to mine. I hadn't planned on talking with him until after I was changed, but I figured now was as good of a time as any.

Are you listening to my thoughts?

He nodded.

I was planning on coming to see you after I was changed, but since you're here there's something I wanted to tell you. I don't hold any hard feelings toward Teresa, Alexander or Travis for what they did. They took advantage of an opportunity to feed—the same as I'll be doing with my family. I don't know how I could blame them for doing something I've justified for myself. I know you and Sienna have been friends for a long time, and I don't want there to be any animosity between our covens. Please let them know I forgive them.

Stefan folded his muscular arms tightly around my body. After a long hug he leaned back and cupped my chin with his hand. "I've known Sienna for almost two hundred years, and her friendship is the only thing that has gotten me through more rough times than I care to remember. When Alexander told me what happened, I was certain we'd have to move. I just couldn't see how we would ever get past this. You have given me the most precious of gifts." He turned toward Sienna and wiped his eyes. "I see what you mean, my dear. She is indeed special."

I was surprised to see Sienna crying, until I remembered that I'd only told Sandy what I was planning to do.

She took me into a warm embrace. "I love you, my wonderful daughter.

Thank you."

I buried my face into her shoulder and blinked back tears of my own. "I love you too, Mom. What's best for the coven, right?"

"That's right, baby," she choked out, returning to her seat.

Stefan briefly consoled her then shifted his attention back to me. "Brooke, I look forward to welcoming you into your new life. It's been an honor to meet you."

"You too, Stefan." When he turned to leave, I placed my hand on his forearm. "Oh, I know I don't have any right to ask, but I was wondering if you'd do me a favor."

"Of course, what can I do for you?"

My college roommates Angela Stevens and Stacey Andrews mean a lot to me. They spend a lot of time at Antonio's. I'd never say anything, but could you ask your coven to avoid them?

Stefan ran his index finger along the edge of his chin as he thought. "We aren't usually that selective about our prey, as I'm sure you've been told."

"I'm sor– "

He motioned with his hand for me to stop. "My coven will not be pleased to have me place restrictions on their feeding, but I feel it is the least I can do after you so graciously forgave them. Do you have a picture of your friends I could have?"

We hadn't taken any pictures together yet. *Crap.*

"That's okay. Just picture what they look like in your mind."

I thought about us eating at Antonio's, getting ready for the party, meeting with the FBI agents and playing tennis.

His brows furrowed as his head tilted slightly to the side. "What were FBI agents meeting with you about?"

It dawned on me that I hadn't mentioned that to anyone yet. "Our fourth roommate, Wendy, was reported missing by her mom. They asked us some questions about her last Thursday. I never met her, and I didn't know anything about any of this stuff at the time." My eyes darted from Raven to Sienna, wondering if they'd feel like I'd held something back.

"You didn't do anything wrong," Sienna assured me. "Your life's been a whirlwind the last few days– there's no way you could tell us everything. Stefan, do you know if your family was involved with this?"

"When was she reported missing?"

I tried to recall everything the agents had told me. "Her mom called the police ten days ago, but the last time she spoke with Wendy was the Friday before I arrived at school."

"Thank God," Sienna blurted out. Realizing how that sounded, she quickly continued. "I mean, I hope she's okay, but if she didn't disappear until two weeks ago, then at least Stefan's family wasn't involved."

"I thought we fed every seven to ten days," I said, grasping to follow her logic.

"Never in the same area– not even in the same city."

Stefan briefly closed his eyes then shook his head in resignation. "I'm afraid we did feed on a young woman that night. That's why I wasn't with my coven when Brooke was attacked– we were supposed to go to Providence that Saturday. What did she look like?"

I'd only glanced at the picture for a second. "All I can remember is that she had strawberry-blonde hair and was on the heavy side."

"Sounds like her," Stefan said. "Did they say anything else that may be helpful?"

"Just that it was the third missing person's case in the area in the last month, and that we should be careful while they check into it." I couldn't think of anything else to add.

Sienna was shocked. "Please tell me that your coven is not behind all of these disappearances."

He ran his fingers through his long hair and lowered his head. "I wish I could, my dear, but I'm beginning to wonder just how often they've been feeding without me. I will straighten this out and punish those responsible. I know the risk this poses to all of us."

"Oh shit! They took DNA samples from me!" My whole body began to tremble as I thought of the repercussions.

Sandy gave me a confused look. "You didn't have anything to do with this. What are you worried about?"

"The hospital," Raven responded before I could answer. "They would have taken DNA samples for evidence to try to determine who she was if she died. Once the samples she gave to the F.B.I. are cataloged, the two could easily be matched up. Most state and federal law enforcement databases are linked together."

I buried my face in my hands. What would I tell my dad if he found out I was brutally attacked and left naked in front of a hospital? There's no way he'd let me stay here. But what would happen if he demanded that I come home? It's not like they were going to let me leave, even if I wanted to. *What the hell am I going to do!*

"You're over eighteen, which makes you a legal adult," Sienna said with a reluctant sigh. "If you step forward and tell the hospital that it was you, they'll have no right to share the information with anyone, not even your father. To keep the police from investigating, the best thing to tell them would be that you tried to commit suicide. Privacy rights don't cover criminal investigations."

Just picturing me rotting away in a psych ward with drool running down my chin made me cringe– I was so not liking this plan. "If that's what you decide I'll do it, but if I say I tried to kill myself, won't they have me committed?"

She bit her lip in thought. "You're right. Given the severity of your injuries, they would likely commit you even against your will. As a ward of the state, your father would be told, which would defeat the whole purpose."

I'd never seen Sienna look so troubled. We all sat in silence for a couple of minutes before Raven finally spoke. "The samples the F.B.I. agents took aren't the problem. Removing those would leave unmatched DNA in the evidence collected from Wendy's room, which would actually make things worse.

"What we need to do is get our hands on the samples they took from Jane Doe. With me breaking Brooke out of the hospital, the Boston police will definitely be treating this as a criminal investigation, so we're going to have to move fast. We'll have to get rid of the paper and electronic case files at the police department as well, so that they can't circulate photos of her around campus.

"The good news is it's only been a week, and it's not like this is a murder investigation. I doubt if the assigned detective has done anything beyond a cursory interview of the hospital staff. We'll plan everything out tomorrow." Raven wrestled the frayed napkin from my jittery hands. "I know this sounds complicated, Brooke, but it won't be that hard. I'm just glad this came up now, before it was too late to do anything about it."

Sandy nodded toward Raven. "And that's why she's in charge of our clandestine operations– all that's missing is a self-destructing recording."

I knew I couldn't blame myself for ending up at the hospital, and it's not like I'd provided DNA samples to the F.B.I. out of boredom, but seeing the colossal mess we now faced still filled me with guilt. The fact that Sienna hadn't decided to cut her losses and dump me in an alley somewhere was remarkable. Instead they were going to risk exposing themselves and commit an untold amount of crimes just to get me out of this predicament. I blinked back the tears that filled my glistening eyes. There was no denying I was important to them.

Raven fished a couple tissues out of her purse and grinned as she handed them to me. "Now let's get back to the issue at hand...getting Brooke laid!" They all burst into laughter, which only grew louder when I failed to connect with a punch and almost fell out of my chair.

"Sounds like an interesting night indeed," Stefan said with a chuckle.

"It's not like that! You have to let me explain."

"He knows," Raven cut in. "Getting you to think about why you're dressed like that was part of the reason I said it– a very small part, mind you."

Stefan confirmed what she was saying with a nod. After giving each of us a kiss on both cheeks, he took a polite quarter bow and left.

* * * *

"So, do you see any contenders?" Sandy asked, her eyes busy surveying the landscape.

I began to study the mass of people in front of our table, focusing in on a seriously GQ 'esqe guy who was showing what I hoped was a female friend how to do a jump step. *What about him?*

"Married," Raven and Ruby blurted out together.

Crap - o for one. As I continued sweeping the crowd, I saw the waitress who had served us drinks earlier handing beers to three guys a few tables down. The guy closest to the waitress was hitting on her, and she was clearly enjoying it. He seemed pretty full of himself, which instantly turned me off. The friend to his right was acting like the typical sidekick, laughing at his innuendos with the waitress and slapping hands as they talked about girls walking by. Then I noticed the guy sitting with them. He wasn't chiming in with any of their crude jokes and looked like he couldn't wait to get out of here.

What can you tell me about the guy sitting on the end of the table over there? To my horror everyone turned toward him at once, catching the waitress's attention. She took a seat in macho man's lap to stake her claim. *Real subtle, people. Jesus! You're killing me here!*

After a quick round of muffled giggles Ruby spoke up. "He's a virgin– as far as I can tell, he's never had a girlfriend."

"He's a junior and lives off campus with his family," Sandy added. "He's majoring in chemical engineering. The one flirting with the waitress is his older cousin."

"And your thoughts were right, sis," Raven said. "He dreads going out with them. He's wishing he would've taken his younger brother's offer to watch the *Lord of the Rings* trilogy tonight."

Do his friends give him as much shit as I think they do about being a virgin and not having a girlfriend?

"Yes," Sienna replied flatly. "His cousin thinks he's gay. They only invited him along so they could make fun of him."

Are you picking up anything I should be worried about?

They all concentrated on him for a couple minutes. Finally Ruby spoke. "Only that he's really lonely. If you choose him, you should make sure he doesn't expect a relationship with you."

I can do that. Do you think he'd sleep with me tonight?

"He's not thinking about taking anyone home right now," Raven said. "Once you introduce yourself, we'll be able to tell."

What's his name?

"Daniel. And he actually goes by Daniel, not Dan."

Good enough for me. If tonight can't be special for me, it can sure as hell be special for someone. Wish me luck.

Everyone cheered me on as I stood up and walked toward his table. When I got within a few feet, the jackass cousin started staring at my breasts with a disgusting smirk on his face. I turned and walked behind the sidekick, and then leaned in toward Daniel. "You're Daniel, right? I've seen you around campus. Would you like to dance?"

Only his friends looked more shocked than he did. I smiled and waited for him to recover.

"What's your name?" he finally managed.

"Brooke," I replied, dancing a little in front of him. After an awkward silence, it became apparent that I was going to have to force the issue if I wanted this to go anywhere. I grabbed his hand and pulled him out of his chair. "Let's go!"

As soon as we started to dance I could tell he'd never done this before in his life. All he did was step from side to side, his arms glued at his waist the entire time. I glared at his friends, who were now bent over the table in laughter, and then slid in behind him and leaned up to his ear. "Do you mind if I show you a few things?"

"Sure," he mumbled, flinching slightly from the close proximity of my voice.

Man, this was going to be hard. I seriously thought about searching for someone who wasn't such an introvert, but I couldn't give his friends the satisfaction of seeing him get rejected. Placing my hands on his waist, I cradled my body up against his. "Let yourself feel the rhythm of the music, and then move your hips with it– like this."

I started to swing my hips to the beat and used my hands to keep him with me, relaxing my grip only after he began to move on his own. His timing was off, since he was waiting for me to move rather than going off the music, but at least he was trying. "Much better. Now, instead of waiting to feel my hips move, listen to the music and see if you can pick up on the rhythm I'm following. Even though this stuff sounds fast, it still follows a regular beat."

Before the end of the song his entire face lit up with a childlike smile. "I think I got it!"

"Only one way to find out." Removing my hands from his hips, I backed off a couple of steps and watched– he was right. "Perfect! Now let's get your arms moving. There are no hard and fast rules for what to do, just keep your arms up and let them bounce with the music. Turn around and watch me for a minute."

I closed my eyes and let myself fall into the music. Once I was moving to the tempo with my usual ease, I peeked at him. He was trying to mimic my arm movements, and looked kinda awkward, but not embarrassingly dorky like he had before. "Look at you!" I called out with a smile.

Daniel laughed and shook his head. "Like it's not obvious that I'm copying you."

"You just need to work on changing it up a bit." I motioned toward two girls dancing nearby. "Their movements seem random, don't they? But if you watch long enough, you'll notice that they're repeating the same moves over and over again. They're just disguising it well."

We continued to dance as we watched. He finally turned back toward me. "The blonde does four different sets of moves and changes the order. The brunette is a lot simpler– she only has seven moves."

For someone who'd never danced before, I was amazed at how rapidly he caught on. "Damn. You nailed it! Now see if you can pick up what I do." I settled back into the music and drowned out the fact that he was watching me. About half way through the next song, I heard him speak.

"God, you're tough. I've seen you repeat a couple sets of moves, but I'm seeing new moves all the time. What are you doing?"

"I don't know ahead of time," I yelled over the music. "I have a lot of individual moves that I use, but I let them come out in whatever order feels right with the music. The less you think, the better you'll dance. Just let the beat take over your body. Enough teaching– let's just have fun!"

I quit watching him and let myself enjoy the feeling that dancing always gave me. A couple of songs had passed before we were close together again. I couldn't believe he was the same guy. Daniel blended in perfectly with everyone else on the floor and looked like he'd been club dancing for years. When the song ended we made our way over to an empty table.

"I can't believe how much fun that was!" he shouted.

"I've never seen someone pick it up so fast. You're a natural!"

"Yeah, right– more like you're a hell of a teacher."

"Thanks, Daniel." The affectionate, almost starstruck look in his eyes reminded me of what Ruby had said. If I didn't want to hurt him, I couldn't afford to wait any longer. But like the true blue coward I was, rather than taking the plunge, I chose to study a particularly interesting piece of lint on the floor.

"What's wrong?"

"I need to ask you something that is going to sound really bizarre."

"Okay…." Fear of where this might be headed had him gathering his legs underneath him like a coiled up house cat preparing to leap out of danger.

After a long pause I met his gaze. "You can sleep with me tonight if you want to."

"Jesus, Brooke, we– "

"Please let me finish," I interrupted. "I'm a virgin, which I can't exactly fake, so I've obviously never done anything like this before. If you say yes, I'll expect you to make love to me, and all I can offer you is tonight– it's your choice."

"Why only tonight?" The disappointment and sadness in his words was palpable.

"I wish I could explain, but I'm afraid it's extremely complicated. Part of saying yes is agreeing not to ask questions I can't answer."

We sat in silence for a few uncomfortable seconds before he reached out and took my hand, gripping it like he could make my question disappear if he only squeezed hard enough. "I'm a virgin too. I get my ass ridden constantly for it but I'm not ashamed– I sure as hell didn't come here expecting to go home with someone tonight. I get the feeling that you did, and I just happened to be the guy you picked."

Daniel pressed his forehead against the palm of his free hand and closed his eyes. "Damn it! I really like you, Brooke, but I gotta know why you're so desperate to lose your virginity tonight, and why you can't have a relationship with the person you give it to. If you can't or won't answer those questions, then I'll have to say no."

The stinging pain of rejection filled my chest as I pulled my hand away. How could it hurt this bad to be turned down by someone I just met? Did I really like him that much already? Trying to salvage what little pride I had left, I stood up and turned to leave, tears streaming down my cheeks.

Before I'd even taken a step, Raven sat down next to Daniel and glared at him with an anger I'd never seen in her. "You horse's ass. My beautiful, innocent, loving sister offers you a chance to share a wonderful moment together, one that you'd remember for the rest of your life, and you say no! You want answers to your fucking questions! Fine! I'm taking her to the Mayo clinic tomorrow to start chemotherapy. The doctors only give her a five percent chance of seeing her nineteenth birthday, and she didn't want to die a virgin. That's why it has to be tonight, and why she isn't looking to get involved with anyone."

She paused. Her intense, fuming stare made Daniel lean away and glance down at the table. "She teaches you to dance and you make her cry– you worthless piece of shit!"

In one quick motion Raven had her arm around my shoulders and was rushing me off to the bathroom. I almost had to break into a jog to keep up with her.

"You were awesome, Raven!" I said once we were safely inside. "You should totally be an actress! You had me believing I had cancer, for God sakes. I think Daniel might have wet himself though… Easy on the death stare, sis."

She acknowledged my compliment with a smile. "Now, when we go back out there, we'll head to our table, and you'll look all sad while we console you. Daniel feels terrible. It won't be long at all before he comes to our table to apologize. He seems like a pretty good guy. I was really impressed that he didn't jump on your offer, in spite of how badly he wants to sleep with you."

Seeing my expression, Raven cupped my chin with her hand. "I can tell that you're into him too. It's nice that your first time can be with someone you like, but be careful not to get too attached– this really does have to be a one-time thing."

"I know," I whispered. "I thought I was going to have to block out memories of sleeping with some disgusting pig tonight. I wasn't ready for this."

* * * *

When we got back to our table, everyone sprung to their feet and smothered me in their arms, really laying it on thick. In order to keep from laughing, I thought about how twisted it was that I'd meet such a great guy, tonight of all nights. Someone who might have been the love of my life was being reduced to a one-night stand. I wasn't that into Greek mythology, but if there was a goddess of love, I must have really pissed her off somehow. My family's expressions changed from mock sympathy to real concern when they noticed that I was crying.

As Raven predicted, Daniel quickly approached our table. I pulled out a wad of Kleenex and wiped my cheeks, and then turned to face him. Raven and Sienna took my hands in theirs, making it clear that I wasn't going anywhere– he'd have to speak in front of them.

Daniel bravely put his hand on my shoulder. "I'm so sorry that you have cancer, Brooke, and that I forced your sister to tell me. I wanted to know because I really like you, and I wish there could be more to our relationship than just one night. Of course I'm attracted to you. I mean, look at you– you're like a supermodel. If you can forgive me, I'd be honored to take you home with me tonight."

"Thanks, Daniel… I really like you too." I wanted to introduce him to everyone, but I wasn't sure if they'd want him to know their names.

Sienna gave me a subtle nod.

"You've met my sister Raven. These are our friends– Sienna, Sandy and Ruby." They all gave him a warm greeting.

"I'm sorry about before," Raven said. "I'm pretty protective of my little sister. I hope you can understand."

"Absolutely," he assured her. "I have three younger brothers myself. If anyone messed with them, they'd have me to deal with. My family means a lot to me too."

Daniel paused, blood rushing to his face. "Brooke, this is going to sound really bad, but I rode with my friends, so I don't have a car to take you in. And um…I live with my family, so I can't exactly take you to my house. I'd offer to take you to a hotel in a cab, but to be honest, I don't have that much money on me."

I could only imagine how hard it must have been for him to admit that in front of everyone. I felt terrible.

Before I could think of what to say Raven stood up and wrapped her arms around him. "Your honesty is admirable. We already have rooms reserved at the Sheraton, and we'll give you a ride to the hotel, along with money for a cab to take you wherever you'd like to go in the morning. Since you live at home, you may want to ask your friends if they'll cover for you, then call and let your parents know before it gets too late."

Daniel seemed taken aback by Raven's affection and thorough planning. "Um… Yeah– good idea." He flashed me a passionate smile. "Be right back."

We all burst out laughing when he ignored his jackass cousin's attempt at a high five. After a brief conversation with them, he stepped away and pulled out his cell phone. My heart began to race. In a few minutes I was going to be having sex for the first time in my life, with a guy I had never even kissed.

* * * *

Daniel and I climbed into the far back bench seat of Raven's Navigator. Sandy and Ruby were in the second row, only a couple feet in front of us. Raven turned up the music on the front speakers to give us some privacy, but rather than ignoring my family, Daniel reached out to them. He asked Ruby and Sandy several questions and had them both laughing by the time we were back on the highway.

Raven turned off the radio and listened as he talked about how much his brothers were looking forward to Halloween. His oldest brother, Nate– the one who'd asked him to watch Lord of the Rings– was thirteen and was obsessed with dragons. Craig was ten and was going as Anakin Skywalker. I just about choked when he said that his seven-year-old brother, Justin, was going as a vampire, but everyone else just laughed and asked about his costume. Daniel had us all in tears when he confessed that he wasn't wearing any underwear, and then colorfully described how Raven had scared the hell out of him earlier. By the time we got to the hotel, I was totally at ease.

Raven dropped Daniel and me off in front of the lobby then went around back to park, leaving us alone. "Your sister and your friends are really cool. I'm glad I got a chance to meet them."

"Me too."

"What floor?" he asked, stepping into the elevator behind me.

Dangerous Waters

I pulled the keycard out of my purse. "Ah...seventeen— we're in 1726."

The elevator doors closed. Daniel gazed at my face, and for a moment we both froze, overwhelmed by the palpable sexual tension between us. His soft brown eyes were soothing and inviting, almost drawing me into a trance of his own. He had thick black hair that was sexy as hell, a strong chin and a tough, masculine face.

His fingers stroked my cheek and glided down my neck, causing my breathing to accelerate. I lunged forward, thrusting my mouth against his. Daniel hoisted me up and pressed my body against the back wall as I wrapped my legs around his waist. After clenching his fist in my hair, he leaned my head back and fervently kissed my neck. When I felt his right hand drift down to my breasts, I let out an enthusiastic groan.

The ding of the elevator sent me scrambling to the corner just before a mother and two kids stepped in. She glared accusingly at us and turned her kids to face the doorway. I snorted when I spotted one of my shoes lying on the floor near her feet.

Daniel's eyes locked on mine, and both of us stared at each other like fighters anxiously awaiting the next round. By the time the elevator stopped on the fifteenth floor, I was exhaling pant-like breaths.

As soon as they stepped off, I jumped into his arms, my tongue parting his lips and entering his sweet, wet mouth. Our kisses grew more primal, almost violent. When the door opened, he carried me out, still wrapped around him.

"My shoe," I muttered breathlessly.

Daniel slid me down to my feet and put his arm between the doors to keep them from closing. I kicked off my other shoe and scampered down the hall with him close behind.

When I finally got the stupid key card to work, he picked me up from behind and spun me around. We crashed into the bathroom wall, wiping out the coffee machine and almost falling into the closet. After unzipping his jacket, I grabbed both sides of his gray button down shirt and yanked them apart, sending buttons flying across the room. He took three steps forward and flung me onto the bed.

Daniel unbuttoned his sleeves and removed what was left of his mangled dress shirt. Then he pulled his white t-shirt up over his head, revealing a muscular chest and tight abdomen that I so wasn't expecting. Maybe Aphrodite didn't hate me so much after all. I unfastened his jeans and slid them down over his hips. He hurriedly kicked them off while I undid my belt and tossed it to the floor.

I felt his hands grip the bottom of my dress. He slowly peeled it off of me, revealing the black teddy, garter belts and thigh high stockings underneath. Daniel glanced at my bandaged wrists, which I'd totally forgotten about, and gave me a sympathetic look. I wasn't sure how he thought this figured into my cancer treatment, but I was grateful not to have to make up an excuse.

"You're so beautiful," he whispered, leaning forward to kiss my lips. "I keep expecting to wake up."

I grinned appreciatively at him. "Can you excuse me for a minute?"

He laughed and gave my butt a playful slap. "Hurry back."

After jumping off the bed, I located my purse under the luggage rack and scurried into the bathroom. I leaned against the sink, closed my eyes and took a couple deep breaths. *Daniel's a great guy. Even if I didn't have to do this I'd still want to—this feels right.*

My nerves settled, I touched up my makeup, injected the cream and grabbed several condoms out of my purse. When I opened the door, Daniel was lying on his side facing me, completely naked. My eyes darted down to his groin. He grinned as he took in my awed expression.

I enjoyed the view for a few more seconds, and then bounded back to the bed, dropping the condoms on the nightstand and sitting down next to him. "Daniel, I can't afford to get pregnant, as that would seriously complicate my treatment. I need you to be super careful. Can you do that for me?"

He ran the back of his fingers along my cheek. "I'll make sure I pull out before I'm done, and I'll stop right away if it comes off. I promise."

I shot him a seductive look and moved my hands slowly up his thighs. Once he rolled onto his back I knelt down over top of him. My fingers glided across his stomach and up between his legs, tracing like a feather across the sensitive skin of his cock. It sprang to life, elongating in response to my touch. Seeing the full size of him was a little intimidating. Was all of that really going to fit inside me? My legs clenched protectively together at the thought.

Not that it wasn't a huge turn on. The trembling tip stood less than an inch from my waiting lips, silently begging to feel the warmth and wetness of my mouth. I closed the distance and placed a whisper of a kiss against his foreskin. Daniel's knees shot wide apart as he let out a fierce groan. Encouraged by his eager response, I ran the tip of my tongue up and down the shaft, cherishing the taste of his hot, salty skin. Each lick drove him wild. Daniel began to thrust in anticipation of my next soft caress, only to be frustrated by my intentionally sporadic timing. Without even realizing it I was testing him– seeing if he'd force me like Logan had. Daniel's hands had torn the sheets from both corners of the bed and were gripping them so tightly that his knuckles had blanched white, but he made no move to take control. The troubled memories from my past faded along with my fear. I took as much as I could fit of him into my mouth and began to suck, massaging his sack with my hand. His breathing shifted to almost a growl, and his hips rocked forward. Knowing that he was close to finishing, I moved my mouth up to the head and flicked my tongue across the underside of the tip. I felt him start to convulse and pulled my face away, just before he climaxed all over his chest.

Wet towel in hand, I lay down next to him and cleaned up the mess I'd made. When I finished, he rolled over so that he was partly on top of me and tenderly stoked my hair. "My God, that was incredible."

I placed my hand behind his neck and pulled his head down to steal a kiss. He kissed me back more intensely, and then tilted my head to the side and worked his way down my neck, his lips spread apart just enough to allow his tongue to soothe my searing skin. After unzipping my teddy, he slid it down almost to my waist, exposing my breasts. He mumbled something like "you're so beautiful" as he continued his trail of kisses along my neckline and across my chest. I squirmed and let out a catlike mewl when the tip of his tongue slid up the side of my breast and over the nipple. After several clumsy but nonetheless pleasurable licks, almost my entire breast slipped into his mouth. He began to suckle while his right hand glided over my nylons and between my legs, enticing me to spread them apart. When I obliged, he ran his fingertips along my inner thighs and slowly, almost teasingly, stroked my pussy through the thin black lace. I pressed myself up against his hand, begging for more.

Daniel let out a soft chuckle as he unsnapped the crotch of my teddy. "I don't know, I think I should make you hold out a little longer. Let you enjoy it – like you did for me."

All I could manage was a pleading whimper as he lightly tugged on my pubic hair. Damn him. I'd never felt less in control or quite so helpless. My body was his. I was so wet that when he finally penetrated me with his finger, it slid in all the way to his knuckles. At first he did little more than slide it in and out like a pencil, but he soon figured out that rotating a finger inside me had far more effect. As if he suddenly remembered that he had two hands, Daniel began to explore my outer folds with his thumb and fingers. I clenched my fists in the sheets and bit my lip, trying to stifle the screams that were rumbling up my throat, but when he forced a second finger into me, it was too much. My body was on fire. Unable to wait a second longer, I arched my back and shouted "fuck me!" at the top of my lungs.

Daniel snapped his head up and almost fell off the bed, causing us both to burst into laughter, and then grabbed a condom off the table and went to work trying to open it. I watched him fumble with it for as long as I could stand before sitting up and snatching it away. *Sandy was right—all thumbs.*

I took out the lubricated condom and rolled it onto him, my eyes widening when it ran out well before he did. As I lay back down, I raised my legs high up against my chest. Daniel slid forward and placed his knees outside my hips. We exchanged several deep, lustful kisses before he eased himself into me. It was so tight. Every inch stretched me wider, making it a struggle to accommodate his massive girth. Daniel stopped with little more than his head inside and waited for me, only pushing deeper when I nodded. I soon reached my limit and pressed back against his pelvis with my hands. Taking that as a firm stopping point, he withdrew his cock almost completely before penetrating me again. The feel of him stretching me out, stimulating my entire vagina with every thrust, had me driving my head back into my pillow. I began to rock my hips, timing them with his thrusts, and felt a sharp, almost burning pain. Sensing what had just happened, Daniel tenderly pressed his lips against mine. I was no longer a virgin.

Round two started with him snatching me up off the bed. I wrapped my arms and legs around him as we tumbled into the nightstand, knocking over the lamp. He pinned my back against the wall, took hold of my thighs and entered me again. After several minutes I began to scream with every breath and slam myself against him, driving his cock in even further. Suddenly my whole body went rigid. My core gripped him tight as my body convulsed in wild spasms and fluid seeped out between my legs.

As soon as it was over, we both collapsed on the bed. Still breathing heavily, Daniel stretched out and placed his hands under his pillow. I curled my body into his, resting my head on his chest.

"You're amazing," he said, bringing his arm down around my shoulders. "Meeting you is the best thing that's ever happened to me."

My lips quickly found his, and we locked in another long embrace. I wanted to tell him everything, even what I was going to become, but I knew it was pointless. He'd never believe me, and even if he did, I'd just be signing his death warrant. Not that he'd want to see me again if my new family didn't kill him. In the real world, finding out that your girlfriend was destined to become a blood sucking monster would pretty much be a deal breaker. It made me sick to keep lying to him after what we'd just shared, but I knew that I had to. "Thanks for making tonight so special– I wish to God that I had more time to spend with you. You're the greatest guy I've ever met. Please don't be sad when I'm gone."

I heard Daniel sniffling and looked up to see him wiping his eyes. He turned on his side and held me tight against him. "Don't give up, Brooke. You have to fight. The doctors could be wrong about your chances. They don't know you– they haven't seen how full of life you are."

I buried my face in his chest and wept, almost wishing that Raven's lie was true. At least then I'd have a five percent chance of seeing him again. After several minutes had passed, I finally regained my composure. "Daniel, I need to prepare myself for what's coming– I don't have much time left."

When he opened his mouth to reply I put my finger to his lips. "Please, just hold me." He curled his strong arms around my back and nuzzled his face against my neck as both of us cried.

When I woke up he was gone. I found a note folded in half on his pillow, written on hotel stationary.

Brooke,

I'm sorry for not saying goodbye, but I thought it would just make it harder on both of us.
I know you aren't looking for a relationship right now, but if you ever change your mind please call me.
You don't have to go through this alone.
I will never forget you,
    Daniel

His full name, address, email and phone numbers were on the back of the paper. I knew I could never see him again, but I couldn't make myself rip up his note, so I tucked it into my purse, climbed back in bed and cried myself to sleep.

Several hours later I awoke to the sound of someone knocking on the door. It took me almost ten minutes to drag myself out of bed and slide my dress back on. When I undid the lock and pulled the door open, Raven was waiting for me in the hallway. She didn't offer any comforting words, but the compassion in her eyes made it clear she understood the horrible pain I was in. I felt a tear escape down my cheek as she reached out and took me in her arms.

"I love him, Raven!" I managed to get out between sobs.

"I know. Try to focus on remembering how wonderful last night was, and that your first time was with a great guy who really cared about you."

"I'll try." After a short pause I eagerly looked up at her. I had to tell someone how unbelievable it had felt. "Aren't you going to ask me how it was?"

Raven snorted. "I think everyone on floors fifteen thru nineteen knows how it was– we were fighting for pillows to cover our ears."

"Hey!" I shouted, my cheeks turning beet red.

Raven placed her hands on both sides of my face and kissed my forehead. "Let's go home."

* * * *

The ride home took my embarrassment to new heights. When we stopped at the first light, Sandy slithered up against the door like a Vegas pole dancer, stared at the guy in the car next to us and yelled "You're cute… Fuck me!!"

They all burst out laughing so hard that they were gasping for air as I hid my face in shame. Every couple miles someone would make up their own take on it, and they'd start rolling with laughter all over again. After a while they didn't even make sense anymore, but that just seemed to make them funnier. By the time we were halfway home even I was laughing.

"You can all go to hell!"

Chapter Twelve
Fight Or Flight

"Would you stop already?" Teresa grumbled, glaring at her ever-pacing brother. "No one's following us. Relax."

Travis finished scanning Beacon Street and ducked back into the alleyway. "God damn it! Do you ever listen? I told you we had to cool it for a while. What the hell were you thinking?"

"The bitch spilled her drink on me."

He sighed and tiredly rubbed his eyes. Arguing with her was like trying to reason with a bratty three-year-old grabbing candy in a grocery checkout line. "So we're homeless because someone accidentally got Diet Coke on your shirt?"

"Quit being such a queen," Teresa said with a huff. "You know Stefan thinks of us as his kids, which is totally weird by the way. All he'll do is make us listen to his *rules* again. If you wouldn't have talked me into running, we'd probably be watching TV by now."

"If Stefan and Alexander just wanted to talk, they would've waited until we got back, not raided our feeding room like a two-man S.W.A.T. team. This is serious, Terr. If they find us, they're going to kill us."

For the first time in as long as he could remember, his snarky, narcissistic sister looked vulnerable. She crossed her arms to conceal her jittery hands and looked into his eyes. "So what do we do? I'm not living on the street again, or in the skuzzy-ass hotels we used to stay in."

Travis placed a comforting hand on his baby sister's shoulder. "Things aren't like they used to be, sis. Even you have to admit that Stefan taught us a hell of a lot. Once we get out of town, we can trance a bank manager and get all the money we need. I thought we'd head south– you always wanted to see Orlando."

Acting as if he hadn't even spoken, Teresa shrugged off his hand and headed further down the dimly lit alley, veering around overflowing dumpsters and piles of loose garbage before slumping back against the brick wall behind her. "And what about the skank who started all this? We just leave her to her fairy-tale life, sipping wine in her mansion? No fucking way."

Anger coursed through his veins at his sister's jealousy and unfounded arrogance. "Wake up!" Travis screamed, shaking her shoulders so violently that her teeth rattled. "You think you can take her? You don't know jack shit. Raven's been training for almost two hundred years, Einstein. She'd tear your ass apart like a piñata."

Teresa rolled her eyes and pushed his hands away. "Not Raven, you douche. I'm talking about Emily."

"Emily? What the hell did she do?"

"If she wouldn't have wandered up to us like a lost puppy, we would never have fed with Alexander there, and Stefan would still be clueless. The bitch led Raven right to our door."

"Oh come on. That's a reach, even for you. Raven lied to her about our scent. You're really going to blame her for that?"

She shot her brother a disgusted look. "I knew making her strip was a bad idea. All it takes is a flash of boobs and you turn to mush. Are you ever going to grow a pair? You'd still be Keri's lapdog if it wasn't for me."

"Don't."

"Oooh, don't talk about my precious Keri," Teresa mocked. "God, you're a pussy. She was never going to turn you, and you know it."

Travis looked away to conceal the pain on his face. Sometimes he questioned whether there was anything decent left in his sister at all. Every year she became darker and even more detached. "That doesn't mean I wanted her to die. I loved her. Doesn't that mean anything to you?"

"Love shmove. You wanted to become immortal. I did you a favor when I torched her."

"A favor? Are you serious? I asked her to marry me that night!" He caught just a hint of a smile on Teresa's lips and froze. "You knew– that's why you did it, isn't it?"

"Yeah, ri– "

Like a stroke of lightning Travis smashed his fist into the brick wall just to the right of her head, opening up a gaping hole into the vacant building behind her. "Don't you fucking lie to me! I swear to God I'll kill you!"

Teresa calmly ducked out from under his arm and dusted the debris off her shirt. "So what if I did know about your pathetic little proposal? Did you forget your promise to our parents, dear brother? Ten years is a long time. Remember the ambulance ride? Mom coughing up blood, and Dad, well, Dad wasn't doing much of anything come to think of it. Hard to blame the guy, since he had a piece of metal stuck in his head. You promised them that you'd always look out for me– swore on your life actually. Where did I fit in your little family? You really think Keri would've let me keep living with you? She hated me."

Travis collapsed to the ground and clutched his knees to his chest, tears stinging at his eyes. Hearing his sister's twisted rationale for taking away the woman who'd turned his life around was unbearable. "How can you say that? She paid for you to go back to school. She even decked out your room with all the shit on your insane 'must-have' list. She was going to ask you to be her maid of honor."

"And when was she going to make me her sister? That's right. Never. All she had to do was say yes."

"Yes? Yes to what?" He stared at her in total confusion until it suddenly dawned on him. "Our walk in the park– you followed us."

"Of course. I'd only been pushing you to ask her for, like, three years."

"So when she said she'd marry me, but she would never change me– "

"I knew I had to take matters into my own hands," Teresa finished. "I figured she'd never be more distracted than that night. Boy was I right. She didn't even wake up until the gas splashed her face. Once I lit the match, all she could do is run around screaming. I'm glad you were at class. It was kinda gross watching her face melt away."

Memories of that horrible night flooded his mind. The rancid stench of burnt flesh and hair when he walked through the door had made him gag. He'd raced upstairs, terrified that his sister had fallen asleep with her bong and died in the resulting fire, only to find her calmly watching TV with his fiancé's charred corpse lying at her feet. "You are seriously messed up," he muttered without meeting her ice cold eyes. "You know that, right?"

Teresa wrapped a strand of her curly blonde hair around her finger. "Whatever. We're immortal now– that's all that matters."

They both slipped back into the shadows when two figures emerged at the end of the alley, continuing on without even a glance in their direction. He found it hard to even look at Teresa now that he understood what had truly happened that night, and how easily he'd been manipulated into playing his part, but in the end it changed nothing. He'd never go back on his vow to their parents. Protecting her was his penance. "It's too dangerous for us to stay here," Travis said. "Will you at least come with me to Florida?"

"Once I choke the last breath out of that little whore, you can take me wherever you want."

Travis slicked back his long, brown hair. "Fine. But if we're doing this, we do it my way. Agreed?"

She raised her shoulders in an indifferent shrug. "As long as she dies, I'm good with whatever."

"Their house is only a few miles from here. It's surrounded by woods, so there are plenty of spots where we'll be able to hear what's going on inside without risking being seen. As soon as she's left alone, you can have your fun, but we're waiting as long as it takes for that to happen. Even Sandy has had decades of training, and I'm not dying for your stupid vendetta."

"Hi ho, hi ho, off to kill a bitch we go," Teresa sang out, dancing down the alley ahead of him like a schoolgirl.

Chapter Thirteen
Black Ops

It was past noon by the time I managed to get my mind off of Daniel long enough to take a shower and make my way into the kitchen. Sienna and the rest of my new family were gathered around the kitchen table, apparently plotting our heist. I was anxious to join them, but I was also starving, so I made myself an omelet and some hash browns and took a seat next to Raven. They were all studying two hand-drawn diagrams. "What are those?" I asked, feeling somewhat guilty for making them take time to catch me up.

"The one on top is the medical records floor of the hospital," Raven explained, pushing them over to me. "The other one shows the two labs where the DNA samples are stored."

"How did you get these?" Everything was labeled and color coded, down to each individual shelf.

"We went on a little reconnaissance trip after we got back from the hotel. Once we found the right floors, it was just a matter of time until enough employees walked by for us to get a good layout of the rooms from their minds. We also got these." Raven tossed two medical badges on the table. "They'll get us in wherever we need to go."

"What if they catch us on camera?"

"First of all, you're not going anywhere near the hospital." Raven took the diagrams back as if she'd just revoked my viewing privileges. "As for the cameras, Ruby's got that covered. Sienna and I will be wearing the same scrubs as the nurse's aides on our respective floors. Combined with the valid badges, no one will suspect a thing."

My eyes darted to Ruby. "You can hack into their security feeds?"

"Piece of cake– I won't even have to leave the house. After I disable their cameras, I'll delete the digital recordings along with any electronic information they have on Jane Doe."

"How? They must have a firewall of some kind." I was hardly Best Buy Geek Squad material, but I did know a little about computers.

"It was too easy really," Ruby said with a grin. "All I had to do was hop on a vacant nurse's station out of camera view and crash their system. Once the technical support guy logged in, I got his admin ID and password, along with the server information. He wasn't the brightest guy in the world, but eventually he discovered the obvious trail I'd left behind and called security. Listening in on their thoughts while they talked about checking the camera feeds for people walking down the hall in the last thirty minutes gave me everything else I needed."

"Our own little Chloe," I teased. I wasn't sure if they knew who the seriously cranky tech girl on *24* was until I heard them laughing.

"I hope I'm not that bitchy."

"No way!" I assured her.

After I'd downed about half my omelet, I paused and looked up at everyone. "What about the records at the police station?"

"That's where you and I come in," Sandy replied, handing me a pay-as-you-go cell phone. "You'll need to call the Boston Police Department at four-thirty and tell them that you have information on the woman who was dumped in front of the hospital naked last Friday. When they transfer you to the detective who's handling the case, say that you'll meet him at five. Don't worry. You won't actually have to go. I'll be waiting on the same floor, in the women's restroom just outside the entrance to the Bureau of Investigative Services. Once I figure out who it is, I'll take control of his body and shred the file." She took a big swig of cherry-flavored water and resumed working on her doodling, shading in the features of an elegant up-do hairstyle on the legal pad in front of her.

"Then what?" I prodded.

Sandy crooked her head. "Um… Go home? Maybe grab a fountain pop on the way?"

"You know what I mean, smart-ass. We're just going to leave him standing there? Won't he wonder what just happened to him?"

"Let him— it's not like he's going to think 'Gee, I must have been tranced by a vampire.' Besides, he's never even going to see me."

"Actually, Brooke's got a point," Raven cut in. "Causing a distraction afterwards would take some of the focus off the file, and would allow you to slip out without being noticed."

Sandy snorted. "Yeah… That's almost what she meant."

"Does it *really* matter who gets credit for the idea?" Sienna chided, clearly frustrated that we weren't taking this more seriously. Her light rebuke made us all snap to attention.

"Sorry Mom," Sandy said. "What if I made him collapse on the floor and flail around like he's having a seizure?"

Raven nodded her approval. "That should work."

"While you guys are doing that, I'll be removing all of their electronic records on Jane Doe," Ruby added. "Unlike the hospital, I'm in their system a lot– I probably know it better than they do."

She glanced at the cell phone Sandy had given me. "You'll need to go somewhere to make the call. They wouldn't be able to trace the number back to us, since we paid cash and used a fake ID, but they could triangulate the location the call is coming from. Once you hang up, take the battery out and bring it back with you."

"Got it." I was glad to have some part in this, even if it was just making a phone call.

"Only one problem," Raven said, not directing her comments toward anyone in particular. "Our entire plan depends on the detective not being able to sense that someone is manipulating his body– "

"Which we're far from certain is the case," Sienna finished for her. "I've never considered it something worth studying, since we only trance those we intend to kill."

I thought back through each of the times I'd been tranced, trying to recall if I ever felt their presence in my mind. Raven had told me what she was going to do, so I knew she was doing it. Same with Sandy and Ruby. Even when I was attacked, there wasn't any doubt as to who was behind it, not with me walking straight toward her. Trying to separate what I knew from what I could actually feel was impossible, like showing someone an ace of clubs, then turning it face down and asking if they had any psychic instinct as to which card it was.

"Would you mind if we did a test on you?" Raven asked.

"Not at all." It's not like it was painful or anything, and I was just as curious as they were to find out.

She smiled and tousled my hair. "Thanks, sis. Go into the living room and sit so you can't see any of us. Once you're ready we'll trance you. If you can tell who's doing it, or hear the person's thoughts, then you can sense our presence in your mind."

I scampered into the living room and plopped down on the section of the couch that faced away from the kitchen. "Take your best shot."

In an instant my body was taken from me. My eyes drifted shut as my legs rose up onto the couch and my upper body reclined, sinking into a pile of throw pillows. I searched my mind for any clue as to who was controlling me, but all I had was the now familiar feeling of REM sleep, with my brain detached from my body.

I remembered Raven saying that vampires could sense how much a human was fighting them. Maybe if I tried to resist, I'd pick something up. After clearing everything else from my mind, I focused on opening my eyes, visualizing them rising like window shades. Within seconds the detached feeling morphed into more of a stinging numbness, like a foot I'd been sitting on for too long. Then my eyelashes began to flicker. With one last mental push I broke through, catching a quick glimpse of the room before being plunged back into darkness. The thoughts that accompanied the foreign but now very clear command to close my eyes left little doubt as to who'd closed them— it was Ruby.

By the time I realized I was free from her trance, everyone was gathered around me. It felt like someone had hit me between the eyes with a sledgehammer. "Damn, Ruby, you're strong," I said, sitting up and rubbing my temples.

She arched her brows. "How did you know it was me?"

Given the techie jargon I'd picked up, that was a no brainer. "I doubt if anyone else in the family would be thinking about setting up a secure FTP connection."

No one said a word. They were all staring at me like a third arm had just sprouted out of my neck. "What?"

Sienna took a seat next to me and placed her hand on my knee. "In all my years, I've never heard of a human taking back control of their body from a vampire. What you just did is not supposed to be possible."

"Maybe Ruby wasn't really trying that hard, since she didn't expect me to fight her," I replied, hoping to avoid being labeled as some kind of freak.

"Actually I was concentrating more than ever to see if I could make you hear my thoughts," Ruby countered. "I've never felt anything like that before— I was still connected to your mind, but I had no control. The surprise you felt when your eyes opened is the only thing that allowed me to close them again."

I picked at the hem of my jeans, not wanting to express the only other theory I had, but knowing I already was just by thinking about it. "Sienna told me that the strength of vampire's abilities varies based on their genetics. Maybe your trance ability isn't as strong as most vampires."

"Certainly a plausible explanation," Sienna said, no doubt trying to alleviate some of the guilt I was feeling for thinking it. "But Ruby's ability is well above average. I've seen her trance people from further away than I can."

I was out of explanations. *Great. So I'm a freak.* "Well, I won't be doing it again anytime soon. My head is friggin' killing me. And our plan should still work– I didn't detect anything until after I took back control."

Sienna slowly raked her fingers through her hair and let it fall down over her left shoulder. "We can't take that chance. We'll have to think of another way to get the file from the police without hurting anyone."

"Couldn't Sandy just read his mind and make sure he doesn't suspect anything?" I wondered.

"What if he does?" Sandy said, crossing her arms and leaning back against the couch. "That wouldn't leave us a lot of options."

"I know– I really don't think he will though. If I'm wrong, I guess you'd have to make him shoot himself or something." I couldn't believe I was actually suggesting that they kill someone just to keep me out of trouble. Maybe becoming a vampire would cost me my soul after all.

Sienna tilted my chin up to look at her. "All that shows is that your mind is adjusting to your new life– it doesn't make you evil, sweetheart. And while there are far less traumatic ways Sandy can intervene than using his revolver, for the most part, your idea is brilliant. If he has no idea what's happening to him, then we'll stick with our original plan, but if Sandy picks up anything alarming, she'll stop his heart as soon as he finishes shredding the file."

Our conversation made me realize how much I'd learned about what vampires could do and how unusual it must be for a human to know so much about them. Maybe that explained why I was able to break Ruby's trance. Maybe I just figured out how to fight it from being put under so many times. Most humans would never be around to experience a second trance, let alone a sixth, and they definitely wouldn't have a chance to ask questions. The more I thought about it, the more convinced I became. There wasn't anything special about me– I'd just been given the opportunity to learn.

Sienna let out a defeated sigh. "You're probably right. If your ability was genetic, it should've manifested itself when you were attacked. Do you really think you could completely resist being tranced now?"

"Maybe– if my head doesn't explode first." I expected to hear at least some laughter. No one showed even the slightest hint of a smile. "What the hell? Why are you all pissed at me?"

"I'm sorry, baby," Sienna muttered. "I know you're confused, and I can sense how much pain you're in, but I'm afraid this can't wait."

It was obvious that she was going to trance me whether I agreed to it or not. I gave her a defiant growl. "Fine. When we're done, I'm raiding my pain pill stash and going to bed. Try to keep me from going to my room."

My arms dropped limp to my sides as the familiar feeling surrounded my mind. Rather than trying to fight through it, I focused on clearing away the numbing haze and felt it recede almost immediately. With only a little more effort than would usually be required, I stood up and headed off toward my room. After a couple of steps I felt the sensation leave my body entirely and I knew Sienna had given up.

The sound of someone bursting into tears brought me up short. When I turned I saw Ruby, Sandy and Raven comforting Sienna, who was now doubled over on the couch with her face buried in her hands. I raced to her side, slid in front of Ruby and threw my arms around Sienna. "What's wrong, Mom? Talk to me!"

"I won't do it!" she wailed. "I can't!"

"Somebody tell me what's wrong!" I demanded, glaring at Raven.

The mournful, hopeless look on her face made me shudder. She was studying my features the way people do at a funeral, when they know they're never going to see their loved one again. "I never should have suggested experimenting on you. This is all my fault. I'm sorry, Brooke– I'm so sorry!" Her whole body shook as she cried.

For the first time since I joined them, I was truly scared. "What's…all your fault?"

Sienna wiped her eyes, and took a couple of deep breaths to regain her composure. "My sweet daughter. The knowledge you've gained, that we caused you to gain, is a threat to all of our kind. The mere existence of someone with your ability presents a grave risk to all vampires."

"You don't…trust me? You think– I'd betray you?" A butcher knife being plunged into my chest couldn't have hurt this bad. I'd given her access to a piece of my heart that had been walled off almost my entire life, and now she was ripping it to shreds.

"I don't question your loyalty now, but I fear that your human ties are just too strong. If your father was attacked, or even Brittney for that matter, you'd be consumed with hate and anger, along with an overwhelming sense of guilt. You'd never forgive yourself for not teaching them how to break our trance. Your self-loathing would only be surpassed by the hatred you'd feel toward us, for not allowing you to protect them. If it got to that point, it's hard to say what you'd be capable of doing."

The pain in my chest shifted to anger. All of the talk about me being her daughter, saying that she loved me, and taking an oath to defend me with her life was complete bullshit. I voluntarily subjected myself to being tranced, and now she wanted to punish me for what I learned from it– unbelievable. I hadn't made any attempt to warn my dad or my friends, even though I knew Stacey and Angie were in danger. I hadn't told the police or the FBI anything, not even when I was mad at Raven for lying to me, and there was a police officer standing just outside my room. I'd been nothing but faithful.

Forcefully pulling out of her arms, I stood up and wheeled around to face her. "I just want you to know that I actually meant the oath I gave you. I would never have done anything to hurt you, or put our family at risk. Well, I guess I should say *your* family, since apparently I'm not a part of it. 'You'll be loved until the very last beat of my heart'… What a joke. Let's get this over with."

I stormed off down the hallway, removing my rugby hoodie and ripping the bandages from my wrists. With a heave I sent the door to the feeding room crashing into the wall, then hopped up on the gurney and lay down on my back. An overwhelming sense of abandonment exploded from deep within me, consuming everything in its path until I was just an empty shell. I couldn't cry or scream. I couldn't do anything other than lie there, silently waiting for my life to end. When Sienna finally entered, I closed my eyes and turned my head away from the door.

"Please look at me," she said, placing her hand on my cheek.

"I really thought you loved me."

"I do, baby. We all do. Which is why, regardless of what I should do, what my duties are to this coven and to our kind, there's no way I could ever hurt you. I'm so sorry for what I said out there, and for even considering acting upon it. I hope someday you can find it in your heart to forgive me. As a sign of how much I love and trust you, I'm giving you the choice to join our family or return to your human life– I'll deal with Stefan."

I sat up, arching my brows in disbelief. "You'd let me leave? Go back to Michigan?"

She looked wounded, like my words had knocked the breath from her. "Yes, Emily. You can go home."

I thought about how much it would mean to me to have my dad fully back in my life again. There's no way I could go to BU anymore, but I could make up some story about how Boston was too big for me and go to college somewhere closer to home. I wouldn't have to kill anyone or drink blood for the rest of my life, and I'd be able to live in one place for as long as I wanted to. I could pursue the career I'd always dreamed of, get married, and even have kids someday if I wanted to. I might even be able to see Daniel again.

The cuts on my wrists would be a problem. Regardless of whether I said that I was attacked or that I tried to kill myself, my dad would never let me out of his sight again. And I'd still have the mess at the hospital to deal with, not to mention all of the lies I'd told everyone. Trying to come up with a plausible explanation for everything that didn't implicate Raven would be almost impossible.

And even if I somehow managed to lie my way through it all successfully, going back home would mean never seeing Raven, Sienna, Ruby or Sandy again. I'd only known them for a few days, but we'd shared so much together, life altering events that would always be a part of me. Through some unbelievable twist of fate, I'd been given three wonderful sisters and a mother who loved me. How could I just walk away from that? How could I possibly go the rest of my life without ever seeing them again?

I gazed into her puffy, tear filled eyes, catching just a faint glint of hope amongst the sea of guilt and sorrow. "My name is Brooke, Mom, and I am home."

"Oh, my sweet baby!" Sienna cried out, lifting me off the gurney to crush me against her ribs. "Thank you. I love you so much."

"I– can't– breathe," I said, only half joking. She kissed me on the forehead, my nose and both cheeks before placing a very motherly kiss on my lips. When she finally pulled back, Sandy, Raven and Ruby joined in, smothering me in their own warm hugs.

"That was the choice I always wanted to offer you," Raven whispered, still grasping me firmly in her arms.

My fingers brushed Raven's face, lifting her chin until she met me stern look. "I'm no longer here because of an agreement you made, or because my only other choice was death. I've decided this is the life I want. So let go of the guilt."

She managed a weak grin as she blinked away tears. "I'll try, baby sister, if you'll promise me something in return. Never speak of what you can do to anyone, not even after you're changed. If Stefan or any other vampire found out, they'd kill you, no questions asked, regardless of what deal they have with us.

Dangerous Waters

We're talking total Vegas rules here. And for your safety and ours, we're going to have to keep you at the house until you're changed, since your thoughts would betray your secret."

I flashed her a smile. Vegas rules as in, what happens in Vegas stays in Vegas. "I think I can handle that."

"I'll never get used to how resilient you are," Sienna said, looking almost awestruck. "Now go to your room– you're grounded!"

I lowered my chin and stomped off toward my room, doing my best irate thirteen-year-old impression. After a couple of steps I stopped and turned back toward her. "What about the phone call to the police at four-thirty?"

She chewed on her lip as she thought. "We'll go ahead with what we planned. Try to leave by four and head south. I'll print out directions for you and put them on the table. When it gets to be about four-twenty, look for a crowded parking lot to make the call from. Don't get out of your car, and keep the doors locked. As soon as you're done, come straight home."

"I will," I promised. "I'm going to try to get some rest before I go."

After taking one of my leftover pain pills, I set my alarm for 3:30 p.m. and crawled into bed. With my head throbbing the way it was, I had little hope of sleeping, but I figured the dark, quiet room might help me feel better. Sienna came in soon after I was in bed.

"Could you leave the lights off?" I pleaded.

"Of course, honey." She sat on the edge of my bed, bandaging my wrists while she sang a beautiful Irish lullaby. "Rest tired eyes a while. Sweet is thy baby's smile. Angels are guarding and they watch o'er thee. Sleep, sleep, grah mo chree. Here on you mamma's knee. Angels are guarding. And they watch o'er thee– " Before she'd finished I was asleep.

It felt like only a few minutes had passed before I heard the annoying buzzing in my ears. I repeatedly clubbed at the alarm until it shut off. I felt like hell– the brief sleep and pain medication had done nothing to ease my headache. As much as I wanted to crawl back under the covers, I knew I had to get moving. I sat up and put my shoes back on and stuffed my wallet, keys and cell phone into my purse.

When I got to the kitchen table, I saw a pile of stuff waiting for me. The cell phone and driving directions were underneath the hoodie I'd tossed on the floor earlier, along with detailed instructions. I slid my shirt back on while I glanced them over– our plan hadn't changed.

* * * *

"I still don't get why we just don't grab her when she comes out," Teresa grumbled, fidgeting impatiently at her door handle.

Travis gave her a sideways glance. "Did you not hear the part where she can't be tranced anymore? If she even got off a shriek, Ruby would be on our asses in a second. I think you can wait a few minutes until she stops to make the call."

"I guess." She motioned toward a towering oak, whose shadow darkened the end of the private drive. "After she's dead we should hang her from that tree – kind of a welcome home present for the rest of her pathetic family."

"I don't give a shit what you do with her," Travis snapped. "But you can forget your little victory dance. We're never coming back here again."

"How do you walk around with that three-foot stick up your ass?"

"Fuck you."

"I'm serious, Trav," Teresa said, turning to face him. "Since when do I have to talk you into having some fun? You're acting like Stefan, for Christ sakes."

He sighed and glanced away. "We've never messed around with vamps before. I just don't want anything to happen to you."

She let out a short little snort. "Damn, you really take that oath thing seriously."

"Don't you remember what caused the accident? *I* killed our parents, Terr." The remorse he could never fully escape rose up out of his gut, threatening to swallow him in another crippling depression. "That promise is the only reason I'm still here."

Teresa placed her hand on his thigh. "You were a kid. Besides, you only covered his eyes for like a second. He didn't have to jerk the wheel like that."

"Can we talk about something else?" Travis tried to discreetly rub his tears away, like he was just hunting down an errant eyelash.

Teresa gathered her curly blonde hair at the back of her head and secured it with a hair band. She was dressed entirely in black, as if they were cat burglars and it wasn't broad daylight outside. Her long sleeve turtleneck left her midriff exposed, of course. Travis wasn't sure if she even owned anything that covered her stomach. Not since she'd had her naval pierced, anyway. "Want to hear what I have planned for the little bitch? That ought to cheer ya up."

He chuckled under his breath. "So you're giving up on hanging her from the tree?"

"This is way better," she said with a wicked grin. "We're going to take her with us. I mean, you scored this awesome van, we might as well use it."

Travis mumbled an obscenity under his breath. Every time he caved and tried to appease one of his sister's crazy-ass ideas, they just snowballed. Nothing was ever enough for her. "For how long? You promised you'd come with me to Florida."

"And I will. What's wrong with bringing along some food and entertainment? I saw the way you touched her when she was on the table. Tell me you wouldn't like to fuck her."

Travis flushed, his cheeks turning every shade of pink, but he didn't say a word. Admitting that he'd thought of Emily each morning as he fondled himself would only encourage his sister.

"That's what I thought. After I knock her out, we'll throw her in the back, and then swing by Home Depot. You built custom bikes– I'm sure you can rig something up to confine her." Teresa glanced down between his legs and giggled.

"Not so patient now, are we?"

* * * *

Dumping everything into the passenger seat of my Camry, I hopped in and took off down the private drive. The traffic was pretty light on Randolph Avenue, allowing me to reach I-93 West in less than fifteen minutes. After merging into traffic on 24 South, I continued on to Central Street, taking the exit and heading west. I was kind of winging it, since the directions had only shown me how to get on I-24, but I figured this exit was as good as any. I'd gone several miles before I began to worry. All I could see were an endless string of subdivisions. Sienna had wanted me to call from a crowded, commercial lot, but this was clearly a residential area, and I was running out of time. Just when I was about to pull into the next vacant driveway, a large YMCA complex appeared on the right. I pulled in and parked near the back, sandwiching between two other cars.

It was almost 4:30. I nervously read through the instructions again, found the number to call and typed it in.

A lady answered on the third ring. "Boston Police Department, how may I direct your call?"

"I have some information on the unidentified woman that was dropped off in front of Massachusetts General Hospital with her wrists slit last Friday," I said, my heart pounding like a drum.

"What is your name, miss?" she asked.

So far the call was going exactly as they'd predicted. "I would prefer to remain anonymous."

"Please hold...."

After sitting on hold for what seemed like an hour, I started to panic. It was almost 4:40– Sandy would definitely have expected the detective to have taken my call by now. "Come on, come on!" I yelled, pounding the dashboard with my fist.

Suddenly a man's voice blared through the phone, and I jumped. "Bureau of Investigative Services. Snyder speaking."

"I have some information on the unidentified woman who was dropped off in front of Massachusetts General Hospital with her wrists slit last Friday," I repeated.

"Okay."

"Are you the detective in charge of the case?"

"Yes. My name is Sergeant Detective Adam Snyder. Please go ahead."

"Not over the phone. Can I meet you in twenty minutes?"

"Sure," he replied. "Where would you like to meet?"

"I'll come to the station."

"Could I get your name?"

"When I get there. I'll see you at five." I hung up, removed the battery and pulled my phone out to check for messages– nothing.

My mind was so preoccupied that I only half glanced at the rearview mirror before pulling out, almost backing into a cherry red Jeep Wrangler. The owner thanked me with a blast of his horn and what I was sure was a slew of obscenities, weaved around my bumper and barreled out of the parking lot. I was still watching him over my right shoulder when something else caught my eye, a flash of movement off to my left. It was nothing more than a blur, but it was more than my frazzled nerves could take. I stepped on the gas and shot backward at breakneck speed, then slammed on the brakes, flipped it into drive and sped off, the accelerator flat on the floor.

* * * *

"Follow her!" Teresa screamed, slamming the van door behind her.

Travis shifted into gear and raced toward the exit, but had to wait for several cars to pass before turning left onto Central Avenue. "Mind telling me how you managed to fuck that up?"

"The dumb bitch almost hit the Jeep I was using for cover. When he laid on his horn I had to back off– half the parking lot was looking at us."

"Did she see you?" He glared at her when she didn't answer. "Damn it! Did she see you or not!"

"I don't know… She might have. Something scared the shit out of her."

Travis recklessly pulled off to the side of the road, going up and over the curb. "I knew this was a dumb idea! Fuck!"

"What the hell? You're losing her, you idiot!"

He wheeled and grabbed her chin, pinning her head against the glass. "This is over! Do you hear me! When Sienna finds out, she's going to have every vampire on the east coast hunting us down. You can forget about Florida. Thanks to you we get to hide out in bum-fuck Arkansas, staring at picturesque views of cotton fields for the next ten years."

She giggled. "Sooie!"

Travis laughed in spite of himself. From the time they were kids, his sister always knew just how far she could push him, and exactly what to say to pull him back from the edge when his anger boiled over. He released his grip and tried to straighten out her scrunched up T-shirt. "Sorry."

"I know. So do you really think we need to hide out? I'm not even sure she saw me."

"At least for a couple months– long enough for them to think we've left for good."

Chapter Fourteen
Mission Critical

As soon as I parked, I raced into the house and called out for Ruby.

"In here!" she replied.

I followed her voice down the hall to the reinforced metal door at the end. It stood slightly ajar, the first time I'd even seen it open, and a thin bead of light was spilling out into the hallway. I nudged it aside, and stepped into what felt like a walk-in cooler. The room had a raised platform floor and black metal grates for a ceiling. Two racks of servers stood in the center, surrounded by several computers, a network hub, a couple of multi-function printers and some other stuff I couldn't identify.

Ruby spun around in her high-backed leather office chair to face me, pulling out her white iPod ear buds. Her light gray, loose-knit sweater had a see-through design, leaving her olive colored skin and black silk bra exposed. The sinewy curves of her ballerina shaped body were breathtaking. "Hey sis, welcome to my war room."

I just stood there with my jaw open. "This is amazing. You've got more stuff in this one room than my entire high school had."

"Yeah, it's quite the setup," she agreed. "Have you worked with computers much?"

"I had some programming classes in high school. I helped out in the computer lab a few times too," I said, taking a seat next to her.

"Cool. You probably recognize a lot of this stuff then."

I gave her a little laugh. "Some of it. How are things going?"

"So far so good. I just finished with the police department records. The cameras at the hospital have been disabled, and all the recordings since last Friday have been erased. All I have to do now is delete their data on Jane Doe."

Within a few seconds a Massachusetts General Hospital login screen appeared. After she logged onto the server, she opened up an SQL session, ran a query to identify table names, took some notes on data dependencies and executed several delete statements. It appeared that she was wiping out everything that had been inserted or updated since last Thursday. Not exactly a pinpoint strike, but definitely efficient.

"Is that it?" I asked in disbelief.

"Not quite– I need to delete their database backups as well." She brought up a file list on the server and removed the entire backup subfolder. Then she logged off and shut down her computer.

"How do you keep them from tracing what was done back to this computer?" She had to be covering her tracks, but how someone would actually go about doing that was beyond me.

"I have so much to teach you," she teased, patting me on the shoulder. "Our servers are ghosted through three different countries and four anonymous login services. Our IP address is changed every fifteen minutes, we use true two hundred fifty-six bit encryption and we have multiple firewalls that the CIA couldn't penetrate."

"Damn. Screw Chloe, you rock!"

Ruby stretched her arms up above her head. "Thanks. How did the call go?"

"Let's see, I had to scramble to find a busy location to call from, I was put on hold for ten minutes, I almost backed into a jeep, and I totally freaked out when I was leaving. Other than that, it went awesome. I hope Sandy was able to wait long enough to find out who answered my call. Have you heard from anyone?"

"Nope." She arched her brows slightly and shook her head. "And unless something goes horribly wrong, I won't. The last thing we want to do is leave a trail of calls that links everyone together."

I pulled my phone out and checked the time for at least the fourth time since we'd started talking. "When do you think they'll get back?"

"Sandy should have been out of the police station by five, regardless of what she had to do, so I'd say another five to ten minutes at most. It's a little tougher to predict for Sienna and Raven, since they have to search a couple places, and they need to wait until rooms are empty to access them." Ruby patted my knee, trying to calm my nerves. "Everything's going to be fine, really. I know this is all new to you, but this is a walk in the park compared to some of the things we've done."

"Thanks Ruby." I smacked my lips together, trying to wet them with my tongue. Between the pain medication and the stress, my mouth was as dry as cotton. "I'm going to get something to drink. Would you like anything?"

"I'm pretty much done in here. I'll come with you."

After grabbing drinks out of the fridge, we took a seat at the table. "Do you mind if I ask some questions about vampire stuff?"

She gave me a good natured, but somewhat frustrated laugh as she swept her fingers through her jet black hair. "You don't know how weird it is to be on the other side of this conversation. To have your whole life boiled down to a single word. We were all just as human as you are once, Brooke. Try not to forget that. But I get what it's like. I peppered Raven and Sienna with questions for weeks when I joined them. What would you like to know?"

She was right. If someone played a word association game with me and said the name of any of my new family members, the first word out of my mouth would be "vampire." It was just a virus. How stupid was it for me to let that be what defined them? I needed to make more of an effort to get to know who they really were. "Sorry, Ruby, I can't wait to get to know you better. Thanks for putting up with me."

She took a swig of her water and gestured with her hand, encouraging me to get on with it.

"It's been a couple of days since you fed. Raven told me that we need to feed every seven to ten days, and that we would get really weak and eventually die if we didn't, but what does it feel like in-between feedings? What do you feel like right now?"

Ruby thought for a moment while she drummed her fingers against the side of her bottle. "It's not like you get weaker by the day. After the fifth or sixth day you start to feel lethargic, and your urge to feed gets a lot stronger. The longest I've ever gone is sixteen days– that was miserable. Sienna had to hold me up while I fed."

"Why did you go so long?"

"I took a trip to Hawaii with a friend. We were only supposed to be gone for nine days, but the airport was closed due to a tropical storm. I was so determined not to kill someone just for me to feed on that I almost didn't make it home. It was really stupid of me."

My thoughtful gaze met her eyes. There was a difference between taking down prey when necessary to survive– like any other predator– and being ruthless or wasteful about it. Every person we fed on was going to leave people behind that cared about them– a sister, a mother, an aunt, a husband. That would be hard enough to deal with without the additional guilt of knowing they could have easily been spared. "I can understand that. I hope I don't ever totally quit caring about people."

"You don't." Ruby sounded almost penitent. She took another swig of her water and forced a smile. "So what other questions do you have?"

"I know I'm going to be in excruciating pain for like twenty-four hours when I'm changed, but how long will it take me to get used to my new mental abilities? How long did it take you to learn to trance someone or read their mind?"

"You'll practice your new powers on the first few people we feed on after you're changed. It may seem cruel, like we're playing with them, but it's the only safe way for you to learn. It took me a couple of months before I could reliably trance someone. You'll pick up the mind reading faster. The key there is to learn to filter out thoughts you don't care about. At first it's overwhelming to go out in public– the noise from all of their thoughts is deafening."

She placed her delicate hand on my cheek, rubbing her thumb gently from my nose to my ear along the underside of my eye. "I don't mean to scare you, Brooke, but the transformation is absolute hell. I could cut your fingers off a quarter inch at a time, and you'd beg me to do the same to your arms and legs rather than experience the pain you're going to endure. The worst part is that you never pass out or go into shock. Well, that and the fact that your brain becomes a million times more sensitive while you're being tortured. On top of everything else, in order to keep you from injuring yourself, you'll be tightly bound to a custom-built bed, so you won't even be able to move. All I can say to comfort you is that you'll survive– all of us have– and once it's over you'll be our sister for eternity."

"Sounds awesome," I replied, my voice dripping with sarcasm. "Thanks for being so honest. Hopefully I won't be as scared since I have some idea what to expect. I'm sure listening to twenty-four hours of me screaming isn't going to be a lot of fun for you guys either."

Ruby glanced sheepishly at the table.

"What? You don't think I'll be screaming? Sorry to disappoint you, sis, but I'm not that tough."

"Actually your mouth will be strapped shut with a special mouthpiece in it. That's the only way we can keep you from swallowing or biting your tongue. You'll be able to make muffled noises in your throat, but that's about it. Don't worry though, you'll still be able to communicate with us through your thoughts up until the last couple of hours."

This just kept getting better and better. I wouldn't even be able to talk. I snorted as I thought about what was likely to be going through my mind. "You may not like what I have to communicate."

She laughed. "You couldn't do any worse than me. I think I accused Raven and Sienna of torturing me for their own sadistic pleasure, told them I dreaded the day I met them, and wished they'd both burn in hell. It didn't even faze them. It's kind of like childbirth I guess, where the mother has a free pass."

Ruby paused and turned her head toward the door. "Sandy's home."

At least a full minute later, I heard a car rumble up the driveway and pull into the garage. "How'd you do that?"

"Her Dodge Charger has a pretty distinct sound. I can usually pick it up before she turns onto our drive."

Sandy had just stepped through the doorway when I leapt into her arms. She took a step back as she caught me, and then started to laugh. "Nice to see you too."

"I'm so glad you're home safe," I whispered, giving her a tight hug. I hadn't realized how worried I'd been about her until now. My whole body relaxed in her arms, melting into our embrace.

She ran her fingers along my jaw line, hesitated for just a second, and then leaned forward and kissed me on the cheek. "Thanks."

"How did it go?" I asked while we made our way back to the table. "They kept me on hold forever. Were you able to locate the detective okay?"

"Yep, and he already had the file with him. They had an industrial shredder in the back, so I was able to shred everything in two handfuls. After I made him collapse and close his eyes, he was freaking out, of course, but there was nothing on his mind that concerned me. I was just about to release him."

"What happened?" Ruby asked before I could.

"He thought about how odd it was that this would happen right after someone called about the case, and that it had to be related somehow. I'm sorry, Brooke, but I didn't have a choice at that point. I kept his heart from beating for almost ten minutes, until I was sure he was dead."

"That's okay." It scared me that I could justify his death so easily. It didn't even bother me that she'd killed him. If anything, I was kind of relieved. Ruby's earlier assurance that we maintained our empathetic views toward humanity rang hollow. I was clearly not the same person anymore.

Sandy put her hand on my shoulder. "Like Sienna said earlier, all that shows is how completely you've accepted your new life. You're willing to do whatever it takes to protect our family."

"I guess that makes sense," I muttered, still unconvinced that my apparent lack of a conscience for human life wasn't tied to something much darker.

Dangerous Waters

She turned her attention to Ruby. "So how did things go here?"

Ruby took a swig of her water and gave Sandy a ho-hum sideways nod of her head. "Same ole, same ole. It only took about twenty minutes. Brooke got home early enough to watch me finish up."

I couldn't believe how mundanely Ruby had described what she did. "You should have seen her! She made everything look so easy. She's a friggin genius."

Sandy flashed her a smile as she retrieved her own bottle of raspberry flavored water from the fridge and plopped back in her seat. "I've seen her in action a few times, not that I can ever follow what she's doing."

When my stomach let out a loud growl, we all started to laugh. I threw on some water to boil, poured some spaghetti sauce into a pot to simmer and started to dice up some mushrooms and zucchini. "So Sandy, what other fun surprises do I have to look forward to when I'm changed, other than being bound to a bed and gagged?"

"Well, you'll be blind and deaf as well– does that count?" Sandy shot back without missing a beat.

"Are you kidding! Why?"

"When the cells in your eyes and ears are being mutated, it does weird things to your vision and hearing," she explained, absently picking at the label on her bottle with her fingernail. "It's a lot less traumatic to wait until the change is completed, then gradually let you experience your new senses. Sienna will put ointment in your eyes and tape them shut like they do for surgeries. And you'll be wearing noise reduction headphones, in addition to construction-grade ear plugs."

I slid the vegetables into the sauce, poured some penne into the boiling water and returned to the table. "Anything else?" I was almost afraid to ask.

"Those are the big ones," Ruby assured me. "You'll have a catheter obviously, given how long you'll be in bed."

"And you'll be naked," Sandy added. "Sienna needs to be able to check for the first sign of injury, and clothes just get in the way. We'll have the heat turned up so you're comfortable."

As I sat waiting for the noodles to boil I remembered a question that had been bugging me since my walk with Raven yesterday. "I know I'll drink infected blood to start my transformation. But it can't come from any of you, or you'd never heal. Where will we get the blood?"

Sandy lifted her cashmere V-neck sweater over her head and sat it on the table next to her water. Her sweater had dip-dyed sleeves, transitioning from solid black to a light gray around the wrists. I'd been drooling over it since this morning. The low-cut, spaghetti strap cami she wore underneath left most of her breasts exposed, which were glistening with sweat. "When one of us dies, the blood is preserved. After it dries and turns into a powder, it's put into vials and sealed. The virus can survive in dried blood indefinitely, and when a little is added to fresh human blood it quickly infects it. You'll be drinking our brother Colt's blood, just as Ruby and I did."

Colt. Whenever anyone mentioned his name, they said it with such solemn reverence. "Raven talked so affectionately about him. Do you mind if I ask how he died? I don't mean to be disrespectful."

Ruby and Sandy exchanged a pointed look before Ruby placed her hand over mine. "Sienna and Raven have a hard time talking about it, so I'm glad that you asked us. From what I've pieced together, Colt, Raven and Sienna were living in England at the time. It was 1860, and two guys that were acquaintances of Sienna's from Ireland had come to visit her. I don't remember their names. Sienna was never really that close to them, but they'd known her a very long time.

"One night, when Sienna and Colt had gone to town to get supplies, things got out of hand, and they tried to force Raven to have sex with them. She resisted fiercely at first, but they threatened to kill Sienna if she didn't cooperate. Raven was still lying naked on the bedroom floor crying when Colt came in. He took one look at her and launched himself at the larger of the two men. Colt was built like an ox and had experience fighting other vampires, but they'd fought together for centuries. Before Colt could finish off the larger man, his friend had cut several deep wounds into his back and neck. It was all Colt could do to kill him before he collapsed.

"Raven and Sienna blame themselves of course, but there's nothing they could've done. I think they feel like they'd be replacing Colt if they added a male to our coven." Ruby brushed her hair behind her ear and let out a deep sigh. "But that's just my theory as to why we don't have any brothers."

"Oh my God! Raven was…raped? Jesus!" Tears stung at my eyes as I imagined Raven, lying naked and crying on the floor while they took turns brutalizing her. "Those sick, fucking bastards!"

When the timer went off for my noodles I shot a disgusted look toward the kitchen— food was the last thing on my mind. I thought about dumping it all into the sink, but I didn't want to waste food they'd bought for me, so I drained the noodles and poured them into a bowl, placed the sauce on top and threw it in the fridge.

A split second after, Sandy and Ruby jumped up from their chairs. I heard the front door crash into the wall.

"Sandy! Ruby! We need blood, now!" Raven screamed.

I darted into the living room and saw Raven holding Sienna's limp body in her arms. She was alarmingly pale, and her lips had taken on the grayish-blue hue of a corpse.

"What happened!" Ruby cried out.

"I don't know! Grab the first person you see and get back here. She's dying!"

I didn't need to hear anything more. I rushed to Raven's side and raised my right arm in the air as she sat Sienna down on the floor. "Cut me!"

Her eyes locked on mine. "Brooke, we can find– "

"Damn it! We don't have time to argue!" I fired back, cutting her off. "Now do it, or I'll grab a steak knife and do it myself!"

Knowing that I was right, Raven reluctantly took hold of my wrist, pushed my shirt up and ripped off the bandages. Her face filled with compassion as she reopened my wound, cutting just deep enough for blood to start flowing.

She held my wrist over Sienna's mouth and gently spread her lips apart. I could tell that she was breathing from the slight rise of her chest, but it was very shallow.

"Please feed, Sienna! Oh God, please!" I shouted, seeing the blood pouring out of the corners of her slack mouth. Her lips moved slightly.

"You need to swallow," Raven commanded.

Sienna took a hard gulp then opened her mouth for more. This time she swallowed as soon as it was full. I was overcome with happiness when she wrapped her lips around my wrist and began to feed. Her strength was slowly returning, but she still looked so pale.

Without any warning she opened her mouth and snapped it shut like a bear trap, burying her teeth deep into my arm. I screamed in agony and collapsed to the floor.

"You're feeding on Brooke!" Raven shrieked. "You're hurting her!" She pushed down on Sienna's chin while she held her forehead, trying to pry my wrist free, but it was hopeless. There was no sign of recognition in her eyes. Sienna was acting on a pure instinct to survive, feasting on my torn-apart wrist like a wolverine.

"It's okay," I mouthed, the words coming out blurred together.

"Brooke, she may need more blood than…than you can give her."

I knew what she meant– than I can give her without dying. With a great deal of effort, I lifted my head and placed it in Sienna's lap. "I promised to defend her with my life. She can have as much as she needs. I love you, Mom." The room went black.

Chapter Fifteen
Two Steps Back

"Brooke? Brooke?" I heard someone calling.

I slowly opened my eyes and saw a shadow of a figure standing over me. My face tightened into a grimace from the fierce pain in my arm. I tried to pull it free from whatever was holding it, but it wouldn't budge. "Please stop!" I begged as something sharp punctured my flesh.

"I know it hurts, but try to remain as still as you can," Sienna said, caressing my cheek.

"Sienna?" I mumbled, still half in a daze.

"Yes, honey, I'm right here."

After several blinks I managed to focus on her grief stricken face. "Are you okay?"

She sniffled and wiped her eyes. "You almost die, and the first thing you think about when you wake up is whether I'm all right. Yes, my precious daughter, thanks to you I'm okay– you saved my life." She bent down and gave me a kiss, and then picked up a glass of orange juice off the nightstand. "Can you drink this for me?"

I took the glass from her and guzzled it down.

"That's a good girl. I wish I could give you something for the pain, but it'd be too dangerous given how much blood you lost. I was hoping you wouldn't regain consciousness until we were done. I'm sorry sweetheart, but we need to finish closing you up."

"Could you trance me?" Since I didn't remember feeling any pain when I was attacked, I figured vampires must be able to block the pain signals from getting to the brain if they wanted to.

"Your assumption is correct. That would allow us to block the pain. Can you still be tranced?"

"Yep. I have to fight to break through it– I won't fight you."

The familiar haze filled my head and my body went limp. Seconds later I felt my right arm being lifted in the air. I knew if I thought about what I wanted to do, Sienna would make the movements for me.

Who's with me? My head immediately turned to my right. Raven was sitting in a chair next to my bed with a small metal table in front of her.

Hi, Raven! This was kind of fun.

Raven snorted and shook her head. "Only you could make a game out of being tranced." I laughed in my mind and was surprised to hear laughter leave my mouth. Sienna was pretty good at the whole translation thing.

My wrist was concealed by a paper drape like they use in hospitals for surgeries. Raven was wearing a surgical gown and mask along with latex gloves. *How bad is it?*

"It took us a while, but we were finally able to stop the bleeding," Raven replied. "The original laceration looks pretty good. I'm very concerned about the bite though– it went all the way to the bone on both sides, and cracked your radius. It's only a hairline fracture, so it should heal okay without a cast. Given the amount of mangled tissue I removed, there's bound to be at least some nerve damage. I don't want to alarm you, but you may lose some function in your hand. I'm sure a hospital could have done a lot better. Unfortunately that wasn't an option this time."

Sienna was so overcome with shame that she lost control of my mind. Before I realized I could talk, she ran from the room in tears.

"Can you try to get her to come back? I need to talk to her."

"Of course… Just hold your arm still." After Raven got up she covered my arm, pulled her mask down and gazed into my eyes. "I could never repay you for what you did. You didn't just save Sienna's life– you saved our whole family. You're the best, sis."

She kissed me on the forehead and left the room. My arm was killing me, but I did my best to keep from moving it. As worried as I was about my hand, I was far angrier with myself for not being smart enough to offer my left arm. Having to learn to do everything left-handed at my age was going to be a nightmare. I tried to wipe the thoughts from my mind when I heard them coming down the hall.

Sienna stopped just inside the doorway and peered at me, waiting for some kind of reaction. I patted the bed to reassure her. "Come sit with me."

"I'll never forgive myself for this," she muttered, placing her arm over my waist. "I wish to God I would have died. I can't bear what I've done to you."

I reached my left arm out and took her hand. "I would've given my life to save you– this is nothing. Please promise me that you won't feel bad about what happened today ever again. The fact that you're still here talking to me makes this one of the best days of my life."

Dangerous Waters

"Thank you, baby," she said, forcing a faint smile. "I can't promise that, but I'll try. You are the kindest, most loving person I've met in a very long time."

Raven sat back down in her chair, pulling on a fresh pair of gloves before lifting her mask into place.

I turned toward Sienna, my lips lifted into my most cheesy, playful grin. "Trance me, Mom!"

They both laughed as Sienna took control of my body. I felt Raven lift my right arm back onto the steel table, and then all feeling from my arm was cut off.

Do you know what happened to you earlier? I asked.

Sienna turned my head to look at her. "Not really. I'd destroyed the blood and hair samples, and was about to leave when I was asked to help position a patient for a series of X-rays. It seemed simple enough, and I couldn't exactly say no, since I was supposed to be a nurse's aide. Even though I stood in the control room during each X-ray, by the time I got back to Raven's truck, I felt drained. Raven asked me what was wrong, but at the time I just thought I was tired. The last thing I remember is leaning up against the door and closing my eyes. I've never heard of radiation having any effect on our kind– we have a lot of research to do. In the meantime, none of us will be going anywhere near a hospital."

Weird. I'm glad that you at least know what to avoid until we figure it out. Did you have any trouble getting the records, Raven?

"Nope, but I had the far easier job. We knew right where the records would be. I just walked into the room, took the file and walked out– it was that easy. It took a while to find a secluded shredder, but even with that I was in and out in fifteen minutes."

How did you learn to do medical stuff?

"This probably won't be too comforting, but my only hands-on experience came as a nurse for British soldiers in Canada during the war of 1812. I've studied several fields of science and medicine in college though."

She was right. Knowing her last operation was over two hundred years ago wasn't comforting at all. An image ran though my mind of her cutting through my arm with a blood crusted hacksaw like they used in the civil war. If it wasn't for the fact that I'd already felt my hand– and the lack of seeing a hacksaw anywhere– I would have been terrified.

"Okay– you're all stitched up. Before I wrap it let's see how much movement you have. Don't be scared if it's limited. It should continue to improve as the swelling goes down and the nerves heal."

I felt the haze leave my mind and let out a gasp, recoiling from the pain.

"I know it hurts like hell, but try to move your fingers for me," Raven instructed, rubbing my shoulder in support.

I stared at my hand and tried to make a fist. My thumb and two outside fingers moved a couple of inches, almost touching in the middle, but the other two fingers were totally unresponsive. Even though I wanted to be strong for Sienna, I couldn't fight back the tears– my right hand was all but useless. I'd been trying to prepare myself for what it'd be like to have superhuman physical abilities once I was changed. Now I'd have to get used to being crippled. "That's not too bad. And it'll get even better, right, Raven?" I said, as upbeat as I could manage. I was sure they'd already read my thoughts, but I had to try.

"Actually that's way more movement than I was expecting to see this soon. That's a great sign." Raven wasn't any more convincing– her voice was shaky and she couldn't hide that she was crying. Sienna buried her face in her hands and started to weep.

"Sienna, I know I can't lie to you," I confessed. "I'm terrified about what this will mean for my life as a vampire, and sad that I won't be able to play tennis or do a lot of the things I used to enjoy. It's going to take me a long time to get used to this, and there will be a lot of days when I'm feeling sorry for myself. I wish I could keep those thoughts from you, but I can't, at least not for a few more weeks. I love you, and I need you to help me through this."

Sienna held me tight against her chest. "I'm so sorry I did this to you. I'll do everything I can to help you recover. It's going to be really hard, sweetie. You're going to have to fight through the pain and frustration, and keep pushing yourself to do even more each day. You have to get better. You just…have to."

Her distraught look made it clear that far more was at stake with my rehabilitation than how much function I regained in my hand. Anything short of my full recovery would leave an unbearable albatross around her neck. "I'll try my best," I whispered.

When Raven removed the drape from my arm, I turned to inspect the wound. Crescent shaped ridges of jagged skin now covered both ends of the incision, and there were several deep depressions where flesh had been removed. Feeling a bit nauseous, I diverted my eyes while she wrapped it. "When can I take pain pills?"

"Your blood pressure was eighty-five over fifty the last time I took it, which is still dangerously low." Raven ran hear glove covered fingers across my brow, brushing the hair back from my eyes. "I can't give you anything for the pain until that gets back to at least a hundred over sixty. It would help if you ate something. Does anything sound good?"

The pasta I'd made earlier came to mind, but I didn't feel up to a heavy meal. "Maybe some scrambled eggs and a pop tart?"

"Coming right up," Sienna called out, hopping up from the bed and leaving the room.

As soon as she was gone, Raven started to laugh. "It'd be safer for you if I help her. I don't think she's cooked anything in over nine hundred years."

"Good call, sis. Thanks."

Sienna returned a few minutes later and sat a large tray over my lap. In addition to the eggs and pop tarts, there was a tall glass of orange juice and three pieces of toast. I instinctively reached for the glass with my right hand before wincing with pain. "Oops," I said as I forced a smile.

After I drank down most of the orange juice and finished the pop tarts, I picked up the fork with my left hand. Sienna watched me anxiously as I tasted the eggs. They were really good. Not too dry, with a little cheddar cheese mixed in.

"I made them myself," she boasted, grinning from ear to ear.

"They're yummy! Where'd you learn to make them?"

"My mother taught me to cook when I was young. It's a lot easier to cook with the equipment we have now than it was back then."

Hearing her mention her childhood made me eager to know more– I had so many questions.

"I can't wait to share some of my stories with you, but you need to get some rest." As she took the plate away, I was surprised to see that I'd eaten everything. "Guess I was hungrier than I thought."

"I saw the noodles in the fridge– it'd been a long time since you ate anything." Sienna paused and studied my face. "I'm glad that Ruby told you what happened to Colt and Raven. You remind me a lot of him, you know."

"I do? How?"

She sat the tray down and took a seat on the edge of the bed, lifting my left hand into her lap. Love emanated from the laugh lines of her smile-scrunched freckled cheeks to the bright spark in her green eyes. "There's nothing that he wouldn't do for Raven and I. He never complained or asked for anything, and always made light of his own problems. Colt found the good in everyone and gave his heart freely and completely. He was the most devoted, loving son I could ever have hoped for." She lifted up my chin and kissed me on the forehead. "Now get some sleep."

When she turned to leave I called after her. "Sienna?"

"Yes, baby?"

"This is embarrassing, but could you help me go to the bathroom? I feel pretty lightheaded."

"Of course." She gently lifted me out of bed, and then let me steady myself on her while I walked to the bathroom. Peeing in front of her was beyond awkward, but it beat the alternative of doing a face plant on the tile floor. After I'd finished, she helped me stand up and pulled my underwear and pants into place. We both laughed at my pathetic attempt to brush my teeth with my left hand. Once I was back in bed she gave me a quick kiss and left the room. Moments later I was asleep.

Chapter Sixteen
Sienna

"I can't do it!" I shouted, chucking the butter knife in anger. It clanged against the side of the sink before careening off onto the floor. I glared at the mutilated bread I'd tried to butter with my right hand.

"It's only been two weeks. You've made tremendous progress, sweetheart. Here's two new pieces of bread. Let's try again." Sienna patiently handed me a clean knife and flashed me an encouraging smile.

My hand had gotten a lot better. I now had feeling in all of my fingers, and I could even make a loose fist. It was still weak, and I didn't have anywhere near the dexterity I used to. Even so, I could see improvement every day.

Since it was hard for me to pinch my thumb and index finger together, I'd been wrapping my thumb around my fingers instead. Clearly that wasn't going to work. I couldn't baby myself anymore. Using my left hand, I straightened my index finger and pushed my thumb onto the other side of the knife. It hurt, but I was able to maintain my grip while I stuck the knife into the butter. I picked up a piece of bread and tried to glide the knife gently and evenly across it. My body bounced up and down with excitement when it reached the other side without tearing.

Sienna nestled my head against her shoulder, affectionately kissing the top of my head. "I'm so proud of you."

It seemed silly to be celebrating something so simple, but I knew that a week ago I wouldn't even have been able to pick up the knife, let alone use it for anything. After I finished making my toasted cheese sandwich, I grabbed some potato chips and milk and sat down at the table.

I kept glancing at her like a hopeful puppy begging for table scraps while I nibbled on my sandwich.

"Okay... I guess you've earned it," she said with a laugh, brushing her reddish-blonde hair back from her eyes. "Feel free to interrupt with any questions that you have."

Sienna had held off on telling me about her past to use the stories as a reward for me being diligent with my therapy. I leaned forward in my seat and eagerly nodded my head, anxious to finally hear about her life.

"I was born in 1088 in Limerick, Ireland. It's a small island between the Shannon and Abbey rivers. We had a large farm with beautiful rolling green hills covered with crops, cows, pigs and sheep." She rested her chin on her heavily calloused hand, gazing off into the distance as if her farm once again stretched out before her. "I had two older sisters, Alyson and Ana, and a younger brother, Aed. Ana was named after my mother."

"Your name was Aillenn right?"

Sienna grinned. "That's right. Aillenn Inghean Dhomnaill, which means daughter of Domnall, my father. He was a simple but loving man. Even though he was exhausted by the time he came in from the fields, he'd take time each night to read and sing to us until we fell asleep. My sisters and I filled our days with chores: feeding the animals, milking the cows, making bread, butter, clothes and soap, and helping my mother in the kitchen. It sounds like a tough life, but we all enjoyed it. My mother taught us to read and write, but that was the extent of our schooling.

"My first memory of Archill was when I was five. He lived on a farm a few miles from us. His father was good friends with my dad and brought him along one day on a visit. He walked right up to me and yanked on my pony-tail. I think he expected me to cry, but I slapped him hard across the face instead. After he rubbed his cheek, he gazed into my eyes and smiled— oh, what a smile he had. He never missed a visit after that.

"We were married when I was seventeen in a beautiful ceremony on the hillside of our farm overlooking the river. My mother and sisters sewed my dress by hand. Our wedding gift from my parents was a piece of their land so we could build a house of our own. Calling it a house is a bit generous I suppose, since the walls were made of stones and mud and the roof was covered with straw. Archill helped my father tend our fields, and I continued to help my mother and sisters with the daily chores. I felt blessed to have a loving husband and still be so close with my family. While everyone was quite taken with him, my brother Aed and Archill were inseparable. I think he slept at our house more than in his own bed."

I was spellbound. To hear her describe such a long ago time in vivid detail revealed the ancient, unimaginably wise woman hidden beneath the nineteen-year-old body sitting across from me. I couldn't wait to hear more. "What did he look like?"

"He was tall and muscular, with long flowing brown hair down to the middle of his back. He had soft brown eyes and a boyishly handsome face... I still remember the last time he held me." Sienna ran the back of her fingers along her own cheek as she sighed.

"What happened? Did you have kids?"

Her expression turned cold with grief. "About six months after we were married, dozens of heavily armed men rode up to our farm. My dad, Aed and Archill met them in front of my parent's house while my mother, sisters and I hid inside. We all screamed when we heard the fighting start. I tried desperately to get to him, but my mother wouldn't let me go. After the mob killed my husband, brother and father, they took our animals, burned my house along with all of our crops and lit my parent's house on fire with us still inside. We had to wait until we were sure they were gone before we tried to escape." Sienna closed her eyes and took a couple of deep breaths to regain her composure. "The house was full of smoke, and flames were all around us. I picked up my sister Ana and carried her outside before I collapsed in the yard. When I woke up the next day, she was dead. I didn't find my mom and Alyson's bodies until later that afternoon– they never made it out of the house." Her voice broke off and she began to weep.

I slipped out of my chair and took her into my arms, patting her softly on the back. "I'm so sorry, Mom. Who were they? What did they have against your family? Tears streamed down my cheeks as I comforted her.

Sienna wiped her face on the sleeve of her pink scoop-neck tee. I handed her some tissues from the countertop and took my seat while she blew her nose. "A lot of families in the area were not doing as well as we were. One of the old Irish clans that had ruled the town for generations felt threatened by our wealth. They feared that we were going to combine our lands with Archill's family and challenge them for control of the town. It was all nonsense of course. Neither of our families had any interest in politics. My dad had helped build most of the houses of the people who killed him.

"I tried to warn Archill's family but it was too late– the outlying fields of their farm were still smoldering when I arrived. I was barely eighteen, penniless and on my own. Everything we had was either taken or lost in the fire. I didn't even have any clothes other than the filthy, burned dress I was wearing.

"I spent the next few weeks begging for food while I roamed from town to town looking for work. It took almost a month before I managed to get a job at a small inn. It didn't pay anything really, but they fed me twice a day and allowed me to sleep in their barn. Looking back on it, it's hard to say what kept me going. I had nothing to live for and was absolutely miserable.

"Late one night, shortly after I turned nineteen, I was walking down the alley toward the barn when I saw a man and a woman leaning against the wall of the inn. At first I thought they were kissing until he glanced at me and wiped his mouth. The woman's neck was ripped wide open, but she just calmly stood there while blood poured down her chest. She was tranced of course, but I had no idea at the time. I knew at once what he was. We had all heard stories about vampires, and most people believed they were true even if they'd never seen one themselves. It was a barbaric time where murders were commonplace and often went unpunished. Vampires didn't have the need for secrecy that we do now and had no fear of humans. They'd kill in front of other people or in broad daylight if they felt like it.

"I just stood there while he finished feeding– I don't know why I didn't run. When her lifeless body fell to the ground, he headed across the countryside to his home with me following close behind. Once we were inside he told me that he could sense the tremendous pain I was in and all of the hate that I felt for the people who killed my family. He promised that he could give me the power to make them pay for what they'd done if I wanted him to. There was nothing I wanted more. After he retrieved a mug full of blood from the woman's body, he mixed in some powder from a canvass pouch and handed it to me."

"He didn't even ask if you were injured?" I blurted out, totally shocked. "You could have died."

"I don't think he really cared what happened to me," Sienna said flatly. "By the time I recovered from being changed, he was gone."

She distractedly rubbed her hands together as she spoke, messaging the inside of her palm with her thumb. "My new abilities were terrifying. I couldn't pick anything up without breaking it. I flew across the room in a blur whenever I tried to walk, constantly smashing into things. I thought I was going crazy when I started to hear people's thoughts in my head. If I hadn't met Caerell, I doubt I would've survived very long. I was trying to feed for the first time when he saw me. I'd just tackled a woman into a pile of garbage in the alley and slit her throat with a knife. Blood was spraying all over me while I clumsily tried to lick at it. He scared the hell out of me when he let out a gut-wrenching laugh. I stayed with him while he taught me everything I should've learned when I was changed. While I was very grateful, he wasn't particularly kind and had quite a temper, so after two months I headed back out on my own."

Sienna's eyes hardened as her lips pressed into a thin line. "Once I'd mastered my new abilities, it was time for vengeance. We'd all watched the men approach before my mother took me and my sisters inside, and I recognized five of them. As soon as I was back in Limerick, I sought out the head of their clan. After torturing him to get the rest of their names, I viciously slaughtered his entire family. I enjoyed watching them suffer, making him pay for what he'd taken from me. I was a monster fueled only by hate and rage.

"After I killed three more of our attackers, something changed inside me. It no longer felt like I was administering justice. I began to realize that what I was doing was wrong. I saw the fear and innocence in their children's eyes as I killed them– their faces haunted me in my sleep. I was becoming a dark, evil person, and it sickened me. At the same time, I couldn't stand the thought of letting them get away with murdering my family. The only reason I'd even become a vampire was to kill them. I forced myself to keep going, but each time I killed one of them, I felt even more disgusted with myself, until I just couldn't do it anymore. I left Ireland for the first time in my life, riding across the Irish Sea to England in a small ferry boat.

"I eventually made my way to London. It was a big city compared to what I was used to, with almost twenty thousand people then. There were tailors and bakeries along with countless inns. While I knew that I'd always be a vampire, I was determined to find a purpose for my life and to act in a way that would let me feel good about myself again. I took a job as an inn keeper's assistant at one of the larger inns on the edge of town and worked sixteen hours a day, seven days a week. In the evenings I'd sing in the parlor to entertain our guests. After a year the inn keeper retired, and I was offered the position. The job paid well and allowed me to build up a small savings for the first time in my life."

"How'd you feed without anyone noticing?" I said, cocking my head to the side. I highly doubted they had incinerators back then, and with the transportation available at the time, she couldn't exactly jet off to a different city each week.

My reasoned question earned me a smile. "Since I knew how to trance people, it was easy to lead them somewhere secluded to feed. People died unexpectedly all the time back then from things like dysentery and the plague, so the bodies weren't much trouble either. I took care to hide the incision, but it's not like they did autopsies or anything. I fed only when I had to, and did everything I could to minimize their anxiety and pain. I never fed on our guests, and I was very careful not to be seen.

"The elderly lady who owned the inn died three years later. She didn't have any close relatives, so she left the inn to me in what amounted to a will at the time. I sold it after two years, since I knew people would start wondering why I wasn't aging. It was one of the most popular inns in London, and it brought a high price.

"When I left London I crossed the English Channel into France and made my way to Paris. I attended the University of Paris, studying the faculty of arts. While it wasn't exactly what I wanted, you had to graduate from the arts before you could get into law, theology or medicine. I studied fine art, literature and drama– I even learned to dance."

"What kind of dancing?" I asked, my curiosity piqued.

"Unfortunately techno music hadn't been invented yet," Sienna joked. "We learned folk dances like the branle and ronde. I also learned to speak French."

"Cool! Say something in French."

She grinned and kissed my cheek. "Je t'aime, ma fille."

"What does it mean?"

"I love you, my daughter."

I jumped up and gave her a hug. "How would I say 'thank you, I love you too, Mom'?"

"Merci, je t'aime aussi, maman." Her face beamed when I repeated it back to her.

"After I graduated, I opened my own inn in the center of town. It took almost all of the money I had to build it, but I knew I could make it work. Thankfully, it was a huge success. We had dancing and singing in the ballroom every evening. People came from miles around just for the drinks and entertainment, and we filled our rooms each night. I was proud of what I'd accomplished and happy that I felt like myself again. After five years I knew I needed to move on, but I couldn't make myself sell it. My stubbornness almost cost me everything.

"Two years later a friend from the university stopped in with her husband. It'd been over seven years since we saw each other, and I should've been almost thirty. Not surprisingly she was shocked by my appearance. I tried to make light of her comments, but she wasn't buying it. When she thought to herself that I must be a vampire, I knew I had to act. I put her under my trance and pulled her hand up to her stomach like she was going to be sick. Once her husband noticed, I made her walk out the door with him following close behind. After leading her as far away as I could without losing control, I went out into the night after them. I was careful to stay at least fifty yards back while I took her further and further toward the worst part of Paris. Each time her husband reached out to stop her, I motioned him away with her arm. When I felt that we were far enough from the inn, I made her dart down an alley and make sounds like she was throwing up. As soon as he joined her, I rushed up and broke his neck, then crushed my friend's skull against the wall. I'll never forget the look on Maggie's face when I killed her– it still gives me nightmares. I haven't lived in one place for more than five years ever since.

"I waited for six months before I put the inn up for sale. There were so many people competing to buy it that I ended up getting almost twice the asking price. After I left Paris I continued to move from country to country across Europe, opening an inn and selling it every four or five years. It was risky, as someone could have stopped in at any time that had stayed with me long before, but I enjoyed running them, and they were very successful. I was careful not to revisit the same country for at least fifty years and I never went back to the same towns. After a hundred and fifty years I had more money than I could ever spend and decided it was no longer worth the risk."

I had to force myself to take a breath. Based on how long she'd been alive, she'd barely scratched the surface, and she'd already described a more incredible adventure than I could imagine living in ten lifetimes. "But you loved the singing and stuff. Didn't you miss it?"

She lifted my hand to her mouth and kissed my fingers. "For a while I did. Then I recalled how happy I was growing up on our farm in Ireland. It'd been almost a hundred and seventy years since I left. I was tempted to buy our land back, but there were too many painful memories. After searching several different towns, I ended up buying a beautiful fifteen-hundred-acre farm near Waterford that we still own today. I spent the first year remodeling the house and the barn and just enjoying the land. I'd purchased two saddle horses along with the farm and I spent a great deal of time riding. It seemed wasteful to not make use of the fertile soil, but I knew I couldn't manage a working farm by myself, so I hired someone to help me the following spring."

"Was it Colt?" I interrupted, like a child too eager to wait for their father to turn the page of their favorite book.

Sienna's face broke into a warm smile as she laughed. "Yes, honey… although his name was Nicholaus De Marre at the time. He was twenty years old when he responded to my posting in town for a full-time farm hand. I returned from riding one day and found him in the barn fixing the broken stall door. He'd already replaced three broken pieces of railing in the paddock. I hired him on the spot. He had such an easy way about him that we bonded instantly.

We spent the day walking the land while we talked about what crops we'd plant and where we'd run sheep and cattle. When we got back to the barn, I let him dunk me in the water trough for the horses like we'd known each other for years. I could tell that he was attracted to me, but he never forced the issue, and quickly accepted that we could only be friends.

"We plowed and planted three fields that spring, and then built a new barn and pens for the cattle, sheep and pigs we got in the fall. For the first few weeks, he arrived before sun up and worked until well after dark before making the hour-long ride back to town. He was from France and lived alone in a small room above one of the taverns. It didn't seem right to make him ride all that way when I had so many empty rooms in my house– that's what I told myself anyway. The truth was that I cared for him and missed him terribly when he was gone. It felt so good to share my life with someone again."

"How did you hide not eating?" It probably wouldn't have been too hard while he was only working there, but living together? If I didn't know my sisters were vampires, I sure as hell would have been wondering about their eating habits by now, and I'd only been here three weeks.

"I used all the tricks I'd learned through the years, like pretending that I'd just finished eating, or acting like I was in a hurry and grabbing some food to take with me. It worked pretty well for a while. Occasionally he'd have a fleeting thought about how it was odd that I never ate much, but nothing more than that.

"Then one night I came out of my room after my bath to find that he'd made dinner for us. He knew I hadn't eaten at least since breakfast, since we'd spent the entire day together. And we'd just been wrestling around before my bath, so I doubted he'd believe that I was suddenly ill. I couldn't think of any viable excuses so I sat down and ate with him: Lamb chops, potatoes, beans and bread. It tasted incredible– he was quite the cook. After only a few bites I began to feel terrible cramping pains in my stomach. I tried to make it to the end of dinner but it was hopeless. When my stomach started to convulse I darted out the door and raced behind the house to throw up. Of course he followed me.

"I didn't have to read his mind to know that my secret was out– in my rush to get out of his sight I'd moved much too fast. After I finished vomiting I cast a hopeless gaze in his direction. To my surprise, rather than cowering in fear like I expected, Nicholaus pulled me into his arms. He told me that he knew I was a vampire but he didn't care. He loved me and wanted to stay.

"I didn't know what to say. I'd never thought about trusting a human, but I knew I could trust him and that I loved him too. There was no way I could hurt him, not even to protect myself. When I said that I loved him too and that he was welcome to stay, he lifted me into the air and spun me around. We both laughed when I reminded him that I'd just been vomiting.

"We lived together on the farm for three years almost as if nothing had changed. I started to pick up thoughts about him wanting to become a vampire long before he asked. Nicholaus didn't want me to be alone ever again and worried that he wasn't strong enough to protect me. I decided that I'd change him, but only if he fully understood the life he was choosing. I'd tell him everything, even feed in front of him, and then ask if that was truly what he wanted.

"The first time he watched me feed, he threw up almost immediately and ran back home. I was sure that was going to be the end of him wanting to become a vampire, but he joined me again the very next week. On the fifth feeding I got him to drink and I knew he'd made his choice."

"Where'd you get the blood to change him?" I knew that they used dried vampire blood, but based on what she'd told me, she hadn't known any vampires who'd died yet.

"Very observant– I'd only met two other vampires at that point. And since I had no idea how to find the vampire who'd turned me, I went to visit Caerell to see if he could help.

"His old home was in ruins and appeared to have been abandoned for quite some time. I'm not sure why I thought he'd still be living there over a hundred and seventy years later. The town had doubled in size since I left, and all of the familiar places were gone. I figured that if he still lived around there he'd likely be hanging out at one of the pubs. I'd been in town for over a week before I finally spotted him coming out of an alley early one morning, the smell of fresh blood still thick in the air.

"He gave me a pleasant greeting and invited me to visit. When I arrived at his new home, I was surprised to see that he wasn't alone. His monstrous brother Colbán had been living there for several years. He was somewhat friendlier than Caerell, but just as serious."

My jaw fell open when it dawned on me who she was describing– her *old acquaintances* from Ireland.

Sienna placed her hand on my shoulder. "While that wouldn't happen for almost six hundred years, you're right. Unfortunately I had no way to know that at the time. I didn't even meet Raven until 1814.

"I told them about Nicholaus and asked if they could help. Caerell described in detail the precautions I should take beforehand, and then went into a back room and returned with a small pouch. He reminded me of how confused and scared I was when we'd first met, and how he'd taught me to manage my new abilities. I was really thankful for all of his help and invited them to come visit us if they ever made their way to Waterford.

"When I returned home, Nicholaus met me halfway up the trail and pulled me right off my horse. He was sure that something bad had happened and that he was never going to see me again. That's one of the only times I ever saw him cry. Over the next two weeks I did everything that I could to prepare him.

"Watching him go through the change was horrible. He was screaming in agony for almost thirty-six hours. At one point he begged me to kill him, to spare him from any more pain– I completely fell apart after that. As soon as it was over, I sat down next to him and took his hand, but he smothered me in his arms before I could apologize. After a long embrace he told me how much he loved me. Then he thanked me for making him my son.

"Over the next couple of months I taught him how to control his body and move normally, how to filter out others' thoughts, even in crowds, and how to trance people. I'd never tried to describe how to do the things I'd learned to someone else before, and I wasn't very good at it. I tried to follow Caerell's instructions, but when Nicholaus didn't understand, I'd get frustrated and angry at myself for not being able to explain it better. Nicholaus would always comfort me and tell me what a great job I was doing– he was so patient.

"A year after he was changed we moved to Nottingham, England. We let the family that owned the adjacent farm in Waterford use our land and pay the taxes for it out of the profits. We also informed the local magistrate of the arrangement and paid him to 'watch over' our land for us. It was far more difficult to manage properties back then. People didn't respect claims on land like they do now."

"When did you change your names to Sienna and Colt?"

"We began to use aliases when we moved to Nottingham, picking names that were appropriate for the time period whenever we moved. At first we fully assumed each new identity, even calling each other by our new names at home, but after our fifth move we agreed that it was just too confusing. While there was no way around having to go by different names in public, we needed something permanent to use around each other. I wanted our new names to have some significance rather than just being arbitrarily chosen, so I tried to think of things from our lives that we could base them on. After about a week of mulling over potential names I finally came up with Colt– Nicholaus loved it. I tried to make something out of my last name, but gave up after a couple of days and just went with my favorite color."

Sienna laughed when she noticed how attentively I was listening to her. "I think that's enough history for one night– you must be tired."

I hadn't realized how late it'd gotten, but I didn't want her to stop. "We're not even up to 1300 yet! I'm not tired, Sienna, honest! Ruby told me that Colt had experience fighting other vampires before he fought Colbán and Caerell. When? What happened?"

Sienna gave me a wily grin. "When you can ask me in writing using your right hand, I'll tell you all about it."

"But that could be months from now!" I complained.

"Not if you keep working hard like you have been. Wait until you hear about the angry horde that came to kill us in Germany." Before I could reply, Sienna wrapped her arms tightly around me. "Thank you for being such a good listener. You don't know how much it means to me that you really want to know about my life. I love you."

"Je t'aime aussi, maman," I replied.

Chapter Seventeen
We've Got Company

"Help! Help!" I hollered as Raven dragged me out of bed, still wrapped in my covers.

She laughed. "You can yell all you want— you're still working out with me today. We've only got five weeks left to get you in some kind of shape."

Raven yanked the covers out of my arms and tossed them back on the bed, leaving me lying on the cold wooden floor in my panties and undershirt. I'd gotten the green light to work out over a week ago, but I'd managed to avoid it until now. She'd obviously grown tired of my excuses. I rubbed my eyes and slowly meandered toward the closet. "What time is it?"

"Seven a.m. The same time we'll be working out every day until you're changed. I'm afraid your days of sleeping in until eleven are over."

"I guess I have been pretty lazy lately," I admitted. With no schoolwork or job to worry about, I'd settled into a summer-like routine— going to bed after 1:00 a.m., kicking around in my pajamas well into the afternoon— pretty much everything that made my dad start circling help wanted ads in the paper.

"You think?" she said, sarcastically arching her eyebrows.

"Sorry. I know this is important and that you're trying to help me. You won't have to drag me out of bed again."

She flashed me a smile. "That was kinda fun actually." We both giggled.

I threw on my black and pink Lycra lace-up pants and matching camisole top, then followed Raven down the hall to the workout room.

"Whoa!" I gasped as we entered. Now I knew why there were only two doors on the right side of the hall— the room was the size of a basketball court. A small portion in the front had rubber pads covering the floor and was filled with several Nautilus machines, a stationary bike, a stair stepper, a rowing machine and a treadmill. There was a stack of dumbbells and some free weights in the far corner. Everything looked brand new. Bare wood floor covered the rest of the room, and the entire back wall was taken up by several racks of swords. I could tell from the way they were stored that they weren't ornamental.

"What do you do with these?" I asked, stepping forward to take a closer look.

Dangerous Waters

Raven picked up a Samurai sword, took a few steps away and began to whirl the blade around her. Her body twisted and lunged as the sword moved with dizzying speed. She executed a series of no-handed back flips that took her across the entire room. Then she launched herself toward me, tucking into a front roll and ending with the sword at my throat.

"Holy Crap!" I shrieked, stumbling backward. "You're amazing! How'd you learn to do that?"

"Sienna taught each of us. It's the best way to learn to fight and to keep our reflexes sharp. Using swords allows us to fight each other at full speed without any risk of injury. We also do some martial arts training, but all we can do is lightly spar."

"What if you run into each other?"

She snorted. "We're not that fragile. It takes more than incidental body contact to hurt us. We do wear fencing gloves to cover our nails though."

"Did you buy all of that just for me?" I asked, glancing back toward the exercise equipment at the other end of the room.

Raven put her fingers under my chin. "You're a part of this family, and we're each provided with everything that we need. Right now you need to get in shape for your transformation. Are you ready to get started?" She pulled a remote out of the pocket of her yoga pants and flashed it in front of me.

"Bring it on!"

Techno music filled the room, and I impulsively swung my hips to the beat. "Russenmafia– good choice!"

Raven moved two of the rubber mats out into the center of the room, stepped onto one of them and started into an easy, dance-like warm up. I happily danced alongside her. When the first song ended, she shifted into a fast-paced aerobic routine. It was easy to follow, since her moves were in perfect rhythm with the music, but the pace was unrelenting. By the end of the third song, I was drenched with sweat. I pushed myself to keep going for two more songs before flopping on the floor, desperately trying to regain my breath. We took a short break and chugged down some Gatorade before making our way over to the machines.

After I completed two circuits of the five Nautilus machines, Raven held my feet for sit-ups and led me through three sets of curls with five pound dumbbells. I shot her a pleading look as I finished the last set.

"We're almost done," she promised. "You just need to cool down, so you're not too sore tomorrow."

I'd jogged almost a half a mile on the treadmill before Raven picked me up and twirled me around in the air. "Great workout, sis."

"Thanks– I may not be able to walk for a week, but that was fun."

We headed for the kitchen to grab something to drink. Sienna was sitting on the couch in her powder-blue bathrobe, disinterestedly watching the morning news. She turned toward us and smiled. "How was your workout?"

"I'm dead tired, but it felt great. Raven showed me what she can do with a sword too– she's incredible."

"Wait until you see Sienna," Raven cut in. "She fights all three of us at the same time and rarely gets touched."

Sienna's cheeks blushed at the compliment. "I seem to remember losing my favorite shirt to your sword not too long ago, my daughter."

"And when's the last time any of us left the room wearing anything but our underwear?"

"It has been a while," she conceded. We all shared a short laugh.

My body was dripping with sweat, but I decided to grab something to eat before I showered so I could soak in the tub for as long as I wanted. I'd just finished putting pancakes on the griddle when I heard Raven shout from the living room..

"Fuck! Fuck! Fuck! "

"What's wrong?" I asked, my attention still on my cooking.

"So you heard it too." Sienna's eerily calm, Dexter-like voice gave me goose bumps. "I was hoping I'd imagined the way the engine missed when it hit third gear."

"I can take her out the ba– "

"It's too late for that," Sienna cut in. "He's already close enough to read Brooke's thoughts. We'll have to fight."

I flipped off the griddle and darted into the living room.

Sandy and Ruby hurdled the second floor railing and raced to Sienna's side, their shapes little more than a blur. Suddenly I was catapulted off my feet into the back wall. I let out a wheeze as my body crumbled to the floor. By the time I'd regained my breath Raven and Sandy had taken up defensive positions in front of me. Sienna and Ruby stood crouched, ready to pounce, on opposite sides of the front door.

"What's going on!" I yelled, growing even more hysterical.

Raven spared me a quick glance over her shoulder. "Stefan's here."

The pieces suddenly clicked into place with horrifying clarity. Stefan was about to discover I could no longer be tranced. And in order to protect me from what they viewed as an inevitable attack, my family was going to kill him, with several of them likely dying in the process. "And you're just going to ambush him? He's Sienna's friend– maybe he'd understand!"

Raven turned to face me, kneeling down on the floor. "It's our best chance to kill him without any of us getting hurt. We can't risk talking to him first. Now please, sis, be quiet. He just parked his car."

There was no way I was just going to sit back and watch while my family fought for their lives, especially not when I didn't even agree it was necessary. "Stefan! Stay outside on the porch! I have something I need to tell you!" I shouted as loud as I could.

Everyone was stunned into silence.

Their eyes bored into me as I quickly climbed to my feet, and I felt an overwhelming need to explain myself. Raven and Sandy looked like they wanted to play rock-papers-scissors to see who'd get the honor of tearing my throat out. But what was far more disturbing was the sheer disappointment on Sienna's face, like she'd expected so much more from me. "I'm not trying to be a martyr– I really think I can make him understand."

Raven placed her hand on my chest and pressed me back against the wall. "Bullshit. You think we'd rather have you die than one of us. I guess you forgot the part about doing what was best for the coven, that or you're just too selfish to care. You think you're being heroic? Making us bear the loss of our sister. You're hurting us worse than he ever could."

"So if Sienna and Ruby died fighting Stefan, you'd still think it was worth it?"

"They wouldn't have," she snapped.

I eased out from behind her none-too-gentle grip so I could address my entire family. "That's not the point. Look, I know you guys love me, but you've only known me for a few weeks. Of course you mean more to each other than I do."

"Does a mother love her newborn infant any less than her other children?" Sienna argued, crossing her arms over her chest. "Time has *nothing* to do with it. You're my daughter. That's all that matters."

Crap. I was so losing this argument. "Maybe you're right. I'm sorry for screwing everything up. I still feel like Stefan will understand though. I couldn't live with myself if I didn't at least try to talk with him."

Sienna tossed her robe onto the couch and pulled her strawberry-blonde hair up into a tight pony-tail. Even in a slinky pink cami top and panties, she looked deadly. "Raven, take Brooke into the hall and stand guard at the end. Ruby, take the kitchen entrance. Sandy, the stairway. Once I let him in I'm going to ask that he kneel and allow me to grip his throat from behind. If he complies, Brooke can have her talk, but if he makes even a single aggressive maneuver, close in. We'll have him surrounded."

We all got into position, Sienna gliding to the door like a cat. "Stefan, I know you heard all of that, and that wasn't by accident. I love you, my dear friend. All I want to do is talk."

Sienna peered through the peep hole, unbolted the door and flung it open. Stefan stood with his back to her, his hands clasped behind his neck. "As do I– I would rip my own throat out before I harmed you, my love."

He allowed her to guide him into the living room, took a seat on the floor and spread his legs out wide, giving himself no leverage to get up. Sienna tilted his head back, placed her nails at his throat and nodded to Raven.

Sandy and Ruby took flanking positions as we advanced, leaving only my backside unprotected. When we reached the couch closest to Stefan, Raven motioned for me to stand behind it.

"Brooke? What's all this about?" he asked. Before I could answer, he read my thoughts. "That's not possible."

"I'm afraid it is. But I'd never tell anyone. I'd never do anything that could hurt my family."

"Would you mind showing me?" He flinched when Sienna tensed her grip. "Easy, dear– I won't harm her."

"You could explode blood vessels in her brain before she even realizes she's tranced."

"Yes, I could," he admitted. "I'm giving you my word as your friend that I won't."

"It's okay, Sienna," I muttered, stepping out from behind Raven. "I trust him." I gazed into his eyes and felt him take control of my body. After pushing back the haze from my mind I kneeled down submissively in front of him, and then looked up at his shocked face.

"I don't believe it. That's amazing!" he said, bursting into laughter.

"So you don't want to kill me?"

Stefan cocked his head. "Kill you? Why would I want to do that?"

"Don't play ignorant," Sienna chided. "You know how serious this is."

"The knowledge Brooke possesses is a threat to all of us– but you were right to trust her with it. I've never seen anyone as devoted to their coven as she is. The fact that she could no longer be tranced is not all that I captured from her mind. She freely sacrificed herself to save your life and was willing to confront me alone rather than risk anyone else getting hurt. By speaking up the way she did, she also saved my life." Stefan paused as he regarded me, dipping his head in a respectful nod. "I wish I could trust anyone in my coven half as much as I trust her."

Sienna stepped back and withdrew her hand from his throat. "I should have had more faith in you. I'm sorry."

"There's no need for that," Stefan said, rising to his feet in one fluid motion. "Brooke's your daughter, and you had good reason to perceive me as a threat– I would've expected nothing less. I'm afraid I do have some troubling news to share though."

I got up and followed everyone to the couches, taking a seat next to Sandy. Sienna and Raven sat on the opposite couch, across from Stefan.

"After we met at the bar that night, I went home and confronted Alexander. He was adamant that he'd never fed without me before. When I asked if Travis or Teresa had, he told me to ask them myself. I didn't need to, as their guilt was obvious on Alexander's face. We both set out to look for them, starting with the abandoned building where Brooke was taken.

"I could smell the fresh blood before I even entered the basement. The young woman they'd been feeding on only moments before was still alive, gurgling and choking on her own blood– they'd slit her throat from ear to ear. We finished her off, disposed of the body and continued to search the rest of the night and the entire day. Neither of us has seen them since.

"I'm afraid that I have no control over them anymore, and that their carelessness is jeopardizing all of us. I no longer consider them a part of my family. I'm sorry I've done such a poor job leading my coven."

Sienna took his hand in her own. "It was very gracious of you to open your home to them in the first place. I've never tried to take in anyone who'd already been changed, let alone a brother and sister. You offered them a chance at a better life. It's not your fault they weren't smart enough to take advantage of it. I assume you want them dealt with if we see them?"

"Just follow them and give me a call. They're my responsibility." He turned to face me. "I never got a chance to mention your friends to them, although in hindsight that's probably a good thing– they would've likely killed them out of spite. I'll be sure to tell Alexander."

I let out a huge sigh of relief. Given their history with me, I was sure he was right. "Thanks, Stefan."

As soon as he left, I headed for the tub. My whole body ached, and I was already so tight that it hurt to walk. Seeing the three-foot hole in the plaster where I'd hit the wall only made it feel worse. "So who threw me through the wall anyway?"

"Sorry about that," Raven said. "I was in such a hurry that I didn't think about how fast I was moving when I picked you up. I should've held onto you longer."

"Good lesson in kinetic energy," I joked.

Sandy rolled her eyes. "Seriously? Physics humor? You're such a dork."

"I know you love me," I shot back with a smile.

She snorted. "That could change."

Chapter Eighteen
Raven

I got undressed and brushed my teeth while the steaming hot water filled the tub. After I climbed in, I searched all around, trying to figure out how to turn on the jets. There were three touch controls on the outside of the tub, but they only had arrows on them.

Okay, this is embarrassing, but could someone show me how to use this tub? I thought, hoping to at least avoid having to yell or walk into the living room. There was a soft knock on the bathroom door a few seconds later. "It's open."

Raven was already laughing when she entered. "This is super complicated, so try to follow along okay? See the little stick figure guy? The button with the three curvy arrows going toward his neck activates the jets for your neck. And the one with three arrows going toward his back? You'd think it'd be for your legs, but I'll be damned if it doesn't turn on the jets for your back."

I glanced at the controls again. Sure enough, there were little stick-figure bodies next to the lines I'd seen. *Crap.* "Thanks, smart ass."

"Don't mention it," she said with a toothy grin. "Now that I'm here, do you mind if I join you?"

"Come on in." It seemed a little *communal* to be sharing a bath, but there was plenty of room, and she'd already seen me naked several times. I no longer felt self-conscious around any of them.

Raven undressed and climbed in while I switched on the jets. The water felt wonderful– my entire body was being messaged at the same time. I took a deep relaxing breath and closed my eyes.

"Damn. Look at your wrists."

I lifted my arms out of the sudsy water and peered at them. It'd been a month since I was attacked and fed on by Sienna. I'd stopped bandaging my wrists almost two weeks ago and had noticed that the skin was getting smoother, but I was still astonished by what I saw now. All that remained of the lacerations and bite marks were bright pink scars. My right wrist still had deep indentations from the loss of tissue, but I'd have those for life. "Oh my God, they're totally healed."

"The scars are still bright pink, so not quite, but they're getting there.

Another four or five weeks and you'll be ready." Raven reached out and took my hands. "Are you excited?"

My transformation had seemed so far off until now. I'd been focusing so much on my therapy that I really hadn't even thought about it lately. In roughly thirty-five days, I'd no longer be human. I'd be drinking people's blood to sustain myself and would never eat food again. My body and mind would be capable of doing unbelievable things, I'd never age, and my whole family could potentially live forever.

As unnerving as some of those thoughts were, the purgatory type life I'd been stuck in since making my choice was worse. "I feel like I'm living in two worlds right now, without fully belonging in either of them. When I look at you, Sandy, Ruby and Sienna, I see my sisters and my mother, but until I'm changed physically I haven't truly joined this family. Not that the transformation process doesn't scare the hell out of me. And I know it will take a while, but I can't wait to learn how to fight and control my new abilities, so I feel more like I fit in."

Raven dismissed my fears with a disarming smile. "You'll be a vamp before you know it. And with all of us here to teach you, it won't take long at all for you to catch on to things. Especially given how coordinated and graceful you are already."

My mind wandered as I gazed at the smooth lines of her heart-shaped face. She was more than just beautiful. Her pointed chin, perfectly proportioned nose and pronounced cheekbones gave her almost a sculpted look, like a goddess come to life. I wanted to know everything about her.

She gave me a playful groan, straightening up in the tub to rest her back more solidly against the wall. "I think I'm in for a long bath."

My entire face lit up as I leaned forward and hugged my knees, eager to hear about my sister's life.

"I was born in 1795 in Quebec City. My parents moved there from Britain before I was born, shortly after the French had been defeated. We lived above a small shop they ran in the market area of town, on the edge of the St. Lawrence River. My father made a terrible salesman. If he wasn't giving merchandise away to one of the slew of beggars, he was trading it for far less than it was worth. Thankfully caring for our horses, pigs and chickens occupied most of his time."

"Did you have a horse?" I could just picture her in riding pants and knee boots, elegantly mounted on a wild black stallion while she galloped across the open pasture and meadows.

Dangerous Waters

She laughed at my *Black Beauty* inspired fantasy. "Her name was Chestnut. She was a gorgeous bay mare with a jet black mane and a thin white stripe along her nose. Man did she love to be ridden, especially once I'd learned to canter. At fourteen hands she was barely more than a pony, which made her perfect for my undersized, nine-year-old body. I had to get up extra early so I could clean her stall, feed her, brush her down and fill her water bucket before helping my mother with breakfast. Not that I minded. I went riding almost every afternoon, following the river bottom miles downstream to a small farm market. The elderly woman who owned it was friends with my mother and would pretend to look the other way while I swiped a carrot or an apple for Chestnut.

"Each morning after breakfast my mother would spend hours haggling with the local farmers, taking in milk, eggs, butter and whatever else they'd brought with them in exchange for the metal ware, spices, fabric and other goods we'd imported from France. I spent the bulk of my day cleaning and stocking shelves while she waited on customers. At night me and my father would tend the animals while my mother cooked, and then we'd all settle around the fire. My mother loved to read, especially Ann Radcliffe novels, and would spend hours curled up in her oversized leather chair reading to me. My dad busied himself with paying bills and writing correspondence at his desk, pretending not to listen, but I'd catch him sitting idle at the suspenseful parts.

"My mother's headaches began shortly after I turned fourteen. They were infrequent at first, and only required her to lie down for an hour or so, but by late fall she was bedridden. Our doctor was convinced her poor eyesight was to blame, that she'd spent too much time reading in the dim lamplight. Even if he hadn't been so misguided, there's no way they could have treated a brain tumor at the time– the first attempt at such a surgery didn't occur for another eighty years. He gave her remedies for the pain, but there was little else any of us could do.

"To make ends meet my dad started delivering goods for the local merchants and fur traders to Montreal, going away for several days at a time. I did my best to run the shop on my own, but I was only a child. The same people that had traded fairly with my mother for years wasted no time profiting from our hardship, demanding ridiculous payments for the simplest of things, or taking what they wanted without even attempting to barter. In less than a month the shelves were empty. My father's income barely kept food on the table, and he had to sell Chestnut to help us make it through the winter."

"I'm sorry about your mom. I can't believe the people that knew her so well would be so evil to her daughter. Did you get to say goodbye to Chestnut at least?" I couldn't exactly fault her father for selling her horse when they were starving, but to not let Raven get any kind of closure would be cruel.

Raven captured one of my feet, which were angled inside her own legs, and patted it with her hand. "Thanks. And I did. Before he left for Montreal, my father let me spend the entire weekend in the barn, riding Chestnut and sleeping next to her on bales of hay in her stall." Her lip trembled as her face took on a far more solemn appearance. "I'd just gotten my mother to sleep the next night when I heard glass shatter downstairs. My father wasn't due back for days, and by that point my mother was too weak to even stand. She'd shown me where she kept our butcher knife, and told me that if I ever got scared, I should take it and hide in my closet. My heart was beating so fast I could barely breathe, but I tiptoed into the kitchen and took the butcher knife out from beneath the sink. Whoever had broken the window was now inside the shop and was heading straight for the doorway to our loft.

"There was no way I could hide when my mom was so helpless. I ran to her room and waited behind the door, hoping that whoever it was would just take what they wanted and leave. Each creak of a stair made me jump. My whole body was shaking, and I was holding the knife so tightly in my hand that my skin had turned pale. When the door to our loft opened, a little whimper of a yelp escaped my lips. The walking stopped. Sure that they'd heard me, I slammed my free hand over my mouth and began to cry. The intruder started moving again, and headed straight for my mother's room at a brisk pace. I gazed at my mother, remembering all of the happy times we'd shared together. I was only fifteen but I'd had a good life. When the bedroom door flew open I pounced, driving the knife with both hands deep into the man's back. He cried out and collapsed to the floor with me landing on top of him. It wasn't until I got up that I recognized my father's coat– "

Raven's voice broke off as she turned her back to me and buried her face in her hands. I scrambled across the tub and nestled up against her, gently rocking her trembling body while she cried.

"You know he doesn't blame you. He probably felt terrible for scaring you so bad. Regardless of why he broke the window, he had to have realized what you would think– home alone with your invalid mother. He should have been yelling that it was him from the second he opened the door to the shop."

Still sniffling, Raven leaned back and wiped her eyes. "Without even thinking I pulled the knife out– which knowing what I do now was probably the worst thing I could have done– and tried to press a towel against his back to stop the bleeding while I screamed for help. He stayed conscious for a few minutes, long enough to explain what had happened to our neighbor and ensure I wasn't punished for what I'd done. He'd gotten mugged on his way to Montreal. They took everything– his carriage, the horses, and everything from his pockets. One of the men said they'd been following him since he left our house, and that they might have to pay his daughter a visit on the way back through town. It was hours before he found someone willing to give him a ride. By then he was sure he'd be too late."

"So he wasn't sure what he'd be walking into," I concluded. "Then he heard you cry out and came running." She solemnly nodded her head, and I tucked a few loose strands of her damp golden hair behind her ear. "It's not your fault, Raven. It was just a tragic accident."

"That's what the local magistrate said. Not that it did anything to ease my guilt, or made my father any less dead." She closed her eyes and let out a long, slow breath. "Taking care of my mother kept me going for a while. I had to beg for food just to feed her, rarely getting enough to eat anything myself. The bills piled up. And while the bank wasn't quite callous enough to take our house while I cared for my mother, they had no problem throwing me out when she died the next spring."

"What about your mom's friend? The one with the farm market?" If she was willing to turn a blind eye while Raven pilfered her shelves for Chestnut, I couldn't image her turning her back when Raven needed her the most.

Raven stretched out her legs and lowered herself deeper into the water, resuming her earlier position while I returned to my own end of the tub. "She offered to take me in. She even convinced me to give it a try for a while. But my endless depression soon frustrated her. I rarely left the attic she'd converted for me to live in, and I never spoke. I'd eat if she forced me to, but even then it was only a couple bites. After a month went by without any improvement in my condition, her patience waned. I was sent packing with nothing but the handful of undersized dresses I'd brought with me. Given that I was destitute and only sixteen, my options were kind of limited, so when I stumbled across a recruiting office I decided to join the British army as a nurse's aide.

"After spending three days in the back of a covered wagon, we arrived at one of the converted farm houses they were using as a field hospital, only a few miles behind the front lines. The house itself was a giant two-story, French-inspired colonial, with white siding, dozens of glass, shutter-style windows, ornamental molding and three chimneys protruding from the roof. The staff lived two to a room, occupying each of the ten small bedrooms. My roommate was a chubby French girl who spoke only broken English. Not that it would have mattered. I made no effort to speak to her or anyone else except to answer direct questions. We were dressed in low-neck gowns and petticoats with a shift underneath, and were required to wear our hair in a mass of curls.

"We spent our days caring for the wounded– bathing and feeding them, changing their bandages, and seeing to their treatments. As we became more experienced we were asked to assist with surgeries, debride wounds and administer sutures. Abhigail, the head nurse, was a tyrant of a woman. She thought nothing of slapping us across the face if we talked back or made mistakes and often sent us to bed without food or water. Whenever she caught me crying, she'd drag me by the hair into the corner, lift my skirts, and beat my shift-covered bottom with the cane she carried, saying that if I was going to cry like a baby she'd treat me like one. Rather than suffer her abuse, I quickly learned to suppress my sullen mood during the day.

"My roommate, Genevieve, wasn't as fortunate. She often complained about my persistent crying, and was finally moved to a different room when a space freed up. Even though we'd lived together for almost two years, we hadn't become anything close to friends. But being alone for hours each night only deepened my depression. Her bed didn't go unused for long. A lot of the soldiers flirted with me of course, being a young and fairly attractive woman. Until then I'd always been quick to rebuff them. I'd become so starved for attention of any kind that even lust was welcome. I started taking advantage of private moments, letting them kiss me or rubbing them during their bath, and often let the more able-bodied ones bed me with little more than a name. Abhigail pretended not to notice for months– she was probably just glad that something had finally shut me up– but when the other girls complained of my special treatment, she had to act.

"When I came down for breakfast one morning the entire staff was waiting for me in the dining hall. She dragged me to the front of the room, stripped me down to my shift and beat me with her cane until I passed out. When I woke up, I was chained to the floor in a dark, musky old cellar. My head had been shaven, and my entire body was covered with cuts and bruises. I spent almost four months locked away in that hole, begging them to kill me."

Tears stung at my eyes as I placed my hand on her knee, praying for the appropriate words to ease her pain. "So rather than trying to understand why you were so depressed and get you some help, she chose to beat you. Then when you reached out to the only people willing to offer any kind of comfort, she threw you in a fucking dungeon. That's almost fair. Christ."

The corners of Raven's mouth rose in a somewhat reluctant grin. "I'm not sure I was quite as innocent as your summation portrayed me to be, but thank you, my sister."

She took my hand from her knee and held it firmly against her thigh. "In the spring of 1814 I left Canada for the first time, slowly heading south through Maine and New Hampshire before finally ending up in Boston. My hair was still short– kind of like Sandy's, actually– but it was cute, and I had little trouble finding willing suitors in the local taverns. I shared my body with them in exchange for a free meal, a bath and a place to spend the night. Some of the men even bought me a dress or a fancy hat and would ask me to keep them company at their table before we went to bed. I'd become a prostitute without even realizing it.

"You'd think that would mean that I was my own boss, at least. I soon found out that Boston's popular taverns were prime real estate for women in my new trade, and the local talent didn't take too kindly to an outsider stealing their clients away. After having a knife held to my throat, I agreed to become one of Lady Monique's whores. That wasn't her real name, obviously, and I was soon given my own persona, as a naughty chambermaid named Lady Anna. I was dressed in revealing gowns each night that left most of my breasts exposed, with a little maid's bonnet tied around my chin. I'd pretend to dust, wipe down the counter or sweep the floor, only to be scolded by Lady Monique for my sloppy work. She'd take me over her knee, raise my skirts to reveal my black, thigh high stockings and naked bottom, and then lightly spank me in front of all the potential clients, pausing to ask the crowd if I'd learned my lesson yet. It never took more than a few seconds before one of them wanted to join in, forking over the steep price Lady Monique demanded for a night with me. As word spread from town to town, people starting traveling great distances to observe our little show, driving the price even higher. I was kept in the finest clothes and treated like a prized mare."

Rather than being repulsed by the unexpected turn in her story, I found myself incredibly turned on. I was soon lost in a fantasy, with me dressed as a naughty chambermaid while Sandy held me over her knee, showing everyone in the bar what a bad little girl I'd been. I could almost feel her hand smack against my naked butt. When Raven snorted, I looked up to find her pointedly glancing downward with her brows raised. I was mortified when I realized that the hand she wasn't holding was buried between my legs. I yanked it away and curled myself into a ball, so embarrassed that tears soon filled my eyes. If Sandy hadn't already heard my thoughts, she would the next time I ran into her. There's no way I could keep living here. "Please kill me."

I could feel her arms wrap around my shoulders as she pulled me into a hug. "I thought the best I could hope for was that you might understand what led me to become a prostitute, even if you'd never look at me quite the same way again. Instead you display such an open mind that you find the eroticism in it. You're truly remarkable, Brooke. And as for your little fantasy, I won't elaborate – so don't ask me to– but trust me when I tell you that Sandy will be flattered."

What was that supposed to mean? Yeah, she was cool about our kiss earlier, and my little daydream that led up to it, but this was a whole different league. At least part of me wanted to sleep with her. Raven's expression made it clear that follow-up questions were off the table, so I chose to get us back on track, hoping the last two minutes would be magically purged from my mind. "How did you meet Sienna?" If she was twenty when she was turned, it had to be soon.

"The tavern I worked in had local musicians and singers perform on Saturday nights, trying to appeal to a more diverse crowd. Most of them were awful, and were quickly drowned out by the boos and jeers of the raucous crowd, so when I saw this freckled face young Irish girl take the stage in her fancy red gown, I felt sorry for her. Then she started to sing. After only a few notes of her perfectly pitched, soothing tenor voice, the crowd fell silent. She worked the room like an experienced performer, shifting from soft love ballads to more upbeat numbers with a practiced ease, sensing the mood of the crowd.

"Lady Monique and the rest of us stood with gaping mouths, shooing away anyone who bothered us. Even the bartenders were mesmerized– not that anyone was even attempting to order drinks. It was like Sienna had cast a spell over the entire room. When she finished, the crowd erupted in applause like we were in an upscale theatre rather than a fairly trashy tavern. The sound was deafening as they demanded an encore. Sienna obliged, singing a haunting French song that sent chills up my spine. I doubt if more than a handful of people in the sizeable crowd spoke the language, but that didn't seem to matter. Her voice spoke to your soul.

"A handsome, well-built man decked out in a stylish black suit took her arm as she finished, guiding her to a reserved table near the back while he discouraged anyone from getting too close with a menacing glare. With the musical entertainment wrapped up, it was time for me to go to work. I sauntered over to the end of the bar and began my routine, taking a rag from the bartender and starting to wipe down the counter as I swayed my hips. The catcalls and shouts were intermittent at first– probably because half the people were still staring at Sienna– but by the time I'd reached the other end of the bar the place was roaring again.

"Lady Monique appeared on cue, drawing her own round of applause from the crowd. When she did the little tsk-tsk motion with her finger and pointed to the wet spot I'd intentionally left behind, the place went nuts. She asked the crowd what she should do with poor Lady Anna, and they all played their part, yelling that she should spank or beat me. I acted appalled, which only made the calls grow louder. Finally Lady Monique took a seat in the chair that had been brought out for this part of our act, and I sulked as I trudged over to her. I obediently sank to my knees at her command and bent across her lap to receive my punishment. Just as she raised my skirts the room fell silent. I was baffled. Usually this was the part of the show where I could barely hear myself think.

"My skirts were tugged down around my legs as someone lifted me from behind, standing me back on my feet. I turned to find Colt glaring at Lady Monique like he was going to decapitate her. Her face had gone so pasty white against her fiery red hair that it looked like she'd donned clown makeup. Sienna was holding me none to gently by the elbow. She asked how much it would cost to buy me out of whatever contract Lady Monique had me under. When Lady Monique finally recovered enough to speak, she burst into laughter, telling Sienna that I was worth fifty grand if I was worth a penny. Colt pulled a satchel of gold coins out of his suit pocket and tossed three times that amount in her lap. Before I even knew what was happening, they were escorting me out to their luxurious carriage.

"Going from being a whore to a slave was a little offsetting to say the least, but after seeing the gold Colt flashed and their carriage, I figured it'd have to be a step up. Besides, it wasn't like Colt was hard to look at. If he wanted me all to himself, I wasn't about to complain. After he helped Sienna into the carriage, he took my hand, guiding me as I climbed in across from her. When Colt sat down next to me I figured it was time to start earning my keep, and nestled my body up against his side. He shoved me away like I was a leper. I cast Sienna a confused look, wondering what the hell they'd bought me for, and she claimed that her father had been friends with my parents. After my mother became deathly ill, he'd promised my father that he'd look out for me should anything happen to him as well. Her father had supposedly spent years looking for me before succumbing to typhus. She and her brother had picked up the search, only to hear stories of my act and find that I lived in their own hometown.

"At first I rolled my eyes at their ridiculous story– I mean, come on, what are the odds that a family that was looking for me in Canada would just so happen to live in the town I'd settled in hundreds of miles away?– but when I asked her probing questions about my parents and my childhood, her responses were flawless. She told me that they were hoping I would stay with them, as my father had wished, but I was under no obligation to do so. If I didn't like living there, I could leave anytime I wanted, and they would set me up with my own trust fund regardless. I kept waiting for someone to pinch me. After all the horrible things I'd endured, I was being plucked from society's cesspool of bottom feeders to live a charmed life as a spoiled rich girl. It was too good to be true.

"And I'd only managed to keep my depression at bay by making my life so degrading that I couldn't bear to think of my parents at all, for fear of what they'd think of me. The life they promised would leave me far too idle. In some ways, the fact that their father had been friends with my parents added a whole new level of pain. Knowing my past, they'd be looking at me each day with the same *poor Elizabeth* expression in their eyes that they had now. I wasn't sure I could handle being Elizabeth Black again.

"As the carriage lurched forward and got underway, Sienna told me they'd arranged twice-a-week sessions with Boston's top psychiatrist, hoping that I'd allow them to provide the counseling they were certain I'd need from what they'd learned about my childhood. I couldn't see much of a downside, so I nodded my head and stared blankly out the carriage window while the horses made the seventeen mile trek to their home– the same house we live in now, although it was totally remodeled five years ago.

"Things were awkward at first, having found myself living with people I'd never met, but when Sienna took us riding the next morning, I began to loosen up. Colt took to me like a big brother almost instantly, lacing my boots for me and helping me up into the saddle. We were brushing down the horses after our ride– teasing each other about who'd won our little impromptu race– when he called me Lizzy for the first time. The name stuck. I soon had a horse of my own, a palomino mare named Trudy. We went riding every day except when we had to make the trip into town for my therapy sessions.

"Doctor Carmichael was an older man, in his late sixties, with a bald head and thick rimmed glasses. Sienna had filled him in on everything that had happened to me, from accidentally killing my father, to caring for my dying mother, and being beaten and imprisoned. She'd even told him about my years spent as a prostitute. I guess I could have felt like she'd betrayed my trust, but having everything out on the table let me fast forward to beating my depression rather than taking years just to tell him about the causes.

"The biggest thing I learned was to not keep things bottled up. As part of my therapy, I had to spend hours each night telling Colt and Sienna about my mom and dad, and not just the pleasant things. I had to go into details about her brain cancer and what I did to take care of her, and tell them both what happened the night of my father's death. The next phase was just as hard, describing what it was like each day in that cellar. I'd never cried that much in my life, but after three months passed, I found that the overwhelming guilt and pain I'd kept sealed inside was gone. For the first time since losing my parents, I felt like I was part of a family.

"Sienna began to expose me to their true nature soon after. I'd always wondered about their strange scent, and thought it odd that they never ate in front of me, but it's not like vampirism was the first thing that jumped to mind, not even back in the early nineteenth century. I could also tell they weren't brother and sister– not by blood anyway– as they looked and acted almost nothing alike. When I started asking questions, they answered them. At first their answers were vague, leaving plenty of gray area to claim they didn't mean what it sounded like if I didn't take it well, but as I gained more knowledge and asked more direct questions, they told me the truth, including how they'd lied to me the night they took me home from the tavern.

"I couldn't even look at them for a while. I felt so betrayed after finally opening up my heart. But over time I got past the stigma associated with the term "vampire" and forced myself to consider all they had done for me. They'd taken me in and helped me move past the darkest moments of my life, allowing me to be truly happy again. My closets overflowed with expensive new clothes, and if I even glanced twice at an item while we shopped, Sienna bought it for me. Sienna was more serious than Colt, but they both had a surprising sense of humor, and we shared so much in common that living together was easy. The days we'd spent riding were among my most cherished memories, and listening to Sienna sing felt almost like a religious experience. Aside from my parents, they were the most loving people I'd ever met.

"Sienna asked me if I wanted to become her daughter early the following summer. I'd managed to watch them feed a couple times by then, but they'd never presented me with any kind of ultimatum. Even now she didn't come right out and say it, but I could tell that if I refused, I'd be asked to leave the only home I'd known since being thrown out of my parent's house after my mom died. There's nothing I wouldn't have done to stay with them.

"The thought of feeding off of and killing people didn't bother me. Not that I'd enjoy it or anything, but I hadn't been emotionally attached to anyone since my parents died. As I told you earlier, the only part of the decision I struggled with was never being able to have children. I'd always looked forward to telling my child about how wonderful their grandparents had been, and figured that sharing a long life with them would somehow make up for how I'd been shortchanged. In the end I had to accept that my life was intrinsically tied to theirs. Sienna and Colt had become my family. I couldn't walk away from everyone I loved just for the hypothetical possibility of someday having a child of my own.

"I fed for the first time a few days later. We didn't have a naming ceremony back then, but I did make a similar vow to both of them before I received my new name. Sienna had to constantly chide Colt for continuing to call me Lizzy. He never did stop doing it. I think he enjoyed egging her on.

"Just after midnight on June thirteenth, Sienna woke me up and prepared me for my transformation. She tried a couple of new things based on her experience with Colt, binding me to my bed to reduce the risk of me hurting myself, and strapping my mouth shut to keep me from screaming. Not even the passing of almost two hundred years has dulled my memory of the pain.

"Once I'd adjusted we moved to a small town just outside of Hartford so I could attend the Litchfield female academy. It was one of the only colleges that admitted women at the time that wasn't just a finishing school. I focused on the sciences, studying biology, chemistry and math, but I enjoyed my literature and logic courses the most. I graduated four years later and began to help Sienna manage our investments.

"Sienna and Colt created a corporation called Brown holdings shortly after they came to the US in the beginning of the nineteenth century. While we've modified the charter several times since then, it's still one of the companies we use today. We invested heavily in textile mills, import/export companies and banks, quickly amassing a sizable fortune. Sienna always demanded a face-to-face meeting with the executives of the companies who wanted us to invest. It only took a few minutes for us to uncover everything: how confident they were, what they were hiding, how much they were willing to offer, future plans–more information than they'd ever willingly disclose. It was easy to make the right choices with complete transparency.

"We moved to Philadelphia just before Christmas in 1820. Sienna had a friend who lived southwest of town near the Delaware River. Suzanne was known for the elaborate black-tie vampire-only New Year's Eve parties she threw. It was by far the largest gathering held each year and gave everyone a chance to catch up with friends from across the globe. It wasn't uncommon for a thousand people or more to attend, some coming from as far away as China and the Middle East. Everyone was careful to feed before they arrived, and to leave before they had to feed again, to avoid bringing any unwanted attention to the gathering. Sienna and Colt hadn't been to one since I joined them and were excited to see everyone again.

"They introduced me to hundreds of people, Sienna beaming with a mother's pride the entire time. At the time I only spoke English, which made it almost impossible to communicate without Sienna or Colt translating for me. The party continued into the early hours of the morning, with drinking and dancing and endless conversation. When things finally died down around four a.m., I was too tired to sleep, so I headed up to the third floor to watch the sunrise through the large bay windows that faced the river.

"As the first signs of light broke the horizon I heard an alluring French voice behind me. I had no idea what he was saying, but as soon as I glanced at him I remembered meeting earlier. I noticed that he was motioning toward the far end of the couch, so I patted it with my hand. He took a seat next to me, and then lifted up my hair and whispered a poetic sounding sentence that had me swooning. I assumed he was complimenting it and thanked him.

"He had a long, slender body with dark hair and thick stubble on his face and neck. He looked young, maybe eighteen, but his face had lost all of its boyish features. He was wearing a thick wool sweater and worn, comfortable trousers. I was jealous that he'd thought to bring a change of clothes, as I was still wearing my ankle length gown and heels. He'd looked handsome earlier in his cloak, double-breasted waistcoat, and breeches, but not seductively tempting like he did now.

"Seeing my gaze, he leaned back against the arm of the couch and motioned me over to him. I kicked off my shoes and curled my body into his with my head resting against his firm chest. He held my hand as I drifted asleep. That was the first time I met my Edmund."

"Your Edmund? Tell me everything!" I leaned closer to her, wrapping my arms around my knees. After all she'd been through I was happy to hear she'd met someone, even if it was bound to end badly, given that he wasn't still around.

Raven blushed and gave me a coy smile. "When we woke we spent the entire day together, walking through the snow along the river, sharing drinks at a little café, shopping and catching a play at the Walnut Street Theatre, all the while trying to communicate with simple gestures and expressions. Sometimes we'd talk in English and French without trying to be understood, just to hear the sound of each other's voice. As the sun dipped below the horizon, Edmund walked me to the steps of our home and gave me a long, passionate kiss. When he finally stepped back, he handed me a note, written in French of course, and whispered 'Tu vas me manquer, mon amour.' As soon as he was out of sight, I raced inside and asked Sienna what it meant, repeating it the best I could. Her eyes welled up when she said 'I will miss you, my love.'

"The letter contained his address along with a small note saying how happy he was to have met me and that he'd write soon. Sienna and Colt began to teach me French the next day. For six months that's the only language they'd speak, breaking into English only to translate when necessary. After the first couple of months they demanded that I speak French exclusively as well. They helped me read the first few letters I received from Edmund and write my replies to him, teaching me the unfamiliar words he'd used and proofreading to correct my mistakes. When our letters got more intimate, I quit asking for help all together.

"In July Edmund asked me to come visit him. Sienna and Colt were overjoyed, but they were also worried about me making the journey alone. At the time it was still a thirty-day voyage by ship across the Atlantic, which meant I'd have to feed at least three times while on the boat. Even though we'd just moved to Philadelphia, they agreed that it'd be best for all of us to make the trip together.

"We worked with Edmund to purchase a beautiful estate along the River Leiz in Montpellier, only a few miles from where he lived. It was late September before everything was finalized and we were able to make the trip over. As soon as I stepped off the boat I leaped into his waiting arms— it felt so good to hold him again. My mouth eagerly found his as his hands drifted down my back and firmly gripped my butt, pulling me hard against him. Only Colt's less than subtle clearing of his throat stopped us from going further right there on the pier.

Dangerous Waters

"Edmund had planned to take me to the theatre at the Place de la Comédie, followed by dancing and drinks, but it was all we could do to make it back to his house. He was living with his mother and an older man, whom I'd met at the party, in a large Greek revival style home. Thankfully we had the entire east wing to ourselves. Given his gentle nature, I was concerned that he might be too passive in bed, but that fear dissipated when he took me with a raw, almost savage hunger. I didn't realize how loud I'd been until I met his mother the next morning.

"When Edmund and I approached her at the table she flashed us a warm smile and said 'S'il vous plaît dis moi la prochaine fois que tu veux faire la peau a un chat vivant, et Allie et moi partirons de la maison,' which means 'Please let me know the next time you want to skin a cat alive, and Allie and I will leave the house.'"

"Oh my God!" I blurted out, bursting into laughter. "What'd you do?"

"I don't think I've ever been quite that embarrassed before. I curled into Edmund's side and hid my face in his shirt. His mom didn't know I spoke French, so she couldn't figure out what I was reacting to until I replied 'Le chat fait ses excuses,' which means 'the cat apologizes.' She felt horrible and begged me to forgive her, saying that she was only teasing her son. I told her not to worry, and that I thought it was quite funny.

"As the months went by we spent more and more time together, even going on trips alone to Paris and London. I knew that I loved with him, but I'd never worked up the courage to tell him about my father or the time I'd spent as a prostitute, and we were long past the point where you'd expect such things to have been shared. The secret was like a cancer, eating away at our relationship as I walled off the parts of my life I was starting to feel ashamed of again. I'd worked too hard to let go of my guilt. If we were going to have a future together, I'd have to tell him.

"In early April Edmund said that he had a surprise for me and asked me to meet him at an address in town later that afternoon. When I arrived at the small house near the center of town, the door was open. Edmund was dressed in the suit he'd worn the night we met in Philadelphia, and was down on one knee with an open jewelry box in his hand. I ran into the house, screaming yes over and over again until I dove into his waiting arms. We spent the rest of the night privately celebrating as we familiarized ourselves with all three of the bedrooms along with the kitchen floor. As I lay in his arms the next morning, I knew I couldn't wait any longer. Gathering all of my courage, I leaned up on an elbow, laid my arm across his chest and told him everything.

"While I spoke, he remained perfectly calm with kind of a stoic look on his face. When he still hadn't said anything for several seconds after I'd finished, my heart began to race. He finally looked at me, and in an ice-cold voice asked me if I seriously expected him to marry a whore. I was so dumbstruck that I just sat there, half draped across his chest, until he pressed his hand into my face and threw me backward into the wall– "

Her tears started to flow, and Raven crawled back into my waiting arms, crying softly against my shoulder. The more I tried to comfort her with kind words, the harder she cried, so I finally gave up talking and just held my grief stricken sister.

She'd endured an impossibly hard life full of tragic events, any one of which most woman would never recover from, Look at how messed up I was just from losing my mom. She'd had to care for her mother as she withered away, on top of dealing with accidentally killing her father, being beaten and imprisoned, being raped and having the only love of her life throw her heartfelt confessions back in her face. The fact that Raven had coped with it all made me respect her more than anyone I had ever known. She was a resilient, courageous warrior with an inner strength I could only hope to emulate some day.

After several minutes she sat back and gave me a small, forced smile. "I think that's about all the sharing I'm up to for tonight. Do you mind if we talk about something a little more upbeat?"

She was still sitting close to me, so I leaned forward and kissed her on the cheek. "You name it."

"What would you like for your birthday?"

I curled my brows as I looked at her, surprised that she wouldn't have picked up the date from my mind by now. "I'll be changed before then– it isn't until December seventeenth."

"I know when you were born, ya goof," she said with a laugh. "We celebrate the day we became a vampire as our new birthday. Since you won't be in any shape to celebrate on the actual day this year, we thought we'd do it ahead of time. It needs to be early enough to allow you to recover from anything minor that might happen, so we planned to have it next week."

"Sweet! Let's tear the roof off this bitch!" I couldn't wait to dance with them again.

Raven snorted. "I think that expression died about ten years ago, sis. But yeah, we figured dancing would be a big part of your party. What else would you like to do?"

I curled my lips, trying to think of other things we could do without leaving the house. Suddenly the perfect idea came to me. "Before the dance party, I want each of us to pick out our favorite movie of all time. We'll watch them all together in a big movie marathon with pizza and popcorn."

"I like it– you can learn a lot about someone from their taste in theatre. You still haven't told me what you'd like for a gift though."

After all that I'd heard about the family's wealth, I knew I could probably ask for anything, but I'd never been materialistic. My dad had always provided me with the things I really needed, or I'd worked to buy them for myself. I'd have to get used to having closets full of new clothes, and at some point my Camry would need to be replaced, due to its high mileage and tie back to my former life, but I was determined not to become a spoiled little diva. I didn't need a bunch of gaudy jewelry I'd never wear, a $1,000 handbag or $600 shoes.

As I thought about my values growing up, I realized how much I had in common with my new family. While they had plenty of nice things, they weren't flashy about it, and they were all very down to earth. Rather than just sitting back and living off the family money, they went to college and worked toward goals they'd set for themselves. My dad would love all of them... I eagerly snatched up her hands as the thought hit me. "I'd like you all to meet my dad after I'm changed."

Raven's brow furrowed in concern. "I'd love to meet your father, as I'm sure all of us would. Having us there would help you relax as well." She paused and studied my face.

"But," I said, interpreting her hesitation.

"Spending several days in close quarters with a human will be risky. It would only take one slip for him to see your wrists, and avoiding every situation where he'd expect us to eat with him will be difficult. He's bound to detect our scent with all of us there, and you'll still be a very young vampire, lacking the discipline and control that comes with time. We'd never hurt him regardless of what he suspected, but if he accused us of doing something to you, things could get very complicated for all of us."

I peered off into the distance, thinking about what she was saying. My wrists shouldn't be a problem. It'd be late December, so I'd normally be wearing sweaters and long sleeve shirts anyway. Meals were a huge concern, but hiding my lack of appetite would be even harder if I were alone– at least this way I had a built-in excuse for someone else I could've eaten with. There was no doubt that he could notice our scent or see me move unnaturally fast as well. Raven was right, visiting him would be risky, but it'd be less of a risk if they were there. And while I knew I'd have to leave him behind someday, I couldn't bear the thought of never seeing him again– not yet.

Raven's lips widened into an affectionate smile. "Looks like we're all going to Traverse City for Christmas."

"Thanks, Raven! I know he's going to love you guys!"

She laughed. "It's going to feel weird calling you Emme again."

"God, that's right– that name sounds so foreign already."

Chapter Nineteen
Dead Presidents

Teresa flung herself into the waist-high pile of money stacked between the two hotel beds, throwing it up into the air like confetti. "How much do you think is here?"

Travis glanced at the catatonic, middle-aged man sitting in the armchair in the corner. "Mr. Senior Vice President thinks it's north of three hundred grand. Fuck, I knew it'd be worth the trip to Denver. I think he deserves a cut. What about you, sis?"

Teresa sauntered over to the chair. After hiking her black leather skirt up to the top of her thighs, she sat in his lap, straddling him. "Unfortunately poor old Jonathan isn't going to be around long enough to spend it. He has his heart set on hanging himself tonight."

"Please don't kill me!" Jonathan begged, having been granted the ability to speak. "My wife's pregnant with our first child. They're all I care about. I won't say anything. I swear."

"No need to worry about the fam, Jonny. They've been dead for hours. Seems finding out it wasn't your baby was just too much for you to take. I thought stabbing her twenty times in the stomach was a little over the top, but she was fucking half the neighborhood, so hey, who am I to judge?"

Seeing the sadistic gleam in her manic eyes, he buried his hands in his hair and screamed. "Oh God! Kristine… You sick bastards! I hope you both burn in hell!"

Teresa leaned forward and kissed him on the neck just below the jaw line, leaving a bright cherry stain from her heavily coated lips. "Once you realized what you'd done, you decided to rob your bank and take off for Mexico. You had a few hours to kill before the flight, so you brought a prostitute back to your hotel room to get even. Then everything caught up with you and, well, you know the rest."

His lips pressed into a thin line as his gaze bore into her, pure hatred emanating off of him in waves. "They'll never believe any of this, you psychotic bitch."

"Really? Which part? I'm not kidding about her sleeping around. It'd be faster for me to tell you who she hasn't fucked on your street. Remember her trip to Bermuda last spring? Sorry. Never left your sub. Your golf pal Kenny spent the week pounding her raw and became a proud daddy. As for the hooker thing, you couldn't keep your hands off me when we were checking in. And with me dressed like this?" Teresa motioned toward her costume brunette wig, caked on make-up and skimpy outfit that left most of her boobs hanging out. "I'm pretty sure they bought I was a whore."

"Your wife died in her bed without a struggle and with no sign of forced entry," Travis added. "And your fingerprints are all over the murder weapon. The police will find your ticket to Cancun on top of your bag over there, which also has over ten grand stuffed into the bottom. They'll figure you wired the rest into an account somewhere."

"Not to mention the suicide note you're going to leave that confesses to everything." Teresa let out a snide little giggle. "Damn, Trav. We're pretty good at this."

All hope left Jonathan's eyes as he realized that the whole country would believe every word of their story. Teresa reached down and unzipped his pants, sliding her hand inside. "It's not all bad news– I am going to give you a hand job first. We need some cum for the forensic team to find."

He was rock hard after only a couple strokes, in spite of his rage-filled protests, and ejaculated into her hand a few minutes later. She walked over to the bed they'd torn the covers off earlier and spread it around in the sheets.

Jonathan took a seat at the desk, grabbed the hotel stationary tablet and started to write while Teresa spoke, taking dictation for his own death. When the two-page letter was finished, he ripped the sheets out of the notepad and placed them on top of his bag before carrying his chair into the bathroom. He climbed up on it, pushed the white ceiling tile aside, and then looped his belt around his throat. After tying the other end to the iron water pipe above, he kicked the chair out from underneath his body. The tips of his toes dangled across the floor as he slowly choked to death.

Chapter Twenty
Happy Birthday to Me

My arms stretched out lazily over my head as I rolled over onto my back and yawned. Suddenly panicked at how rested I felt, I spun my head around to peer at the clock on my iHome.

"Eight-thirty? Damn it." I extracted myself from the cocoon of covers I'd nestled into and sat up, yelping when my feet hit the cool wooden floor. In spite of my general hatred for doing anything before 10:00 a.m., I'd managed to be on-time for our early-morning workout sessions every day for the past week– until today, that is. As I slipped on a pair of running pants, I heard a tap on the door.

"I'll be right there!"

Raven opened the door and casually leaned back against the door frame. "I turned off your alarm. I thought I'd give you the day off since we're celebrating your birthday."

"Oh… Thanks. It felt good to sleep in." I lumbered over and sat down on the edge of the bed. "So what movies did everyone pick?"

"It's a surprise," she said with a smirk. "Besides, you've got gifts to open first."

I playfully reached out my arms. "Bring 'em on!"

Raven snorted as she took a seat next to me. "You're such a goofball. Everyone's out getting 'breakfast' right now. I was hoping we'd be finished before you woke up."

Memories of the night I fed with them flashed through my mind– I could almost taste the warm blood in my mouth. They'd fed several times since then, but I'd never felt any desire to join them until now. I slowly looked up at her. "Could I…join you?"

"Of course, my little vamp sister," she said, placing her hand under my chin. "What a symbolically appropriate way to start your first birthday. I wish I would've thought of it. Better sharpen your fangs– they should be back any minute."

I gave her the most menacing snarl I could manage before we both burst out laughing. "Think I have time for a shower?"

"I'm afraid not– I can hear their car pulling up now."

"Okay." I darted into the bathroom. The shower could wait, but my bladder was another story.

The front door swung open just after I joined Raven in the back of the living room. Sandy flashed us a smile as she entered with Sienna and Ruby following close behind. I could tell by the stern expression on Ruby's face that she was controlling the middle-aged, massive male in her wake. He towered over her, standing at least 6'4", and was well over 300 pounds. The Patriots jersey and navy-blue sweats he was sporting resembled my dad's typical Sunday afternoon outfit, which wasn't really an image I needed given what we were about to do.

I was still trying to shake that disturbing thought when Raven took hold of my wrist and pulled me along behind her. By the time we entered the feeding room, the man was lying on the gurney with his feet dangling awkwardly over the end. Sienna and Ruby stood on either side, waiting for him to get settled. His eyes drifted shut. Raising his left arm, Sienna sliced her nails across his wrist and lifted it to her mouth.

As I watched her gorge in his blood, my pulse skyrocketed, forcing me to inhale through my mouth like I'd just finished doing wind sprints after practice. The first time I'd fed it had been a spur of the moment decision made out of desperation as I fought for my own survival. I'd never even considered that I might *enjoy* it. Now I knew the strange kind of high that awaited me. The anticipation had me impatiently rocking my foot. *How are they all so calm?*

Raven leaned over so her lips were directly against my ear. "If you were to kiss Sandy a thousand more times over the next hundred years, do you think the last kiss would make you feel as excited as you did the first time you kissed her?"

"Ah…no." My cheeks burned with embarrassment, recalling the smell of her sweet breath and the feel of her soft, supple lips.

"It's just like that," Raven continued. "To you, this is all still new and exotic. And while you'll always get a good feeling from feeding, the novelty of it will wear off over time."

I get your point, but did you have to use that analogy? Now I'm thinking about feeding and kissing Sandy! Sandy glanced back at us, trying unsuccessfully to smother a laugh.

Sienna and Ruby finished feeding a couple minutes later. They waited for Sandy and Raven to take their place before joining me in the back of the room. Sienna kissed me on the forehead and took hold of my hand while Ruby looked on, her own hand fidgeting by her side. Her face beamed when I laced my fingers through hers.

Having consumed her fill, Sandy laid the man's arm down and wiped the blood from her lips. Raven finished moments later and motioned me forward.

My heart violently crashed against my ribs like it was threatening to break through at any moment. I floated to Raven in a daze, unaware of my feet even touching the floor. When I felt his wrist press against my quivering lips, I locked on and began to suck, sending hot, coppery liquid flooding into my mouth. I ravenously swallowed it down, and an intoxicating mix of adrenaline and endorphins coursed through my body. After several minutes I staggered back and tried to clear my head.

"That was intense." As I turned toward Raven I caught a slight movement out of the corner of my eye, causing my focus to shift back to the man lying on the table. I jumped when I saw his chest rise. "Jesus, he's not dead."

"That happens sometimes with larger people." Sienna gave Raven a slight nod, and in one fluid motion she stepped forward and snapped his neck.

I shuddered, taking an involuntary step away from her. "Oh."

"None of us like to take such a direct hand in their death," Sienna said, bracing my shoulders to support my now wobbly legs. "But it's the cleanest and most humane way to handle these situations."

"I understand." Seeing Raven commit such a violent act right in front of me was definitely harder than watching someone die from being fed upon, but I knew she'd only done what was necessary to prevent him from suffering any further. Like a buffalo culled from the herd by a wolf pack, his fate had been sealed the moment they'd chosen him. I was a predator now. I needed to come to terms with that.

Sienna grinned and ruffled my hair, trying to brighten my now somber mood. "You'd better get cleaned up, birthday girl– we've got a big day ahead of us."

* * * *

After a long, hot shower I brushed my teeth and gargled (twice), and then slid into my fluffy pink bathrobe and headed toward my closet. When I stepped past my bed I noticed the giant red ribbon and bow hanging across the middle of my closet door. I scampered across the floor, anxious to find out what was inside.

"Holy crap!" Every shelf, rack and cubbyhole of the cavernous room was full. There were at least 30 pairs of shoes along with row after row of skirts, tops and dresses. I sifted through the rack closest to me and discovered that they were almost all styles I would've picked out for myself. This wasn't just a matter of backing a moving van up to the nearest Saks Fifth Avenue and stuffing it full of clothes. Someone had put a lot of thought into each item that they'd selected, keeping my tastes in mind.

"Happy birthday," Sandy called out from behind me.

I bounded over and leaped into her outstretched arms. "Thank you! They're all so beautiful. How'd you know what I'd like?"

"I'm a quick learner." Her sultry voice sent an electric current through me like I'd taken hold of a downed power line. She brushed the wayward bangs back from my eyes and lowered her mouth to my waiting lips. After teasing them apart with the tip of her tongue she nipped at my bottom lip, and then gave me a slow, tender kiss that turned me to mush. When her hands slipped under my robe and began to travel up the back of my bare thighs I groaned into her mouth. "See what I mean?" She let out a cute little squeak of a laugh and sat me back on my feet.

I had no idea what was happening between us, but ever since my fantasy we'd been exchanging increasingly steamy embraces. And I'd noticed that she didn't refer to me as her sister anymore.

She took hold of the lapels of my robe and pulled me toward her, claiming my mouth again with her full, pouty lips. "As for your taste in clothing, it was pretty easy really— all I had to do was pay attention to your thoughts about the clothes we've worn over the last five weeks, combine that with what you already owned, and voila, the essence of Brooke is born!" We both giggled.

"Jeans, shorts, t-shirts and the rest of your casual stuff is in the dressers in the back," Sandy added. "The navy blue tub in front of the dressers is full of workout clothes. You'll go through them in no time once you start learning to fight."

"What's it like? Are you ever scared?" I was eager to start my training, but the image of Raven tumbling across the floor in a blur before pressing the steel of her blade against my throat made me shiver. I couldn't imagine myself ever been skilled enough to repel such an attack.

"At first I was terrified. It's hard to convince yourself that you don't need to fear having a three-foot sword slice across your neck until you get hit with it several times. That's why you won't even have a sword for your first lesson. You'll just run around screaming while Sienna hits you over and over again. That may sound like torture, but you can't learn while you're afraid."

I snorted as I pictured me running for my life in the workout room while Sienna kept clubbing me over the head with her sword like I was in a Tom and Jerry cartoon.

Sandy burst out laughing. "That is so what it's like!"

We collapsed on top of each other in gut-wrenching laughter until we were both gasping for air. Just as I was beginning to catch my breath, Sienna stepped into the room.

"Run, Brooke, run!" Sandy hollered.

We both lost it, laughing even harder than before while I recounted the Tom and Jerry image of our swordfight in my mind, embellishing it even further. Sienna gave us kind of a what-am-I-going-to-do-with-you-two shake of her head as she joined in.

When we finally recovered Sandy and I got up and sat on the end of my bed. Sienna stood facing me with her right hand behind her back. "Are you ready for my gift?"

"Definitely!"

She brought her hand forward, revealing a notepad and pen. "I'm afraid I need all replies in writing."

I was baffled. It'd only been two weeks since I scribbled a completely illegible note in an effort to get her to continue her life story (per the terms of our deal). I flexed my fingers, feeling a little stiffness in two of them. If I couldn't do this, I'd probably start bawling, which was the last thing I wanted to happen today.

"You haven't missed a therapy session since then, and you're a lot stronger now. Please try," Sienna said, setting them in my lap.

Holding the pad with my left hand, I let out a deep sigh and nervously lifted the pen.

I'm ready for my gift, Mom.

"Look! I did it!" I yelled, bouncing up and down on the bed. Sandy and Sienna squeezed me between their arms.

"I knew you could do it, honey. And now for your gift– "

"You're going to love this. It's frickin awesome!" Sandy blurted out as Sienna left the room.

When she returned, she handed me a large white brochure with nothing but the word "Kelser" on the front. Intrigued, I quickly flipped it open. The inside pages had "Kelser Indoor Tennis Club" written across the top and were covered with pictures of people playing tennis.

I fought back tears. I knew my wrist would never be strong enough to play tennis again, not even recreationally.

Sienna caressed my cheek with the back of her hand. "You can't as a human. Once you're a vampire, your wrist will be able to crush a racquet handle like a twig."

"Raven told me that our scent was too strong when we sweat to be around anyone."

"It's true that we can't play around other people," she agreed, her spiral-curled ringlets bouncing as she nodded. The look wasn't exactly flattering on her – she kind of looked like Annie– but I knew better than to critique Sandy's latest creation. "But that's not because of our scent– sweating doesn't have any effect on that. Raven couldn't be honest with you at the time since you didn't know what she was. When we play sports it's easy to get caught up in the competition and forget that people are watching. It wouldn't take more than a few minutes for everyone in the building to know that we weren't human."

I felt like she was talking in circles. "So how can we play?"

"By ensuring that there's no one else in the building," she said with a wide grin.

I examined the brochure in more detail: 28 tennis courts, thirty-eight dollars per hour. "Seriously? For how long?"

Sandy leaped off the bed and started taking mock tennis swings in the air. "As long as we want– we own it!"

I stared at Sienna in complete shock. A club like this would have to cost millions.

"Don't worry about the money, sweetheart. It's a great investment for us," Sienna reassured me. "They're one of the top clubs in Boston and cleared over two million in profit last year."

Not only was I going to be able to play tennis again, something I'd given up all hope of doing, I was getting to play with my new family. "You don't know how much this means to me."

"It's the least I could do after you worked so hard to get better. No one will be happier to see you play tennis again than I will."

Watching Sandy step forward and follow through like she'd just hit a serve made me giggle. "Your footwork is terrible."

"I'm taking you down, Brooke!" she shot back at me.

Dangerous Waters

"Have you guys ever played before?"

"Raven and I used to play all the time until we met Ruby," Sienna said. "We had so much fun teaching her to defend herself that sword fighting kind of took over as our new sport. We've talked about playing countless times since then, but we never have."

"That's right– Raven told me that she played seriously for a while," I remembered. "How'd your matches usually go?"

Sienna fussed with my damp, messy hair while she spoke, trying to untangle it with her fingers. "Raven was always more aggressive than I was, going for aces on serves and winners on returns. Because of that she always had more unforced errors as well. Long rallies tended to frustrate her, and her impatience led to careless mistakes. If she was really on her game, she'd beat me handily, but most of the time I'd nudge her out in close sets."

"God this is going to be fun!" Her description alone let me know that I'd have my hands full with her and Raven. I couldn't wait to teach Ruby and Sandy to play too.

"We'll let you get dressed," Sienna said, getting to her feet. "I'll try to keep Raven and Ruby at bay, but you may want to hurry."

I gave them both a big hug and raced to my closet. A beautiful strapless Ombré silk dress had caught my eye earlier, and I hastily leafed through the rack until I found it again. It had a pleated bodice cinched by a gem and varied in color from the top to bottom, going from a dark gray on top to almost a sheer white. While it was way too elegant for our movie marathon, I couldn't wait to dance in it later. Near the far end of the first row of shoes, I spotted a pair of champagne colored Jimmy Choo metallic slingbacks that matched the dress perfectly. "Ah hell, so I like six hundred dollar shoes," I said to myself. I didn't even want to think about how much the dress cost.

I laid my evening outfit on my bed, and then began to search for something cute to wear during the day. I was tempted to just throw on a pair of jeans and a t-shirt, but it seemed wrong to go with something so everyday when I had so many new things to choose from. Even the casual clothes in the dressers were fashionable. I almost settled on a pair of stretch Jodhpur riding pants before I found a cute black fleece jumpsuit sitting on top of the drawer below. It had a draped neckline and racer back (which would allow the white tank I'd wear underneath it to show), with rolled cuffs on the bottom.

Raven walked in just as I was finishing up my makeup. "You call that hurrying?"

"Hey, I had a whole closet of stuff to go through," I argued before turning to show off my outfit.

"That's really cute— I may have to borrow it sometime."

"Help yourself." I gestured toward the bed. "Look what I picked out for later."

Raven walked over and held the dress up to her. "That's going to look amazing on you. And these shoes are perfect for it. Jimmy Choo's?" She raised her eyebrows with mock accusation.

"I know, I know— so much for my big 'down to earth' speech. What can I say? They're gorgeous."

She laughed. "That they are." Raven laid the dress down on the bed then came up and stood behind me. "Do you trust me?"

"Completely."

She pulled a black silk scarf out of her pocket, folded it into a blindfold and placed it over my eyes. "Come with me." Raven took my hand and led me down the hall and across the living room. I could hear Sienna and Sandy talking in the kitchen.

"Where's Ruby?" I asked as we approached the door.

"Picking up the movies and pizza. Pepperoni, double mushroom, Canadian bacon and double cheese right?"

"Exactly. How'd you know?"

"When you mentioned that you wanted pizza for your birthday, you thought of your favorite toppings. That's how I knew what movie to get for you as well. Good choice by the way. That would definitely be in my top five."

"Mind telling me what I chose?"

"I'm surprised you don't know. Your mind jumped to it immediately when you mentioned having us pick out our favorites. What would you say your favorite movie is?"

There were so many movies that I liked— I never had an easy time picking out a favorite. How could my unconscious mind be so sure of something that my conscious mind couldn't decide on? If I went by which one I'd seen the most, it'd have to be *Dances with Wolves*. I never made it to the end without crying.

"See, that wasn't so hard," Raven teased. "As for your other question, when we consciously think about things, our mind debates and challenges our initial impressions in order to validate them. Our conscious thoughts are also subject to our moods and frame of mind. You could have easily picked something other than *Dances with Wolves* if you'd just watched it recently, or you were in the mood for a comedy, even though it's clearly your favorite."

Are you going to miss being able to read my mind?

I could feel her squeeze my hand. "I have to admit it'll take some getting used to. As comfortable and resourceful as you've been sharing your thoughts, I think you might miss us being able to do it a bit too."

I will. It's been kinda fun really—except for a couple of thoughts that I wish to God none of you had heard.

Raven led me through the door, down the porch steps and across the creek stone walkway to the circle drive in front of the house. "Are you ready?" she said, untying my blindfold.

I eagerly nodded my head and she pulled the scarf away. A silver Mercedes M-class SUV was parked along the curb with a giant red bow on top of the roof. "Is it a– "

"Hybrid? Of course, sis– give me some credit. It has the highest fuel efficiency I could find in something large enough for us all to ride in."

"I love it!" I shouted, opening the driver's side door and climbing in. The dark gray interior was offset by wood trim around the gear shift and center console. The seats were covered in a luxuriously soft leather just a couple of shades lighter than the carpet and dash. I activated the built-in GPS navigation system and scrolled through a couple of menus before flipping on the XM satellite radio.

"It also has an external plug in for your iPod. There's a TV back here too," Raven added from the back seat.

"This is kick-ass!" I gripped the leather wrapped steering wheel like I was flying down the road. "Can I take it for a ride?"

Raven handed me the keys. "Just to the end of our road– Ruby isn't finished making the registration 'official' yet."

"Who's it registered to?"

She snorted. "Brooke Davis, of course."

"Of course," I said with a laugh. So my fake ID wasn't so fake after all. The engine hummed quietly as I shifted it into drive and headed down the driveway. The steering was effortless, and the ride was incredibly smooth. I turned onto the side street and accelerated.

"Brooke," Raven scolded lightly.

"You're no fun," I complained.

"In addition to not having a valid registration, you don't have your license with you, and the car isn't insured yet."

"Okay, I'll be good." I slowed down and pulled into the next driveway to turn around.

"Oh, I almost forgot the second part of your gift." Raven leaned forward between the front seats and opened up the center console.

"Second part? I think you're covered with the new Mercedes," I joked, glancing down into the open compartment. A bundle of Delta plane tickets lay on top. "We're going to Traverse City!" I pulled one of the tickets open to try to find a date. "When do we leave?"

"They're open-ended– we'll finalize the dates once we see how long it takes you to adjust."

"Thanks, Raven. You're the best." As the car rolled to a stop back in front of the house I could see her biting her lip and staring off into the distance. "What's wrong?"

"I don't know if I should say anything or not."

I turned around so I could see her without craning my neck. "About what?"

After a long pause she finally released the seatbelt she'd taken hostage and looked at me. "Ruby's concerned that you're not going to like her gift. She made me promise not to say anything, but I really think you need to know to avoid hurting her feelings."

"That's crazy. I'd love anything that she gave me."

"I'm sure you would, but this may seem a little bizarre to you, and if you even think that for a second, she'll pick up on it and be crushed."

"What is it?" I felt terrible asking, since I was sure Ruby would want to surprise me, but I couldn't think of any other way to prepare myself if it really was something odd.

"That's why I hesitated to mention it– even if you have an entirely positive reaction, she'll be able to tell that you already knew. Ruby's planned a whole day together for just you and her so that you can get to know each other better. She wants to take you to the Museum of Science, the New England aquarium and the Natick Mall."

I cocked my head to the side. "That sounds awesome. Why would either of you be worried that I wouldn't like that?"

She tried to resume strangling the passenger seatbelt, but I blocked her hand, so she settled for nervously pulling on her braid. "I knew you'd like that part. It's the second part of her gift that I'm concerned about. I know Ruby hasn't told you much about her past yet, and you think of her as a techie genius, but she was actually a professional artist before she joined our family. She concentrated mostly on oil paintings and charcoal drawings. You should Google Mary Jewel sometime– you'll find images of several of her paintings online. Some of them went for over a thousand, which was a lot of money at the time. Her specialty was the human form."

"She wants to do a painting of me?" I guessed.

Raven's eyes met mine as her cheeks flushed. "A certain kind of painting, yes."

"She wants to paint me naked?!" As much as I hated to admit it, this was beyond bizarre. It was downright creepy.

Her face filled with sadness and disappointment at my reaction. "It might seem that way, but if Rembrandt or Monet offered to create a one-of-a-kind painting for you for your birthday, how special would that be? The naked body is just the form that she works with. Please try to understand."

I felt like an ass. Instead of playing it safe and just buying me something expensive, Ruby was going out of her way to make me an intimate and personalized gift that would help me get to know her better at the same time. Not that I had any idea where I'd put the thing when it was finished. "I'm sorry. It's an extremely thoughtful gift. What will I do with it though? I'm not a prude or anything, but I don't exactly want a Playboy picture of me on public display."

Raven rolled her eyes. "Her paintings aren't pornographic. She paints her subjects in natural poses, like lying in bed or curling up with a blanket by the fire. Whatever prop the person has strategically covers their privates, while still leaving plenty of skin exposed– they're sensual and on the erotic side but not at all crude. Mine usually hangs above the fireplace in my room. It's one of the only things I take with me whenever we move. Ruby asked us to take them down before you moved in so she could get to know you before opening up about her past."

"You all have one?" I said, picturing her in the poses she'd described.

"Yep. She even made one of Colt based off our descriptions. It hangs next to Sienna's in her room. In mine I'm lying in bed on my left side. A black satin sheet comes up between my legs and over my right arm, which is drooped casually across my body to cover my nipples. I look so comfortable, like I'm enjoying a cool breeze on a hot summer night."

"That sounds beautiful. Can I see it?"

"Of course, sis," she replied. "But not until after she does your painting."

211

My mind went to work thinking of potential poses. I wanted it to be something natural, something I'd typically do. I never slept in the nude– except for the night with Daniel at least– and there's no way I'd be casually strolling around the house naked even if I lived alone. The only time I was really comfortable naked was when I was taking a bath. I imagined myself in the whirlpool with some strategically placed suds covering the bottom of my breasts and privates while my arms and left leg rested on top of the tub. The room would be filled with soft candlelight, which would flicker across my bare skin.

Raven ran the back of her fingers along my cheek. "I've seen how serene you look relaxing in the tub. That will make for a striking image. I knew you'd love her gift once you understood it."

Ruby's blue Cadillac Escalade pulled up the drive just as Raven and I stepped onto the porch. Rather than fruitlessly trying to hide my thoughts, I ran up and threw my arms around her. "Thank you so much, Ruby. I'm really looking forward to our day together, and I've got a great idea for my painting."

Ruby shot an accusatory glare toward Raven, who was still standing on the porch. Her expression softened when she read my mind and discovered how much I truly loved her gift.

I gazed into her dark brown eyes with a wide grin on my face. "So what do you think, Ms. Artiste? Will it make a good setting for my painting?"

"It'll be perfect– absolutely perfect." After a long embrace, she leaned back and smiled. "So what'd you think when she first told you?"

I snorted. "Honestly? I wondered why my sister wanted to turn me into a Playboy centerfold. It took me a while to catch on to the artistic nature of your paintings."

"I'm actually glad Raven told you," Ruby said. "I drove around for an extra half hour trying to come up with the right way to explain it. I finally decided to chicken out and show you their paintings, then offer to do one for you if you liked them."

I burst into laughter, thinking about how much easier that would have been. "Well, I really didn't catch on to the type of paintings that you do until Raven described hers. I think seeing them first would've avoided a lot of confusion."

Ruby went around to the passenger side and picked up a large pizza, a Best Buy bag and a box of microwave popcorn.

"Can I help?" I offered, peering into the bag.

She grabbed it with her right hand and tucked it behind her back. "No snooping!"

"Let's go, troublemaker," Raven said, hoisting me over her shoulder.

"Hey, put me down!" I yelled with mock protest. She carried me into the living room, plopped me down on the couch and took a seat on the far end.

"Movie time! Who wants to go first?"

"Since it's your birthday, I thought we'd start with yours," Sienna replied.

"Has everyone seen it?" I was hoping at least one of them hadn't.

"Only Raven and Sandy," Ruby answered from the kitchen. "The description on the box sounds interesting."

Sienna laughed. "How can you go wrong with Kevin Costner?"

"Ain't that the truth!" Raven agreed, lying back against the end of the couch suggestively. "He's welcome in my Teepee anytime."

I chucked an accent pillow at her, which she easily caught and tucked behind her head. "Thanks, sis."

After grabbing three slices of pizza and a large glass of Diet Dew, I nestled into the couch next to Raven. The 60-inch OLED screen and surround sound made the room feel like a theatre. Ruby tossed flavored waters to Sandy, Raven and Sienna, and then dimmed the lights and sat down next to me.

I began to weep when the Pawnee Indians killed the disgusting but lovable wagon driver and took his mules. Sienna handed me and Ruby some Kleenex, then placed the box on the table. "That may not be enough," I said, wiping my eyes.

Everyone watched intently as Lieutenant Dunbar befriended Two Socks the wolf and tried to establish a rapport with the leaders of the Sioux tribe. By the time he met his beloved Stands With a Fist I could tell they were as engrossed in the movie as I was.

I felt disgusted when he left to retrieve his journal from the old Army fort, knowing what was to come. When the soldiers escorting him to his court-marshal shot Two Socks, we all reached for more tissues.

It dawned on me as Dances with Wolves and Stands With a Fist rode off together at the end that the plot pretty much outlined the last seven weeks of my life. He'd befriended a group of people who were different than he was, fell in love with them, risked his life to protect them and eventually became one of them. I'd never been a big believer in fate, but it seemed an incredible coincidence that my favorite movie would so closely predict my future.

"I agree that it's not just a coincidence," Sienna said. "But not for the reasons that you're thinking. It wasn't fate or destiny that brought you to us. You identify closely with his character, a kind, open-minded person searching for something more in life. That's why you like the movie so much, and why you were willing to join us."

"That makes sense I guess. So what'd you guys think?"

Ruby motioned toward the pile of tissues on the table in front of her. "Do you have to ask?"

"It was so nice to see a western told from a more balanced point of view," Sienna commented. "How did they film the scenes in the plains with the Buffalo? Was that all computer generated?"

"Actually they were shot in Fort Pierre, South Dakota using thirty five hundred real buffalo. They stampeded them past seven different cameras five times during the eight days they had to shoot the scenes."

"Please don't ask her to name the buffalo," Raven said, dramatically burying her head under a pillow. Giggles and squeals filled the room as we wrestled on the couch. When we finally separated, Sandy got up and removed the DVD.

"Who's next?" I asked.

"Your choices are *Sleepless in Seattle*, *The Horse Whisperer*, *Gone with the Wind* or *The Good, the Bad and the Ugly*," Ruby replied.

"I'm not going to pick!" If I did, I'd end up choosing someone's favorite movie last.

Raven flashed a mischievous grin. "*Sleepless in Seattle* it is."

"Damn it! That's not fair."

Sandy pulled her movie out of the bag, held it above her head like a Wimbledon trophy and did a little victory dance. "I knew she loved me the most."

"Bite me!" I shot back at her.

"I'm kinda full from breakfast, but I guess I could use a snack." She flashed her teeth and took a step toward me. I snorted, and they all joined me in laughter.

We all got up to take a break, and I headed to the kitchen to make some popcorn. It made me feel like a pig to be the only one eating anything, but I always loved munching on stuff when I watched movies. Giving up food was not going to be easy. Raven shook her head when I plopped down on the couch with a giant tub of popcorn in my lap. "What?" I said innocently, shoveling a handful into my mouth.

"Live it up, birthday girl."

Dangerous Waters

I defiantly grabbed several more kernels and stuffed them in, my cheeks stretching out like a squirrel. I knew she was going to make me pay for this in the morning.

It only took me a few minutes to recognize that the character Tom Hanks played was extremely similar to my dad. His wife died of cancer when their son, Jonah, was six. He was devastated by the loss of his wife and didn't even think about dating again. Although he was a devoted father to his son, he was only a shell of his former self. After a while I didn't even see Tom Hanks when I looked at the screen. I just saw my dad, filled with the pain that he'd tried to mask my entire life.

As the story progressed toward the predictable happy ending, I was taken aback by the lengths Jonah went to in order to find someone special for his father. I knew he was just a fictional character in a movie, but he still made me think about how selfish I'd been growing up.

While I was always there for my dad and tried to make life as easy as possible for him by staying out of trouble, I never encouraged him to date. I counted on him being totally devoted to me. He'd spent almost all his free time and spare money carting me around to tennis camps, riding lessons, Girl Scout outings and a million other things without ever complaining. If that wasn't bad enough, as I got older I began to treat his dedication like a burden I had to bear. How many times had I whined to Britt about not being able to go out because it was my father's "stupid" movie night, or bitched about my dad "forcing" me to go fishing again? Then the second I graduated from high school, I moved as far away from him as I could. Nice. The guy devotes the last thirteen years of his life to raising me and that's how I repay him. And now I was becoming a vampire, which meant I wouldn't see him at all in a couple years, and would never give him a grandchild. I couldn't even stand the thought of leaving Sienna and my sisters behind, but what about him? I'd done nothing but make one selfish decision after another my entire life. He deserved so much better than me.

I was still mentally chastising myself when Sienna sidled up to me and kissed the top of my head. "How could you think such things? You're one of the most loving, selfless people I've ever known."

"Then how could I use him like that?" I blinked back the tears that were burning at the corners of my eyes.

"You didn't use him, Brooke. In addition to being an angel of a daughter, you became his best friend and companion. You're the only reason he has any semblance of a normal life."

I leaned back and peered into her tranquil green eyes. "What choice did he have? I never let him try to find anyone else."

She sighed, her face contorting with pain. "It'd be nice to think that there's more than one true love out there for all of us, and that we're all capable of loving again. Sometimes people love so deeply, down to their very soul, that they're simply not capable of opening their heart up again. I tried with Stefan. Even though I love everything about him, and hundreds of years had passed since I lost Archill, I couldn't make myself fall in love with him. If I ever could've loved again, I would have chosen him."

Sienna affectionately tucked my hair behind my ear. "I think your father's the same way. There's nothing you could've done to get him to date again, not that it was your responsibility in the first place. As for the comments you made to your friends about not wanting to do things with him, you know those were only excuses. Just like every other teenager in the world, you didn't want to admit that you enjoyed doing things with your parents. And if I've learned anything about your father from what you've told me and from your thoughts, he's tremendously proud of you for getting into such a prestigious university, and for always having the courage to pursue your dreams, wherever they may take you."

"How do you always know what to say to make me feel better?" I asked, managing a faint smile.

She cradled my head tenderly against her chest. "Just part of being a mother, my sweet child."

"I'm sorry about Stefan."

"I really hurt him when I ended things between us. The fact that we're still such close friends shows what a remarkable person he is." She pulled back and blotted my eyes with the Kleenex in her hand. "We can watch the rest of the movies tomorrow. Your sisters and I will get to work turning this place into a club while you change."

"Ten minutes, tops!" I promised, already halfway down the hall. After changing into the elegant ombré silk dress and designer heels I'd picked out earlier, I quickly touched up my makeup. I was about to step away from the mirror when my reflection gave me pause. My ultra-chic hair was cropped short around my face. You'd be hard-pressed to find a supermodel anywhere in Paris donning a more fashionable dress or heels. I now owned a Mercedes and had access to a bottomless bank account, our own cruise ship, a private tennis club and mansions all over the world. My fiery hot trysts with Sandy had me seriously questioning my sexuality. Oh, and let's not forget that I'd already participated in killing two people. I hadn't just starting answering to a different name. I'd assumed an entirely new life.

Chapter Twenty-One
Body Paint

  I took a deep breath and untied my robe. Ruby gave me a reassuring smile as I slid the cotton fabric over my shoulders, letting it pool at my feet on the floor. I stood naked in front of my sister for a few seconds, trying to get used to the idea that she was going to be staring at my body for hours, and then stepped down into the steaming hot tub. The glow of soft candlelight filled the room along with a soothing lavender scent. Ruby sat on a stool behind an easel that supported a large, horizontally aligned canvas. She mixed colors on her palette while I turned on the jets and assumed the position for my pose. Resting my arms on top of the tub brought my breasts completely out of the water. As if that wasn't bad enough, having my left leg draped over the side raised my pelvis so high off the bottom that my privates were clearly visible.

  Ruby snorted when I began to frantically search for some bubble bath. "I can paint suds in where they need to be, sis– they don't actually have to be there."

  "Oh." A fresh wave of heat danced across my cheeks, making them burn.

  "Find a relaxing position and let me know when you're ready. It's okay to move around a little, just try to resume the same pose when you're done."

  "How should I have my hair?" I ran my fingers through it, pushing it back behind my ears.

  She curled her lips up in thought. "I think it'd look great wet and combed straight back."

  "That sounds good."

  Ruby stepped out from behind the easel, grabbed a wide tooth comb off the sink and sat down behind me. "Close your eyes," she whispered before soaking my hair. The deliciously warm water streamed down my face and carried away some of my anxiety. I leaned my head back and sighed.

  Once she finished combing my hair, I settled back into my pose. The contoured bottom of the tub made it easy to get comfortable. I just couldn't decide how to hold my head. *Should I lean it against the back and close my eyes like I'm asleep or stare off into the distance like I'm lost in thought?*

  "Definitely the latter," Ruby said. "You have such beautiful eyes– it'd be a shame to have them closed."

"Thanks. I think I'm ready."

"I was born in 1911 in New Yor– " Ruby stopped mid-sentence when I lurched forward in eager anticipation of her story. "Painting here!" she called out, holding her brush in the air for emphasis.

"Oh… Sorry." I shot her a heartfelt gaze and resumed my pose.

After a short pause she continued. "I was born in 1911 in New York City. My parents were socialites, to say the least. I don't believe either one of them ever worked a day in their lives. My father was an heir to the Jewel fortune amassed by my great grandparents.

"I was their only child. I attended only the finest private schools growing up and spent my free time being paraded about from one elitist get-together to another like their little trophy. I rarely saw my parents when we were at home– raising me was pretty much outsourced to our army of nannies, tutors and house staff. When I turned sixteen, I was sent off to the Dana Hall boarding school where I spent the next three years.

"After graduating from High School, I attended Wellesley College right here in Boston. The college campus is actually beautiful. It's situated on five hundred acres with a lake, woodlands and open meadows. I'll have to take you there sometime."

"I'd like that."

Ruby flashed me a smile. "While I despised my parents for forcing me to go there at first, it ended up being the best thing they ever did. That's where I discovered my love of art. Visual arts classes were strongly encouraged as freshmen electives, so I signed up for two of them. By the end of the first semester I knew that I wanted to be an artist and changed my major to studio art. My parents didn't really care what I majored in. Their only purpose for sending me there was for me to find some Ivy League guy from a well-to-do family to marry. No daughter of theirs would ever work for a living.

"Toward the end of my junior year I was selected, along with three other students, to exhibit works at a local gallery. We each got to showcase five of our paintings. My instructor chose two abstract pieces I'd done during my sophomore year to go along with the Post-Impressionist and Realist paintings I'd chosen.

"On the last day of the exhibition, Edward Hopper– he was like the Serena Williams of American realist painters– stopped in unannounced to check out our work. By the time he got to my paintings, my heart was in my throat. I held my breath as he slowly made his way from one painting to the next without saying a word. When he was finished, he turned to my instructor and asked if he could meet the artist. After a quick introduction he praised my work and invited me to continue my studies with him in New York. I instantly accepted, of course. To my knowledge, he'd never taken anyone on as a student.

"My parents went berserk when I told them. Not only had I failed to find someone to marry, but now I wasn't even going to graduate. They threatened to cut me off entirely if I didn't finish school. When I moved into a flat in New York to study with him two weeks later, they followed through on their threat.

"After two years Edward and I agreed that I was ready to paint professionally. He set me up with my own small studio and helped to get several of the works I'd done while studying with him exhibited in galleries throughout New York. In exchange, I gave him seventy-five percent of the proceeds from the six paintings that I sold the first year. There's no way any reputable gallery would've considered showing the work of someone fresh out of art school if I wasn't his protégé."

Ruby dipped her brush and continued her smooth strokes, her eyes intently focused on the canvas. Every few seconds she'd cast a quick glance my way, checking her image, and observing the subtle features of my body.

"By the end of 1935, galleries were competing to show my work. I'd begun to focus on capturing the elegance and beauty of the human form, offering to create custom pieces for high-end clients. My mother called for the first time in over three years to ask me to attend a party they were throwing. Some of their friends had purchased paintings of mine and were just dying to meet me. All of a sudden I was their 'darling' daughter again– their phony display made me sick. I reminded her of how they'd disowned me when I left school and never spoke with either of them again.

"I met Sienna and Raven at an exhibit in December of 1936. Sienna wanted to commission three paintings for her and needed them completed as soon as possible. When I explained to her that I had a backlog of five other paintings, she offered me fifteen thousand to start immediately. There was no way I could turn that down. The most I'd ever received for a painting before was fifteen hundred.

"I came to their house in New York for the first time less than a week later. After they gave me a quick tour, we spent hours getting to know each other. They were unbelievably perceptive, almost as if they could read my mind." We both glanced at each other and laughed.

"I shared everything with them, things I hadn't even told Edward in the two years we spent together. We exchanged hugs before I left like we'd been friends for years.

"When I arrived the next morning, Sienna was lying naked on the floor in the living room next to a roaring fire. Of all the paintings I've ever done, hers is still my favorite. She was so comfortable around me that it put me totally at ease, even with Raven watching intently over my shoulder. When I showed the painting to her late that evening, she broke down in tears, threw her arms around me and gave me a kiss. I was a bit taken aback by the outpouring of affection, having come from such a cold family.

"She invited me back the next day to help her hang it. The three of us ended up spending the entire day together shopping and going to a Broadway play. I repeatedly refused to let them buy me things, but my protests didn't do any good. When I unpacked my bags later that night, all of the items I'd put back were in there.

"I stopped by early the next morning to thank them and work on Raven's portrait if she had time. After a quick knock on the door, I let myself in, like Sienna had asked me to do the day before. Seconds later I heard a door down the hall slam shut. I thought maybe I'd caught them in the shower, so I took a seat on the couch to wait. After twenty minutes went by, I was sure I'd done something wrong. I wrote out a note apologizing for stopping by unannounced and asked them to call when they wanted to resume working on the paintings. I also thanked them for the generous gifts, thinking that maybe they'd expected a call the night before. I was pretty shaken up by the time I got back to my loft. They were actually in the middle of feeding, but several weeks passed before I found that out.

"Sienna called shortly after I got home and frantically apologized. She said that Raven had been ill that morning, and she'd gone into town to get things for her. Raven had tried to get out of bed to come meet me, but she felt too weak. Sienna is far too pure of heart to be any good at lying. Even if I hadn't heard voices in the room after the door closed, I wouldn't have believed her. Nevertheless, I was relieved that she wasn't angry with me and figured that something personal must have been going on that she didn't want to discuss. She asked me to stop by the following morning, and I happily accepted.

"Sienna wrapped her arms around me when I arrived and apologized again. To be polite, I asked if Raven was feeling better, which of course she was. As soon as we were inside, Raven told me all about her idea for her pose. She was so excited that she practically dragged me into her room. Raven told me everything about herself as I worked, as much as she could at the time, anyway. Sienna stepped into the room just as I was putting the finishing touches on it and was so happy that she twirled me around in the air. You know how beautiful Raven is, but she's absolutely stunning in that portrait."

"I can't wait to see it." After hearing both of them describe Raven's painting, the buildup was killing me.

"Wait until you see your own," Ruby said with a smile. "You're truly breathtaking."

"If my painting's breathtaking, then you must be taking a lot of artistic license," I teased. "I didn't know you were going for a Post-Impressionist work."

She veered her hand away from the canvas mid stroke and broke out in laughter. "I have to commend your use of the terminology, sis, but you have a really distorted view of yourself. You were plenty attractive when we met. Now your arms and legs are more toned. I'd kill to have the definition in my abs that you do, and your new hairstyle goes so much better with your face."

"That's really nice of you to say," I muttered, not buying a word of it.

She shook her head. "You don't believe me do you? Set aside what you *think* you look like, and really take a look at yourself."

I tried to do as she asked, glancing down at my left arm from an almost detached viewpoint, and was a little surprised to see clearly defined muscles bulging out of it. My eyes darted to my left leg, which was flexing to keep my lower body from swaying in the water. It was just as firm. I'd been working out with Raven every day for over a month, but the changes to my physique had been so gradual that I really hadn't taken much notice of them. "Damn."

"See what I mean? Look at your stomach for God sakes."

I peeked at my chiseled stomach, which resembled something straight out of an abdominal machine infomercial. "I'd noticed my clothes were getting looser. And I could certainly feel these." I patted my firm stomach muscles. "I guess I just didn't realize I'd changed quite this much."

"The last two weeks it's really begun to show. I know it'll take some getting used to, but you look beautiful."

"Thanks, Ruby."

She nodded her head and resumed her work. "Where did I leave off anyway?"

"Sienna was swinging you around in the air after finishing Raven's portrait," I reminded her.

Dangerous Waters

"Oh yeah, thanks. I spent over a week making several charcoal sketches of Colt, trying to get a good image of him from their descriptions. Let's just say I'm not cut out to be a forensic artist. They finally said that I had it down perfectly, but I think they were just being kind. I really wish I could've seen a picture of him.

"I took the features that they liked the most from a few of the drawings and tried to incorporate them into his painting. I'd never tried to do a portrait-style painting without a model before, and it was tremendously difficult for me. When I was finished, Raven and Sienna told me how happy they were and swore that the portrait was an amazing likeness of him, but I could tell they were disappointed. They'd talked so glowingly about Colt while we were doing the sketches and were both so excited, like they expected my painting to bring a small piece of him back to life. Even though it made Sienna really upset, I refused to let her pay me for it.

"I'd gotten to know both of them so well during the two weeks I spent working on their paintings that they'd become my closest friends, but I had no idea if they felt the same way. They'd hired me to do a job for them, which was now complete. For all I knew, that was their only interest in me. I went into the spare bedroom and packed up my supplies.

"After I'd tucked the wide part of my easel under my right arm and picked up my bags, I heard Sienna enter the room behind me. I spun around as she stepped forward to hug me, right into the pointed top of my easel. She hit it with such force that she knocked me onto my back. When I recovered, Sienna was standing over me, unharmed except for a tear in her blouse near her stomach. The long center support of my easel, which was over two-inches thick, was splintered into dozens of small pieces, like it'd been driven into a brick wall. I tried to sit up and felt a sharp pain in my right arm— it'd been broken just above the wrist. I couldn't understand how Sienna hadn't been injured given the force of the collision.

"They rushed me to the hospital and stayed with me the entire time I was there. When I woke up from surgery, I had a cast from my hand to my elbow, which meant that I wouldn't be able to paint for at least six weeks. For the next month we were inseparable. By the end of the first week, I had so much of my stuff at their house that I'd basically moved in with them. I'd never been happier in my life.

"I came home from getting groceries one afternoon and found Sienna and Raven sitting at the table waiting for me. They told me that they were going to be moving to France in a couple of weeks. I was crushed. I loved them both like sisters and couldn't imagine my life without them. I all but begged them to stay, but it didn't do any good. When I went back to my loft that night, my whole life fell apart. Everything had seemed so perfect before I met them. I was really proud of what I'd accomplished and had always enjoyed the independence and freedom that I had. Now I just felt totally alone.

"After I didn't leave my loft or answer the phone for a week, Raven and Sienna stopped by and knocked on the door until I let them in. I looked like hell. I hadn't bathed in days, I was still wearing my pajamas at two in the afternoon, and there were dirty dishes and clothes all over the apartment. I couldn't make myself care about anything anymore. When they saw how depressed I'd become, they both began to cry. They took me in their arms and told me how much they loved me, and that they wished there was some way I could stay with them. I hadn't thought about going with them before then, but there wasn't any reason that I couldn't move to France– as an artist it'd be one of the best moves I could make.

"When I asked if I could come along, Sienna gave me a warm embrace and said that nothing would please her more, but I'd have to join her family if I wanted to live with them. I was so confused– she was talking like she wanted to adopt me or something. As far as I knew I was seven years older than she was. She asked me to take a seat on the couch so she could explain.

"Sienna opened her mouth a couple of times like she was going to say something. Then she just sat there, staring at the floor. Seeing that she was getting nowhere, Raven decided to take a more direct approach. Without any hesitation she sat down next to me, peered into my eyes and told me that they were vampires. I just laughed and playfully pushed her shoulder. Then I glanced at Sienna. Her face filled with shock at what Raven had blurted out. I didn't know what kind of sick joke they were playing on me, but it seemed beyond cruel when I was already suffering. I demanded to know why they were making fun of me, and then attempted to run off to my room where I could burst into tears without an audience. After my third step, my body stopped, turned around and sat back on the couch.

"It took a while for them to calm me down enough to release me from their trance, but once I was free, we spent the entire afternoon talking. They went into great detail about every aspect of their lives and openly answered all of my questions. When we finished, Sienna told me that joining her family was my choice, and that they'd always love me regardless of what I decided. If I joined them, I'd have to assume a new identity, which would mean the end of my professional painting career.

"As I sat thinking about everything I'd just heard, I realized that they were still the same people I'd spent the last two months with, the same people I loved. And what I'd always enjoyed about painting was the way that it made me feel, how it allowed me to express myself. I never thought of art as a business. I didn't need to exhibit or sell my work– as long as I could continue to paint. That's all that mattered to me. I'd seen a glimpse of what my life would be like without them during the past week, and I wanted no part of it. Picking up on my thoughts, Sienna pulled me into her arms and called me her daughter for the first time.

"They'd lived in New York for over five years already, but Sienna thought it'd be best to wait until after I was changed before we moved. While I worked with them to strengthen my arm and prepare for my transformation, I finished the five paintings I'd been commissioned to do, the last paintings that Mary Jewel ever produced."

Ruby's olive-colored cheeks took on a rosy hue as she dipped her brush into the whites and grays she'd mixed, her gaze focused somewhere south of my waist. Bring on the bubbles.

"I'm afraid I didn't take to feeding like you did. The first time I watched them I didn't even make it to the bathroom before throwing up. It was almost three weeks before I tried again, and I got sick even faster the second time. I didn't think they were monsters or anything– I just couldn't stand the sight of blood or the thought of drinking it. Sienna was getting really worried. She wouldn't change me unless I fed with them first."

"What'd you do?" I took the opportunity to work some of the stiffness out of my neck before glancing sideways at her.

"Since watching obviously wasn't helping, I thought I might as well just try feeding. The next time they fed, I went first. Raven blindfolded me and held the woman's wrist up to my mouth while I swallowed a couple of mouthfuls. It tasted gross, but I managed to keep it down.

"Sienna held my naming ceremony later that night. I wish I still had the dress Raven gave me. It was a navy blue floor-length gown with a square neck and a slender waistline. The sleeves came down about half way to my elbow and were puffed on the shoulders. Combined with the extravagant necklace, bracelets and earrings, I felt like royalty. You have me to thank for the blood part of the ceremony. To show them that I really was willing to give my life like I'd pledged, I cut my palm with a letter opener and held it up to Raven's mouth. She was reluctant at first, but then she drank from me, as did Sienna.

"On the last day of March, Sienna carefully checked my body and determined that I was ready. She bound me to my bed and strapped my mouth shut just like she'd done for Raven, and then blindfolded me and placed cotton in my ears. I was also the first to go naked, since Sienna had some trouble checking Raven's body for injury with the straps cinching her robe to her body. On the upside, the urinary catheter had been invented by then, so I didn't have to pee into a bedpan.

"As it turns out, the blindfold really didn't do any good— I could open my eyes and look right through it. That's why we use the medical tape now. Your fitted mouthpiece will be a hell of a lot more comfortable than having your teeth smashed together with leather straps around your chin. Other than that, you'll be going through basically the same preparation process that I did.

"It took almost thirty hours for me to complete the change. Raven had tried to tell me what to expect, but I didn't think it would be as bad as she was making it out to be. I didn't listen to her like I should have. As soon as I swallowed the blood, I started to panic. I felt as if a hundred knives were being jabbed into my stomach. My heart raced dangerously fast, and I struggled to get enough air through my nose. I was sure that I was going to die. That's why I was so candid with you earlier about how much it's going to hurt. You really do need to prepare yourself. Don't stick your head in the sand like I did."

"This might be a stupid question," I said, putting my arms and left leg back in the hot tub to rest. "But if everyone can still read my mind until the transformation is almost finished, why couldn't someone just trance me and block all the pain?"

She gave me a thoughtful look. "That's certainly not a stupid question— it seems logical enough. Unfortunately, in order for us to trance people they need to have stable brain processes that we can both detect and manipulate. The change is like electroshock therapy. Your brain is overwhelmed with signals from your body that it doesn't understand, and your brain cells themselves are being mutated. There's just too much instability for us to control. Our ability to read your mind will also be greatly diminished, even in the beginning of the process. All we'll be able to pick up are your conscious thoughts."

"Crap," I grumbled. "It was worth a try."

"Absolutely." We both giggled while I resumed my pose.

"By the time we were ready to move, war was looming in Europe, so we went to Dallas instead. Sienna converted an entire room into a decked-out art studio for me. For the first time since college, I was free to paint whatever I wanted. I didn't need to worry about damaging my image, what the art critics would think or whether or not someone would buy them. It was liberating. The walls were soon filled with various styles of paintings, from scenic landscapes to some of the best abstract pieces I've ever done."

I was struck by how much of her human life had revolved around her artwork– her rocky relationship with her parents, moving to New York, starting her own business, becoming famous, and meeting Raven and Sienna. There'd been no mention of falling in love or any lifelong friends she'd been forced to leave behind. Sienna had used it to ease her transition, just like buying a horse for Raven or, in my case, a sprawling tennis club, but if the lack of paintings on our rather plain walls was any indication, her artwork seemed to play a very small part in her life now. Could eternal life make you grow tired of even your most passionate interests? Would I grow to hate dancing and playing tennis after seventy or eighty years? What if I didn't find new things I was interested in to replace them?

"That's why belonging to a tight-knit coven is so important," Ruby responded to my increasingly panicked train of thought. "Vampires that try the whole lone wolf thing never last more than a few decades. Having all that time to themselves slowly drives them insane. Eventually, they either start living so wildly that other vampires in the area have to put them down or they just let themselves fade away. I still enjoy painting occasionally, but it's just one of dozens of hobbies I have now. We constantly throw ourselves into new things as a family and encourage each other to branch out. For me, that started with learning to fight.

Sienna worked with me every day on basic sword techniques, physical maneuvers and sparring. After about a month Raven joined in, and I got my first taste of live combat. Even though I was way out of my league, it was by far the most enjoyable thing that I'd ever done. You're going to love it. You'll discover things your body can do that will just blow you away."

Raven had made it out like they trained constantly, so I was surprised I hadn't gotten a chance to watch by now. "I've been dying to see you guys go at it."

"We talked about letting you watch, but Sienna decided it just wasn't worth the risk. Things get really crazy in there." Ruby paused and gave me a devious grin. "Luckily, you sleep like a rock."

"Damn it!" I splashed my fist angrily into the water. "I've been waiting for a month for you guys to fight, and you've been doing it the whole time?"

Ruby gazed tenderly into my eyes. "You won't have to wait much longer– you'll be a vampire in just over a week."

This was it– my last week as a human. I'd already started to drag out my meals, knowing that it might be the last time I ate that particular food. "Is there anything I need to do differently the last few days?"

"We'll take you to get your legs, armpits and bikini area waxed tomorrow. You'll also need to wear multiple layers of clothing to give you some extra padding in case you bump into anything. You won't be working out anymore or doing anything physical at all. But the hardest thing by far will be your diet.

"Even though your transformation isn't until Monday, you won't get any solid food after Wednesday. You'll be placed on a full liquid diet on Thursday and Friday, clear liquids only on Saturday and will get nothing but water on Sunday. You'll have the added pleasure of getting an enema on Saturday and Sunday to clean out anything that's left. I know all that may sound crazy, but if you had any food in your stomach you'd throw up during the transformation, which could kill you. And while undigested food in your intestines would likely pass through okay, there's no sense taking a chance. If you were to develop a blockage, it'd be fatal."

"Sounds won-der-ful," I said, drawing it out for extra sarcastic effect. *When am I going to learn to quit asking questions?*

After a couple minutes of silence I glanced up at Ruby. It didn't appear like she planned to continue her story, and there was still so much I wanted to know. "So who's the guy in the picture next to your bed?"

The corners of her mouth rose up in a droll smile. "That would be my husband, Kelly."

My brows shot up to my hairline. So much for her supposed lack of a love life. "Your what?"

She laughed. "You heard me right– we got married in 1978. The trip to Hawaii I told you about earlier was for our honeymoon. I guess you could say we have a pretty unconventional marriage. We get together for two to three weeks several times a year, taking turns between him coming to stay with us and me going to live with his coven. We go on a couple trips alone each year as well. We're both extremely close to our families and decided together that we'd be happier this way. I'll warn ya, Brooke, when we do get together, I have a hard time keeping my hands off of him. Raven just about moved out the last time he visited."

I didn't doubt that given their lengthy separations. The thought of having a pseudo-brother was kind of exciting. "When do I get to meet him?"

"Very soon actually– he's flying in on December first. Adding a member to one of our families means a great deal to both of us."

"Awesome! How'd you guys meet?"

"Sandy introduced us. Well, technically Maria Glass did I guess. It was 1970. We were living in Los Angeles at the time and had just met Maria. I'll let her explain how we met. One night at a beach party, she introduced us to a friend of hers who she surfed with. Even though they'd been friends for several years, she had no idea Kelly was a vampire. I thought he was nice and incredibly hot, but nothing happened between us right away. Kelly came to visit Sandy several times after she joined our family. We began to spend more and more time together when he stopped by until he finally built up the courage to ask me out. I was worried about what Sandy would think, but she couldn't have been happier for us. She was my maid of honor at our wedding."

"Who else is in Kelly's family?" Given her marriage, I assumed we'd be spending quite a bit of time with our in-laws. Hopefully our families got along okay.

"He has two brothers, Kevin and Chris, and a younger sister named Melanie. Cody is the Patriarch of his coven. Melanie loves it when I come to visit. I think she gets pretty tired of being surrounded by guys all of the time."

"I bet. It'd be cool to have a brother, but there's no way I'd want to be the only girl."

"Now that you know I'm married, there's something I've been dying to show you." Ruby hurried over to me and held out her left hand. "It's been really hard not wearing it for the last two months, but I knew it'd prompt a lot of questions. I wanted to have a chance to get to know you first."

Her ring was white gold and had a huge round center stone with two pear-shaped side stones. "Damn, girl! That's quite a rock."

"He claims that he picked it out all by himself, but I'm pretty sure Sandy helped him." Ruby admired her ring for a moment longer then walked back to her easel.

"So when did you get into computers?" On the surface it seemed odd that a former artist would pursue such a technical profession, but writing code and configuring systems required plenty of creativity in their own right. Just look at all the brilliant minds who entertained themselves by developing viruses capable of crippling billion dollar companies.

"Sandy got me a Macintosh for my birthday when they first came out in the eighties. I took to it right away. Computers were starting to be used more and more at government facilities, colleges, hospitals and police stations. We needed to be able to access their systems in order to make life easier for us. I got my bachelor's degree in computer science from the University of Washington in 1990, but I've taught myself far more than I ever learned in school.

"That just about does it," Ruby said, inspecting her work. "You can get out now. I'll step out for a minute to let you freshen up and get dressed, but don't peek until I come back, okay?"

"I'll be good," I promised. If I happened to catch a glimpse as I walked into my bedroom, it'd be purely accidental."

"Brooke!" Ruby scolded from the hallway.

Okay, okay—I won't look! Being covert around here was impossible. Everyone gathered in my bedroom just as I finished getting dressed.

"Close your eyes." Ruby whispered. When I complied, I heard her step into the bathroom to retrieve the painting.

Sienna gasped when she brought it into the room. "Oh Ruby, it's beautiful!"

"Brooke's going to love it!" Sandy added.

"Can I see it?" I shouted impatiently.

Ruby giggled, leaning her head up to my ear. "Open up, sis."

As soon as I opened my eyes, I was speechless. Beautiful didn't even begin to describe it. The scene was painted in exquisite detail, but it didn't just capture what I'd looked like lying in the tub like a picture. Everything I'd felt was somehow embedded within the paint. As I studied the portrait, my mind drifted off into peaceful bliss.

I didn't realize that I was crying until Ruby stepped in front of me and wiped my cheeks. "I'm so happy you like it."

Chapter Twenty-Two
The Last Supper

"Are you sure you wouldn't rather have Sienna help you?" Sandy asked with a panicked expression on her face. "I was never much of a cook, and this looks really complicated."

"No backing out now– you've already seen the Water's secret lasagna recipe!" We both laughed.

I'd gotten my grandma's recipe from my dad early that morning. He was a bit surprised, since I'd never shown any great interest in cooking, but there was no way I was going to settle for anything less for my last meal. She'd always made lasagna for me when she came to visit on my birthday. I remembered watching her throw it together as she carried on a conversation– no measuring, no checking and re-checking the recipe. I don't even know if you could call this a recipe. A pinch, an oversized handful, add to taste, a fair amount… How the hell was I supposed to decipher this?

Sandy giggled. "You're not exactly instilling confidence in me, girl."

Smiling, I stopped slicing up the zucchini and turned toward her. "Sandy, I don't mean to– "

"I know," she interrupted before I could finish the sentence, obviously aware of what I was about to ask even without reading my mind. "I'm sorry I haven't opened up to you before now. I guess I've been putting it off because it's hard for me to talk about the early years of my life. Just thinking about that time brings back a lot of painful memories."

"Oh God, I'm sorry."

She placed her finger and thumb under my chin, silencing my concern. "There's nothing to be sorry about. I want to share this with you.

"I was born in 1949 in North Carolina. Though I wouldn't really say I'm from there since we moved when I was three. My dad was in the Army, so we moved around a lot when I was young. He wasn't the stereotypical drill sergeant father. He was goofy and loving and had a great sense of humor. He always managed to bring out the lighter side in my mom, who was a little more uptight than he was. She'd get a job on base wherever we moved– house cleaning, child care, whatever was available. We never had a dime to spare, but we were happy.

"Shortly after I turned thirteen, we moved to Los Angeles and lived off base for the first time. My dad was planning to retire in a couple of years, and they'd always wanted to live in California. It was awesome– there were three beaches within a ten minute drive of our house. Even though it scared my mom to death, I began to take surfing lessons right away. I pretty much lived at the beach from then on, quickly making friends with all the locals. My dad filed his retirement papers in February of 1965 and was due to be released from active duty by the end of the year.

"A week after he filed, we received a notice that his unit was being deployed to Vietnam, and he wouldn't be allowed to retire until he served a full four-year tour. We were devastated. He was forty-four years old and had already served two tours in Korea. The night before he left, we went for a long walk along the beach. He told me how hard it was on my mom when he was deployed before, and asked me to watch over her while he was gone. I was only sixteen, but I promised him that I would.

"After he left we wrote letters to him every day. Each week he'd send us three letters in return: one to each of us that we were to keep private and one that we read together. I tried to calm my mom down when we didn't receive our letters the first week of September, but when nothing arrived the following week, we were both terrified. His commanding officer at the base came to our house late that Sunday. They weren't…even able to recover his body." Sandy covered her eyes with her hand as she began to tear up, taking deep, shaky breaths.

"I'm so sorry, Sandy." I pulled her forward and cradled her head against my chest, giving her soft pats on the back.

When her eyes lifted to meet mine, they were full of pain, and her lips were still quivering. "God… I didn't think it'd be this hard."

Needing a break, Sandy drained the lasagna noodles and coated them with olive oil while I stirred the sauce in the Crockpot. After combining the parmesan, ricotta and mozzarella cheeses, I got out a large glass pan. We layered the noodles, cheese mixture, hamburger, vegetables and sauce, and then topped it with a thick layer of mozzarella before throwing it in the oven.

We both leaned up against the counter, and Sandy reached over and took my hand. "My mother really fell apart after he died. She started to drink obsessively and stay out most of the night. Whenever she wasn't drunk, she was crying. I tried to help out as much as I could, making her meals, cleaning up after her, doing the laundry and encouraging her to stop drinking.

Dangerous Waters

Unfortunately things just kept getting worse.

"She brought Dennis home for the first time about six months later. He was an ex-convict and even a bigger drunk than she was. At first I left whenever he came around, but before long he'd moved in with us. Less than a week had passed before they got into a huge fight. After about an hour of yelling at each other, he called my mom a worthless whore and slapped her hard across the face. I couldn't stand to see him treat her like that. I jumped up from the couch and pushed him with all my strength, knocking him to the floor. When he got up, he punched me so hard that I blacked out until the next morning. I pleaded with my mom to call the police, but she wouldn't do it. She said that the fight was my fault and that I shouldn't have provoked him. I didn't know what to do. I had to find a way to save her.

"One night after I got home from the beach, he cornered me in the living room and announced that they were getting married. When I begged my mom not to do it, he grabbed me by the hair, threw me down and put his knee in my stomach to pin me there. He screamed that he expected his daughter to respect him, and then hit me twice in the face. My nose and lip were bleeding when he let me up, but I stared right back at him and shouted that I'd rather be dead than be his daughter. After he beat me severely, he threw me out of the house and told me that if he ever saw me again, I'd get my wish.

"I was only seventeen and I was homeless. As scared as I was of him, I knew I couldn't just leave everything I owned behind. I waited until I was sure they'd passed out, and then snuck into the house and got all of the stuff out of my room. After my car was packed, I went into their bedroom, kissed my mom on the cheek and told her that I loved her. That was the last time that I ever saw her.

"I drove to my best friend Julie's house in Santa Monica, waking her entire family up at three a.m. Her dad was good friends with my father, so I was hoping that he'd take me in. Julie had told him about my previous run in with Dennis, but he was still shocked when he saw my face. It took several hours of pleading with him and his wife before I managed to talk them out of calling the police. I was so scared of what Dennis would do to my mom and Julie's family if they turned him in.

"They told me that I was more than welcome to stay with them as long as I wanted to. They had a three-bedroom home with three kids, so space was tight. Julie's younger sister Katie, who'd been sharing the room with her, moved into the other bedroom with her older brother Jack. He was eighteen, so I'm sure he wasn't too thrilled to be sharing his room with an eleven-year-old girl, but he never complained."

I giggled. "Gee, I wonder why. A horny eighteen-year-old boy sees a hot seventeen-year-old girl move in, and you think he's going to complain?"

"Good point," she said with a grin.

"I started working part-time with Julie at the surf shop where we met while I finished up my senior year in high school. After graduation, I enrolled at a beauty school to become a hair stylist. I'd always enjoyed playing around with my friend's hair. Shortly after I got my license, I leased a work station from a hair salon near Zuma Beach. Julie's parents bought me most of the startup supplies I needed as a graduation present. It was great to be able to set my own hours so I could still work at the surf shop and enjoy the beach.

"On a Saturday morning in early June three girls– obviously not locals– came into the surf shop and started asking me all kinds of questions about surfing. I was the only one in the store at the time, and the place was packed like it was every Saturday, so I was trying to do a hundred things at once.

"You have to keep in mind that we had outsiders come in all the time who'd talk your ear off for four hours and not buy anything, or would return everything the next day after they tried it once. We learned to make things hard on them to make sure they were serious before we wasted a lot of our time. So I glanced up from the board I was waxing and told them as rudely as possible to hurry along to their nail appointments or lunch at the club and let me get back to work. You should've seen Sienna's face– I swear to God she thought about ripping my throat out right then and there in front of everyone.

"I heard her whisper something to Raven as they left the store about how she was sorry this had to happen on her birthday. I ran out the door after them to apologize, and then spent as much time as I could with them during the rest of the morning. After helping them pick out everything they needed, I gave them the insider price that we usually reserved for locals. When they asked me if I knew anyone that could help them learn, I offered to show them the basics myself when I got off work. Sienna gave me a warm hug before they left, which made me feel a lot better.

"It was almost four p.m. by the time I met them. After changing into our wetsuits, we made our way down to the beach to practice paddle-out and pop-up maneuvers in the sand. It usually takes beginners at least twenty minutes to get the hang of it, so I was stunned when they all nailed their first three attempts. Since they had that down, I took them into the water to practice on a couple of small waves near shore. They were all talking smack to each other, who was going to stay on the longest and be the first one up. I could tell they were having a great time.

"We waded out about seventy yards and waited for the next set to come in. When we all paddled to catch the first wave, I couldn't believe that I was struggling to keep up with them. That was nothing compared to the surprise I felt when they all popped up onto their boards and rode their first wave all the way to the shore. Granted, the waves at Zuma aren't monsters– it's where most kids learn– but I'd never heard of anyone learning to surf that fast. It'd taken me almost a week to stay on for any length of time.

"After their third wave they asked me where we could go for more of a challenge. I offered to take them to Huntington Beach the next morning and exchanged their Malibu surf boards for thrusters, which are shorter and have three fins instead of one to allow you to make quick moves. We met at the beach at six a.m. I took them to the north side of the pier, which has much smaller waves, and showed them how to pivot and turn to ride up the face of a wave and back down into the barrel. In spite of their physical gifts, they all fell several times during their first few runs, but by eight a.m. they looked like they'd been surfing for years.

"Even though I'd promised, I was hesitant to take them to the south side of the pier– the double breaking waves are a challenge even for expert surfers. I'd waited almost five years before I felt confident enough to surf there, and this was only their second day. I spotted Gina and Eric on the beach, two of my surfing buddies, and asked them to evaluate Ruby, Raven and Sienna on our next run. When we got back, they gave me a nod and made the quarter-mile walk with us down the beach. We all bit it a couple times, some of the falls were pretty nasty, but there was no doubt they belonged. By the last run they were nailing maneuvers that I still had a hard time with. I couldn't believe they were already better than I was.

"We had such a good time hanging out together all day that I invited them to the beach party that we were throwing late that night. These were always 'locals only,' but Gina and Eric liked them too, so I was sure it'd be okay. I was dead tired, but somehow I managed to put nine hours in at the salon before getting some sleep and making my way back to the surf shop to meet them. After exchanging hugs, Sienna took me aside and thanked me again for everything I'd done for them. I told her how great it was spending the day with them and that I hoped we could continue to do stuff together. I couldn't have been happier when she asked if tomorrow was too soon.

"Almost everyone I knew was gathered around the bonfire when we arrived. Gina and Eric told everybody how Raven, Ruby and Sienna had held their own on south pier on their second day of surfing. Just like that, they were 'in.' Julie scampered up to me and smiled when I introduced her as my sister. Kelly followed shortly after, picking me up and twirling me around before giving me a soft kiss on the cheek.

At that time, I couldn't understand why Sienna, Ruby and Raven were so shocked. He was the one who taught me to surf when I was thirteen, and we'd been close friends ever since. As confused as I was by their reaction, I was even more startled by his. He stood in front of me almost defensively while I introduced them, acknowledging them only with a slight nod of his head. I slowly made my way around the rest of the circle, trying not to leave anyone out in the mass of people.

"We spent the rest of the night drinking, dancing and just kicking back on the beach. After far too many beers, several of us decided to go skinny dipping. When I woke up a few hours later, I was fully clothed and had a blanket over me. I couldn't remember even finding my clothes again, let alone putting them on, and I sure as hell hadn't brought a blanket with me.

"I made my way over to Sienna and Kelly, who were sitting alone by the fire. They both greeted me fondly, but whatever they'd been discussing was dropped. Since I was falling asleep, I decided to head home. Sienna jingled my keys in front of me and said that I wasn't driving myself anywhere. I was too tired to argue so I agreed to let her take me, with Ruby and Raven following behind.

"I'd moved out of Julie's parent's house when I got my job at the hair salon and was living in a low rent apartment in a pretty seedy part of LA. The place was a complete dump, but it was all I could afford within driving distance of the beach. Julie was staying in the dorms at UCLA, and the rest of my friends were either still living at home or even more broke than I was.

"Sienna grew more concerned with every turn we took. By the time we pulled up in front of my building I swear there were tears in her eyes. She insisted on walking me to my door, which I didn't mind since I was still pretty hammered. After she helped me into bed, I noticed her inspecting the apartment on her way out.

"When I got out of work at the hair salon the next day, Sienna was waiting in the parking lot. She told me that she'd gotten me a gift, but I'd have to follow her out to their house to get it. I figured they were throwing me a party or something and willingly went along. After a short drive, we turned onto the Ventura freeway and headed out to Agoura Hills, which is just north of Malibu and Zuma Beach. When she pulled into a sprawling estate, I figured she'd missed her turn, until the iron gates began to open. I followed behind her in disbelief while we made our way up the circle drive to their beautiful two-story Victorian inspired mansion.

"Ruby and Raven came out to greet me, and Sienna led us all on a tour of their home. After slowly making our way through all of the gorgeous rooms downstairs, we went up a marble staircase to the second floor. There was a large red bow on the first door on the left side of the hall. When I peered at Sienna, she just smiled and told me to open it. The room was amazing of course, with all of the amenities you'd expect in one of our bedrooms, but what caught my eye at the time were the things from my apartment. I hurried over to the closet, and sure enough, all of my clothes were in there.

"I really didn't understand what was going on. Three girls I liked a lot but had only known for two days had moved me into their house without even asking me. It's not like I had any sentimental feelings for the shithole I was living in, but I almost felt like I'd been kidnapped. When I turned back around, all of Sienna's excitement was gone, replaced with sadness and pain from my reaction. I thought about what she'd seen when she drove me home the night before and how much it had bothered her. Apparently she didn't want her new friend living in a place like that and was willing to open her home up to me. I threw my arms around her and thanked her for her generous gift. Sienna happily pointed out that both of my jobs were within a twenty minute drive, along with all of our favorite beaches.

"The rest of the summer flew by. When I wasn't working, we were at the beach, surfing five or six times a week. All of my friends loved them, especially Gina and Eric. Eric followed Raven around like a lovesick puppy most of the time, but never managed to get anywhere with her. Gina was a freshman studying fine art at USC and was just starting to learn to paint. Before long she was at our house almost as much as I was, working with Ruby in her studio. Ruby loved having a protégé to teach— I don't think I've ever seen Ruby as happy as she was that summer. Gina went on to become a successful artist in her own right. We have a couple of her paintings hanging in our LA house."

"What about their scent?" I was surprised that they'd bring people into their house so freely, even into closed bedrooms.

Sandy grinned. "Since all of us smelled like a combination of surf wax, tanning oil and sea salt, they didn't need to worry about anyone detecting their scent. LA is really the easiest place for us to live.

"On my natural birthday, October fifth, Sienna, Ruby and Raven planned a private party for me at our house and a huge get together with all of our friends later that night on the beach. I had a couple hours' worth of work to do at the surf shop to finish closing up for the winter, but I thought I'd be able to get out by eleven at the latest. Sienna dropped me off since she had some shopping to do anyway.

"I worked as fast as I could, anxious to get on with the fun part of my day. By ten-thirty the windows were boarded up, and everything was locked up tight. Sienna wasn't back yet, so I decided to take a walk on the beach. As I crossed the parking lot, an old beat up station wagon came barreling up the driveway right toward me. I managed to dive into the bushes to avoid being hit, but when the car screeched to a stop right against the curb, I was trapped.

"By the time I got to my feet, Dennis's hands were around my throat. He beat me mercilessly while he asked me over and over again where my mom was. I had no idea of course– I hadn't spoken to her since the night I left. The surf shop sat up on a hill from the main road so no one could see us, and the traffic noise drowned out my screams. He lifted me up in the air and slammed me down on the cement, causing my head to whip back against the concrete. After straddling my body with his legs, he continued to pound my face. I tried to raise my arms to protect myself, but he had them pinned under him. Once I could no longer move he got up and began kicking me in the ribs. When I started to cough up blood, I knew he was going to kill me.

"I'm not sure how I stayed conscious, but I suddenly realized that he'd stopped beating me and was talking to someone else. I opened my eyes and saw Sienna standing in front of him. I tried to scream for her to run, but all I managed to do was cough up more blood. Then she attacked. In a blur of motion both of his legs were severed at the knees before his entire body was launched over sixty feet in the air, crashing against the garbage bin at the end of the parking lot. There wasn't any doubt he was dead.

"Sienna rushed me to the hospital where I flat lined twice before they stabilized me. I had four broken ribs along with a broken nose, cheekbone and jaw, and a severe concussion. One of my ribs had punctured my lung, which almost killed me. When I woke up the next morning, Sienna was sitting next to the bed. She hesitantly reached out to take my hand, afraid of how I'd react.

Dangerous Waters

After what I'd seen I knew she wasn't human, but I didn't care– she was a hero to me. She'd saved my life and killed the bastard who had tortured me and my mom for years. I couldn't speak, but I tightly squeezed her hand. She leaned over, kissed me on the forehead and told me how much she loved me. It took four surgeries and over two weeks in the hospital before I was finally ready to go home.

"Sienna told the police that she hit Dennis with her car when she saw him assaulting me. Given the damage to his body, they believed her. The investigation was closed as soon as they were able to speak with me. After corroborating her story, I explained what happened before Sienna arrived, and then told them about the incidents at my parent's house a few years earlier. Based on the extent of my injuries, the District Attorney concluded that his death was justifiable homicide and charges were never filed. If I wouldn't have been so badly injured, I'm sure Sienna would've just disposed of his body and said she found me that way, but she knew she didn't have time. All she thought about was saving me.

"Sienna told me what she was on the way home from the hospital. Compared to the body snatching alien image that had been running through my mind, being a vampire almost seemed normal. I nonchalantly replied 'Oh... okay,' like she'd mentioned that we needed to stop for milk on the way home. She looked so bewildered by my reaction that I couldn't keep from laughing, even though it killed my ribs. Sienna went on to explain everything to me, including what would happen when we got home and the choice I'd have to make once I got better.

"Once she got me settled into bed, Ruby and Raven joined her, and they each put me under their trance. Even though they weren't meeting me for the first time, like the night Raven brought you home, it was still important for me to demonstrate my trust now that I knew what they were. My feelings for them hadn't changed– they were my family, and I loved and trusted them completely.

"I tried to watch them feed for the first time a couple of days later. At first everything was fine. Ruby and Sienna began to feed, and, much like you, I couldn't believe how natural it seemed. The sight of blood didn't bother me and neither did watching them drink it. I even wondered what it would taste like. Then I glanced at the young woman they were feeding on and thought about everyone who would miss her: parents, brothers and sisters, friends, maybe even a husband. God, what if she was someone's mother? Before I even realized what I was doing, I was begging them to stop.

"Sienna quickly tranced me and walked me out of the room. Once we were in my bedroom, she released me and motioned for me to sit next to her on the bed. I started to apologize for what I'd done, but she just smiled and kissed me on the cheek. She said that she still felt remorse for each person that she fed upon, and that if that ever stopped, she would truly feel like a monster. She explained how she'd learned to cope with her new life by finding a sense of purpose and helping those in need. She told me about the tens of thousands of people they'd saved with their charity during various natural disasters, and the hundreds of thousands more who had benefited from the scientific and medical research that they'd funded.

"I thought about what she said for several days. By the time they fed again, I'd decided to join them. When Sienna handed the man's arm to me, I placed my lips on his wrist and swallowed several mouthfuls of blood. As soon as I'd finished, they all welcomed me to the family.

"I received my new name later that night in a ritual that was pretty much identical to yours. I'll never forget the black, floor-length halter-neck dress that Ruby dressed me in. It was so beautiful.

"After being home from the hospital for three weeks, I was able to chew without any pain, but it took almost two months before my ribs quit bothering me. By the end of November I'd fully recovered from the attack. I spent the next six weeks working with Sienna and Raven to rebuild my strength and prepare for my transformation.

"We celebrated my vampire birthday the third week of December, three weeks ahead of the planned date. Raven got me tons of new clothes, and Sienna bought me my first new car, a gorgeous red jaguar convertible. My most memorable gift by far though was from Ruby. Her painting of me lying naked in the sand on Zuma Beach is still the most precious thing that I own. I'm on my belly looking at her with my legs crossed and raised up behind me. My arms are positioned under me, lifting my upper body off the ground. I can almost feel the sand on my body when I stare at it."

"That sounds beautiful. When can I see it?" I'd already seen the rest of their paintings, which were all even more stunning than I'd imagined.

"It's in my closet– you can help me hang it up after dinner tonight."

"Cool." With any luck hanging her painting wasn't all we'd be doing. The sensual look in her eyes was almost enough to make me skip dinner entirely.

Sandy traced my lower lip with her thumb, and then stole a quick kiss before she continued. "On January eleventh Sienna looked me over and prepared me for my transformation. We used a custom-built bed with more comfortable straps, and I got to wear a fitted mouth guard and have my eyes taped shut, but other than that my preparation was the same as Ruby's. When it was finally over I was shocked to hear that only twenty-two hours had passed– it felt like it'd been at least a week. After what happened to Ruby, everyone made sure I knew what to expect going in and that I wasn't making light of it. To mentally prepare myself I used the pain I'd felt after Dennis almost killed me as kind of a benchmark and assumed I would feel even worse than that. It sounds weird to say this, but I wish you had something similar to think about. It really seemed to help me. As bad as the pain was, I was never afraid and managed to stay relatively calm."

"What about when Sienna bit me and broke my arm?" I asked, trying to get some kind of gauge of how that would compare.

Sandy thought for a moment. "If that's the most pain you've ever been in, then it's probably the best thing for you to use, but that's not even close to what you'll feel."

I'd collapsed and just about fainted from the overwhelming pain. If that was nothing compared to what I was about to go through, I needed to spend a lot more time preparing myself. Sandy nodded her head in agreement.

"Two days after I was changed, Kelly stopped by to visit. He twirled me around and kissed me the same way he always did and asked how his little magpie was doing. I instantly felt like myself again. After my naming ceremony, Sienna had told me that Kelly was a vampire, when she was sure I was going to join them. She also explained why he reacted the way he did on the beach when he first met them, how protective he felt toward me. When Sienna and Kelly spoke after the beach party that night, she promised that they wouldn't expose themselves to me or harm me in any way. After I was attacked, Sienna told Kelly what happened and got his permission to offer me the choice. While he never wanted me to become a vampire, he thanked her for saving my life and gave her his blessing."

I looked up at her with a smirk. "His little magpie?"

She grinned. "When I was a teenager I hated the name Maria, so my friends used to call me Maggie. Kelly started calling me his little magpie when he was giving me surfing lessons, and the name just kind of stuck.

"Feeding was incredibly difficult for me at first. Sienna had told me how much our corporations donated each year and all of the research they did, but I knew they'd be doing that whether I was a vampire or not. In order to ease my guilt I needed to find something I could do myself to make a difference. Sienna encouraged me to find a cause that I felt strongly about and come up with a way that we could help.

"When I thought about my life, I realized how drastically things changed when my father was killed, how my mom and I didn't have anyone to turn to. If we would've been provided with ongoing counseling along with financial help, everything might have been different. My mom never would have become an alcoholic or met Dennis. She could have gone back to school and gotten a job to support us on her own.

"After doing some research on charities and government programs, I found that there was nothing out there that provided the type of help I had in mind for families that had lost a loved one through military service. I didn't want just another charity funded by the family money though. I was determined to raise at least some of the money myself.

"When I told Sienna about my idea, she went right to work. She setup a meeting with the lawyers, accountants and business executives who handled all of our philanthropic work in the US and helped me prepare a presentation to share with them. I was so nervous– I'd never had any training in business or public speaking. She worked with me for weeks before we flew to New York for our meeting.

"The first part of the pitch was a personal testimonial. I told them all about what had happened to me and my mom after my father was killed and how there was no one there to provide the help that we had so desperately needed. Then I went over my ideas, how we could recruit counselors, therapists and other volunteers and solicit donations to fund the new charity. I don't know if it was my speech or them knowing who had introduced me, but everyone loved the idea. I spent the next year working with them to sign up volunteers, open our regional offices and launch our public awareness campaign. It was exhausting work, but I loved it. I got to meet so many of the families that benefited from the help we were providing, and I could tell that we were already making a real difference.

"The first year our corporations provided over seventy percent of the money, but by the end of the third year, outside donations accounted for over half. Today we have over fifteen thousand volunteers and have several offices in all fifty states. Private donations now account for over ninety percent of our funding. The only statistic that matters to me though is that we've already helped over ten thousand families. While I had to quit being involved in the daily operations in 1977, I still do what I can behind the scenes to help."

"God Sandy, that's awesome. I'm really impressed."

"Thanks."

Sandy buttered the French bread and sprinkled it with garlic powder while I mixed the vinegar and olive oil for the dressing. After we stuck the bread in the oven, she headed toward the living room.

"There's no hubby I should know about, is there?" I called after her, only half-kidding. Getting my sisters to talk about the guys in their lives was like trying to break a Russian spy.

She turned back toward me and laughed. "Definitely not. My love life has pretty much been snoozeville so far, a couple of crazy weekends, but nothing serious."

"What's the deal?"

The playfulness in her face was replaced with confusion. "The deal?"

"You guys are all like 'Oh, Brooke, you'll meet hundreds of hot vamps.' Either the dating pool has been seriously exaggerated, or you're not telling me everything. I'm not even in your league, so if you can't land at least one boyfriend in almost forty years, I'm pretty much screwed."

"I'm...." Sandy began before dropping her gaze to her feet. "We're not– fishing in the same pool."

"Um, what?"

"I'm gay, Brooke. It was really shitty of me to keep that from you, especially since we've been flirting around so much, but I hope that doesn't change how you feel about me."

I just stood there, trying to wrap my head around what she was saying. The fact that she liked women wasn't a surprise– she was obviously into kissing me – I guess I'd just figured she was bi-curious like I was. "But in the car on the way to the club, you told me what to do, with condoms and stuff."

"I experimented a lot in high school. I had a good idea which way I was leaning by the end of tenth grade, but I continued to hook up with guys once in a while even after I was changed. I guess I was hoping I'd grow out of it. I didn't."

"So does this mean– "

She pressed her lips to mine, cutting me off mid-sentence. "Only you can answer that. And you're going to need time and plenty of experiences to do so. I'm not going to push you, or make ultimatums about not seeing other people. I hope you find that your feelings toward me are more than just curiosity, but if that's all it turns out to be, then I'll be happy to have helped you discover yourself. The only thing I won't tolerate is you being ashamed of your sexuality or trying to hide it. If we're going to take things any further between us, it's going to be done out in the open."

Regardless of whether they already knew, the thought of telling Sienna and the rest of my family that I was bisexual terrified me. But there was no denying how I felt. My whole body came alive when we touched. Even now I was staring at her glistening lips like a starved dog. "I'm okay with that." Suddenly the kitchen felt like it was a thousand degrees. My hands were sweating, and I was trembling so bad I had to lean back against the counter to steady myself. "I know you can't eat any of this," I said, desperate to change the subject. "But would you taste a bite of the lasagna with me when it's done?"

"I'd love to see how we did. Just don't be offended when I spit it out."

I snorted. "Deal."

I mixed up the salad and sat it on the table while I waited for the lasagna and garlic bread to finish cooking. I'd avoided eating anything all day so I could pig out as much as possible, maybe even coming back for seconds sometime before midnight if they let me. That was assuming it would turn out, of course. It'd really suck if my last meal consisted of garlic bread and salad. I leaned up to the oven door and breathed in deeply– at least it smelled good.

When the timer went off, I pulled everything out of the oven and sat it all on a wire rack to cool. The wonderful aroma made my mouth water, and the mozzarella was nice and melted on top, just the way I liked it. Once I'd finished my salad, I hurried back into the kitchen and placed an enormous piece on my plate. Even though I knew she'd only be able to chew one bite for a couple of seconds, I decided to cut Sandy a piece too.

"Come and get it!" I yelled, carrying our plates to the table. I was overjoyed when all of them came into the dining room.

Sienna locked her arms around my waist. "This is one meal that we'd never let you eat alone."

I bounced around the table, seating everyone like a maître d', and then cut three more pieces and poured them each a glass of water. After carrying everything to the table, I took a seat and anxiously waited for their reactions.

Sandy picked up her fork and took the first bite. She slid the food around in her mouth for several seconds, and then discreetly discarded it into her napkin. After rinsing her mouth, she wrapped her arm around my shoulders. "I think we did it. Damn that's good!"

Dangerous Waters

Ruby, Sienna and Raven each took a bite, savoring it for as long as they could.

When Sienna finished, she glanced at both of us. "You two are quite the team in the kitchen. I've never tasted lasagna before, but that was delicious."

"Thanks, Mom," we replied, almost in unison.

"Ah crap," Raven grumbled. "Tastes good going down too."

Ruby mouthed an obscenity under her breath. "You're not the only one. Oh well, if we're going to get sick, we might as well enjoy it. Pass me a piece of garlic bread."

"I'm sorry, you guys," I said. From what Sienna and Raven had told me, they were in for a rough night.

Raven handed a piece of bread to Ruby and took another huge bite. "Don't be– this is totally worth it." Ruby nodded her head in agreement.

I ran my fork down into the lasagna and took my first bite. It was good… really good. It may not have tasted exactly like my grandma's, but it was extremely close. I eagerly took another bite.

"All right!" Sandy cheered, giving me a high five.

I downed about half of the enormous piece I'd given myself along with three pieces of garlic bread, and then pushed back from the table– completely stuffed. I knew there was no way I'd be hungry again before midnight even if they would've let me eat again. I forced one more bite into my mouth and chewed it as slowly as I could, knowing that it was the last solid food I'd ever eat.

Chapter Twenty-Three
The Endless Day

"Time to get up, honey," Sienna whispered, softly nudging my shoulder.

I rubbed my eyes and yawned. "What time is it?"

"About four a.m. I know you're tired, but we need to get started. The longer you're in bed, the higher the risk that you'll develop blood clots before the change is completed."

I crawled out from under my covers and sat up next to her. Now that I was awake, the hunger pains returned in force. I'd planned to spend yesterday mentally preparing myself, but I found it hard to think about anything other than how hungry I was.

Sienna swept the disheveled hair out of my eyes and handed me a large glass of water. "I need you to drink this. It won't help much with the hunger, but this is the last opportunity you'll have to drink anything for at least twenty hours."

I looked at the glass with disgust. After drinking nothing but water for the last day, I'd never been so sick of it in my life, but I gulped it down and headed for the bathroom.

"Remember not to brush your teeth," Sienna reminded me when I finished washing my hands.

"Oh yeah, thanks," I said, closing the cabinet door I'd already opened half way. My hands started to shake as I removed my pajamas and slid my panties off. I took a deep breath and returned to the side of the bed, standing naked in front of her. Sienna gave me a comforting smile, and then began to closely inspect every inch of my body, from the top of my scalp to the skin between my toes.

"How are you feeling?" she asked, pressing down on the lymph nodes in my neck.

"Good." I was a nervous wreck, but I didn't feel sick or anything.

Sienna leaned in toward my mouth. "Open wide."

I opened up as wide as I could while she used a dental mirror to check my gums, teeth and tongue for any swelling or bleeding. When she was finished, she lifted my hands and looked over my nails. They were just over an inch in length

– long enough to be deadly, but not so long that I'd look like a freak. I couldn't wait to get rid of the cotton gloves that I'd worn for the last week to keep from accidentally scratching myself.

Sienna held my hands in hers, her bright eyes sparkling. "Everything looks good. Are you ready to become a vampire?"

"As ready as I'll ever be." I couldn't wait to be a vampire– it was the becoming part that scared the shit out of me.

She guided me down the hall and into the feeding room. The gurney had been replaced with a queen-sized bed that had several padded straps hanging off of it. "Go ahead and jump up on the bed. Try to align yourself with the straps so you're in the right position."

"Got it." The short end of the straps that contained the fasteners made a body-shaped outline which I easily fit myself into.

Sienna returned wearing medical gloves and holding a thin clear tube. "Okay, Brooke, I need you to spread your legs apart and lift your knees in the air."

I held my knees against my chest while she guided the catheter into me, doing my best to ignore the burning sensation as it inched its way up my urethra and into my bladder. Sienna stood up and hooked the other end of the tube to a clear bag, which she hung off the end of the bed.

After lowering my legs, she bound them into place with straps above my ankles, below and above my knees and at the very top of my thighs. The straps were tighter than I thought they'd be, but the soft padding made it bearable. Sienna continued working her way up my body, fastening straps above my hips, across my stomach and just below my breasts. My arms were secured next, with straps across the top of my hands, at my wrists, just above and below my elbows and under my shoulders. Sienna lifted a Y-shaped strap over my head, guided it down between my breasts and locked it into the strap going around my chest. When she was finished, everything below my neck was immobilized.

"She's ready," Sienna called out to the living room. Moments later all of my sisters joined me at my side.

Raven bent down and kissed me on the cheek. "I know how scary this is, but everything's going to be okay. I'll be right here the entire time."

"Thanks, Raven. Regardless of what I may think during the next few hours, I couldn't be happier to be doing this."

Sandy slowly traced her fingertips along the exposed skin on my side. When they grazed across my breast my nipples hardened, and I had to bite my lip to stifle a moan. This was so unfair. My naked, bound body was being played with like some feature attraction in an S&M exhibit, and my whole family was watching me get off on it. Showing no mercy, she bent down and gave me a deep, passionate kiss that sent my insides reeling.

"That ought to give you something better to think about," she teased. The room filled with laughter.

"Don't think I'm not going to get you back for this!" I said, still laughing.

"Promises, promises."

My cheeks burned with heat. Sandy had demanded that our relationship be out in the open. You couldn't get much more open than this. Her public display had taken the burden off me to confess words that still caught in my throat.

"Remember," she continued. "No matter how bad the pain gets, it's normal. Try to relax and just let it take its course."

"I'll try. Oh, and Sandy," I said when she took a step away. "Thanks."

She nodded, flashing an insightful smile.

Ruby reached down and tucked a couple of loose clumps of hair behind my ear. "Thank you for opening your heart up to me and becoming my friend. I can't wait for Kelly to meet you. I love you."

"I love you too, Ruby." Like a flood gate opening up, the tears began to flow, streaming down my cheeks in waves.

"My sweet angel," Sienna said, putting her fingers under my chin and kissing me on the forehead. "You're the most loving, selfless, devoted child a mother could ever hope for. Rather than just joining our family, you transformed it into something far better than it ever was before."

She reached into her pocket and pulled out a silver Celtic cross necklace that had a large green amber jewel in the center. "This is very old, handed down through many generations to my mother, one of the only things I was able to salvage from the fire. I've spoken to your sisters, and we'd all be honored to have you wear it."

"It's beautiful," I said between sniffles. "I'll cherish this for the rest of my life."

She wiped my cheeks and leaned forward and placed it around my neck. The silver chain was longer than my mother's, allowing the cross pendent to rest comfortably beneath it.

"Thank you– for everything," I muttered. "I love you so much, Mom."

Sienna cuddled up against me, and then took earplugs out of a small plastic bag, placing them in my ears and covering them with noise reduction headphones. The sound of my own breathing began to echo in the eerie silence. She held my eyelids open and squeezed ointment into my eyes, letting me blink a couple of times before taping them shut. I let out an anxious sigh when I felt her lean my head forward and touch my lips– this was it. As soon as my jaw fell open, cold blood poured into my mouth. After my third swallow the cup was taken away and the mouth guard was put in place. I could feel straps being placed over my forehead and under my chin, completely locking down my head.

It hit me. My whole body tensed as my guts twisted inside like they were being ripped apart. I tried to scream, but no air could escape my lips, so the sound came out as little more than a high-pitched whimper. The wave of excruciating pain began to spread outward from my abdomen, doubling in strength with every new cell it reached. It had only been seconds and my resolve was faltering. I wasn't strong enough to survive this.

My entire chest contracted, forcing the air out of my body. I frantically tried to breathe, but I felt like my lungs had been filled with sand. With every attempt I grew more desperate. On the edge of blacking out, I took my final gasps, like the fish I'd watched slowly suffocate in the bottom of my dad's boat. *Something's really wrong! My chest! I can't breathe! I'm dying!* I expected them to rip the mouth guard out and start CPR, but their only reaction was to take hold of my hands and caress my face, trying to comfort me and urge me on. I took three more sharp snorts through my nose, and like being handed a cup of ice cold water after crossing the most barren of deserts, precious, life-giving air returned to my lungs. My breathing was rapid and shallow, but at least I was breathing again.

When the virus reached my heart it went into wild, irregular contractions before seizing. Pressure exploded inside my chest, and I let out another blood curdling squeal. Even that indescribable pain was instantly drowned out by the lightning bolt that shot up my spine and into my brain. Having lost all control of my mind, my body started to twitch in violent spasms. Random images flooded my head: my mom breastfeeding me, the merry go round at my grade school, my dad teaching me to ride a bike. It was like watching a jumbled slide show in my own brain.

As I regained some control, I felt the pain spread into my shoulders and hips. My eyes were pounding inside my skull like a Slurpee brain freeze on steroids. Instead of wondering whether I could survive this for a second longer, I was beginning to question why I would want to. If you were sentenced to death in the electric chair, would you be grateful if it took hours to kill you instead of seconds? How could I have thought that joining them would be worth this? Nothing would be– not even bringing my mom back from the grave.

The general pain sensations coming from every part of my body were becoming infinitely more precise. Instead of receiving thousands of distinct signals, I was now receiving millions. It felt like my flesh was being boiled away in acid while hundreds of people continuously stabbed me with jagged hunting knives.

Just as I was about to beg them to put me out of my misery, a strange buffering sensation enveloped my mind. I could still tell my body was in intense pain, but it was more of a detached awareness rather than something I was fully experiencing. Almost like someone had turned the pain dimmer switch down from "pure, unimaginable hell" to "having bamboo shoved under your fingernails." If this was just some kind of endorphin high, I hoped it would last as long as possible.

Please tell me it doesn't get any worse, I thought, somewhat rhetorically.

I was surprised when I heard Sienna answer me. "You're at the worst of it, honey. You're doing really well."

How can I hear you?

"The headphones and earplugs only help to dull your increased sense of hearing. Before it's over you'll be able to clearly hear us talking in the living room even with your door closed."

Could you sing to me? I recalled how she'd helped me fall asleep after the first time I fought through Ruby's trance.

"Of course." Sienna's beautiful voice filled the room as she sang my favorite Irish lullaby. I focused on it, trying to ignore everything else in my mind.

When the fourth song ended, a different voice began to sing. *Raven?* I guessed. It didn't really sound like her, but I'd never heard her sing before.

"Does that sound okay? Sienna went to get something to drink."

It's beautiful. I didn't understand the words since she was singing in French, but it had a soothing melody. *I can't believe how much this hurts. How long has it been?*

"Try not to think about it– you're doing great."

Please? Not knowing is way worse than anything you could tell me.

There was a long pause, as if her desire to please me was at war with her own better judgment. "You're about four hours into it."

I have twenty more hours of this shit! No fucking way! Kill me, Raven. If I mean anything to you at all please do this for me. Don't make me suffer anymore.

Dangerous Waters

"There it is!" she said with a laugh. "I was beginning to worry about you. The rest of us were begging to die within minutes. Trust me, there's nothing you could say that we'd listen to right now. Just try to relax and hang in there."

You think this is funny? Fuck you, you skanky-ass bitch! You ruined my whole life! I wish Sienna would have let you rot away in that tavern with the rest of the whores!

After a prolonged silence, Raven's breathing shifted to gasps and wheezes– it was clear she was choking back tears. The infinitely small rational part of me felt horrible for what I'd said, but it was a faint whisper among a crowd of thousands.

"You know she doesn't mean that," Sienna whispered to her from somewhere near the doorway. "No more than you meant what you said to me when you were in her position."

"That doesn't make it any easier to hear. I'm sorry– " Her footfalls faded as she darted from the room.

Sienna stepped forward and glided her fingers along my cheek. "Try not to beat yourself up, honey. She'll be okay. None of this matters in the end."

I couldn't make myself care whether she forgave me or jumped out in front of a bus. All that mattered was the pain. While the dulling effect from the mind-haze seemed to be holding, my body had adjusted to it. A tub of boiling water would feel cool to the skin if you'd jumped out of a geothermal pool, but in the end the water's still boiling. I started trying to hold my breath to see if I could suffocate myself. Sienna screamed at me to stop, but that just made me more determined.

Then everything changed. I was lying in chest-deep water inside a cave. The stone floors were bare except for the back corner of the room, where there was a thick bed of jaguar furs. Several wooden torches affixed to the walls cast a warm glow over the water. I knew this couldn't possibly be real, but it was unlike any dream I'd ever had before. I could feel the water rush across my skin and smell the fumes from the fire. The images I was seeing weren't flashes or a mishmash of garbled thoughts– they were crystal clear. I was simultaneously seeing through my eyes and watching me, like having two camera angles of the same scene.

Or was it me? There was a noticeable resemblance in the face, and the hair color was pretty close, but there was something strange about the eyes. They were light green rather than hazel and had pupils shaped like a cat's. Whoever she was, I could tell from the scent that she was a vampire. And based on the fire torches and furs for a bed, she was living like a bazillion years ago.

Three women walked through the narrow opening to her chamber, dressed in tanned hides with rope around their waists. She flashed them a smile. After they disrobed they joined her in the small pool and began to scrub her body with a mixture of flower petals and some kind of animal fat. Feeling their hands scrub my body brought me back inside of her.

The women never made eye contact. The grace of their movements and unmistakable scent made it clear that they were vampires as well. Then the woman washing my left side briefly glanced at my face. I noticed two things instantly – her pupils weren't slit shaped like mine, and she was extremely nervous. The image terrified me.

In one fluid motion my left hand raked across her throat, sending her decapitated head flying into the carved stone wall. My feet shot up under me as the girl on my right sprang. Her strike was lightning quick; far faster than any human was capable of, but slow motion compared to mine. I grabbed her right arm around the wrist, ripped it out of the socket and punched clean through her chest. As her mangled body crumpled into the pool, nails dug into my neck. I tried to launch myself toward the doorway, but it was too late. The woman who'd been washing my hair tore out my throat. I fell face down into the water. Dead.

When I came to, I was lunging against the straps.

"What's wrong, baby!" Sienna cried out.

I think I was…dreaming.

"I wondered why you were quiet for so long," she said with relief. "What'd you dream about?"

It was awful! I was living in a cave back in the Stone Age and was some kind of weird cat-eyed vampire who had vampires for slaves. They came in to give me a bath and attacked me. I killed two of them before my throat got ripped out.

Sienna couldn't keep from laughing. "You'll have to tell me later– you sound like you're on a cell phone going through a tunnel. And I can't believe I'm about to say this, but try to stay awake from here on out. I've never heard of someone being able to sleep during their transformation before."

As I fully regained consciousness, I discovered that the pain had eased slightly. My arms, legs and head were still in agony, but the rest of my body felt fine. I had to be near the end.

Sienna brushed my sweat-drenched hair back and gave me a loving kiss. "It shouldn't take more than a couple of hours for you to complete the change.

Dangerous Waters

Once you're no longer in any pain, just tap your fingers on the bed, and we'll get you out of there. Can you do it now for me so I know you understand?"

I lifted the fingers of my right hand as far as I could off the bed and tapped them twice.

"Perfect. You're going to begin to feel a different kind of hunger soon. Rather than being driven by an empty stomach, this will be more of an urge for energy, kind of like when you're really tired driving and you know you need some caffeine. As soon as your transformation is complete, you'll need to drink your fill to help replenish your body."

The pain was becoming more and more distal, shifting into my lower arms and legs, then just my hands and feet. My eyes were no longer bothering me, and the pressure in my head had begun to ease. As I waited for it to end, I noticed an odd craving growing stronger in my mind. It was similar to the urge I got to slam a Gatorade after wearing myself out playing tennis, but I knew I wasn't just thirsty. By the time the last of the pain subsided, I was beyond exhausted. Remembering Sienna's signal, I raised my fingers and tapped them on the bed.

"Okay, I need you to listen carefully," Sienna commanded after removing the headphones and earplugs. "Once we remove the straps don't try to move. I'll lift your legs in the air for you and we'll hold them there while we remove the catheter. Just try to let your whole body relax and let us do everything."

I tapped my hand again to let them know I understood. Within seconds all of the straps were off and my mouth guard was removed. I let my body go limp while they lifted my knees and removed the catheter.

Once the tape was peeled off, I slowly opened my eyes, blinking to get them to focus. I glanced at Ruby, who was standing near the back of the room, and could easily make out the individual threads on her cashmere sweater. Her hair, which had always looked solid black, actually had countless minute variations in color. My reality had gone from a black and white TV to HD. "Holy crap!"

Ruby flashed me an uneasy smile. "What?"

"Your hair's so beautiful! I never noticed all of the different colors before."

"Wait until you go outside," she said with a laugh. "It's a whole new world."

Sienna put her hand on my shoulder. "I want you to try to sit up now. You're going to notice that your body moves a lot differently than you're used to. We'll spend the next few days working with you, but for now just try to move as slowly as you can."

I placed the palm of my right hand near my side and tried to push myself up as I kicked my legs over the side of the bed. Instead of just raising my upper body into a sitting position, the slight push off of my arm sent me flying several feet into the air. Combined with the kick of my legs I ended up making a catlike inverted leap, landing on my feet a good ten feet from the bed. They were all grinning, like that was exactly what they expected to happen.

Sienna walked over and wrapped a bathrobe around me, easing my arms through the sleeves. "Now that you know what happens when you try to move normally, let's try it again. This time you need to really concentrate on slowing yourself down. Try to break each movement into several small parts and pause between each of them. Set your feet down gently like you're trying to walk across a floor of eggs without breaking them. When you're ready, I want you to take one step back toward the bed."

Very slowly, I shifted my weight onto my right foot, pushed my left knee forward, rotated up onto the balls of my left foot, and then lifted it up in the air. After reaching my left foot forward, I sat my heel on the floor, gradually transferring my weight onto it. I repeated the process in reverse, placing my right foot next to my left.

"I did it!"

"That was perfect!" Sienna praised. "Now take three more steps just like it and try to sit down on the bed."

I methodically made my way across the floor as if I was walking in a mine field. After slowly turning around, I placed my hands on the edge of the bed. Rather than using one big push, I raised myself up onto it like a gymnast lifts herself into a handstand on the balance beam. When I was suspended over the bed, I gradually lowered my body down into place.

"That's enough practice for now." Sienna handed me a large plastic pitcher filled with blood. "You must be starving."

The aroma was intoxicating. I closed my eyes and breathed the scent deeply into my lungs. My mouth started to water as I lifted the pitcher to my lips and slowly drank it down, savoring every gulp. I could actually taste the sugars, proteins and minerals the blood contained and could feel the energy flowing into my body– maybe I wouldn't miss food so much after all. "That tastes…incredible."

Raven wiped the blood from my mouth and licked it off her fingers. "Wait until you get your first taste of fresh blood. This is only a day old, but it tastes like garbage compared to blood taken straight from the vein."

"I'm a vampire," I muttered, somewhat in shock.

Sienna placed her hands on both sides of my face and kissed me on the forehead. "You're my daughter. Welcome to your new life."

Chapter Twenty-Four
Mind Games

I continued my slow retreat while Sienna patiently stalked me like a lioness in the tall savanna grass. It seemed like I was successfully eluding her, but her widening grin made me nervous. She began to twirl her fifty-inch Claymore sword around her body at incredible speed. It had a twisted redwood handle and brass cross sets angling down toward the blade. My muscles tensed as I prepared for her attack.

Sienna lunged forward and took a roundhouse-style swing toward the base of my neck. I ducked and felt a gush of wind blow through my hair as her sword passed within inches of my head. While I'd succeeded in dodging her initial attack, she was now right on top of me. I tried to launch myself into a forward roll, but it was too late. Her sword came down across my back from my left shoulder all the way to my right hip. Even though I could tell that I wasn't injured, I instinctively reached behind me to check for blood. When I stood up, my now mangled black running tank top fell down around my elbows. I snorted and pulled it the rest of the way off.

"You see, sweetheart, there's nothing to be afraid of," Sienna reassured me, placing the razor sharp blade against the side of my neck. Every instinct inside me was screaming for me to run, but I knew this lesson wasn't going to end until I'd proven that I was no longer afraid. My entire body started to shake as I took the end of her sword and guided it down to my midsection. While the thought of being impaled by a four foot sword wasn't much more enticing than being beheaded, having her take a full swing at my neck was more than I could handle right now. I anxiously stood my ground while she pulled back and drove her sword into my stomach, shattering it into several pieces that rained down onto the wooden floor.

"Oh my God!" I shouted, picking up one of the shards of metal. "That's too cool!"

Sienna affectionately caressed my face. "That was very brave of you. Next time I'll start teaching you to fight."

After jumping in the shower, I spent a few hours surfing the web for Christmas and birthday gifts, then grabbed my phone and flopped on my bed.

Dangerous Waters

We were flying to Traverse City in three weeks, and I still hadn't told my dad anything, not even that they were coming with me. Raven scheduled the flights late the night before after watching me like a hawk the entire day– kind of like a fourteen-hour final exam– making sure I'd learned to control my new body. In less than four days, moving like a human had become second nature to me, thanks to all of their help. I could feel the nerves building in my stomach as the phone began to ring.

"Hi, honey!"

"Hi, Dad, any snow up there yet?"

"It is December you know," he replied with a chuckle. "We've already got two-foot snow banks. How's school going?"

"Good. Final exams are coming up in a couple of weeks, so I've got a lot of studying to do." I actually had no idea when finals were, but I figured they had to be before Christmas sometime.

"When do I get to see you?"

"Only three more weeks! I'm flying in on the twenty-first."

"You're flying?" I could hear the confusion in his voice. He knew I wasn't working yet, and that I'd never charge something that expensive on my emergency credit card without asking him first.

"Raven's family does a lot of business travel, so they have tons of frequent flyer miles. They decided to fly all of us up there as her Christmas gift."

"Who all is coming?" he wondered.

"All of us! Me, Raven, Sienna, Ruby and Sandy. Is that okay?"

"Of course, sweetie. We'll squeeze 'em in somewhere. Besides, it'll give me a chance to get to know them." My dad had always been cool with my friends. Brittney still stopped by to visit him whenever she could.

"You might not recognize me," I said, making it sound like a joke.

He laughed. "It has been a while– I'll hold up a sign at the airport."

"Just look for a girl with short brown hair."

"You cut your hair?"

I'd begged him since the end of my freshman year to let me get highlights put in, and I'd never worn my hair short, so it wasn't surprising that he was confused. "Sandy did it for me. She's like an amazing hair stylist. I love it!"

"Well, that's all that matters to me. Maybe she can give me a trim while she's here."

"I'm sure she'd love to." I pictured the parted-down-the-side dorky business haircut he'd worn for as long as I could remember. Maybe Sandy could finally get him to try something different.

As I leaned my head back against the pillow, my untied bathrobe fell open, drooping loosely off my shoulders. I glanced down at my lean, muscular body. The obvious change in my physique would be difficult to hide, even with bulky sweatshirts. "We've been working out a lot too. The Rec center is awesome."

"It looked nice," he agreed. "Sounds like you're having a lot of fun."

"You know it!"

"So should I get turkey or ham for Christmas dinner?"

I was speechless. Even though we always ate a giant Christmas dinner together, it had completely escaped my mind.

"Honey, what would your friends like better, turkey or ham?"

"I wouldn't go to a lot of trouble, Dad. We just grab something on the go most of the time."

"Emily," he said sternly. "If your friends are staying with us on Christmas, they're going to be treated to a proper Christmas dinner. Now which would they like?"

Crap. It was never good when he used that tone. "Turkey," I mumbled in defeat. Our trip hadn't even begun yet and it was already a disaster.

"Turkey it is. We'll give them a meal they won't forget!" He was certainly right about that– they were going to kill me.

"I'll make ya a deal," I said as an idea came to me.

"What's that?"

"If I talk them into the whole 'formal Christmas dinner' thing, then you have to let us fend for ourselves the rest of the time we're up there."

"But– "

"No buts," I interrupted. "Take it or leave it."

"I guess that's fair…if you give me some good gift ideas for them."

"You don't need to get them anything, Dad."

He chuckled. "Take it or leave it."

"You win." If I knew my new family at all, I was sure he'd end up buried in gifts anyway. Maybe he wouldn't feel so embarrassed if he got them something in return. "I'll send you an email in a couple of days."

"I love you, sweetheart."

"Love you too. Bye"

I covered my head with my pillow while I thought about how I was going to break the news to my family. Even though my dad wasn't the most observant guy in the world, he was sure to notice five girls puking their guts out for several hours. And it'd be hard to pass it off as food poisoning with him feeling fine. Combined with never seeing us eat anything else and my drastic weight loss, he was bound to conclude that we were bulimic or anorexic.

"What's wrong?" Raven asked, taking a seat next to me.

I nervously lifted the pillow. "I just spoke with my dad. I really screwed up."

"What happened?"

"Everything was going good at first. He bought my explanation about cashing in your frequent flyer miles, and he's really excited to meet you guys. He was a little surprised that I cut my hair, but it's nothing to be alarmed about. He even joked that Sandy could give him a trim while we're up there."

"I'm sure she'd be happy to."

"That's what I said. I also told him that I'd been working out a lot so he wouldn't be shocked when he saw me. Then he asked me what you guys wanted for Christmas dinner."

"Oh," she muttered. "What'd you tell him?"

"At first I couldn't think of anything. When he pressed me for an answer I told him not to make a big deal about it, but he wouldn't let it go. I finally caved in and told him turkey."

Raven slowly ran her fingers through her hair and blew out a breath. "This is bad."

"I know! I did manage to get him to agree to let us fend for ourselves the rest of the time though."

"Really?" she asked, shooting me a skeptical look.

"Yeah… Will that help?"

"Definitely. There are a lot of tricks we can use if we only have to get through one meal."

"Like what?"

She grinned. "Sleight of hand for the most part. One of us will get his attention while the people outside of his view discard a reasonable amount of food. It'll be easy to know when to move since we'll all be able to read his mind. We'll keep him talking and constantly pass food around, the more commotion the better. He'll think we're all having seconds by the time we're done. The hardest part will be letting him watch each of us take a few bites. As you saw a couple weeks ago, it's easy to swallow unintentionally."

"What will we do with all the food?"

Raven chewed her lip in thought. "We'll all wear loose-fitting dresses that are about knee length. We'll attach a long, narrow pouch to our upper thighs so that it expands when we spread our legs apart. Once we're sitting down we'll discretely pull up the front of our dresses and open the pouch. Given how fast we can move, it'll only take a fraction of a second for us to grab a bite of food off our plate and drop it between our legs. What type of kitchen table do you have?"

"It's an oval shaped wood table. It has two leafs you can put in but we never use them."

"That's perfect. We'll use both extensions and have your dad sit on one of the ends. You and Sandy will sit the furthest away from him on each side to give you some cover and the most time to maneuver. Ruby and I will also sit on the side in the seats closer to him. Sienna will take the most difficult position, on the end of the table directly across from him."

"I think that might work," I said with relief.

She reached out and ruffled my hair. "You did good. This will be far easier than trying to make up excuses for every meal."

"I hope so. He's getting each of you a present too."

"That's really sweet. We'll make sure that Santa is good to him, sis. You're lucky to have such a thoughtful dad. I can't wait to meet him."

"He's the best," I said proudly. "I know he is going to love you guys."

Raven glanced at what I was wearing. "You'd better throw some clothes on – they should be back soon."

I jumped up and headed for my closet. It'd been a week since my transformation, and I could feel the hunger growing stronger inside me. I needed blood. As anxious as I was to feed, I was even more eager to learn how to trance people and read their minds. After throwing on my pink-trimmed camouflage lounge pants and a pink long-sleeve t-shirt, I went to join Raven in the living room.

"I want to make sure you're prepared for what will happen tonight," Raven said after I took a seat next to her on the couch. "You'll start to hear thoughts enter your mind before they even get inside the house. I know we had a lot of fun reading your mind, but people we bring home are as scared as you were when Teresa tranced you in the alley. They plead for their lives and think about all of the loved ones they're leaving behind. It can really make you feel like a monster. It won't be easy, especially given how kindhearted you are, but you need to find a way to harden yourself so you can learn what we need to teach you."

Dangerous Waters

My enthusiasm instantly vanished. I'd never thought about what I'd be hearing them think tonight. I recalled the frantic pleas and prayers I'd made when I was attacked. There's no way I'd be able to listen to thoughts like that without breaking down in tears. "I'll try," I whispered, lowering my head.

Raven lifted my chin up and gazed into my eyes. "I'm not asking you to change who you are– that's what I love most about you. But in order to survive we need to feed, and in order to feed we need to be able to distance ourselves emotionally from those that we feed upon."

I hadn't memorized the sound of all of our cars yet, but I could clearly hear Ruby's Escalade slowing down to turn onto our drive. "They're here."

"Not bad, sis," Raven said, nudging my shoulder.

As soon as Ruby pulled up in front of the house, thoughts began pouring into my mind. *Where am I? Why are they doing this to me? I love you, Jeremy. Jenny has choir practice tonight. Our trip to Florida. I yelled at her this morning. I was supposed to call Allison today. I don't want to die! We never should have moved here. What are they going to do to me? I told him I wanted to stay in Denver. Why can't I move my body? Please, God, please save me! She needs me. Did they drug me?* It was extremely disorienting. I cast Raven a helpless glance while I massaged my suddenly aching temples.

"Now you see why we don't go out in public right away after we're changed. Don't worry, after a while you won't even hear their thoughts unless you choose to," Raven assured me.

Sandy nodded her head slightly as she entered and continued on toward the feeding room with a woman in her early forties following close behind. She was wearing a brown polyester knee-length skirt and a matching, three-quarter sleeve, single-button jacket with a lace undershirt. She looked professional, like a business executive, and was fairly attractive for her age. After Ruby joined Sandy in the feeding room, Raven, Sienna and I walked into my bedroom and sat on the end of the bed.

"I'm really proud of you for how strong you're being," Sienna said, patting my knee.

"Thanks. I'm really trying."

Sienna reached out and took my hand. "Let's start by having you tell me everything that you hear her thinking. Don't try to summarize or restate it in any way. Just repeat it."

"Okay." I'd been trying to ignore her thoughts, but the noise was deafening in my head.

"It must be past five. Jeremy will be home soon. Are they going to rob me? We're out of milk. He'll call if I'm not there. Why am I just sitting here? They were all young women. Where did the others go? Why is no one saying anything? They must have slipped that date rape drug into my coffee. Maybe the police can trace it. What do they want from me? Steve can do it. Who are they? I'm supposed to be picking Jenny up. I hope he calls him. They'll never find it. Think Jeremy. I don't want to die. Why did I cheat on him? It's in my inside pocket– "

Raven darted past me, flying down the hall and into the feeding room.

"She's got a cell phone hidden on her," Sienna explained, shaking her head and swearing under her breath. "I can't believe I was that careless."

Raven returned moments later, still wiping what was left of the woman's phone off of her hands. "The last call she'd made or received was over three hours ago. We should be okay."

Sienna relaxed and turned back toward me. "Okay, I didn't expect that much excitement, but that was good, honey. You're already retrieving some of her subconscious thoughts. Now I'll teach you how to follow chains of thought so that you can make sense out of what you're hearing and obtain far more information."

"There was more?" I asked in disbelief. I was sure I'd repeated everything that entered my mind.

She grinned. "Steve is her brother and is a detective in the Boston Police Department. She had a cell phone in her purse that was a throw away, in case she was ever attacked or kidnapped. That's why we didn't search any further. She cheated on Jeremy last week in her office with her assistant Alex. Jenny is fourteen and plays the clarinet. She and her husband have tickets to fly to Destin in three weeks for their twenty-year anniversary."

My eyes widened in amazement. "Teach me!" Raven and Sienna laughed at my enthusiasm.

"This time, instead of passively listening, I want you to focus your mind on a particular thought that you hear. Once you're concentrating hard enough, you'll begin to receive her subconscious thoughts. You'll still hear everything she's consciously thinking about, but it'll seem muted or dull compared to what you're focusing on. In time you'll learn to listen in on multiple lines of thought simultaneously, but for now we'll stick with one. Once you pick a thought to follow, let us know so we can follow along and see if we detect anything that you miss."

"Got it." I closed my eyes and started listening to the noise in my head again. *How did they know? Oh God, I'm going to die. She didn't even have to look for it. How did she crush it like that? He's going to find out. She knew right where it was. I'm sorry, Allie...* "That one."

As soon as I honed in on that particular thought the noise in my head faded to a whisper. Moments later a stream of thoughts far clearer than anything I'd heard before flooded my mind. *How could I kick my own daughter out of my house? She was only eighteen. So what if she got arrested. Like I didn't smoke pot when I was young. I'm such a hypocrite. She forged my name on some checks. Jeremy was right to check her into the treatment center. Why did I take her out of there? She was getting better. I missed her so much. She got Jenny high. How could she do that? She was only thirteen. Why did we have to go to that stupid reunion? She would've never thrown that party. I overreacted. I should've taken her back to the treatment center. At least she finally called me. Now I know where she is. I need to tell her to come home.*

Almost as if she had quit talking, the string of thoughts abruptly ended. "She kicked her daughter Allison out of the house when she was eighteen for getting her younger daughter Jenny high at a party she threw while they were at a reunion. Allison had been arrested earlier and had forged her mom's name on some checks. Jeremy had checked her into a treatment center, and she was getting better until her mom took her home again. Her mom feels like a hypocrite, since she smoked pot when she was young as well. Allison recently called and let her mom know where she was. Her mom wants to ask her to come home."

Sienna arched her brows in surprise. "Very good."

I glanced away and bit down on my lip as I thought about what I'd said. This family was dealing with so much already, and now they were going to be without their mother. I fought back the tears that were stinging at my eyes, remembering what Raven told me. If I allowed myself to care about them, I'd never be able to feed. "Did I miss anything?" I asked, forcing a smile.

"Nope," Raven said. "That was perfect."

Sienna wrapped her arm around my side and kissed me on the forehead. "Now we need to teach you to quiet others' thoughts in your mind. To help you learn we'll distract you with menial exercises that function like isolating a particular thought– anything your mind is not directed toward will be greatly suppressed. Your brain will eventually learn to suppress anything you're not paying attention to rather than suppressing everything *except* what you're concentrating on, but that'll take a while."

Raven shot me a competitive grin. "Would you like spelling or math?"

"Math," I answered quickly– my horrendous spelling made crossword puzzles almost impossible.

"This is going to kind of be like rapid fire. The questions themselves won't be difficult, but you'll need to pay attention in order to keep up."

"Bring it on, sis!" I challenged.

Raven launched into an endless string of simple math problems, all building upon each other. I was barely able to respond to one question before she hit me with another. After a couple of minutes, the woman's thoughts all but vanished from my mind. We repeated the exercise several times until the response was almost immediate. Each time it took longer and longer for her thoughts to return.

Sienna then had me practice distracting myself by thinking about something in detail: what I wanted to bring on our trip, what I was going to get Sandy for her birthday…anything to occupy my mind. I still had to focus on something in order to suppress her thoughts, but it was fairly easy to do.

When I finished we got up and made our way into the feeding room. Sandy and Ruby were standing on either side of the woman, who was sitting on the floor Indian style facing the doorway. Raven made her way over to Sandy while Sienna and I walked right up to the woman, stopping less than two feet from her.

"The first thing I want you to work on is just learning to put someone under your trance," Sienna instructed. "As soon as you have control of her, I want you to let her go. Don't try to make her do anything or manipulate her subconscious thoughts in any way. Do you understand?"

I nodded my head, recalling what they'd told me about how easy it was to kill someone if you didn't let their subconscious thoughts pass through your mind.

"Once Sandy releases her, I want you to lock in on her brain activity, the electrical impulses going into and out of her mind. This is different than focusing on her thoughts. Just stare into her eyes and direct your mind toward the signals that enter your brain. When you can see, hear and feel what she's experiencing, she's under your trance. Are you ready?"

I took a couple of deep breaths, and then gazed into her eyes. "Yep."

As soon as Sandy released her, I was overwhelmed with bizarre physical sensations. I was looking at myself as clearly as if the images were coming from my own eyes, my feet were numb from sitting on them too long and I was ordering my body to get up and run from the room. The feeling was similar to the dream I had when I was being changed, except that I was experiencing two separate realities simultaneously, rather than one reality from two different viewpoints.

"Release her, Brooke," Sienna commanded.

I quickly glanced away, breaking the trance. The woman didn't even have a chance to flinch before Sandy was back in control. "Sorry. It was so confusing– I couldn't separate our minds."

Sienna stroked my hair. "There's nothing to apologize for. You did fine. This time, as soon as you have her tranced, I want you to locate the almost constant signals that you feel leaving her mind. They'll be easy to identify, as they control her key bodily functions. Once you find them, you need to allow them to pass through your mind to her body. I know that sounds complicated, but you'll be able to feel yourself blocking them. Let us know when you're ready."

Complicated? Was she serious? Landing a 747 without any training would be complicated. This sounded downright impossible. Maybe if I had several minutes to get used to the feeling of having someone tranced and could slowly dig through her brain. How long could she go without her heart beating before she died… A few seconds? Gee, no pressure or anything. "I'll give it a try. Yell at me or something if I'm taking too long."

As soon as I finished my sentence she was under my control. I ignored the incoming signals from her eyes and the rest of her body and focused entirely on what was leaving her brain. My mind decoded each impulse instantly: commands to move her legs, to scream and to look away from me. Then I detected a group of repeating signals coming from deeper within her mind. The first one I identified controlled the contractions of her heart muscle. *Bingo.* Just like Sienna had said, as soon as they were isolated, I became aware of my thoughts to block them. Allowing them to pass through my mind was no more difficult than deciding not to clap my hands.

I knew that was all Sienna had asked me to do, but she was stable, and I was eager to find out if I could make her move. Supposedly all I had to do was think about what I wanted her body to do, and my brain would send the signals to make it happen. I thought about uncrossing her legs, since I knew they were bothering her, and watched in amazement as they unfolded. I could feel the painful tingling sensations returning to her brain from her numb feet. After straightening them out flat on the floor, I turned away and felt the connection break.

Before I was fully aware of myself again, my body was being twirled around in the air. Sienna held me tightly in her arms with a glowing smile on her face. "That was outstanding! I didn't think we'd get anywhere near that far tonight."

"Thanks, Mom." As excited as I was to be trying out my newfound abilities, the images of the woman looking at me in horror while I turned her into my puppet were burned in my mind.

Sienna took my hand and led me to the front of the room. "We'll pick up from there the next time we feed."

Sandy directed the woman up onto the gurney, and then stood in the back next to Raven. Ruby assumed her usual position at the left side of the gurney while Sienna stood behind me on the right. The woman's eyes slowly closed, and she seemed at peace. I knew it was just a façade but I chose to believe it, focusing on my hunger until her thoughts were again silenced in my mind.

"Go ahead," Sienna said, encouraging me.

I picked up her left arm and slid the sleeve of her jacket up past her elbow. Since she was wearing a watch, I placed my nails higher up on her forearm, then pushed gently and slid them across, cutting deeply into her flesh. The smell of fresh blood saturated the room, arousing in me an animalistic urge to feed. Within seconds a heavenly, almost decadent taste filled my mouth. Raven was right– the blood I drank right after I was changed was like sewer water compared to this. I could actually feel my body being rejuvenated as I gorged in her blood. When my stomach was uncomfortably full, I handed her arm to Sienna and walked over to stand next to Raven.

"Is there any left?" Raven teased.

Since Ruby finished a lot sooner than I did, I figured she was probably only half joking. I'd need to make sure that I didn't take more than my share or one of us could end up going hungry. "Sorry, I kinda pigged out," I whispered.

Raven put her arm around my shoulders and smiled. "Everybody does their first time. Don't worry about it."

Chapter Twenty-Five
Dodge, Parry and Thrust

"This one?" I asked, reaching for a basket-hilted broadsword. It was about three feet long, was double edged and had a fairly wide blade.

"That's it," Sienna said.

I lifted the sword off the rack and began to swipe it through the air. It felt weightless, like I was holding a toothpick. The rush I'd gotten from learning to trance people the day before was nothing compared to this. After almost three months of waiting, I wasn't just going to see my first fight– I was going to be in it, going head to head with Sienna.

Knowing that the clothes I wore today were doomed, I'd dressed for the occasion, throwing on an Old Navy t-shirt from high school that was now far too big and black spandex leggings that were ripped above the knee. I rolled my eyes when I saw what Sienna was wearing– a red, lace trimmed V-neck cami and light blue cargo capri pants.

She turned her head to the side. "What?"

"Look at you!" I replied with mock disgust. "You didn't even bother to change. Aren't those your favorite pants?"

"Yes, they are," she said, grinning confidently. "And they still will be tomorrow."

I giggled. Even though I knew she was trying to arouse my competitive spirit, I was as sure of that as she was.

"There are a couple of things we need to go over before we start. You need to keep safety first and foremost in your mind at all times. While there's nothing you could do with your sword that could hurt me, the same cannot be said for your body. I'll push you to the very edge of what you're capable of, but you always have to stay under control. Never remove your gloves under any circumstances or continue to fight if they're damaged. Never make any punching or kicking motion, not even as a distraction. And never try to tackle, flip, trip, push or otherwise intentionally contact your opponent. At the end of the day, the only thing that truly matters is that we both walk out of here unharmed. Do you understand?"

"I'll be careful, Mom," I promised.

She flashed me a tender smile. "The other key thing to remember is that

I'm not teaching you to fight with a sword— I'm using a sword to teach you to fight. The purpose is not to learn a bunch of fancy sword maneuvers that would win you a fencing competition. Everything we do is geared toward sharpening your reflexes and teaching you what your body is capable of. You've spent the last week learning to limit your movements so that you can function normally and appear human in public. Now you need to learn to unleash your body and harness its power. Let's get started."

After showing me how to hold a sword and correcting my stance, Sienna walked me through a series of defensive blocking techniques, letting me practice each of them several times.

"Are you ready to try some combinations?"

"Bring it on!"

Sienna lunged forward, aiming her saber for the right side of my chest, just below my elbow. I deflected it, only to watch with wide eyes as it whipped toward my head on an upward arc. At the last instant I executed the appropriate block and heard our swords collide. In rapid succession she took a swipe at my right knee and ended with a thrust aimed for my stomach. I somehow managed to defend both.

"Very nice."

Her compliment on my swordsmanship brought a wide smile to my lips. It was like Serena Williams commending my overpowering serve. "Thanks!"

Switching roles, she walked me step-by-step through each of the offensive maneuvers she'd executed. At first my technique was so mechanical that I horribly telegraphed my attacks, but I soon began to feel more comfortable with a sword in my hand.

After our first competitive exchange, Sienna stepped back and shook her head. "So much for my tried-and-true training schedule— it should've taken you at least a month to achieve this level of proficiency. I can't believe I'm about to say this, twenty minutes into your first lesson, but let's see how you do with full-speed combat."

As if someone had flipped a switch, Sienna's entire persona changed. All of the warmth was gone from her now steely expression. She looked deadly. I took a couple of steps back and nervously raised my sword.

Sienna raced forward at amazing speed and brought her sword around toward my neck. An echo filled the room as our swords met. To my surprise, I had no trouble following even her fastest movements. What had appeared as nothing more than a blur when I was human was now crystal clear. While I was still celebrating, she continued on behind me and ran her sword all the way down my back.

"Damn it!" I yelled, angrily tossing my shirt to the floor. First lesson or not, I never enjoyed losing at anything I competed in.

Sienna returned to the center of the room and waited for me to regain my composure. After I settled back into my stance and raised my sword, she slowly advanced.

I studied each of her movements, looking for any opportunity to strike. When her weight shifted onto the balls of her right foot, I darted to her left and executed a downward slicing attack, aiming for the top of her left arm. She ducked, and my sword whipped over her head. Sienna was now crouched into a ball, but I couldn't capitalize on the opportunity as my wild charge had thrown me totally off balance. Before I could recover, I felt her sword slice across the back of my neck.

The result certainly wasn't any better than the first round, but I could tell from the way she'd reacted that I'd caught her off guard. I just needed to maintain better control. As soon as we resumed fighting, Sienna launched herself behind me and took a swing at the back of my right shoulder. I pulled my upper body forward and rolled away from her, springing to my feet just as her long steel blade approached my face. My sword shot up, barely catching hers in time. When I raised it a little further above my head, I knew she was vulnerable.

I took a quick step left and bought my sword down across her chest from her left breast all the way to her right hip. She staggered back, completely stunned, as her shirt fell open.

"Yes!" I lowered a knee and pumped my fist in triumph.

Sienna ripped what was left of her shirt off and glared at me with an animalistic rage in her eyes– now I knew how Sandy felt when they met in the surf shop.

"Sorry," I muttered, my voice trembling. "That was really immature of me. Please don't be mad."

She rubbed her forehead with her glove, the anger slowly bleeding away. "I'm the one who should be apologizing. I should never have reacted like that. I just wasn't expecting that to happen today."

I started to giggle. "Neither did I."

"You analyze your opponent's movements and vulnerabilities very well."

"Nine years of playing tennis."

She grinned. "You ready to go again?"

"Definitely!"

Sienna turned her body sideways and began to walk in a slow circle. I stayed square with her, watching intently for any kind of opening. When I saw her shift her weight to the instep of her right foot, I knew she was about to step toward me with her left. I sprinted to her left, figuring that I'd get behind her, but I'd been duped. Rather than stepping forward, she'd pivoted, anticipating my move. I felt her sword strike the back of my legs just below my butt.

"Tricky," I said, surveying the damage. I could feel my underwear beneath the large flaps of spandex that were now hanging down from my rear.

"Pink lace... Nice!"

Now that Sienna was disguising her moves, I'd have to wait until she committed to them before I could react. That gave her a distinct advantage as long as she initiated the attack. Knowing this, I decided to go on the offensive. Sienna turned sideways like she'd done before, with her left foot facing me, and began to walk. As I continued to watch her circle, I uncovered an inherent flaw in her technique. In order to walk she had to slow her body down to allow herself to move at a human pace. That meant that from the time she began to take a step until it was completed, her reaction time would be greatly diminished.

As soon as she lifted her left foot in the air, I rocketed behind her and swung my sword on a downward angle toward the back of her right leg. Since the toes of her left foot had just touched the ground she was unable to react in time. My sword struck her right hip and went down across the back of her leg, all the way to her calf. Her capri pants fell down her body and bunched up around her left knee. Even her underwear had been cut, leaving the right side of her butt and her right leg totally bare.

I gazed at the remnants of her red, hi-cut panties dangling between her legs. "I like yours better."

Sienna couldn't keep from laughing as she shook her head in utter disbelief. "Looks like we'll be doing team fighting from now on."

I smiled as I pictured Sienna and me, outnumbered, fighting back-to-back against my sisters. "We can take 'em!"

"Generally you have the two best players on opposite teams."

I gave her a skeptical look. All of my sisters had decades of experience fighting with Sienna– there's no way I could be better than them already. This was the first time I'd picked up a sword in my life.

Dangerous Waters

Seeing the doubt in my eyes, she continued. "None of your sisters had any experience with one-on-one physical competition before they were changed. While studying an opponent's every move and seizing on their mistakes is second nature to you, they're still trying to master that. You have a lot to learn, but even now you'd almost certainly fare better in a fight with another vampire than any of them would."

"Please don't tell them that." The last thing I wanted was for them to be jealous of me, or think that I was full of myself.

Sienna wrapped her arm around my shoulders. "I admire your modesty, sweetheart, but it's important for their safety that they know what you're capable of. Besides, it's not like they aren't going to find out for themselves the first time we fight together."

I let out a deep sigh. I knew she was right.

Raven walked in just as Sienna slid her pants the rest of the way off. She glanced at Sienna, who was now wearing nothing but her white Nike tennis shoes, then looked back at me, speechless.

I wheeled around and stuck out my butt. "I didn't fare any better. The only reason I still have pants on is because she kept hitting me above the waist."

"As my current state of attire would suggest, your sister's being rather modest," Sienna countered. "She's all but my equal already."

Raven continued to stare at me in silence, like I was a freak show attraction at the local fair.

"Please don't look at me like that," I said, tears stinging my eyes.

She quickly pulled me into her arms. "I'm sorry– it just caught me off guard. Like sending the cat into the barn after a mouse and having the mouse walk out."

Her golden hair was twisted and pinned in an elegant, elaborate up-dew. "When's the wedding?" I said, my lips curving up in a smile.

She lifted her shoulders in a helpless shrug. "Sandy was bored this morning. It was either this or having her curl it, and the last time she did that it took hours."

I reached down and picked my sword up off the floor. "Would you like to go a couple rounds?"

"I wish I could, but I actually came in here to tell you guys that Stefan and Alexander are here." When Raven saw the horrified expression on our faces, she burst out laughing. "I'll get you both some clothes and make sure they stay in the living room."

Chapter Twenty-Six
Just Visiting

As soon as we were dressed, Sienna and I hurried into the living room. Raven was sitting by herself on the couch across from Stefan and Alexander. It didn't look like Ruby and Sandy were back yet from picking Kelly up at the airport.

Stefan leaped to his feet when he saw us and pulled me into a tight embrace. "It's so nice to see you again, my dear. Welcome to your new life."

"Thank you, Stefan," I said with a warm smile. "It's good to see you too."

"So how was your first lesson?"

I started to giggle when I caught him taking a peek at my clothes. "Well, this isn't what I was wearing when I went in there."

He chuckled. "I would've been surprised if it was."

"You should be surprised," Sienna chimed in, undermining my attempt to be humble yet again. "This isn't what I was wearing either."

He stared skeptically at her. "Surely you're toying with me."

"No joke, my love— Brooke is quite gifted."

Stefan tucked my hair behind my ear and kissed me on the forehead. "The more I learn about you, the more curious I become. You are truly extraordinary." I could feel the blood rush to my cheeks as I gave him a bashful smile.

He took my hand and led me over to Alexander, who was still sitting on the couch. He stood, and I noticed that he was a good four inches taller than Stefan and at least twice as wide through the chest. I didn't remember him being so massive.

"Hi, Brooke," he said, his hands fidgeting at his sides.

I stepped forward and gave him a hug. "Thank you."

His face filled with confusion. "For what?"

"For sparing my life…and for not tearing my best friend apart when she tried to save me." I turned to Raven. "What were ya thinkin', sis? He's huge!"

"I was praying that diplomacy worked," Raven said with an almost deadpan delivery. The room filled with laughter.

I waited until I had Alexander's attention, and then slapped him lightly on the cheek. "That's for checking out my body when I was on the table."

He flashed me a devilish grin. "It was worth a slap." I pushed his shoulder, but he didn't budge an inch.

"Any sign of Travis or Teresa?" Sienna asked.

"Nothing so far," Stefan admitted. "But there haven't been any missing person cases reported in Boston since the night they left, so I think it's safe to assume they're gone."

"They could just be feeding somewhere else."

"Of course, but based on their past behavior, I think that's unlikely. They never understood why we take the precautions that we do. Their refusal to change is what led to all of this."

"I agree," Sienna conceded. "Besides, even if they are still in the area, if they're being more careful about how they feed, then there's nothing to worry about anyway."

Stefan turned back toward me. "I find myself yet again in your debt. Rather than merely accepting my son's apology, you befriended him. I dare say he is smitten with you. You are a wonder, my child."

"Dad!" Alexander groaned in embarrassment. I snorted and glanced up at his now beet-red face. Even though I wasn't attracted to him– mainly due to his ginormous size– I hoped we could become good friends.

Stefan shrugged his shoulders innocently. "What?"

"Please ignore him," Alexander begged.

"So you don't…like me?" I choked out with as much pain in my voice as I could manage while keeping a straight face. His eyes quickly met mine. He looked completely bewildered, like a rat trapped in a maze. Unable to hold it any longer, I burst out laughing.

"Oh…you!" He shook his head at me with a you-are-so-gonna-pay-for-that look on his face. Seeing that he had a sense of humor, I decided to push him a little further.

"What's wrong, darling?" I closed my eyes and smacked my lips, making kissing noises at him.

Suddenly his lips pressed against mine. My eyes flew open in shock, and I pushed back against his chest. He gave me another tender kiss, eroding my resolve. No longer protesting, I gripped his shirt with both hands and eagerly placed my lower lip between his. His strong arms wrapped tightly around me as our kiss deepened. When he finally pulled away I staggered back, speechless.

"Nothing, my love," he replied cockily.

Crap. He's so not my type. So why do I want to rip his shirt off right now?

"Get a room!" Raven teased. Now I was the one blushing.

Alexander gazed intently at me, trying to gauge my reaction. His smugness had been replaced with genuine concern. I took his hand and held it against my side. I knew almost nothing about him, but there was no denying how right it had felt when he kissed me.

"I'm afraid we must be going," Stefan said, motioning for Alexander to join him.

"Can't you stay a little longer?" Sienna pleaded. "Kelly should be here any minute."

"As much as I would like to, I'm afraid we have a plane of our own to catch. We're going to spend some time in Sydney over the holidays. I'll be sure to stop by the next time he's in town." Stefan stepped past Alexander and took me into his arms. "Enjoy your trip home. It would be an honor to meet your father someday."

"I'd love that– I'm sure he'll come out to visit me sometime this summer. Have fun in Australia." He took my hands and kissed me on both cheeks.

As Stefan said goodbye to Raven and Sienna, Alexander leaned in close to me. "Would you…I mean," he mumbled hesitantly. The unexpected shyness was kinda cute and helped to offset his intimidating build.

"Go out with you? Yes," I responded, letting him off the hook. Sandy had encouraged me to see other people. I could only hope that she meant what she said.

I was instantly engulfed in a giant bear hug. When he finally loosened his grip, I leaned up and touched my lips to his. "When will you be back?"

"January tenth."

His eyes widened when my hand shot into his jeans, retrieving the cell phone that I'd felt press against me. After entering my number, I slid it back in his pocket and gave him another soft kiss. "January tenth," I repeated.

"So what do you guys think of Alex?" I asked as soon as I was sure they were out of hearing range. I was hoping he'd let me call him that– Alexander was a mouthful.

"Alex?" Raven questioned with a smirk on her face. "He's a hell of a guy when he's not threatening to tear my head off."

"Come on… Seriously!"

Sienna lovingly ran her fingers through my hair. "He seems really nice. You two are cute together."

"He's got a good sense of humor in spite of his shyness," Raven added.

Dangerous Waters

"And even though he's built like a freight train, he's remarkably gentle with you. He kind of reminds me of a teddy bear."

"He does!" Okay… Maybe a grizzly bear, but still. "What do you know about him?"

"Not as much as I should, given that he's my best friend's only child," Sienna said. "Stefan met him in 1875 when he was living in Norfolk. Alexander had lost both of his parents during the civil war and was working at a local shipyard, spending his nights on the street or wherever he could find shelter. Stefan gave him a place to stay, and they soon were close friends. Alexander became a vampire the following spring– I believe he was twenty-one at the time. Before the transformation, Stefan spent an entire week with us so I could teach him everything that I'd learned from Colt and Raven's transformations. You're related in a sense, as Alexander also drank Colt's blood. It was just the two of them until about a year ago, when they met Travis and Teresa."

"They're here!" Raven shouted. We all went out onto the porch to wait for them.

Just as Ruby's Escalade came to a stop, Sandy hopped out and pulled the luggage from the trunk. Kelly joined her moments later, insisting on carrying the two largest suitcases himself. Ruby and Sandy laughed at his chivalrous gesture– like any of us needed help carrying *anything*.

Kelly was about six feet tall with a trim sculpted body and light brown wavy hair combed back away from his face. He had a dark golden tan, sapphire blue eyes, a strong jaw and chiseled cheek bones. Ruby was right– he was hot.

"Damn," I whispered admiringly under my breath.

Raven giggled. "You said it, sis."

Unable to wait any longer, we all went out into the yard to meet them.

"Hi, sweetheart!" Sienna hollered.

He picked her up and held her close to his chest. "God it's good to see you, Mom– it's been way too long."

As soon as they parted, Raven leapt into his arms. "Welcome home, bro. I really missed you."

Kelly kissed her on the cheek and slid her back onto her feet. "And you must be Brooke."

"It's nice to meet you, Kelly," I said, taking an awkward step forward.

He pulled me into a tight hug, and then leaned back and flashed me a to-die-for Hollywood smile. "So how are you adjusting to things?"

"Pretty good. It's easy for me to move normally now. I've still got a lot to learn about trancing people and suppressing thoughts, but I had fun practicing yesterday."

"Good to hear. I'm really looking forward to helping Sienna with your training the next couple weeks."

Sienna glanced at me, her eyes full of a mother's pride. "She left out the part where she totally de-clothed me in her first fighting lesson this morning."

Sandy, Ruby and Kelly all stared at me in complete silence. I could feel my cheeks burning and buried my face in my hands.

Kelly reached down and gently lifted my chin. "Really?"

I knew Sienna wouldn't let me lie, but I could at least tell them the whole truth. She was making it out like I mopped the floor with her. "Sienna hit me with her sword more times than I hit her, so she won regardless of who had more clothes on at the end. And now that she's seen how I fight, I'm sure she'll adjust her strategy and kick my ass even worse the next time."

"There isn't a conceited bone in your body, is there?" Kelly said approvingly. "I've fought against Sienna several times, and even with my physical advantages I've only managed to strike her twice. You have a gift, Brooke. That's nothing to be ashamed of."

"Thanks."

"My little ninja warrior," Sandy teased, leaning over to give me a quick kiss.

I took her hand as we all followed Raven up the creek stone walkway and onto the porch. After opening the door, Raven spun around and shot me a devious grin. "I almost forgot… She's got a boyfriend too."

Sandy looked back and forth between us in shock. "Jesus, how long were we gone?"

I tried to punch Raven, but she was using Kelly as a shield, dancing behind him like a fighter. Giving up, I rolled my eyes and let out an aggravated sigh. "We haven't even gone out on a date yet, so I'd hardly call Alex my boyfriend."

"Who's Alex?" Ruby wondered. "Alexander? Stefan's Alexander?"

I nodded my head.

"But isn't he the one that– " Ruby grabbed Kelly's arm, cutting him off. His face broke into a wide smile. "Interesting."

"I know it seems weird, but he's actually a pretty cool guy," I explained. "And if you think about it, what he did was kind of amazing. If he would've barged into our house and demanded that we let him walk out with the girl we were feeding on, that wouldn't have been a very pleasant conversation either. I'm sure Sienna would've handled it without threatening him, but I doubt if we would've let him leave with her."

"I would have certainly called Stefan and tried to defuse the situation, but I agree with you, Brooke," Sienna said. "If she was just a friend of his, there's no way he would have left here with her. Your mind is capable of a level of objectivity that is truly uncanny."

"So you two have a date?" Sandy's question brought me up short. It wasn't accusatory– she sounded genuinely curious– but her smile didn't quite conceal the hurt in her eyes.

"I don't know how they managed to set it up with their tongues in each other's mouths the entire time, but somehow they pulled it off," Raven joked.

I'd had enough. I faked to my left and got her to step just far enough out from behind Kelly to tackle her into the couch. Our squeals and giggles filled the room as we wrestled around on the floor.

"You give!" I hollered, smothering her face with an accent pillow.

"Okay! Okay!" As soon as I lifted the pillow, she yelled "Oh! Alex!" then started kissing the air. Before I could react, she hooked my right leg and flipped me onto my back, pinning my arms by my sides with her knees.

"Say he's your boyfriend!" she demanded.

"No!" I squealed, trying to free my arms while using only a human amount of force.

She picked up the pillow and mashed it in my face. "Say it!"

I was laughing so hard that I couldn't breathe. "I give."

She slowly pulled the pillow back, ready to smother me again if I didn't surrender. "He's my boyfriend," I said in a weak voice.

She grinned, enjoying her victory. "Who is?"

"Alex is my boyfriend," I whispered, even quieter than the first time.

She shoved the pillow into my face again. "What was that?"

"Alex is my boyfriend!" I screamed. Raven collapsed next to me, both of us struggling to catch our breath.

After we got back to our feet, I walked up to Kelly and took his hand. "You have to see the painting Ruby made me for my birthday!"

Ruby gave me an apprehensive look. "You don't mind?"

"Why would I? It's beautiful." Her face lit up. It was obvious how badly she wanted to show it to him.

I pulled Kelly along with me while I scampered into my room with Ruby following close behind. "Ignore the mess," I called out as I flipped on the lights. I hadn't bothered to make the bed yet, my pajamas from last night were still lying near the bathroom, and my workout clothes from the blue plastic bin were tossed all over the floor.

I'd decided to hang my painting in the center of the left wall so that I could see it from my bed, the loveseat and the chair.

As soon as Kelly saw it, he let out a gasp. "Oh, honey."

Ruby went along with him when he hurried over to get a better view. "It's unbelievably lifelike and detailed of course, but what I'll never understand is how you're able to capture the atmosphere and the surroundings in your work. After just looking at your painting, I feel as relaxed as I would if I'd just gotten out of the bath myself." Ruby pulled his head down and stole a long, hot kiss.

Kelly lifted his left arm up in the air, inviting me to join them, and wrapped it around my shoulders when I reached his side. "Not to mention how incredibly beautiful the subject of the painting is."

"Thanks. Did Ruby tell you what else she got me?"

"No, she didn't." He cast Ruby a sideways glance. She smiled and kissed him again.

"When we get back from Traverse City she's taking me out to the New England Aquarium, the Museum of Science and the Natick collection. We're going to spend the whole day together."

"Ruby told me how much you like animals and that you're majoring in conservation biology. You two should have a great time."

"You know it!"

"So what else did you get?" Kelly asked. "I know first birthdays are pretty wild around here."

"That's for sure," I agreed. "Raven got me the silver Mercedes in the driveway and plane tickets for all of us to go to Traverse City. Sandy got me a whole closet full of beautiful new clothes, and Sienna bought us a tennis club in Boston so we can all play tennis together."

"I heard you were quite the high school phenom. You made it all the way to the singles championship this summer, didn't you?"

"Yeah." I frowned, recalling the pounding that I'd taken. "I lost zero-six, one-six. I didn't even win a point in over half the games. It was humiliating."

"You were playing the number one seed in the state who hadn't lost all year," Ruby countered, arguing supportively on my behalf.

Okay, someone had done some surfing on the web. I gave her an appreciative smile. "I don't mean to pout. It's just kind of a painful memory. My dad got tickets for all of his friends and the people from his work to come down to Midland for the finals. He had to be so embarrassed watching me get pummeled like that."

Kelly still had an arm around each of us. Ruby reached her right arm around my left side, initiating kind of a group hug. "When your father was watching his little girl play for the state championship, I'm sure he had several emotions running through his mind, but I guarantee embarrassment wasn't one of them."

I could feel my eyes welling up. "Anyway, I still love to play tennis, and I can't wait to play with everybody. So is your sister Melanie the newest member of your family?"

"Actually, Chris is," Kelly said. "He just became a vampire three years ago. Kevin was already living with Cody when I met them in 1904. Melanie joined us in 1983."

"I'd love to meet them."

He grinned. "They're looking forward to meeting you as well."

"Looking forward?" Ruby challenged, raising her eyebrows at him. "Demanding is more like it."

Kelly kissed her on the top of her head. "Let's just say they're really hoping that you'll join Ruby when she comes out to visit me in February."

"Sounds awesome! Do you think you could teach me to surf while I'm out there?"

He laughed and gave my body a little squeeze. "Of course– I'll have you up riding waves with us in no time."

"Sweet! You've got quite a guy here, sis."

Ruby wrapped her hands around Kelly's neck and gazed into his mesmerizing blue eyes. "No argument there."

I was amazed by the passion they still felt for each other after being married for twelve years. When they held each other, I could tell that the rest of the world disappeared. Watching them filled me with a hopeless longing that made my insides ache. The only one who'd every made me feel that way was the one person I could never see again.

Chapter Twenty-Seven
New Moves

Sandy leaned against my doorway and pulled one of her legs up behind her to stretch. "You ready?"

"I hope so." Except for my brief fight with Sienna, I'd spent my entire time as a vampire acting human. I couldn't wait to fight her again, but sword fighting was only one component of my training.

It was just past 6:00 a.m. when Sandy and I walked across the backyard. The ground was illuminated by the quarter moon, which cast far more light than my new eyes required. It was a little chilly, maybe the high twenties, but there wasn't any snow yet.

I bent down and grabbed the back of my calves, stretching out my hamstrings. "So where are we going?"

"There's a nice beach about nine miles from here on Quincy bay. I thought we could watch the sunrise."

"Cool. I've never seen the sunrise over the ocean before. How long do you think it will take us to get there?"

"Even with us jogging the last mile at human speed, we should be there in less than fifteen minutes."

My jaw fell open. "How fast can we go?"

"At an easy jog, like we'll be doing this morning, we'll still top fifty."

"Miles per hour?"

She grinned. "That's nothing– we can sprint for long distances at close to two hundred and can get up to around three-fifty for short bursts."

"And you know this…how?"

"We had fun goofing around with a radar gun a few years ago."

"So who's the fastest?" Knowing my new family, even if they started out with a scientific purpose in mind, their experiments would've morphed into a competition.

She gave me a cute little smile. "Raven still claims that I cheated, but I had the top speed for a sprint at two hundred and six. Sienna blew us all away on the lunge moves, with several of hers breaking four hundred."

"Holy crap! You could pass me in my Mercedes with it floored."

"Pretty cool, huh. Wait until you see what it feels like."

"I can't wait!" I finished stretching my quads and my groin, and then got back to my feet. "Ready when you are."

"We're going to start out following the trail that goes to the Blue Hills reservation pond. Once we reach the pond we'll head north. There isn't really a trail to follow, but it's pretty easy to weave your way through the trees. When we reach the edge of the reservation, we'll cross over a golf course and go through the Milton cemetery before we hit the Neponset River. From there we'll head east along the riverbank all the way to Quincy Shore Drive. No one lives within sight of the path we'll be taking, but we'll have to walk across two roads while we're following the river and slow to what will feel like a crawl for the last mile to the beach. It's important that you take relatively the same path that I do, especially once we get through the cemetery, as we are narrowly avoiding a couple of subdivisions."

"I'll try to stay behind ya," I promised.

As soon as Sandy started to move, she was across the bridge and out of sight.

"Crap," I blurted out before taking off after her. Even though I was only intending to jog at a nice, easy pace, the ground flew past me at astonishing speed– each of my strides had to be covering at least twenty feet. In just a few seconds I was back on Sandy's heels. "This is too cool!" I shouted. I could hear her giggling in front of me.

When we reached the pond, Sandy veered to her left toward a thick set of pines. She maintained the same pace but significantly shortened her stride, increasing her foot speed to compensate. I immediately followed suit. The reason for the change became apparent as soon as we hit the trees. While my mind had no trouble picking a safe path through the downed trees, thickets and branches, I had to use far more precise footwork.

After a short time jogging through the forest, I noticed that Sandy was taking a much straighter path than I was, making me work a bit harder to keep up with her. I soon learned from watching her that it was easier to hurdle smaller obstacles on the ground than it was to veer around them. Even piles of downed trees three feet high could be cleared with only slightly more effort than a normal step.

As my movements became more routine, I began to relax and take in everything around me. My ears had no trouble distinguishing the slight breeze rustling the pine boughs around us from that of a clearing I was sure lay ahead.

It was effortless to isolate the faint sound of individual insects scurrying along the ground. I could even hear rushing water from the river that was still miles north of us. In addition to the thick scents of pine and earth that were almost overpowering, I could smell the mildew from the moss on the trees and decaying flesh from a carcass that was somewhere off to our east. The scent of Kentucky bluegrass told me that the clearing ahead was likely the golf course.

We rapidly crossed over four different fairways before angling off to our right through a small community park and veering back to our left into the cemetery. Sandy followed the main drive for as long as she could, and then cut across a few plots and into a set of pines. There were several houses on both sides of us while we made our way through the narrow strip of woods that divided the subdivisions, but there was no way anyone would spot us at night in the dense foliage. When we reached the river bottom, we jogged along the bank, staying close to the tree line to break up our silhouettes. As soon as the pines ended, Sandy veered north into a large irrigated farm field and picked up speed. I broke into a brisk jog to stay with her, hurdling five foot wide irrigation channels along the way. The main river was still to our left, but there was a large tributary branching off of it about two thousand yards ahead that wrapped all the way around us to the right. Sandy headed for the narrowest point, which still had to be almost a hundred feet across.

"Sandy!" I yelled in a panic. She'd failed to mention we'd be jumping a river along the way.

"Don't sweat it, Brooke. It's easy!" she hollered back over her shoulder.

I skidded to a stop just short of the river and watched Sandy sail over it with ease, landing a good twenty feet past the far edge.

As soon as she heard that I was no longer behind her, she stopped and doubled back. "What's wrong?"

"I'm scared," I admitted. "I don't really want to go for a swim this morning."

She snorted. "You're such a goof! You could easily jump the main river at its widest point."

"Really?" The widest part I'd seen had to be over 350 feet across.

She just rolled her eyes at me. "Just back up about five hundred yards, slowly accelerate until you reach the pace we had near the end and act like you're hopping over a creek– your body will do the rest."

"Okay," I muttered, already jogging back toward the pines.

When I was about half way across the field, I stopped and turned back toward her. I was tempted to sprint at full speed and put everything I had into the jump to ensure that I cleared the river, but there was a multi-lane highway less than 70 yards behind her. If we could jump anywhere near as far as she was saying, I'd be road kill. I'd have to trust that what she was telling me would work.

After starting out slowly, I built up speed until I was back to a brisk jog. When I reached the riverbank I planted my left foot, pushed off and threw my right leg forward, launching myself at least 30 feet into the air. I easily cleared the river, landing about 50 feet behind Sandy.

"I am so doing that again! Did you see me?"

She scampered over and gave me a quick hug. "There's nothing like your first jump. We'd better get moving though if we want to make the beach before sunrise."

We headed north, tightly hugging the four rows of pines that ran along the highway for cover, and then cut through a larger set of pines before slowing to a walk as we crossed Granite Avenue. We maintained a human pace while we went under I-93 and skirted the edge of three subdivisions. When we reached another golf course we charged forward, following the cart path all the way to Harriet Avenue. Sandy and I jogged side by side the rest of the way, up Newport Avenue to Quincy Shore Drive, then circling around to the beach.

After walking along the shoreline for a couple hundred yards, we reached a nice, secluded spot and plopped down in the sand. The beach was deserted and the small clump of trees behind us shielded us from the sparse traffic on the road.

"That was kick-ass!" I said, bending over to stretch out my legs.

"Totally!"

"How did you learn the route?" The way she'd used all of the available cover made it obvious that she already knew exactly where she was going.

Sandy pulled a water bottle out of her fanny pack, popped the top and took a big swig before handing it to me. "I've been doing that run at least once a week since we moved out here this spring, and I've done something similar to it everywhere we've lived since I was changed. Sienna isn't crazy about my little excursions, since they present some risk of exposing us without serving any real purpose, but she's never tried to stop me. I got Raven and Ruby to join me a couple of times. They never saw the fun in it. Maybe being able to move like that will get boring to me too someday. Right now there's nothing I enjoy more."

Sandy's knee-length aerobic tights clung to her muscular thighs. She had removed her jacket to cool down, and the pink fitted tank she had on underneath left her midriff and most of her breasts exposed. Her skin glistened with sweat, and her short blonde hair was stuck to her forehead. It was all I could do not to pounce on her. I reached out and ran my fingers along her cheek. "I'd love to join you anytime you'd like a partner."

"Do you really mean that?" she asked, carefully studying my face.

I gazed into her pale blue eyes. "Absolutely."

Her face broke into a wide smile as she kissed my hand. "Every Wednesday?"

"Count me in!"

We sat nestled up against each other and watched in silence while a faint orange light in the distance grew stronger. The darkness slowly yielded to the brightening light, with bands of purple, red, orange, yellow and blue reaching higher into the sky. A few minutes later the sun crested the horizon, casting a stunning orange reflection across the water. The sun had a goldish-yellow core surrounded by oval-shaped layers of bright orange and fiery pink. Like a child's drawing, six brilliant yellow streaks extended from the center in a perfect star pattern.

"God, that's so beautiful," I whispered, staring out across the glistening bay.

Sandy wrapped her arm around my waist and nudged my body up against hers. "You're amazing, you know that?"

I let out a content sigh, resting my head on her shoulder. "I think you're pretty amazing too."

After kissing the top of my head, she turned toward me and leaned in, stopping just before our lips touched.

I quickly closed the distance.

The first kiss was little more than a peck, but it sent a scorching wave of heat circulating through my veins. My heart beat so hard that the noise was deafening, like a bass drum going off in my head. She gave me two more soft, intimate kisses before parting my lips and deepening our embrace. When I felt her hand firmly grope me, I locked my fingers in her short blonde hair and nibbled on her lip. Sandy sprung to her knees and laid me down in the sand, kissing and caressing my neck while she unzipped my hoodie.

Her fingertips slowly traced the curve of my jaw, and then slid down my chest. I let out a soft whimper when she lifted up my sports bra and sliced through it with her nails. Her lips found mine again. We shared open-mouthed, lustful kisses while her skilled fingers explored my exposed breasts. She began to twist and pull on my nipples, sending threads of delicious pain through my body. Then her head slid lower and my breast was in her mouth.

Her erotic nips and multi-speed, flickering tongue felt almost criminal– like toys from some adults-only toy box I'd never gotten to play with before. The last trace of my inhibition burned away. All I wanted was for her to rip my pants off and take me right here on the beach. At least that's what I thought until she began to suck. Unlike Daniel, who latched onto my breast like a calf searching for milk, Sandy slid from one hyper-sensitive spot to another. It felt almost like she was giving me a hickey, but with a vibrating sensation mixed in that made my whole body quiver.

"Oh! Oh fuck!" I moaned. She hadn't ventured anywhere near my pussy and I was already going to cum. When she felt my body stiffen, she moved up to my nipple and sent me tumbling over the edge. A wild orgasm claimed me. I thrashed around in the sand and screamed like a banshee while I soaked the crotch of my running pants. As soon as the last convulsion ended, Sandy started to lightly stroke my abdomen with her fingertips, drawing little circles around my navel while she waited for me to recover.

I took a deep breath, letting myself enjoy the serene feeling for just a second longer before sitting up and reaching for the bottom of her tank top. I'd raised it about half way up when Sandy's arms knocked my hands away. Before I could ask what was wrong, she grabbed my hoodie, pulled it back over my shoulders and zipped it up. She'd barely finished when an older couple came into view, walking along the shoreline with a black lab and golden retriever in tow. We gave them a polite wave as they passed.

"That was close," I said, still watching them. The lab kept running circles around the woman, making her trip on the leash.

Sandy jumped up to her feet. "We should probably head back. You've got a big day ahead of you."

"Are you sure? I don't see anyone else around." I reached for her shirt again.

She caught my hands and pulled me up. "I'm sure. I didn't even mean for things to go that– far."

"Meaning, you didn't expect me to have a gigantic orgasm from just playing with my boobs."

Sandy snorted. "Pretty much. Are you sure you're okay? I feel like I'm rushing you."

"I'm fine. No scratch that– I'm far better than fine. That was unbelievable.

Well, at least for me."

She cupped my face and gave me a reassuring kiss. "Please. I'm so wet right now I'll have to peel my panties off by the time we get home."

"Speaking of that." I glanced down at my soaked crotch. "Not that I'm complaining, but this feels kinda gross."

Sandy led me to a public restroom about a quarter mile further down the beach and stood guard at the door. After tossing my panties and shredded sports bra into the trash, I rinsed out the crotch of my pants and rung them dry. I was hoping for an air dryer, but had to settle for a handful of paper towels.

I'd been fantasizing about our first time for so long that, up until now, I was a little afraid the reality of the moment could never measure up. But after seeing what she could do with her tongue and mouth, I wasn't sure I could even survive her going down on me. And I hadn't even gotten to touch her yet. I couldn't wait to have her breast in my mouth, to tease her nipple as she came for me. When I noticed that I was playing with myself again, I let out a laugh. Bi-curious was so out the window.

"Much better," I said, ducking under her outstretched arm blocking the doorway. "Ready for the trip back?"

She tilted my chin up with her hand, and then used her fingers to straighten my hair. "I'm afraid that's going to take longer."

"Why? Do we have to go a different way?"

She grinned. "We have to drive. We can only run when it's dark out."

"That explains it. Hey, I finally get to ride in the Charger."

"Yep, I have my own space in a parking garage about two blocks from here. I've been driving down the night before and running back, but now that you're joining me, we could drive two cars and drop one off."

She had her jacket tied around her waist, which left all that delicious skin on her chest still exposed. I traced my fingers slowly along the edge of her tank, caressing her breast though the thin cotton material. Her nipple hardened beneath my touch. "Or I could ride with you and we could run back together."

Sandy let out a soft little moan. "I was hoping you'd say that."

When we got back to the house, Sienna and Kelly were waiting for me in the training room. I took a lightening quick shower, threw on a pink sports bra and black fitted shorts, slid on my Nike cross-training shoes and hurried down the hall to join them.

In the center of the room toward the front, where the exercise equipment used to be, a large portion of the wooden floor had been removed. The vacated space was occupied by what could only be described as a heavily armored phone booth. Four solid steel square posts stood bolted into the cement floor with thick metal plates attached to each side. The posts were arranged in a rectangle that was roughly the size of a human. Given the two large piles of extra plates stacked up neatly against the wall, I was guessing they were interchangeable.

Sienna flashed me her usual, adoring smile. "How was your jog?"

"It was way cool! I got up to, like, eighty miles an hour and jumped a river."

Kelly chuckled. "Quite a feeling, isn't it?"

"The best." I shifted my attention to the contraption they'd built. "What's that for?"

"That's your opponent," Sienna said with a smirk. "Meet old ironsides."

My eyes widened as I studied the plates more closely. "I'm going to hit that? It must be four inches thick."

"The plates are actually three inches thick," Kelly corrected. "And they're made of a mixture of beryllium, nickel and titanium to produce a tensile strength of a hundred and thirty thousand pounds per square inch. It takes roughly a hundred and fifty thousand pounds of force to cause harm to even the most vulnerable parts of our body. So in order to be in the ball park of how hard you'll have to strike another vampire to injure them, you not only need to hit these plates, you need to punch and kick right through them. The strength of the metal is less than the force required to hurt you, so there's no risk of injuring yourself. That's why we don't use a hundred and fifty thousand psi plates."

Sienna surveyed what I was wearing. "Take your socks and shoes off. I don't think Nike had this in mind."

I giggled as I slid them off, picturing what a Nike vampire commercial would look like.

"As we briefly discussed yesterday, there are several elements of your training," she continued, strolling around the perimeter of the cement floor, her eyes on ironsides. "Sword fighting is designed to sharpen your reflexes and teach you when to strike. Martial arts and sparring will strengthen your defensive skills and teach you how and where to strike. Learning to control your body by practicing physical maneuvers like running, jumping and tumbling is critical for attack and defense. Ironsides serves only one purpose: to teach you how hard to strike."

"Where are we must vulnerable?"

"Generally speaking, you want to target the softest areas of the body with your kicks and punches: the abdomen, the sides below the ribs, the kidneys and throat," Sienna said, touching the corresponding areas on my body. "But our biggest vulnerability of all is our flesh. Using our nails allows us to direct all of our force onto a tiny surface area, making it easy to tear through vampire skin. Even though the wounds themselves are often superficial, they are nonetheless lethal given our inability to heal, and several long gashes across an opponent's back, chest or stomach will cause them to rapidly bleed out. While striking the bony areas of the body like the arms, legs, head and ribs can also inflict damage, it's a last resort, as it presents too great of a risk of injuring yourself."

Kelly turned to face me. "Okay, Brooke. First, pay attention to how I'm holding my hands. Don't clench your fists and never place your thumb inside of your fingers. Keep your hands loose with your fingers curled slightly inward. As you throw a punch, make a loose fist so that you strike your target with your knuckles like this– " Kelly threw a quick jab with his right hand, putting a deep impression in the plate. "Now it's your turn. Don't worry about power for now. Just get the feel for throwing a punch."

I'd practiced something similar in my self-defense class, minus the three inch thick steel plates, of course. I turned sideways with my left foot forward and my feet about shoulder width apart, raising my hands up to just below my chin. As I extended my right arm, I twisted my hips and put my shoulder into it. I was shocked when I saw that my hand had barely left an impression in the steel.

"Damn it! What'd I do wrong?"

"Actually, you did a lot of things right," he said, sounding a bit surprised. "Have you had martial arts training before?"

"Just an eight-week class at the Y this summer. How was that good? I can barely tell where I hit it."

"Your form is excellent, far ahead of where I thought you'd be. Now you just need to learn to harness the power from your body."

"How do I do that?"

Sienna laughed. "That's what we're here to teach you. This isn't something you're going to master in five minutes– it took Sandy almost a month to break through her first plate."

"Oh." I'd assumed that I'd just be able to do it naturally, like I had earlier with running and jumping.

"This time I want you to do the same motions that you did before, but visualize not just striking the surface of the target, but punching clean through it," Kelly instructed. "And you need to explode through your motions like you do when you're sword fighting. Imagine that Sienna's standing in front of you, and she just left her stomach vulnerable. You need to strike before she recovers."

"I see– I need to psych myself up."

"Exactly."

After I got back into my stance, I rocked slightly from side to side, pretending that the plate in front of me was Sienna preparing to attack. Then I pictured her carelessly raising her sword over her head, leaving her entire body exposed. In a fraction of a second I threw all of my weight onto my right foot as I violently twisted my hips and thrust my right arm ahead. A loud, metallic echo filled the room. When I tried to pull my arm back, I felt like someone was holding it. Unsure of what had happened, I looked up at the plate and discovered that my arm was buried all the way up to my elbow. The metal surrounding it was dented in at least a foot, and several hairline cracks splintered off in all directions.

"Yes!" I cheered, throwing my left arm up in the air.

Sienna placed her hand on my shoulder, shaking her head in disbelief. "Okay, so maybe you can master it in five minutes."

I leaned back and tugged on my arm again. "How do I get out?"

"Just step back and pull your arm hard, like you're trying to elbow someone behind you," Kelly replied. "Even though the torn metal is sharp, it can't hurt you."

I peered over my right shoulder, pushed off my left foot and shot my arm backward, easily dislodging it from the hole.

Kelly looped his arms loosely around my back. "I was willing to accept Sienna's explanation for your success fighting against her, as it's logical to assume that your experience playing tennis would be helpful. But given what you just did, I'm convinced there is something more going on with you."

Sienna furrowed her brows. "What do you mean? You think she has some kind of ability?"

"Yes," he said flatly. Kelly stepped back to study me like I was a particularly interesting lab specimen. "I don't have any idea what it is yet, but I'm sure there is something genetic at work here. It's as if she already knows what we're trying to teach her and is just remembering how to do it, not learning it for the first time."

"I agree that Brooke's skills are extraordinary for someone so young, but she was very athletic as a human." The concern in Sienna's eyes made me wonder if having an extra ability was really a good thing. She looked like a mother stuck in denial as a frustrated doctor tried to get her to accept that her child had cancer. "She played several sports in addition to tennis and is an amazing dancer as well. I can't think of a similar vampire to compare her to. Maybe it's normal for someone like her to pick this up so easily."

Kelly firmly placed his hand on her shoulder, trying to make her to see reason. "You know as well as I do that what she just did should have taken weeks, even if she practiced for hours every day. And I don't care how athletically gifted my sister is, there's no way she should've gotten her sword within the same area code as your body for several months, if not years. On top of that, she just happened to be the only human in history that could break our trances and the only vampire I've ever heard of that managed to sleep during their transformation. It's far too much to be chalked up to coincidence."

I gnawed my lip while I tried to follow along. "I don't understand. How could I inherit vampire abilities?"

Kelly took my hand. "Let me clarify, my beautiful and talented sister. I didn't mean to imply that you had vampire ancestors who somehow managed to have children. If I'm right, you have a unique ability that was revived by your transformation, stemming from very old but very human relatives that had some kind of advanced fighting skills embedded within their culture– like those first taught by the Buddhist monks in India, China and Japan. Since control of the mind was a central component of their teaching, that would also explain your ability to break our trance and sleep during your transformation."

The stern set of Sienna's jaw made it clear she still wasn't convinced. "You're forgetting that she could break our trances before she was changed."

"I don't think her ability was entirely dormant, it was just greatly enhanced by her transformation. Just like her sight, hearing and sense of smell. Without even realizing it, I believe she's been tapping into it her entire life."

"That makes a lot of sense…but we don't have anywhere near enough information to conclude anything." Sienna gave me a thoughtful look. "If it's okay with you, I'd like to do a genealogical workup on your family and run a DNA analysis to see what we can learn about your distant relatives."

All I'd wanted since I decided to join my new family was to get through the awkward learning phase and fit in. Instead I felt like they were about to brand a number on my neck so they could easily refer to me in their experiments. "Just don't forget that I'm your daughter, Mom, not some fucking lab rat."

Dangerous Waters

Sienna bent down and gave me a loving kiss on the forehead. "Watch your language or you'll be my *grounded* daughter, but point taken. Any information you can provide on your parents and grandparents would be helpful. Especially their full names and the dates and locations of their birth. I can get your DNA samples from the brushes in your bedroom."

I was about to argue how unfair she was being– that I was hardly the only one in the family to use the F word– until I remembered that I was the only one who was actually a teenager. "I know some of them but I'll get the rest from my dad– I can pretend it's an assignment for class or something."

"That's perfect." Sienna tenderly caressed my cheek. "Are you ready to resume your lesson?"

I nodded.

Kelly replaced the plate I'd destroyed, and then stood next to me. "Since you seem to have a pretty good handle on punching, let's try a simple front kick. Did you practice them in your class?"

"Yep. On the last day we even got to break pine boards."

"Excellent. First show me your form at human speed."

I got back into the karate stance I'd practiced in class, standing about two feet from the steel plate. As I pivoted my hips toward the target, I shifted my weight onto my left foot and lifted my right knee up above my waist. After rocking up onto the balls of my left foot I curled my toes back and snapped my right leg led forward, lightly hitting the plate at about chest level. I slowly pulled my foot back so that my knee was again raised to my waist and returned to my starting position.

Kelly picked me up and twirled me around in the air. "Outstanding!"

"I don't recall Sienna teaching me that move, my love," Ruby said, walking into the room with Sandy and Raven close behind.

He flashed her a smile. "Your sister is unbelievable. She shredded a plate on her second punch."

"It took her two tries? You're slipping, sis!" Raven teased. The room filled with laughter.

"Do you mind if we watch?" Sandy asked. The curiosity and excitement in her eyes made me smile. Maybe being special wouldn't be so bad after all.

"Not at all– just promise not to laugh if my first kick doesn't go so well."

Raven snorted. "I can't promise that. Why do you think we want to watch? Go ironsides!" Raven raised her arms over her head like a cheerleader.

If I did anything less than kick clean through the plate, I knew they'd all be rolling on the floor. Feeling a little flustered, I got back into my stance and tried to settle my mind. I imagined that I was back in the damp, dark room where Teresa and Travis had fed on me. The plate in front of me was Teresa, standing with her back toward me while I placed my mother's necklace around her neck. I forced myself to dwell on the memory until tears streamed down my face. But unlike before, when she turned around and smiled at me, I was no longer under her trance. Teresa's arms hung down at her sides, leaving her totally defenseless.

Rage built inside me as I prepared to launch my attack–

* * * *

I was now crouching in the thick underbrush of the rainforest, seeking cover. What remained of my tribe hid nearby as a wooden warship with three massive white sails pounded the beach and surrounding area with its cannons. My plan to wait in ambush for our iron-clad enemy to reach shore had backfired, and now my people were being slaughtered in droves. Hundred-year-old trees fell like matchsticks under the unrelenting barrage, starting fires and cutting off our escape.

I wore an elaborate headdress and a simple loin cloth made of feathers. Ink patterns of dots and lines adorned my arms and legs– and I was a man. His darkened skin and black hair gave him a Native American appearance, but there was something familiar about his eyes. Most surprising of all, he wasn't a vampire.

His thoughts focused on the woman and five small children that he'd left hidden under tree bows on the other side of the forest. Failing to repel this attack wouldn't just cost him the lives of hundreds of his bravest warriors– his enemy would track down and kill every man, woman and child until his entire tribe was extinct. In his fifty long years and countless battles, he'd never encountered a warship or cannon before. Its devastating power rivaled his own, but he was done cowering in fear.

Lunging out of the forest, I raised my hands out in front of me and let out a fierce battle cry. The skin on my fingertips started to tingle as a brilliant white light arched between them. My entire body was now surging with power, drawn from the billions of atoms that surrounded me. When the mass of pure energy forming near my chest had grown to the width of my body, I thrust my hands toward the midsection of the ship. The light shot forward, ripping through the red wooden planks just above the waterline. A split second later the entire ship exploded in a massive fireball that threw me onto my back–

* * * *

Still half in another world, my right leg rocketed forward faster than I'd ever moved before. A thunderous explosion shook the room like an earthquake and left a terrible ringing sound in my ears. After I recovered from the deafening noise, I realized that I was still standing on both feet. My eyes shot up to the target. The front plate was gone, and there was a volleyball-sized hole in the back plate. "Where'd it go?"

Kelly bent down and picked up a twisted piece of metal off the floor. "Everywhere, like shrapnel from a grenade!"

"Holy shit! She broke the back plate too!" Sandy raced over to inspect the carnage along with the rest of my sisters.

Sienna reached up and wiped a tear from my cheek with her thumb. "What were you thinking about?"

"That was Teresa– and she'd just taken my mom's necklace from me."

She laughed. "That's a relief. I'm not sure I'd want to fight you again if that was me you were picturing." I burst out laughing and gave her a tight hug.

"How much force would it take to do that?" Ruby asked, studying the piece that Kelly was still holding.

"I have no idea." He shook his head as he continued to inspect the twisted metal. "Cody's been using this kind of device to train our family since long before I joined them, and nothing like this has ever happened. The fact that a fragment from the front plate hit the back plate with at least a hundred and thirty thousand pounds of force means that the initial impact must have been several times that high. As fit as your sister is, she doesn't have the muscle tissue to generate that kind of power. There's no doubt that Brooke has a unique genetic ability of some kind, but determining exactly what it is and what all it will allow her to do could take decades."

Now that I'd settled down somewhat, my thoughts drifted back to my crazy ass daydream. What the hell was that? It had felt so real. And just like my dream about the cat-eyed vampire, I was the Native American warrior but also observed him from a birds-eye view. Except this time I was wide awake. I thought about telling Sienna, but even Sandy already seemed a little scared of me. If I told them I was having hallucinations, they'd probably throw me in a cage so I couldn't hurt anyone.

"As exciting as all this is, there's still one more thing Brooke needs to practice today." Sienna motioned toward all the debris. "Let's get this cleaned up so we can continue."

Kelly went to work replacing the front and back plates while Raven, Ruby and Sandy gathered up all of the metal fragments and piled them in the corner.

"There isn't a lot of technique necessary for this one," Sienna continued. "I just want you to dig your nails into the metal and claw downward to get a feel for how hard you need to push to tear through vampire skin. Because you're applying the pressure to a lot smaller surface area, you'll discover that it take far less force to penetrate the plate."

I placed the nails of my right hand against the front plate and pulled downward, pressing hard against them. A burning pain lit up my arm, causing me to grip it tightly against my chest and recoil in fear.

"What's wrong!" Sienna shouted.

I closed my eyes, anxiously waiting for the pain to subside. "It's my wrist."

"Let me see." Raven pulled my left arm away then lifted my right hand up to her chest. "Move your fingers for me."

"Not right now. It's just my muscles– that was way too much pressure on them." When the pain finally eased I flexed my fingers.

"Good. Now bend your wrist." After I twisted my wrist around in both directions without wincing, she began to press her thumbs against the inside of my arm, working her way from my hand all the way to my elbow. "Any sharp pain when I press down?"

"Nope– so am I going to croak?"

She laughed. "I think you'll pull through."

Sienna was still staring blankly at the steel plate. The claw marks I'd left were no more than an eighth of an inch deep, and trailed off after only a couple inches.

"She's okay, Sienna," Kelly reassured her.

"Okay!?" Tears rolled down her cheeks as she turned to glare at him. "Brooke's defenseless because of me. I've maimed my own daughter."

I stepped between them and forced her to look at me. "Please don't feel bad, Mom. I love you. Do you really think I wouldn't be happy to trade some weakness in my wrist for your life?"

"I know you would, baby," she choked out, gazing affectionately into my eyes. "But that doesn't excuse what I did to you. Your forgiveness is the only reason I've been able to bear it."

Dangerous Waters

Kelly grinned, motioning toward the pile of rubble in the corner. "And unless you're volunteering to stand in front of her next kick, I'd hardly say Brooke is defenseless."

Sienna wiped away what was left of her tears with her palm and took a couple of deep breaths. "True."

"Besides, I still have my left hand to claw with." I walked up to the front plate and raked my nails across it, easily tearing half inch deep grooves into the metal.

Sienna reached out and took both of my hands. "I'm going to have to get very creative with your training. There's no way we can risk having you spar with us or do any contact maneuvers, not even roughhousing with your sisters – you're just too powerful to take a chance. We'll have to use more of a kata style, where you learn the moves as part of a routine that you can practice without an opponent.

"I'll continue to sword fight with you for now, since its essential for your development that you practice full speed combat with other vampires. You exhibited complete control during your first lesson, but if you ever move too rapidly for me to follow, like you just did when you pulverized that plate, I'll have to suspend that as well. We'll begin to work with you on your tumbling exercises tomorrow, and we'll utilize ironsides more than we ever have in the past."

I could feel my eyes welling up but Sienna wouldn't let me pull away from her. "Please don't think that I'm punishing you, sweetheart. We just need to take some extra precautions until we gain a better understanding of what your gift allows you to do, and how much control you have over it. And I know it may not feel like it right now, but you truly have been blessed with a gift– one that could save all of our lives someday."

How was this not a punishment? I was getting screwed out of most of my training, and my sisters weren't allowed within ten feet of me. I held my wrists together like they were in shackles. "Sure you don't want to just chain me up in the closet? I mean, I'm so dangerous and out of control, I'd hate to kill someone while I'm trying to brush my teeth."

"You know that's not what I meant."

"Whatever. I'm going to take a bath– unless that's been banned too." I stormed off before she replied.

Chapter Twenty-Eight
Country Living

Travis took one last look at the snow-covered banks of Henry's Fork. His family had spent at least two weeks vacationing near this part of the Snake River every summer, he and his dad fishing while the girls rode horses or browsed for souvenirs. He thought about how good it would feel to hold a fly pole in his hand again– to hear his dad coaching him on just where to cast, how to tempt a reluctant trout or search the shore for mayfly hatchlings in order to select the perfect bait. When he was twelve he'd won their family's big fish contest for the first time, landing a twenty-five-inch Rainbow. His dad had marched him from store to store, proudly showing off his prize and bought him his very own fly tying kit as a reward. Less than ten hours later, both his parents were dead.

He'd spent the next five years bouncing around with his sister from one nightmarish foster home to another before he finally met Keri. She was a guidance counselor at his high school and had latched onto him from the moment they met, as if turning his life around was her personal mission. At first Travis wanted no part in hearing her inspirational bullshit about what a good person he was inside and went out of his way to show her just how wrong she was, but each of his escapades just made her that much more determined. When she put her own career on the line to cover for him, lying about his whereabouts after he broke into the cash register in the cafeteria, he quit pushing her away. Keri told him to get his shit together, and he finally listened. He started attending all of his classes, did his homework and raised his GPA a full point by the end of his junior year.

On Fourth of July weekend, Teresa swiped their foster mom's credit card and took off to Vegas, running up close to a two-thousand-dollar bill. They were back in the placement center for the seventh time on Monday. Thanks to Keri, they weren't there long. Social services was far from thrilled to have a twenty-three-year-old single woman take legal custody of a seventeen- and fifteen-year-old, but she was a counselor, and it wasn't like people were beating their door down to get their hands on two troubled teenagers with checkered pasts.

He slept with her for the first time less than a week later, and they were sharing a bedroom by the time school resumed. Things that Travis dismissed with little more than a passing thought, like Keri's apparent lack of appetite, piqued his sister's curiosity. It wasn't long before she was following Keri whenever she left the house. Keri knew of course and was using Teresa's inquisitiveness to her advantage, waiting until she'd convinced Travis to come along before revealing herself.

In hindsight, his sister's exuberance was a clear warning of things to come, but at the time, he was thrilled that she was so accepting. She began urging him to propose almost immediately. What Teresa had done to achieve her true goal sickened him, but he couldn't bring himself to hate her for it– or even blame her for that matter. His ten-year-old sister had been an easy-going, good-natured kid full of smiles and kisses. He'd killed that girl as surely as he'd killed their parents.

Travis wiped his cheeks on the sleeve of his winter jacket before tossing two of the rabbits he'd caught into the back of their steel-gray H3. He bit into the neck of the third, eagerly gulping down the life-giving fluid. Then he climbed into the truck and started back toward their cabin, wondering if he'd ever see this place again.

* * * *

"Come on, Terr– this isn't funny anymore. Just close your eyes and drink."

Teresa turned her head away from the rabbit in disgust. "I told you, I'm not eating another fucking animal. Get that out of my face before I puke."

"It's been thirteen days– "

"And whose fault is that!" she screamed. "You're the one who won't let me feed."

Travis threw the carcass toward the half-open cabin door, and it smacked into it with a thud. "You know how many people were killed in Idaho Falls last year? Two. That means it'd be a pretty big fucking deal if someone disappeared."

"So we'll go back to Boise."

"Yeah, because it had a whopping four last year– we've already matched that ourselves. And don't even think about Salt Lake City. After your little trance-a-thon in the mall two weeks ago, we're never going there again."

"I'm not the one who moved us here, assbag! Just take me home. Problem solved."

Travis tiredly rubbed his eyes. "It's only been three months. They could still be looking for us."

"If they are, they're not very good at it. I mean, come on. A bank manager cleans out his safe, and then kills himself, and eight people disappear from two hick towns less than three hours apart. I wouldn't exactly say we've been off the grid." Teresa had to steady herself after sitting up on the end of the couch, as if the simple act had taken the last of her strength. The desperate look in her eyes cut through him. "Please, Trav, I hate it here. I'll even eat the stupid bunny."

"Has it really been that bad?" he said, glancing around the small cabin at the seventy-inch flat screen, Xbox One entertainment system, and ultra-plush, deluxe leather couches they'd picked out together.

She reached out and took his hand. "Not all of it. This was our first place – I'll never forget that."

"It's not like we could stay here much longer anyway. Why does it have to be Boston though? It's December. We should go to St. Thomas– or the Bahamas."

Her eyes hardened as she cast him a steely glare. "You know why."

"Emily? You're *still* hung up on her? " He shook his head in frustration. "Let it go already."

"You said I could kill her," Teresa snapped.

"And you fucked it up!" he fired back at her. "It's too late now– if she's still alive, she's a vampire."

"That'll make it even easier. They won't be babysitting her anymore."

He snorted. "This from the girl who got her ass beat all though high school."

She gave him a defiant huff. "I held my own most of the time. Besides, at least I've been in fights. I doubt if her prissy ass has ever thrown a punch in her life."

Travis tugged on his disheveled brown hair while he took several deep breaths to calm himself. "Drop it, okay? I'm not letting you get killed over some psychotic obsession."

"If you *don't* move us back, I'll starve myself to death."

Travis lunged forward, making her cower back into the couch like a submissive dog. "You're blackmailing me! This is horseshit! I'm just trying to keep your dumb ass alive!"

Her lips curled up in a maniacal grin. "Then help me– I'd love to watch you rip out her intestines and make her play with them before she dies."

He let out an exasperated sigh. "I guess I don't have a choice."

Chapter Twenty-Nine
Home Sweet Home

As we taxied up to the terminal, I gazed out the window into the blackness. A light snow was falling into a stiff winter wind, the flakes dancing across the ground in the breeze.

"…on behalf of our Detroit based crew, I'd like to thank you for flying Delta," the captain announced over the intercom. "I hope you enjoy your stay in Traverse City or wherever your final destination may take you. The local time is eleven thirty-four p.m., and the temperature is a crisp seventeen degrees."

The ding of the seatbelt sign being turned off sent people scrambling to grab their bags, crowding the aisle while they waited for the door to be opened. Flying first class from Boston to Detroit had been luxurious, but it meant little on this size of plane. I couldn't wait to get up and stretch my legs. After everyone de-planed, we stood up and gathered our things.

My heart began to race as we made our way up the jet bridge. I could feel a cold sweat dripping down my brow, and my hands were shaking like it was my third day in detox.

Sienna reached out and took my hand. "Relax, sweetheart– everything's going to be fine."

I wanted desperately to believe her, but there were so many things that could go wrong, things that could ruin all of our lives. Sensing that I wasn't ready, Sienna guided us into the woman's restroom, which thankfully was deserted. I darted into the first stall and bent over the toilet, throwing up what little fluid was in my stomach. After rinsing my mouth, I leaned against the sink and splashed some water on my face.

Sandy handed me stack of paper towels, her eyes filled with sympathy. "Feel better?"

"Yep– must have been something I ate." Sandy just shook her head, but I received a few mercy laughs from the others. I was still nervous, but I did feel better. I was ready.

Sienna tucked a chunk of hair behind my ear. "Remember, baby– "

"Emme," I corrected, flashing a smile.

She laughed. "Remember, Emme, try to keep his thoughts suppressed in your mind— it'll help you act a lot more natural. If he thinks anything you need to be concerned about, we'll let you know."

I nodded. It'd been almost a month since my transformation, and I was getting a lot better at suppressing thoughts— the crowds at the airports didn't even bother me. I still had to actively distract myself, but it took very little effort, and the effects lasted for well over an hour.

Since I wasn't wearing any makeup, washing my face hadn't hurt anything. I rarely wore any around the house growing up, so I figured it'd be one less change for him to adjust to. My dolphin hoop earrings and Celtic cross necklace were in my jewelry box at home. Even the clothes I'd packed were things I'd taken with me to college. It felt like I was pretending to be someone else, but "Emme" was a role I'd have to play convincingly if I ever wanted to see my dad again.

We hurried down the hallway and past the security checkpoint. The area was still crowded with passengers and the families greeting them, but David's ratty old Lions jersey was hard to miss. He was waiting just on the other side of the checkpoint, his face beaming.

"Daddy!" I yelled, bounding up to him.

His arms locked around my waist and lifted me off my feet. "God, it's good to see you, honey."

My dad's black hair was combed neatly to the side— like always— and had just a hint of gray around the edges. Ancient looking blue sweat pants with a hole in one knee completed his ensemble.

"Glad to see you dressed up for the occasion."

He gave me my favorite half smile. "You know me."

I turned to introduce my friends, who were now gathered behind me. "Dad, this is Raven, Ruby, Sienna and Sandy."

"Nice to meet you, Mr. Waters," Sienna said, reaching out to shake his hand.

He opened his arms invitingly. "Please, call me David." She stepped forward and gave him a tight hug.

Raven followed suit, adding a kiss on the cheek. "It's great to finally meet you, David. Emme's told us a lot about you."

"And you still came?" It was a tired joke, but everyone laughed anyway.

"Hi, David," Ruby said, nudging past Raven.

He quickly pulled her into his arms. "It's so nice to meet you, Ruby. I hear you're quite the computer genius."

Her cheeks blushed at the compliment. "I wouldn't go that far– I enjoy working with them."

Ruby barely got out of the way before Sandy sprang on top of him, wrapping her hands around his neck. "Hi, Dad!"

"Hi there!" he said, stumbling back a step. "So what do you think? Can you make an old guy look hip?"

She grinned and ran her fingers through his hair. "Absolutely! You'll look like you're twenty-five again."

He chuckled. "I'd settle for thirty-five."

* * * *

Sienna picked up the Lincoln Navigator she'd reserved and pulled around front while the rest of us grabbed our luggage. Sandy, Sienna and Ruby followed as we made the fifteen-minute drive across town, pulling into my dad's driveway just after midnight. We had a small ranch style home with two bedrooms and one-and-a-half baths on an acre lot. The place wasn't anything fancy, but it was located in a nice, quiet neighborhood.

After giving them a brief tour of the house, we piled our luggage into my bedroom and started to get ready for bed. I insisted that Sienna sleep in my room and she reluctantly agreed. Ruby decided to join her when my father offered her his bed, saying that he wouldn't feel right making a grown woman sleep on the floor.

I pulled several blankets out of the closet, layered them on top of the living room carpet and grabbed three sleeping bags and some extra pillows out of the basement. By the time I'd brushed my teeth and said goodnight to my dad, everyone was in bed. I flipped off the lights and climbed into the sleeping bag next to Raven.

As I lay there trying to get comfortable, I suddenly felt a fairly strong urge to feed. We'd just fed before our flight, so I was completely baffled. "Why am I hungry?"

Sandy and Raven burst into laughter, covering their heads with their pillows to try to drown out the noise.

"What's so funny?" I demanded.

Raven lifted her pillow and smiled at me. "What do you smell?"

I took in a deep breath. "Blood."

They both totally lost it, laughing so hard that their whole bodies shook beneath their sleeping bags.

"Stop her, Raven! She's– going to– eat her dad!" Sandy choked out before gasping for air.

"But why can I smell it?" I was tempted to read his thoughts to find out, but there was no telling what else I'd hear.

"Please stop!" Sandy shrieked, pounding her fist into the pillow.

After a couple of minutes Raven regained her composure enough to answered me. "He cut himself shaving, sis."

"Oh… Anyone up for fourth meal?" The room erupted. I could even hear Ruby and Sienna laughing from behind their door.

When we finally settled down I crawled back into my sleeping bag. Even with two blankets underneath, I felt like I was laying on a piece of granite. "Damn, this floor's hard," I muttered. We all cracked up again.

* * * *

Shortly after I fell asleep I felt someone nudging my shoulder. "Time to get up, Brooke."

I rubbed my eyes and peered out the window into the pitch black sky. "Why?"

"Your dad's planning to make breakfast for all of us when he gets up," Raven explained. "We need to get out of here before then so we can say that we already ate. Sienna rented us a suite at the Best Western just down the road."

When I saw that everyone was already dressed, I scrambled out of my sleeping bag and pulled on the jeans and sweatshirt I'd worn yesterday. As soon as I finished, Sienna motioned for me to join her at the kitchen table.

"It'd be good to leave a note for your dad telling him where we went," She whispered. "I know you just woke up, but try to think of somewhere that it'd make sense for us to go so early."

"Today's the twenty-second, right?" I asked, my head still in a fog.

Sienna tilted her head. "Yeah– "

I flipped open the notepad and began to write.

Dad,
Went to the mall to do some Christmas shopping
You know what a sucker I am for early bird sales!
Be back in a while,
  Love ya,
  Emme

"The stores open at six a.m. until the twenty-third," I said while she read my note.

She kissed me on the forehead. "That's perfect."

We walked into our suite less than five minutes later, which wasn't surprising since the Best Western was less than a mile from our house. It had two separate bedrooms, both with two queen-sized beds, a large living room and two full baths. Still half asleep, I ripped off my clothes and crawled into bed, drifting off moments later.

When I finally woke up, Ruby was sitting on the other side of the bed getting dressed, and Raven was blow drying her hair.

"Morning, sleepy head," Raven said.

I flashed her a smile before glancing at the clock– it was almost 11:00. After squirming around anxiously on the end of the bed for a couple of minutes I bounded into the bathroom and sat down to pee.

"Come right in," she said, laying on the sarcasm.

"Sorry, kinda an emergency." After I finished Raven scooted over so I could brush my teeth, and then handed me a dry towel as I stepped into the shower. It was almost noon by the time I was ready to go.

Even though we'd brought our gifts with us, we decided to stop by the Grand Traverse Mall so that we wouldn't walk in empty handed. What started out as a symbolic trip turned into a buying frenzy, all of us hitting the quaint, local shops and loading up on extra gifts for each other. I had no idea how we were going to get all of this stuff on the plane– the bags barely fit in the back of the Navigator.

When we entered our subdivision, the smell of baking chocolate filled the air. I didn't need to read my father's mind to know he was making me a cake. "So much for letting us fend for ourselves."

"It's okay, Brooke– we'll figure something out," Sienna reassured me. "He's throwing you a nineteenth birthday party. Brittney and her younger sister Rachel are helping him decorate."

"Brittney's here?" The last I heard she was planning to spend the week at her parent's condo in Boca with some of her friends from Michigan State.

Raven glanced at me in the rearview mirror. "She wanted to surprise you. She was going to take you to Boyne Mountain to snowboard tomorrow, but now she's worried that you won't want to go with us here."

I gave Sienna a hopeful glance. "Can we?"

She sighed. "It sounds like fun– "

"But," I said, picking up on the reservation in her voice.

"You'll need to be extremely disciplined. You haven't done anything athletic in public yet, and you're very competitive by nature. Unlike surfing, where the wave pretty much dictates how fast we can move, snowboarding will allow us to perform stunts that humans are not capable of. On top of that, you and Brittney have been going snowboarding together for years. That means that she's intimately familiar with your skill level. Not only will you need to act human like the rest of us, you'll also need to limit yourself to what she'd expect Emme to be able to do."

"I will," I promised. "You guys are going to love it! Along with a wicked half pipe and set of jumps, they've got nine kick-ass black-diamond runs."

Sandy slapped hands with me. "Sa-weet!"

"Shopping, snowboarding... I could get used to this!" Ruby chimed in.

The car had barely come to a stop in the driveway when Brittney came tearing out of the house. "Emmy!"

"Hey, Britt!" I replied, opening my arms to catch her. She was just a hair taller than me with a captain-of-the-cheerleading-squad build. Her black hair had natural chocolate-brown highlights and long bangs that drooped across her face. Brittney always had guys falling all over her, but she never let it go to her head.

"I really missed you," she whispered. When she finally leaned back her face lit up. "Look at your hair! Damn! It's gorgeous."

"Thanks. And congrats on making the tennis team. My dad said that you might even get a full ride next year."

"I hope so– I'm only competing in doubles right now. Everyone on the team is incredible."

I took out my cell phone and dangled it in front of her. "You could call me once in a while you know."

She let out a soft little giggle. "Sorry, things just get so crazy at school."

"I hear ya." I could tell by the sudden spike in her heartbeat that Raven and the rest of my family had joined us. "Britt, these are my friends from school– Sandy, Sienna, Ruby and Raven."

"Hey there," she mumbled, giving them a nervous half wave.

Sandy stepped up and wrapped her arm around her neck like she'd known her for years. "So, you've been Emme's best friend for like, a gazillion years. You must have tons of good dirt on her. Spill it, girl!" Everybody started to laugh.

"You mean like when she walked into the men's locker room naked after a meet our junior year?"

"Britt, you swore!" I swatted her back and she quickly danced away from me,

"Do tell." Sandy turned to lead her toward the house, flanked by the rest of my family.

Brittney shot me a mischievous grin. "She'd just finished taking a shower and was off in her own little world, pretty much how she usually acted after a loss. So I'm sitting there half-dressed when I see Emme blow right past our row of lockers and head out the door, wearing nothing but the towel on her head. By the time I pulled on my top and went after her, a loud roar erupted down the hall. I opened the locker room door just as Emme raced inside, holding her hair towel over her boobs. The whole Midland football team got to watch her cute little naked butt bounce all the way down the hall."

"I hate you!"

Brittney continued to joke with them while we walked into the house, completely at ease. Just like that, with one little story, all of the awkwardness between them was gone.

Pink and white crepe streamers were strung from the four corners of the dining room to the ceiling above the kitchen table. Red, white and pink balloons dangled from where they met. Rachel was busy hanging a banner that read "Happy 19th Birthday, Emme!!" A pink table cloth with white trim covered the table, and a small pile of gifts sat on the end of the kitchen counter closest to the dining room. It didn't bother me that the decorations were somewhat juvenile– in my father's eyes, I'd always be his little girl.

"Hi, Emme!" Rachel called out, hopping down from the chair.

I bent down to give her a hug. "Hey, Rae, you're getting so tall. What are you now, nine?"

"Ten," she corrected proudly before gazing at the banner. "Do you like it?"

"It's awesome!"

Her face beamed. "Your dad wanted it to say 'Emily,' but I told him that nobody calls you that except for him."

I giggled, thinking about what it should really say. "Good call."

"I like your hair."

"Thanks. My friend Sandy cut it for me. Have you met her yet?"

She glanced shyly at her feet.

"Well, let's take care of that right now." I took her hand and walked over to the couch where Sandy, Brittney and Ruby were sitting. Raven and Sienna were sitting in the chairs across from them, all of them laughing at whatever Britt had just finished saying.

"Rae, these are my friends: Sandy, Ruby, Sienna and Raven," I said, motioning toward each of them. Everyone gave her a warm greeting.

Encouraged by their friendliness, Rachel walked over to the couch and sat in her sister's lap. "How did you learn to cut hair?" she blurted out, without even waiting for Sandy to finish her sentence.

Sandy abruptly stopped talking and turned her attention toward Rae. "After I graduated from high school I went to beauty school."

"Could you cut my hair like Emme's?"

"Are you trying to get me killed?" Brittney cut in. "You know Mom would never let you get your hair cut that short."

"It's my hair!" Rachel fired back defiantly.

"And my ass. You're not the one she'd be screaming at when we got home."

Seeing her pout, Sandy took Rae's long, wavy black hair in her hands. "I may not be able to cut it, but I'd be happy to give you a nice French braid if you want."

Rae eagerly jumped into her lap. "Cool!"

"Where's my dad?" I asked.

"He got a call from his work, something about a server crashing. He's been in his bedroom on his laptop for about an hour now." I had to fight back a grin when I connected what Brittney was saying to the unpleasant smell in the air.

As if she'd read my mind, Brittney jumped up from the couch. "Oh crap! The cake!" I followed her into the kitchen and pulled it out of the oven.

"I ruined it!" she stared at the petrified lump in her hands. "Your dad's going to kill me."

"Don't worry about it." Even though the cake appeared to be safely beyond salvation, I dumped it into the trash just to make sure and put the pan in the sink to soak. "It's just five hundred less sit ups I'll have to do."

"Like you need to watch what you eat." She pulled up my sweatshirt to make her point, her eyes widening when she noticed my sculpted abs. "Damn, Emme. You been living at the gym or what?"

I tried to nonchalantly pull my shirt down and step away from her, but I couldn't hide how uncomfortable I was. "Pretty much– they have an amazing rec center."

She gave me a bewildered look. "I didn't mean that as an insult. You look hot."

"It's not you," I muttered. "I think I kinda tanked a couple of my finals. I guess I'm feeling guilty about all the working out I've been doing."

"You too?" she said with relief. "My Psych final was a bitch. It seems like whenever I'm not at class, I'm at practice or one of their 'optional' conditioning programs. When I finally get back to my room, I'm so f-ing tired I just want to crawl into bed."

"Only three and a half years to go!" I said as sarcastically as I could manage. We both giggled.

My dad emerged from his bedroom still absorbed in whatever was going on at his work. "I'm sorry, honey. I'm afraid I have to go into work for a while. Our batch scheduling server is down, and payroll goes out tonight. Unless I can get it fixed, I'm going to have to manually kick off all of the jobs and monitor them."

"That's okay, Dad. The party can wait until you get back." He leaned over and kissed me on the top of my head.

"Would you mind if I came along?" Ruby asked, entering the kitchen behind us. "I don't know if I'll be able to help or not, but I'd be happy to try."

"I don't want to take you away from your friends." His voice lacked any conviction. I couldn't believe that he actually wanted her to go. I'd never seen him so stressed over work before.

Ruby grabbed her coat from the hall closet. "It's no trouble. We get to see each other all the time anyway."

Thank you, I mouthed toward Ruby. She flashed me a smile before following him out the door.

Brittney and I walked back into the living room and sat on the couch next to Sandy, who was just finishing Rachel's French braid.

"There ya go kiddo," she said, fastening a red elastic band around the bottom of her pony tail.

Rachel reached up to feel her hair, and then threw her arms around Sandy's neck. "Thanks!"

"You're welcome, sweetie."

Rachel wrinkled her nose. "Hey, you smell like Emme."

"Do you like it?" Sandy asked calmly.

"It smells like flowers. What is it?"

"You've got a good nose. It's a body spray called summer shower. I think it's a little strong myself, but boys seem to like it."

Rachel's eyes widened. "They do?"

"Since when do you care what boys like?" Brittney questioned. "Before I left for school, you told me how gross it was that Josh liked you." Rachel's cheeks blushed and her eyes darted to the floor. "You like him!" Brittney teased.

She giggled. "I try to sit next to him in the cafeteria. He's really cute."

"Rae's got a boyfriend!" I said, lifting her into my lap.

Her head sagged. "He likes Jessica."

Sandy reached out and took her hand. "Do you want to know how to make him forget all about Jessica?"

Rachel's face lit up. "How?"

"As cute as you are, I'm sure there's at least one boy who's always trying to get your attention. Am I right?" Sandy asked, surely having already read her thoughts.

"Yeah... Steven follows me around between classes and always sits next to me, but I don't like him."

"Perfect. When you go back to school on Monday, wear your favorite outfit and instead of ignoring Steven, give him all of your attention, especially when Josh is watching. Make a point of sitting as far away from Josh as you can at lunch and make sure Steven sits next to you."

"Why would that make him like me?"

Brittney snorted. "Oh sis, I've got so much to teach you. If you do like Sandy said, you'll have Josh eating out of your hand in no time. Guys always want what they think they can't have."

After a short pause, Brittney turned toward Raven and Sienna. "So do you guys all go to BU?"

"Just Emme, Raven and I," Sienna replied. "Ruby does information technology work for a medical firm in downtown Boston."

"And I work at a hair salon on the south end of town," Sandy added.

"That's right, you mentioned that you went to beauty school. So how'd you meet them?"

Sandy sat up straighter on the couch, buying her some time to think. "Pure chance. I went to a Red Sox game early last summer with a couple of girls from work, and we just happened to sit next to them. We got to talking and just kind of hit it off."

"What are you majoring in, Brittney?" Sienna asked, smoothly changing the subject.

Britt took a swig of her Diet Coke and sat it back on the coffee table. "Criminal law– I'd like to be a defense attorney like my dad."

"He works for free a lot too," Rachel said with a proud smile.

"You mean he does a lot of pro bono work," Brittney clarified. "His firm donates more hours than any other firm in the state."

"That's very admirable," Sienna praised. "And a very noble profession to go into."

"What are you and Raven going into?"

Sienna hopped up from her chair and made her way toward my bedroom as she answered. "Med school– I'm still trying to decide on a specialty."

"Nice!"

"I'm studying cell biology, molecular biology and genetics," Raven said.

Britt arched her brows slightly, obviously impressed. "That sounds interesting…kind of a medical research scientist?"

She nodded. "Pretty much."

Sienna's voice came from the bedroom. "Emme, do you know if there's any wrapping paper in the house?"

"Her dad has two rolls in his bedroom." Brittney offered before I could respond. "Do you want me to bring them in there?"

"That's okay– we can get them, Britt." Sienna, Sandy and Raven grabbed several bags out of my room and made their way into the kitchen while Brittney and I talked. My dad and Ruby got back just as they finished wrapping my gifts.

"That was quick," I said, leaning forward on the couch so they could see me from the doorway. They'd only been gone about forty-five minutes, and the drive was at least ten minutes each way.

"Thanks to Ruby." The look of total awe on his face almost made me laugh. "She's unbelievable!"

"It was nothing, David. Really," Ruby insisted.

He shook his head at her. "Nothing? Are you kidding me? Not only did she diagnose what was wrong with the scheduling server in about five seconds, something I'd been trying to do for almost two hours, she replaced the faulty NIC card with one out of an older server we were going to decommission, and had the system back up and running in less than ten minutes. Then she gave me a list of all of the jobs that failed to run while the server was down, and manually kicked them off. Oh, I almost forgot. She also modified our job monitoring software to send me alerts on my cell phone when any of our critical jobs fail."

He swept her up in his arms. "I don't know how to thank you. Now I get to spend the next few days with you guys instead of at the office."

"A hug will do just fine," Ruby said, patting his back.

Chapter Thirty
It's My Birthday...Again??

My dad pulled a jar of chocolate frosting out of the pantry and began to search for the cake. "Where'd you put the cake, Britt?"

"I'm so sorry!" she said. "I got to talking with everybody and totally forgot about it. It was pretty much burned to a crisp, so we threw it out."

He chuckled. "I hope birthday ice cream's okay, sweetie."

I peeked at Sienna for some direction and saw her give me a subtle nod. "Works for me."

"We can't eat until after we sing though," he said with a smirk. "Everybody ready?"

I started to giggle when they launched into an off pitch, out-of-synch rendition of "happy birthday to you," and then howled like a dog as they finished. The room filled with laughter. My dad got out chocolate and vanilla ice cream and scooped them into bowls.

"Here ya go, birthday girl!" Sienna called out, handing me a scoop of vanilla. She put her lips up to my ear while she hugged me. "Take a couple bites and spit it back into your bowl when they're not looking. You can just move your spoon around the rest of the time."

Once everyone had started eating I leaned back against the counter, waited until David glanced in my direction and took a small bite. I rolled it around in my mouth until none of them were watching without any trouble, but my attempt to spit it out was a disaster. Not only was it far too loud, melted cream ran all the way down my chin. Sienna made some offhand comment about the snow to my dad while Raven complemented Brittney's shirt, covering for me while I wiped my face. If I couldn't even pull this off when I was in a different room, how the hell was I ever going to get through Christmas dinner? I watched Sienna for a while, hoping to pick up some pointers. Unfortunately, she was so good at it that it was like trying to pick up chess tips from a grand master. Even Sandy made it look effortless. I knew risking another bite without a lot more practice and coaching would be crazy, so I just waited until one of them started to turn their head toward me and shot the empty spoon into my mouth. When enough time had passed I melted what was left in the sink.

Dangerous Waters

"Bring on the presents!" I hollered, taking a seat at the end of the table. With the addition of the gifts from my new family, what had been a small pile now filled up almost the entire countertop.

"I'll play Santa," Raven volunteered. "To Emme, from Sandy."

I flashed Sandy a smile while I opened it. "An iPod touch… Sweet!"

It was silver and had "Sœurs de sang pour l'éternité" engraved on the back. I had no idea what it meant, but I knew better than to ask in front of everyone. If she'd went to the trouble to get it engraved in French, it was probably something we wouldn't want others to hear. I got up and gave her as affectionate of an embrace as I could, given our mixed audience. "This is awesome. Thank you."

Raven handed me a small rectangular box. "This one's from Sienna."

The jewelry box inside contained a sterling silver Celtic bracelet with five different shaped links. I knew it'd go perfectly with the necklace she'd given me. "It's beautiful," I muttered, taking it out of the case.

"It needs to be fitted before you can try it on," Sienna almost yelled, rubbing her thumb across the inside of her left wrist like she was itching it.

I gasped when I realized I'd pulled up my sleeve to try it on. I yanked the sleeve back down before anyone could see my scars. "Thanks, Sienna, I can't wait to wear it."

"That's really pretty," Brittney said. "The design is Celtic, isn't it?"

"Good eye," Sienna praised.

Raven picked up Ruby's gift bag and handed it to me. Inside was a cute purple tote from Bath & Body Works stuffed with tons of products. I jumped up and threw my arms around her. "This smells wonderful. I feel more relaxed already. Thanks."

"To Emmy, from Britt," Raven read out, handing me a large rectangular box. I unwrapped it to find a silver-plated picture frame with the words "Best Friends Forever" embossed in black across the bottom. Inside the frame was a picture from last summer of Britt and me posing in front of our cabin in Yellowstone National Park.

I reached up and wiped away a tear that had rolled down my cheek. *Best Friends Forever.* I'd done nothing but lie to her since we got back from the mall – that's all I'd ever be able to do. We wouldn't even be able to visit each other by the time she graduated.

"What's wrong?" she asked, seeing my tears.

I forced a smile. "Nothing– I just really miss you. This means a lot to me."

Brittney wrapped her arms tightly around me. "Me too. I've got the same picture next to my bed at school."

After I passed the picture around, I pulled out a green Michigan state lightweight hoody with a deep V-neck and a front pouch pocket. "This is cool." I held it up to my chest and pretended to admire it. All I could think about was not seeing Britt get married or have her first baby, not have the chance to see her grow and change and share her life. I managed to blink back my tears and put on a grateful smile.

"I hope it's not too big," she said. "I didn't plan on you losing ten pounds."

I carefully removed my BU sweatshirt, making sure my wrists remained covered by my long sleeve mock turtleneck, sliding it on and modeling it for everyone. It was on the baggy side, but that's how I preferred my sweatshirts anyway. "Fits perfect."

Raven handed me a similarly shaped box. "This one's from Rachel."

"Gee, I wonder what this could be?"

"I'll give you three guesses, and you still won't get it!" Rae challenged.

I playfully raised my eyebrows at her. "Oh really? And what do I get, Ms. Mills, if I get it right?"

Rae chewed on her lip for a few seconds before her eyes lit up. "My dad's getting me a golden retriever puppy for Christmas. I'll name it 'Emily'!" Everyone laughed. Raven and Sienna shot me uneasy looks, unsure of just how far I was going to take this little gag.

"You're on, girl!" It's not like I was guessing a random number between one and one million or anything. I could do this without reading her mind. "Okay… I can tell from the box that it's some type of clothing, and it's too heavy to be shorts or a t-shirt unless there's more than one." I shook the box gently over my head. "Definitely feels like one item. It can't be jeans since it didn't make any noise when I shook it, so that pretty much leaves a sweatshirt or sweatpants. If I know Britt at all I'm sure she'd make your gifts complement each other, so I'm going to say it's a pair of MSU sweat pants."

Rachel's face filled with surprise. "How'd you do that?"

"Just an educated guess, cutie– let's see what they look like." I tore open the box and pulled them out. The green sweats had Spartans spelled out in white lettering running down the left leg. I bounded over to Rachel and squeezed her against my chest. "Thanks, Rae!"

"Should we call my puppy Emily or Emme?" Rachel wondered out loud.

"You don't have to name your dog after me– I was just playing with you."

She giggled. "I kinda like it."

"So do I," Brittney agreed. "I think it's a great name."

I smiled and gazed back at them. It seemed a little strange to have my best friend's family dog named after me, but at least it'd give them something to remember me by.

Luckily Raven handed me a gift before I could jump back on the train to Gloomyville. "This one's from me."

As soon as I'd removed the paper I recognized the sterling silver jewelry box, but it now had "Sœurs de sang pour l'éternité" engraved on the top. I could feel my eyes welling up as I opened it, revealing the stunning diamond hoop earrings. By giving them to me publicly, in front of the only people I'd ever bother to visit, I knew that I'd never have to take them off to come here again. I couldn't deny the sadness of losing my dad and Brittney, but being a part of Sienna's family made the loss almost bearable. Without saying a word, I wrapped my arms around her and began to cry.

"What'd she get you, honey?" my dad asked.

I ignored him and leaned in close to Raven. "What does it say?"

She put her lips directly against my ear and whispered "Sisters in blood for eternity."

"Emily?" David prompted, now with a mixture of concern and confusion.

Being careful to keep the top of the box out of sight, I slid them into my ears and walked over to him. "Look, Dad."

His eyes glistened over as he stared at them. After a few seconds he pulled Raven into his arms. "Thank you," he mumbled into her neck.

"Emme told us how much her necklace means to her, and how badly you both miss her mom," Raven replied. David kissed her on the forehead then turned away and tried to compose himself while Brittney and Rachel oohed and aahed over her gift.

"I'm afraid this is going to be somewhat anti-climatic, but– " David handed me a large box. "Happy birthday, sweetheart."

I ripped open the flaps on the end of the box and pulled out a North Face three-in-one jacket. The inner jacket had white, gray, purple and yellow stripes that looked great inside of the dark purple outer shell. I held it up for everyone then threw my arms around him. "This is really cute– you did good."

"I'm glad you like it, but I can't take the credit. Brittney picked it out of the catalog for me."

"It's designed for snowboarding," Brittney chimed in. "It's got a media pocket, internal goggle pocket, powder skirt and pant-a-locks to attach to your snowboard pants."

"Cool!" I slid it on over my sweatshirt.

"I don't know what you guys may already have planned, but I was wondering if you'd like to go snowboarding at Boyne tomorrow afternoon," Brittney said.

"Sounds awesome!"

"But David promised that we could go ice fishing in the morning," Rae complained. Brittney and I both glanced at him.

"I'll pick you up, sweetie," David assured her. "The yellow bellies are in right now. Ed and Tom from work limited out yesterday in just over an hour."

"What's a yellow belly?" Sandy asked.

"They're large perch that live out in Lake Michigan most of the year," I explained. "Sometimes a school will come into Grand Traverse Bay where it's a lot easier to catch them." Walleye and Bass fishing in the summertime was by far my favorite, but I'd always enjoyed going ice fishing as well.

"Thanks, wilderness girl," Sandy teased.

Hearing the eagerness in my voice, a glimmer of hope crept into my father's eyes. "I didn't think your friends would be interested, but I'd love to have you guys join us."

"I'm in," Brittney said. Even though she'd never been that interested in catching fish, Brittney frequently came along and goofed around on the lake with us.

The corners of Sienna's mouth rose up in a smile. "What time do we leave?"

"All right!" I shouted. "Wait until you guys see the first flag go up. It's a rush."

Ruby gave me a bewildered look. "You put flags up?"

"There are little orange flags on the end of the tip-ups," David clarified.

She snorted. "What's a tip-up?"

"They're kind of like a fishing pole for ice fishing," Raven said. "They have crossing pieces of wood that sit on top of the ice and support a center piece with a reel that goes into the hole. You bend over a thin strip of metal that has a flag on the end of it and attach it to a hook– kind of like a mouse trap. When the fish pulls line out it releases the hook and the flag pops up." I could tell from the amused expression on her face that she hadn't hidden an intense passion for ice fishing from me– she'd just read my dad's mind.

"Do you ice fish, Raven?" David asked, clearly impressed by her answer.

"I'm from Quebec originally."

He chuckled. "That explains it." After a short pause he turned toward Brittney. "We'll pick you guys up at seven if that's okay."

"We'll be ready."

After we gave Brittney and Rae several hugs and a proper send off, I turned my attention to the pressing problem of food. My dad was bound to mention dinner soon. Rather than waiting to turn down an invitation, I preemptively announced our plans to eat at Tony's and promised to bring him something back.

"Your dad is incredible," Raven said as we climbed into the car. "I've only known him for a day and I'm already crazy about him."

"Tell me about it," Ruby agreed. "He's everything I wish my parents would've been."

Sandy placed her hand on my cheek and kissed me, her tongue dancing along the inside of my lips. We'd agreed I was under enough stress this trip without coming out to my dad, but acting like she was just a friend was killing me. It'd been two weeks since our amazing encounter on the beach. There'd been plenty of steamy moments between us since, but they were all of the clothes-on variety, and I was growing more frustrated by the day. "He's as caring and openhearted as you are, and there's not an ounce of malice in him. He loves Brittney and Rachel like they're family."

"He already feels very strongly about us as well," Sienna added.

"I knew he'd love you guys." I'd managed to keep his thoughts suppressed in my mind so far, but I needed to know the truth about how he was doing. "Is he happy?"

Everyone was silent.

"God, he's miserable, isn't he!"

Sienna spun around in her seat and reached behind her, lightly caressing my face. "Unfortunately I was right about him. Losing your mother has left a gaping hole in his heart that nothing could ever fill. He's very loving and strong, but he thinks about her constantly. You're the center of his whole life, and the only reason he's managed to hang on."

"So what happens in four or five years when I can't see him anymore?" I said, wiping my cheeks on the collar of my shirt.

"I don't know, baby," she admitted. "We can buy a few years by moving overseas when you graduate, but he's sure to demand to see you at some point."

"And after a couple dozen excuses why we can't visit each other, he's going to think that I just don't love him anymore. It'll kill him." No one said anything to contradict me.

I drew in a deep breath and closed my eyes, slowly exhaling as Raven pulled into a space near the front of the parking lot. "I'm sorry. It's not like I didn't know I'd have to leave him behind someday. I guess I was just hoping he was getting better."

"We all understand how hard this is for you," Sienna said. "We'll do everything we can to help you stay close for as long as possible."

* * * *

After turning in David's carry out order, we took a seat at a booth and ordered some drinks. Raven unfolded her menu and glanced at it. "So did you guys come here a lot?"

"At least once a week. All of their food's tasty, but the shrimp basket was my favorite. You should see their banana splits– they're ridiculous."

"Are we really going ice fishing tomorrow?" Ruby crossed her arms over her chest and leaned back in her chair. "It must be ten degrees outside."

"We have an ice shanty with a heater so we can warm up if we get cold. And I know it sounds lame, but it's actually a lot of fun. Catching fish is great, but the best part is just goofing around together."

She rolled her eyes, making it obvious that my little sales pitch had failed miserably. "When in Rome."

As soon as the waitress brought the carry out bag to the table, I reached for the check. All of us had debit cards tied to the same bank account that we used for walk-around cash and platinum credit cards for anything larger. Until yesterday the only shopping I'd done was on the internet. Now that I could handle going out in public, I couldn't wait to spend the day in town with Ruby and play tennis again.

* * * *

"Food's on the table, Dad," I called out, setting the bag between a stack of bills and unsorted junk mail.

"I'll be right in!" he yelled from the garage.

Dangerous Waters

We all shed our heavy clothes and headed into the living room. I picked up the clicker and started flipping through the channels. "Hey look!" I said, stopping on HBO's *True Blood*.

Sandy removed her legs from the armrest of the chair she was drooped over, and leaned forward to get a better view. "Cool! I love this show."

"It's like a soap set in a redneck bar," Sienna complained.

One of the people was charred to a crisp and chained to a pole inside the bar, but he was still able to carry on a conversation without any trouble.

"See what I mean…stupid." Sienna glared at me, almost begging me to change the channel. Not wanting to get in the middle of a TV war, I dropped the clicker in her lap.

David walked into the living room carrying his plate. "Is that *True Blood*?"

"I knew you had great taste!" Sandy said, shooting Sienna a taunting smile – there was no way she'd even think about changing the channel now.

Sienna laid the clicker on the coffee table as she got up from the couch. "Take my seat, David. I've got presents to wrap anyway."

"Thanks." He plopped down between Raven and me and put his plate on the table. "Oh, this was a good one!"

I glanced at my dad, who was now totally absorbed in his show. I wondered what he'd do if he knew he was watching it in a room full of vampires.

As soon as the show ended, Sandy got out all of her salon supplies and headed into the kitchen. "Are you ready for your hair cut?"

"You don't have to do that, Sandy," David said, looking more than a little embarrassed. "You must be sick of cutting hair."

"It's no trouble." She spun a kitchen chair around so he'd still be able to see the TV, and then patted the back of it. David placed his dishes in the sink then reluctantly took a seat.

"So how daring are you willing to be?" she asked, snapping a black robe around his neck.

"Well, I need to be able to show my face in the office on Monday."

She snorted. "Gotcha. Are you willing to try something a bit different though?"

"Sure. What do you have in mind?"

Sandy ran her fingers through his hair as she did her cute little lip curl thing. "On the more conservative side, I think a Caesar cut like George Clooney wears would look good on you. If you're willing to be a little more daring though, I think you'd look great with a long crew cut. It'd get rid of all of your gray hair and give you a more youthful appearance while still looking professional."

He let out a loud chuckle. "I like the sound of that. Let's go with the crew cut."

"Good choice." Sandy hugged him around the neck, picked up her clippers and went to work. "So how did you meet Emme's mom?"

In an instant his entire demeanor changed. He closed his eyes and took several deep breaths, trying to retain his composure.

Rather than apologizing like I thought she would, Sandy just stood there waiting for him to answer, as if she was playing some kind of verbal chicken. I knew what she was trying to do, and I loved her for it, but he'd never been able to talk about my mom with anyone— not even me.

After a long and uncomfortable silence, he wiped his eyes and let out a deep sigh. "I was seventeen and had just gotten a summer job at the fishing bridge gift shop in Yellowstone National Park. Anne was nineteen, and it was her third summer working there. She ran the ice cream counter next to the little restaurant. We ate lunch together on my first day and never looked back. On the last night before the season ended, I took her up to our favorite spot on the bluff overlooking Hayden Valley and asked her to marry me."

Sandy put her hand on his shoulder. "That's so romantic! Did you get married there too?"

"We wanted to, but her mother insisted on a formal church wedding." He laughed and shook his head. "You would've thought I was walking *her* down the aisle the way she ran everything. Anne and I got so sick of it by the end that we almost eloped. We had a large ceremony at their family church in Billings, Montana, the following summer. I've got a picture of her in her wedding dress if you'd like to see it."

"I'd love to."

David turned to look at me. "Honey— "

"I'm on it," I said, darting into his bedroom. I couldn't believe how openly he was talking about her, and he was actually smiling. Everyone gathered around as I handed the picture to Sandy.

Sandy gazed intently at it. "She's beautiful."

"She looks just like you, Emme," Raven added. I took a closer look at the picture and noticed my dad doing the same.

"God, she really does," David agreed after studying my face. "You've always reminded me of her, but not this closely. Of course, you're nineteen now, so you're only a year younger than she was in the picture."

"How did you guys end up in Traverse City?" Sienna asked.

"After having her parents' wedding shoved down our throats, she was as anxious as I was to get away from them, so we decided to live in Michigan. I grew up in Charlevoix, but we wanted to start out somewhere new together, so we rented a small house in downtown Traverse City. I started working at the gear manufacturing plant just over a month after our wedding and put her through school at Michigan State. She graduated with a degree in research biology and gave birth to Emily a month later.

"When Emily was about a year old, Anne got her first job doing wolf research on Isle Royale. It was really hard for her to be away from us for two weeks at a time, but she absolutely loved her work. Once it got warm enough, Emily and I came out to visit and spent over a week at the research facility. We even got to nurse a newborn pup they were keeping at the facility because it had a broken leg. She completed her work on the study just before Emily's second birthday. Even though she was highly sought after, Anne chose to take some time off until Emily got a little older. She felt like she was missing out on too much of her childhood."

David squeezed my hand. "If there was ever someone born to be a mother, it was her. As soon as the nurse put your tiny little body in her arms, I saw a love in her eyes that I'd never seen before. Nothing in the world could have made her as happy as you did, sweetheart."

I leaned in kissed him on the cheek. "Thanks."

"In the summer of 1995 they launched a wolf reintroduction program in Yellowstone National Park," David continued, "something Anne had been fighting for her entire life. Even though we both loved it here, we decided that we'd move to Montana so that she could pursue her dream without being away from her family. She'd been offered a research position to help study the wolves once they were released from their acclimation pens." David took a deep breath as his voice started to shake. "She died three weeks before we were going to move."

I quickly wrapped my arms around him as we both let go of the tears we'd been holding back. Sienna, Raven, Ruby and Sandy all comforted us and offered their condolences. After a couple minutes my dad reached up and stroked my hair. "You remind me so much of her, pumpkin– it's almost like the two of you shared the same soul."

After Sandy finished cutting his hair, she escorted him into the guest bathroom. "Oh my God!" he shouted, peering at his reflection in the mirror. "That's unbelievable. I look so…young."

Sandy giggled. "I told ya you'd look like you were twenty-five."

"I don't know if you're a better hair stylist or shrink," he joked. I couldn't remember the last time I'd seen him look so relaxed. The frown lines that I thought were permanently etched in his forehead were gone. "It felt really good to talk about her again. Thank you."

"Anytime. Ever since my dad was killed I've been helping military families that lose a parent get the counseling they need." Sandy paused and intently studied his face. "Do you mind if I give you some rather candid advice?"

David placed his hand on her shoulder. "Not at all. And I'm sorry about your father."

She nodded in acknowledgement of his condolences. "I'd encourage you to talk a lot more about Anne, especially with Emme. I know you've been trying to shield her from your pain, but by refusing to talk about her mother, you've made Emme feel like the topic is off limits. It isn't healthy for either of you to suppress your feelings, and she feels really bad that she knows so little about her mom."

"God, I never thought about it like that," he said, a bit stunned by her bluntness. "There are so many times I wanted to talk with her, but she seemed to be handling it so well. I didn't want to make her dwell on her mother's death just so I could feel better." He paused and slowly rubbed his face with his hands. "It's not going to be easy for me, but I'll certainly try to talk more openly with her from now on."

Sandy leaned up and gave him a kiss on the cheek. "She's lucky to have such an awesome father."

"Thanks, sweetie. I'm sure I've made a million mistakes raising her, but no one could love her more than I do." My dad patted her shoulder then walked back into the living room. "I'm off to bed. I'll get you guys up at six."

After saying goodnight to him, I took a quick shower, changed into a red satin slip I'd been dying to show off, and flopped down on the sleeping bag closest to the TV. Sandy removed her jeans and lay down on her back next to me, dressed only in a navy tank and hi-cut, black lace panties. Her hair was still damp and smelled like apricot shampoo.

"No one has ever gotten him to open up like that," I said, gliding my fingertips along the bare skin above her neckline. "You're incredible."

She turned on her side facing away from me and nonchalantly tucked herself up against my body, as if we weren't both half-naked and this wasn't the first time we'd ever spooned. When I wrapped my arm around her waist, she took my hand and held it up against her chest. "I'm sorry if I went too far in the bathroom or said something you wish I wouldn't have."

"You did great," I assured her. "I could never have said that to him, but it's exactly how I feel."

"Now that he's opened the door, it's important for you to take the initiative – he's not going to change his suppressive habits all by himself."

"I will."

I slid my hand beneath her tank and cupped her soft, perky breast, my fingers lightly teasing her nipple. Our legs intertwined, my knee sliding forward to part hers until I was almost humping her thigh. Raven was due out of the shower any moment, and my dad was only a few feet down the hall. Feeling more than a little voyeuristic, I placed my lips on the curve of her neck below her earlobe, trying to see just how far she'd let me take this.

"Behave," she said with a giggle.

I kissed her again, tightening my fingers around her nipple. "What if I don't want to?"

She removed my hand from underneath her shirt and placed it back on her hip. "Then I can sleep on the couch."

"Ouch. So much for my ability to seduce you– I must really suck at this."

Moving at close to vampire speed, she spun around, rolled me onto my back and pinned my wrists above my head. "You think this is easy for me? You know how many nights I've dreamed that you snuck up to my bedroom after everyone was asleep? How many mornings I've fantasized about you while I got myself off? Having you this close, begging me to go further is like torture."

"Are your fantasies anything like this?" I said, flashing a devilish smile. "Because I gotta say, the whole submissive slave thing is kinda turning me on."

She let out an exasperated gasp. "God, you're impossible!"

"I guess you'll just have to punish me then."

Sandy snorted and we both burst into laughter. After a couple minutes she took my face in her hands and gave me a deep, open-mouthed kiss. "Good night, brat."

"The best." I curled into her side and rested my head on her chest, sighing contently as I drifted off to sleep.

Chapter Thirty-One
When the Cat's Away

"I still think my idea's better," Teresa grunted, holding a tan corduroy skirt up to her waist before tossing it into the open suitcase on top of her old bed.

Travis finished skimming through the leather-bound journal in his hands, latched the solid brass clasp and set it in the growing pile at his feet. "And how long do you think it would take Stefan to find out that we torched his house?"

"Who gives a shit? Maybe it'll make him think twice about fucking with us. Let's see how virtuous that elitist prick is when he's homeless."

"Do I really have to spell this out for you?" He raked his fingers through his hair and turned to face his sister. "One call from him and Emily will be in lockdown for months. Hopefully we'll kill the bitch long before Stefan and Alexander get back from Australia, but we can't risk tipping them off, just in case. Speaking of which, I said you could grab a couple of your favorite outfits – not your whole damn closet. Lose the suitcase too."

Teresa flipped him off, stuffing another dress in her bag just for spite. "Like they're going to notice. God, you're such a douche. Do you even know what the hell you're looking for? You said this was only going to take a minute."

"That's when I thought there was only one of these!" Travis growled, grabbing one of the leather-bound books from the pile at random. "What kind of asshole buys fifty journals that look exactly the same?"

"I told ya he was psycho. And you are too if you think I'm wasting my whole night looking for some lame-ass vamp address book. If they're friends of Stefan, they'd probably kill us on sight anyway."

"We're not hoping to find new BFFs, you moron. Have you ever heard of blackmail? If we find that book, we'll never have to hide again."

She snorted. "Yeah, we're going to blackmail them with their address. Like people couldn't just call 411 or pull out the white pages."

"Okay, smart-ass. You think it's that easy? I'll bet ya ten grand you can't tell me Kelly's address in LA or his cell number. You've got five minutes."

Teresa arched a brow. "Seriously?"

"Four minutes and fifty-four seconds."

Her lips widened into a wicked grin as she whipped out her laptop. Her whitepages.com search for Kelly Mankins returned no results. She tried Cody James, Chris Parker, Kevin Adams and Melanie Weber. Striking out, she switched to Mylife.com, typed in Kelly's email address and executed a reverse lookup. When that came up dry, she Googled him, and then abandoned the laptop and pulled out her iPhone.

"Less than two minutes!" Travis bragged. "And that's with you knowing what city to look in, the names of his family members and his email address."

Ignoring him, she hit 411 and waited for the prompt. When the automated system and the operator confirmed there were no listings for any of the family in the greater Los Angeles area, she swore under her breath. Travis raised his arms in victory. "All right, so it's not that easy to get an address. But we could have just gotten it from Stefan."

"Not even if we tortured him. Didn't you listen to anything he told us? Vampires guard the location of their safe houses with their lives. When coven leaders share it with someone, it's like welcoming them into their family. I guarantee Emily doesn't know where Kelly lives either, even though Ruby's his wife."

Teresa motioned toward the pile of unchecked journals, and Travis tossed one to her to look through. "If their addresses are so fucking top secret, how did you find out where Sienna lived?" She asked as she flipped through the pages. "And why would Stefan risk writing them down at all? They should at least be locked away in a vault somewhere, or password protected on his computer."

"Lucky for us Alexander has a big mouth. And Stefan's carelessness is why he's as good as dead." Travis gave her a smug nod. "But that's just the beginning. Having hundreds of addresses means we can threaten each of them with total exposure. They'll be falling all over themselves to please us."

* * * *

After finishing the pile on the bed, they headed back to Stefan's office to search for more. Travis double checked every drawer of both filing cabinets while Teresa scanned the massive bookcase.

"I don't get it. It has to be here!" Travis slammed the last drawer closed.

"Where did you see it before?"

"Stefan was on the phone, sitting at the breakfast bar and writing in the journal. I managed to read most of a page before he kicked me out. There's no way he'd keep it there, though. It's too out in the open."

"You're sure he was on the phone?" Teresa asked, a spark of excitement dancing in her eyes.

"Yeah. Why?"

"The phone in the kitchen isn't cordless. So he either brought the journal down with him to call right in front of you, when you just said he didn't want you watching– "

"Or someone called and it was within reach of the phone," Travis concluded. He sprung off the bed and swept her up in his arms. "Damn, sis. You're a fucking genius!"

The search in the kitchen was brief, uncovering the ancient leather journal behind a false back in the kitchen cabinet above the fridge. There were over seven hundred names listed, with multiple addresses for each, but at least sixty percent had gravestones next to them.

Teresa grabbed it out of his hands and flipped through it until she found the page for Sienna. "Who's Colt?"

"I guess Raven wasn't her first after all," Travis said, glancing over her shoulder. "Oh, man, look who's listed on the bottom. That must be her new name."

Teresa let out a feral snarl. "Brooke."

Chapter Thirty-Two
Breaking The Ice

"Time to get up, Brooke," Sienna whispered. The smell of sausage, hash browns and eggs filled the room.

"Oh, he didn't," I mumbled, pulling back the cover of my sleeping bag.

She grinned. "Actually I did, but in order for our little ruse to work, we all need to be up and about."

"Sneaky."

I threw on the sweatshirt and sweats I'd gotten for my birthday and went into the kitchen. The sink was full of dirty dishes, and there was some spilled orange juice and bits of food scattered across the kitchen table. It looked very convincing. When I heard my dad lacing up his boots, I made him a plate and sat it on the table. "Come and get it!"

"That smells delicious, honey. Thank you."

"Don't thank me– Sienna got up early and made breakfast for all of us."

"That was really sweet of you." David shoveled a bite of her scrambled eggs and cheese into his mouth. "Oh my God. These eggs are incredible."

Sienna flashed him a warm smile. "I'm glad you like them."

I walked over to the sink and began to rinse our dishes, making sure that he noticed me doing it.

"I can get those later, sweetie," he offered.

"I've got it covered, Dad– just enjoy your breakfast."

* * * *

After stopping to pick up Rachel and Brittney, we bought some minnows and arrived at the empty West Bay Marina just after 7:00.

"Where is everybody?" I asked my dad as we climbed out of the Navigator. Normally once word got out that the fishing was good, the place was packed.

"I don't know," he admitted. "I guess they're getting ready for Christmas. Or maybe they just think it's too cold this morning."

It was bitterly cold, even for Traverse City. The temperature display on the bank sign read seven degrees, and that was without the wind chill. To make things worse, the stiff wind whipped up the snow from the ground and drove it into our faces. Between the five of us, we were wearing every item of winter clothing I had at the house. I had so many layers on I could barely bend my arms. The shanty was going to be really popular today.

We slowly waddled our way out onto the ice with my dad dragging our sled behind him. I used the ice auger as a walking stick while I led the way to our shanty. When we finally arrived, I pulled off my glove and unlocked the door, and then stepped inside and lit the heater.

Brittney leaned down close to me. "There's no way I could talk Rae out of coming today, but this is way too cold for her. She's going to have to stay in the shanty."

"That's okay," I assured her. "We can take turns in here when we get cold. You might as well keep her company for now. Once we get the holes dug out, I'll come by and see how you guys are doing."

"Sounds good."

I stepped outside and gave Rae a hug— she looked half frozen already. "It'll be nice and toasty in there in no time," I promised. She let out a cute little giggle and hurried through the door.

Raven, Sienna, Sandy and I followed my dad toward the open water at the mouth of the bay, stopping about four hundred yards from our shanty. Knowing that the yellow bellies usually schooled along the main drop off closer to shore, I shot him a questioning look. "They're running this deep?"

"Yeah, they're still kind of gathering out here," David replied. "It'll be another couple of weeks before they head in. I had to put extra line on the tip-ups last night to get down far enough."

"We'll drill the holes, Dad, if you want to follow behind and set up the tip-ups," I called out, already walking away. I knew he wouldn't like my plan, since he always insisted on doing the hard work himself.

"I'll do that, sweetheart," he yelled after me. I just kept walking, pretending not to hear him. When he began to unload the sled, I stopped and removed the guard from the augur blade.

Sandy reached out and gripped my arm. "Easy on the muscle there Hercules, breaking his augur in half wouldn't be too discreet."

"Neither would drilling a hole through three feet of ice in ten seconds," Raven added. "Keep it at Emily speed."

"This sucks," I complained, slowly turning the handle of the augur. Even holding myself back, driving the blade through the ice was still effortless. After a couple of minutes, I finished the first hole and handed the augur to Raven, waving my arm around in the air like it was tired.

She hid her face behind her gloved hands and shook her head at my pathetic display. "God, you're a terrible actress." We all burst into laughter.

With the three of us taking turns, we had all ten holes drilled in less than thirty minutes. We made our way back to my dad, who was still working on setting up the fifth tip-up.

"You guys are done already?" he asked, a bit surprised. It would normally take him at least that long to get four holes drilled.

"It was pretty easy with three of us taking turns. The augur was nice and sharp too." I could tell that he'd ground down the blades yesterday– there were fresh scrape marks on the steel and fine metal shavings still hanging from them.

"With the ice being so thick, I figured we could use all the help we could get," David said, clearly pleased with himself for thinking ahead.

After laying two more tip-ups on the ice for my dad, I dragged the sled down to the last hole. With both of us working, we got the rest of the tip-ups in place in only a couple of minutes.

I took the pile of five-gallon buckets off of the back of the sled and flipped them upside down in the snow, right in the middle of the line of tip-ups, and then put boat cushions on top for comfort. When I was finished I picked up the sledge hammer and drove four spike-bottomed metal T-posts into the ice behind them.

"What are those for?" Ruby wondered.

"We do ice fishing in style!" I said, lifting our canvas blind out of the sled. After connecting the metal supports to the T-posts, I pulled the canvas over the frame and tied it into place. Once everyone had taken a seat, I got out our thick wool blanket and spread it over their legs. I gave them each a hand warmer, cracking the first one to show them how to activate it, and then sat down next to Raven and tucked the blanked under my arms. With the wind blocked and all of us sitting so close together, it was almost pleasant.

David placed the minnow bucket back inside the sled to keep it from freezing and gave us a warm smile. "You kids all settled in?"

"Crap! I forgot about Britt and Rae," I shouted before jumping to my feet. Our shanty stood between us and the shoreline, a few hundred yards away. I could see thick white smoke billowing out of the chimney, assuring me that our somewhat temperamental heater was still working okay. I grabbed the sled and slowly made my way over to them.

"Howdy, strangers," I said, ducking my head into the shanty. Brittney and Rachel were stripped down to a single sweatshirt, the tops of their snowmobile suits dangling from their waists. It felt like it was at least 55 inside.

"Emmy! You remembered us!" Brittney teased.

"Sorry it took so long." I took off my winter coat, grabbed the ice pick and went to work breaking out the hole in the center of the shanty. Since Britt wasn't watching me closely, I drove the pick down fairly hard into the ice, breaking through in each spot after only a couple of swings. After about ten minutes, the large rectangle came loose and I guided it under the ice. I setup two lines with bobbers and handed Brittney a net in case they hooked into a Pike. "How about some hot chocolate, munchkin?"

"Definitely!" Rachel replied.

I poured them each a glass from the thermos. "So you gonna catch any fish today or what?"

Her face beamed. "I'm going to catch the first fish, the biggest fish and the most fish!" Brittney and I laughed at her exuberance.

I placed some extra minnows in a Styrofoam cup and sat it on the shelf. "Are you guys okay for a while, Britt? I want to make sure the city folk aren't too miserable."

Brittney placed her hands behind her head like she was basking in the sun. "Oh… I think we'll survive."

I snorted. "I'll be back soon, Tropicana girl."

When I turned to head toward our blind, I noticed that everyone was gathered around one of the tip-ups. I tried to hurry as much as I could without flipping the sled over. Before I was half way back, Ruby lifted a large perch out of the hole. I could hear the enthusiasm in her voice as they celebrated. Given her past, it was unlikely that she'd ever caught a fish before. By the time I reached them, they were already back under the canopy.

David motioned toward the ice. "Check out Ruby's fish. It's a beauty! Over fourteen inches long."

I bumped fists with her. "Way to get us started!"

"That was fun!" she hollered. "I just about fell over when the little flag thingie went up."

"I told ya you'd love it!" Actually, when I saw what the weather was like this morning, I wondered if they'd have any fun at all. It was great to hear them all laughing. I sat down next to Sandy and leaned my body into hers. "You're next, girl."

Dangerous Waters

Less than ten minutes later, two tip-ups went off simultaneously. Sandy and I took off for the far one while everyone else gathered around the tip-up in front of our seats.

When we reached the hole, Sandy plopped down on her knees and glanced up at me. "What do I do?"

"Just lift the tip-up out of the water and put your fingers on the line. If you feel a fish pulling, give it a light tug to set the hook. Once you have him on, pull the line in hand over hand."

Sandy whipped her gloves off, grabbed the tip-up and nervously felt the line. "Holy crap! It's tugging!"

"Cool! Gently set the hook and pull him up."

She gave the line a quick yank and began to lift it out of the water, letting it fall haphazardly across the ice. Before the fish was half way up I could tell that it wasn't a perch.

"Holy shit, Sandy. You've got a Northern!" I yelled, almost as excited as she was.

"What's that? What do I do?"

"You're doing great. Just keep pulling him up nice and slow. A Northern is a kind of pike– this one looks pretty big."

Sandy continued to pull in the line. When the fish got close, I helped to guide his head up through the hole and put my fingers behind his gills to lift him out. It was easily thirty inches long and had a huge belly. "It's a monster!"

"That was friggin awesome!" She proudly held her fish up for everyone to see and scampered ahead of me back to our blind.

"What a fish, Sandy!" After giving her a high five, David took out his measuring tape and held it up to it. "Thirty-three and a half inches. Wow!"

"Look at his gut," I said. "How much do you think he weighs?"

He took the fish from Sandy and lifted it up toward his waist. "He's gotta be at least fifteen pounds. How'd you carry that all the way over here so easily?"

Sandy playfully flexed her arms. "I've got guns!"

He chuckled. "I guess so."

"What did Sienna catch?" I asked, trying to get the focus off of Sandy.

"It got off," Sienna muttered.

David gave her a firm hug around the shoulders. "You'll get him next time."

Even though I'd left Rachel and Brittney only a half an hour ago, I felt guilty having them sit in the shanty all by themselves. Britt had to be bored out of her mind by now. My dad wasn't back from resetting Sandy's tip-up, so we were alone. "Do you guys mind if I hang out with Britt and Rae for a while?"

"Of course not," Sienna said. "I'm sure Britt came along this morning primarily to spend time with you. We're fine, sweetheart– go have fun with your friend."

I threw my arms around her. "Thanks, Mom. I'm so glad you guys are having a good time."

After sliding my gloves back on, I pulled my hood up around my face and trudged off toward the shanty. I was about a quarter of the way across when a sharp squeal cut through the crisp winter air. Even though the shanty was still over three hundred yards away, I knew instantly that it was Rachel. Before I could read their thoughts to see what had happened, Brittney let out a blood curdling scream. *I tripped on my suit. I must have fallen into her. She hit her head on the ice. There's so much blood. Rae's gone! She's under the ice. What should I do? Oh God she's dead! I killed her!*

I sprinted to the shanty at top speed and whipped open the door, sending it careening across the ice. Brittney was blankly staring at the pool of blood, paralyzed by fear. After commanding her to stay where she was, I yanked off my winter coat and boots and dove into the icy water. The stabbing cold squeezed the air from my lungs and sent me scrambling back to the surface. Recovering from the initial shock, I took several gasps, and then breathed in as deeply as I could before I went under again.

I spotted Rachel's blood trail almost immediately, heading with the current toward the mouth of the bay. As my hands pulled backward, I frog kicked with my legs, cutting through the water at amazing speed. Rae's lifeless body soon came into view, sinking deeper and deeper into the inky darkness below me. My body was growing desperate for air, and I hadn't even caught up with her yet. If I couldn't find a faster way out, we were both going to drown.

Then Rae and everything else was gone. I was still underwater, but I wasn't in the bay anymore. My hands were holding onto a log on the bottom of a river and I was...breathing. Well, sort of. Every few seconds I'd take a fresh mouthful of water into my lungs and hold it. The process was extremely uncomfortable and made my chest burn, but somehow I was getting air out of the water. Or *she* was. Just like before, I was submerged completely in some foreign world. I was watching the cat-eyed vampire hide under a log while peering up from the bottom at the people that lined the riverbanks, holding torches and buckets of something that smelled hideous even underwater.

Dangerous Waters

The strange illusion vanished as suddenly as it had appeared. I was back swimming in the bay, and Rae was just ahead of me. When I finally reached her, I wrapped my left arm around her back and pinned her tightly against my chest. I couldn't hold my breath a second longer. Having no other choice, I headed straight for the surface. I took a couple of easy strokes to keep from jolting her body too badly before pulling down with my free hand and kicking as hard as I could. Just before impact, I placed my right arm over her head and leaned my upper body forward to shield her. The ice exploded over me as I torpedoed through it and into the air, landing on my feet about ten yards away…and right in front of my dad.

"Jesus Christ!" he blurted out, lunging backward onto his butt. He frantically backpedaled away from me with his hands and feet while Sienna, Ruby, Raven and Sandy rushed to my side.

I carefully laid Rachel's body down on the ice and collapsed on top of her, coughing up several mouthfuls of water.

"Trance David, Sandy, before he has a heart attack," Sienna ordered.

"Got it," she replied.

"She's not breathing!" I cried out, still lying on top of her limp body. Blood was gushing out of a nasty cut on the side of her head.

"Let us take care of her, baby. Ruby, take Brooke to the car and get her warmed up. We'll be there as soon as we can."

Ruby hoisted me to my feet and began to tear off my clothes. Within seconds I was lying completely naked in the snow.

"S-s-s-h-h-hit I'm cold," I stuttered through my chattering teeth.

"I had to get your wet clothes off," Ruby explained. She bundled me up in the wool blanket, lifted me into her arms and raced for the car. After a couple of strides, I could tell she was keeping it at human speed– a world class sprinter human anyway. As soon as we reached the Navigator, Ruby sat me in the back seat, started it up and turned the heat on full. She crawled over the divider to sit next to me and quickly undressed, throwing her clothes into the far back.

I cocked my head to the side. "What are you doing?"

"We need to wait for them. Nothing will warm you up in this car as fast as my body will." Ruby lay down on the carpeted floor. "Take the blanket off and lie down on top of me."

Since I was wrapped like a mummy, it took me a second to unwind the blanket from my body. My skin was still ice cold. "Sorry," I whispered, pressing up against her bare skin.

She tucked my numb hands under her armpits and wrapped her arms and legs around me, pulling the blanket down over the top of us. After rubbing my body continuously for several minutes she leaned back and glanced at my face. "How do you feel?"

"A lot better. This is really helping."

She flashed me a smile. "That's good to hear. How tired are you?"

My eyelids felt like they weighed several pounds. I knew I could be asleep in an instant. "I feel weird, like I could sleep for a month, but I'm not hungry."

"I was afraid of that," she said, biting her lip. Seeing my panicked expression she continued. "I didn't mean to scare you– you'll be okay. We just need to get you some blood. When something happens that forces our bodies to use a tremendous amount of energy in a short period of time, our hunger isn't triggered like it should be. We end up feeling weak and sleepy but not hungry."

"Kind of like what happened to Sienna when she was exposed to radiation?"

"Exactly."

Now that I was feeling a little better, my attention shifted back to Rae. David and Brittney's thoughts filled my mind, but I couldn't pick up anything from her.

"Why can't I hear Rae's thoughts! Please tell me she's not dead!"

"She's alive, sis," Ruby reassured me. "Listen to your father and Brittney's thoughts. She's breathing again, but she's still unconscious. They're bringing her to the car now."

I could tell from their thoughts that they were both tranced. Brittney was pretty scared but was far more worried about me and Rachel. My father was totally freaking out. While Sandy was keeping his heart calm, his mind was in overdrive, trying to determine exactly what kind of monster I was. "He doesn't even think I'm his daughter."

Ruby caressed my cheek. "I know that's hard to hear, but we haven't had a chance to speak with him yet. His mind is just trying to make sense out of what he saw."

The ramifications of what I'd done hit me like a brick. "I really screwed up, didn't I."

"You did what you had to in order to save her life," Ruby said, gazing into my eyes. "Any of us would've done the same. Regardless of how complicated this gets, you didn't do anything wrong."

Suddenly Ruby lifted me up, spun me around and scooted us back against the third seat. I was now sitting between her legs with her arms wrapped around my chest. She picked up the blanket and pulled it over the top of us just before Raven opened the door. My dad and Brittney climbed into the second row of seats and stared straight ahead, obviously still tranced. Sienna jumped into the back and reached out as Sandy handed Rachel to her. Rae was wrapped up in several layers of their clothes and had a blood-soaked shirt tied around her head. I could tell that she was breathing, but I still wasn't picking up any thoughts from her. As soon as Sandy jumped in, Raven tore out of the parking lot.

"How's Rachel?" I asked.

"She's unconscious but stable," Sienna said. "We need to get her to a hospital as fast as we can. She shouldn't have any brain damage from the lack of oxygen since she's hypothermic and only went about three minutes without breathing, but I'm really concerned about how hard she hit her head on the ice." Sienna put her hand on Ruby's shoulder. "How's she doing?"

"Her heart beat is stronger and her body has warmed up quite a bit, but she's going to need to feed soon," Ruby said.

"When you guys get back to the house, call the airline and get the three of you on the next available flight back to Boston," Sienna instructed. "Do whatever it takes to keep her awake until she feeds. Sandy and I will take care of things here."

Luckily the hospital was only about three miles from the marina. Then again, in a town this size you were never too far from anything. As soon as Raven pulled up in front of the Emergency entrance, Sienna and Sandy jumped out and rushed Rachel inside. Raven sped off before the automatic hospital doors had closed.

Chapter Thirty-Three
You'd Better Sit down for This

When we got to my dad's house, Ruby carried me into my bedroom and helped me get dressed. Once I'd made my way to the couch, she covered me up with two thick blankets, took a seat next to me and pulled my feet up into her lap. Raven handed me a large cup of diet Mt. Dew and sat down on the other side of Ruby. Brittney was seated in the chair across from me, still tranced, but my father was nowhere in sight. "Where's my dad?"

"Lying down on his bed. It'll be easier to talk to them one at a time," Raven explained. "Brittney, I'm sorry we had to do this to you, but we needed to focus on getting Rachel to the hospital. Do you think you can stay calm if we release you? You can just think your response. We can all read your mind."

I'll be okay.

Ruby immediately released her from her trance.

"I'm so sorry, Britt," I muttered.

She swept me up in a smothering hug. "Sorry? Are you kidding me? You almost died saving my sister while I just stood there like a fucking coward."

"You were in shock," I mumbled into her chest.

Brittney leaned back and sighed. "That's no excuse. I'm sure as hell never working as a lifeguard again. Why aren't you in the hospital? You look terrible."

"I'll be okay. Besides, there's nothing a hospital could do for me anyway."

"What…is all of this?" Her frightened eyes searched my face for answers and assurance that she'd be okay. "I mean, how can you guys read my mind and control my body like that? Why can't a hospital do anything for you?"

I took her hand and held it against my chest. "There's no easy way to tell ya this, so I'm just going to say it. Please try not to freak out, okay?"

She let out a nervous laugh. "I'll try."

"We've all been infected with an extremely rare virus," I said, gesturing toward Raven and Ruby. "It's not contagious or anything, so you don't need to worry about catching it. It caused us to become a lot stronger and revived dormant abilities in our minds like telepathy and hypnotism."

Her head cocked to the side. "How did you get infected if it's not contagious?"

Dangerous Waters

"It's complicated." I pulled my sleeves up and showed her my wrists. "After Raven and I became friends I was attacked outside of a restaurant at school. Raven stopped them from killing me, but she had to agree to infect me in order for them to let me live."

"Jesus, Emme! Who attacked you?" Brittney's fingers absently tracing my scars.

I knew I'd beaten around the bush as much as I could. I had to say the word eventually. "Vampires."

Her eyes darted up to mine in disbelief. Seeing that I was serious, she instinctively pulled her hand away. "So now you're a vampire?"

"Yes, but it's not what you think. We're not demons or the undead or any of the other crap you've seen in the movies. It's just a virus, Britt."

"Why didn't you go to the police after Raven saved you? Why would you go through with it?" Brittney took a step toward Raven and shot her an icy glare. "How could you do this to your friend!"

Watching her confront a vampire on my behalf made me beam with pride, even if her accusations were off base. "Easy, tiger. You don't understand. Vampires are a lot stronger than the police, or any other humans, for that matter. After I was attacked, Raven took me into her home and spent the next two months helping me recover. By the time my wrists had healed, I loved all of them. Before I was changed, Sienna risked her entire family to offer me the choice to return to my former life. I chose to become her daughter instead."

Brittney furrowed her brows and bit her bottom lip. "Her daughter? She's the same age as you are."

I snorted. "Actually, she's over nine hundred years old. The changes prevent us from aging– I'll never look any older than I do now."

"Holy crap!" The absolute shock on her face made us all burst into laughter. After a short pause, she gave me a tentative glance. "What about the whole drinking blood thing?"

"That part's true. The virus screws up our digestive system. There's very little I could eat without puking, and even that wouldn't give me any nutrition." I could feel my eyelids growing heavier with every blink. I took another huge gulp of pop, fighting to stay awake.

Brittney propped my chin up with her hand. "You need to get some rest. Why don't you lie down for a while?"

"If she did, she'd never wake up," Ruby replied. "Her body is drained from being in the freezing water. She needs to feed– soon."

Her heart rate soared as Ruby's words sunk in. Horrible images of having her throat torn open raced through her mind when she realized that she might be providing the meal. But concern for me still filled her teary eyes. "I can't lose you. Just tell me what I need to do." Remembering my scars, she pulled up her sleeve and held her wrist near my mouth.

Without realizing it, she'd basically just taken her vow to become my sister, only there wasn't anything hypothetical about the oath she'd sworn. Britt was willing to die for me. I gently pushed her hand away. "I won't do that to you. You could get infected from my saliva."

Raven leaned around Ruby to look at me. "Even if we could get you on the next flight, it'd be almost five hours before you got home. And we can't pump you full of caffeine to keep you awake. You're going to have to feed here. You know we can't safely take someone from a town this small, and the nearest major city is hours away. This is a lot better option for all of us. The chances of her getting infected from your saliva are one in a million. You won't hurt her."

"That means there's a one in a million chance I'd kill her," I countered. "I'm not taking that chance."

"Wouldn't I just turn into a vampire?" Brittney wondered. "I wouldn't mind being nineteen forever."

"If I infected you while you were injured, you'd never heal," I said, my eyes meeting her gaze. "Eventually you'd bleed to death from the small cut on your arm. Besides, you don't know what you're saying. This isn't the kind of choice you make on a whim."

Ruby pulled out her cell phone and called Sienna, putting the call on speaker so we all could hear. "How's Rachel?"

"She's still unconscious, but they did a CT scan and an MRI," Sienna said. "There's no sign of any swelling on the brain yet. They're working on warming her body up now. Her parents should be here any minute."

"Can I come see her?" Brittney asked.

"Of course. I'm sorry we had to take you home for a while first. Raven, can you bring her over?"

"Actually, that's one of the reasons I called," Ruby responded. "Brooke's on the verge of passing out, and we aren't crazy about the idea of grabbing somebody off the street from a town this small. Britt offered to help, but Brooke doesn't want to risk hurting her. Do you think you could swipe an IV and some tubing from a supply closet and meet Raven in the parking lot?"

"Good thinking, Ruby. I'll be out front in five minutes."

"What about– about the radiation?" I said, my voice cracking mid-sentence.

"God, you sound terrible. You don't need to worry about us, baby. We're staying in a waiting room about four floors from radiology."

Raven hopped up off the couch and turned to Ruby. "You've got David?"

Ruby nodded. After concentrating for no more than a second, she shifted her attention back to Brittney. "Is it okay if we draw some blood first? It shouldn't take more than ten minutes. I'll run you up to the hospital as soon as we're done."

"I'm not going anywhere until I know Emme's okay." Her brows scrunched as she looked at Ruby. "Why do you guys keep calling her Brooke?"

I flashed her a smile. "It's kind of a nickname off my last name. Since we don't age, we need to assume new identities every few years. Sienna decided that it'd be less confusing if we had a permanent name to call each other by at home."

"Makes sense…Brooke." The uncertainty in her voice as she uttered my new name made us laugh. It was like she was waiting to see if we'd let her into our secret club.

"Let's do it at the table," Raven called out from the kitchen, swinging the door shut behind her.

Brittney pulled off her sweater and t-shirt off and took a seat. Raven put on a pair of latex gloves, tied a tourniquet around Brittney's upper arm and ripped open a sterilizing pad. After cleaning the skin on the inside of her arm, she inserted the needle and taped it into place, grabbed the other end of the tubing and held it above a large plastic cup. When she removed the tourniquet, blood shot down the tube. As soon as the first cup was full, she handed it to Ruby and began to fill a second.

"Here ya go, sis."

I took the cup from Ruby and hungrily gulped it down, sending a wave of energy streaming into my veins. "Damn. You taste awesome, Britt!" I teased.

"Okay– gross," Brittney said, leaning back in her chair to half scowl at me. "Seriously about to puke now."

Maybe it was a little too soon for jokes, even if she was handling the news of my transformation far better than I expected. Ruby brought me the second cup and took the empty one from my hands. Now that I wasn't in danger of passing out, I wanted to savor my extra meal, but having Britt discover just how into drinking blood I was wouldn't do our friendship any favors. I took a quick peek toward the kitchen. She had her back to me and was watching Raven bandage her arm. Perfect. My eyes drifted shut as I inhaled the intoxicating aroma and slowly drank it down, allowing the succulent flavors to saturate my mouth before every swallow.

"Man, your color's better already."

I jerked my head up and found Britt standing right in front of me. She took a reflexive step back, her mouth, cheeks and eyes contorting into an almost comical bitter beer face. Following her gaze, I quickly ran the back of my arm across my chin to wipe away the offending trail of blood.

"How do you feel?" she asked, her skin taking on an almost greenish hue. If she wasn't serious about being close to puking before, she sure as hell was now. Wonderful.

"Sorry about that– I'm sure you didn't need the visual. I'll be fine thanks to you. You're the best, Britt."

She waved my apology away and managed a smile. "Don't be thinking that things are all weird between us now. I meant what I said before. After what you did this morning, I love you more than I ever have. You'll always be my best friend, regardless of what name you're going by."

Tears pooled in the corner of my eyes. "Thanks, gator. You don't know how happy that makes me. I really am fine now. Please go be with your sister. I'll be down as soon as we talk to my dad."

After pulling me into a suffocating hug, she put her shirts back on and followed Ruby out the door.

I rinsed out both cups, threw the supplies Raven had used to draw Brittney's blood in the trash and sat back down on the couch. My next conversation was going to be hard enough without having a bunch of bloody props lying around. "What do I say to him? He thinks I'm dead."

"Just be yourself and tell him the truth," Raven said. "He loves you more than anything. He'll understand."

I could hear him getting out of bed and opening the door. He walked into the living room and sat down in the chair across from me.

"David, I know how scared and confused you are about what Emily did this morning, not to mention having us take control of your body. I hope you know that we'd never hurt you. In order to minimize the chance of you having a heart attack, it'd probably be best if we answer your questions while you're still tranced. We can read your mind, so all you have to do is think about what you'd like to know."

That's not Emily. Whatever kind of creatures you are, you killed my little girl.

"How can you say that, Dad?" My lower lip trembled as I looked pleadingly into his eyes. "I'm not some stupid alien!"

Raven took my hand to comfort me. "It's okay. David, I assure you, your daughter is alive and well, and is sitting right here next to me."

Bullshit. I know what I saw. She surfaced through three feet of ice like a damn submarine.

"Nobody is denying that. Emily has certain mental and physical abilities as a result of being infected with a rare virus. Your daughter bravely risked her life this morning to save Rachel. Does that sound like something an alien or monster would do?"

Not really. What kind of virus? I've never heard of anything like this before.

"No one that isn't infected has– that's the only reason we're able to survive."

I was leery of jumping back into the conversation since Raven was handling it well, but seeing the remote control on the coffee table gave me an idea. "Do you remember the show you watched with us last night?"

True Blood? What does that have to do with anything? You're not suggesting— His mind raced as he processed our expressions. *I don't believe this! How stupid do you think I am! Vampires? And I'm the God damn Easter Bunny!*

I winced and shriveled into the couch, wishing that it would swallow me beneath the cushions.

"I know how crazy that sounds," Raven said, shooting me a sideways glance. "And to be honest, comparing us to that show isn't a great analogy anyway. Almost none of what you've seen on TV or in the movies is true. There's nothing supernatural or evil about it. It's just a virus."

Virus my ass. Diseases don't give you superpowers, they make you sick. You must have drugged the hot chocolate—I wondered why none of you drank any. Although why you'd do such a thing is beyond me. And all of you were obviously concerned for Rachel. God, this doesn't make any sense. If you're really my daughter, then tell me what song I used to sing to you when I put you to bed at night.

Rather than answer him I started to sing. "In the jungle, the mighty jungle, the lion sleeps tonight." The smirk on Raven's face let me know that I'd just given her prime material to tease me with, but hearing the shift in my father's thoughts was worth it.

Emily? Oh my God... It's really you. But how? How did you break through the ice like that? If I'm not drugged, and you really can do superhuman things, than please show me.

Without saying a word, Raven went into the garage and returned holding an aluminum baseball bat. "This is your bat, correct?"

Yes.

"And would you agree that no ordinary human being could rip an aluminum bat in half with their bare hands?"

I guess so. I mean, maybe if—

"Yes or no," she grumbled. "We can use your car if you require a larger demonstration."

Okay. Yes, I agree.

Raven handed it to me and nodded her head. I placed my hands near the center of the bat and squeezed my fingers down through the metal. Once my fists were closed, I pulled them apart, separating the bat into two mangled pieces.

Holy shit! You're really not—vampires... His thoughts trailed off.

Raven took a seat and gave him a reassuring smile. "So what questions do you have?"

Tell me you don't really drink blood.

She bit her lip and briefly glanced away. "We have to. The virus prevents us from being able to digest food, so we have to take in nutrients in a form that can be readily absorbed into our bloodstream."

Did you turn my daughter into... What she is?

"She saved me, Dad," I said in Raven's defense. "I was attacked the day after I told you my roommate was missing. They would've killed me if it wasn't for her."

I showed him my wrists while I debated what to say next. I didn't want there to be any secrets between us, but expecting him to be okay with me choosing this life seemed ridiculous. "Since I was bitten, Raven talked Sienna into letting me stay with them and helped me adjust to things. I love them all like my sisters. You've seen how great they are."

So you don't kill people to get blood like other vampires? The look on our faces was all the answer he needed. *You're just a bunch of murderers. You make me sick.*

"Thanks for being so open-minded," I snapped back at him. "They saved my life, not to mention that they have foundations and charities all over the world. Remember what Sandy told you? Her dad died in Vietnam, so she started a charity to help families who lost a parent in military service. She's worked with over ten thousand families already, and that's one of the smaller charities we're involved with."

Even if all that's true, and I'm not saying I believe that for a second, it doesn't make up for killing people. What did they do to you? You wouldn't even let me step on a spider growing up. Now you're okay with slaughtering people like pigs? I can't accept that—I won't!

"So you wish I was dead."

My dad's face remained the picture of serenity as he stared blankly back at me from his chair, even as his thoughts were ripping me a part. *I'm not saying that. God, I don't know what I'm saying. This whole thing is insane. I'm glad you're alive, but this is no kind of life. I wanted you to go to college, get married, have a family. What do you have to look forward to now?*

"I'm still going to college to study climatology, and once I graduate I'll be working with global warming researchers just like I always wanted to do."

"And there's no reason she couldn't get married someday," Raven added. "Ruby is."

That's something I guess. But how am I supposed to pretend you're still my innocent little girl? This changes everything. I begged you to come home. Why couldn't you have listened to me!

"Please Daddy!" I cried out, throwing myself into his lap. "I'm still me. I need you! Please don't hate me." All of the emotion I'd been struggling to contain burst free, pouring out in sobs that left me gasping for air.

My dad's arms curled around me, patting my back softly as he spoke. Apparently Raven felt his heart rate had slowed enough to risk releasing him. "I could never hate you, sweetheart. We'll get through this somehow. You're just going to have to give me some time."

I nodded, leaning in for a long hug. "I can do that."

After wiping my cheeks on my sleeve, I got back on my feet. "There are a couple more things you need to know. I'm never going to look any older than I do now. That forces us to change our names every few years, so to make things a little less confusing we refer to each other by the nicknames that Sienna gave each of us."

"I was wondering who the hell Brooke was," he said with a chuckle. "So you're going to stay nineteen forever?"

"As long as I'm alive," I clarified.

He raked his fingers through is crew cut hair, trying to take all of this in. "But if you don't age– "

"We're not immortal," Raven cut in. "There are several things that can kill us, but the most common is fighting with others of our kind."

"One more thing, Dad," I said, leaning my neck up close to him. "Take a deep breath and tell me what you smell."

He peered at me, a bit puzzled, and then reluctantly breathed in. "Are you talking about your perfume? It's kind of strong."

"It's not perfume. It's what all vampires smell like. If you even think you smell that scent when you're alone, start talking with whomever is closest to you and get away from the area as fast as you can. Vampires are careful not to leave witnesses, so there's safety in numbers. Do you understand?"

David stood up and pulled me into a hug, bending down to kiss my head. "Yes, baby, I'll be careful."

When we finally broke apart, Raven placed her hand on his shoulder. "Now that you know about us, you'll be able to see Emme for the rest of your life. We'll fly you out to stay with us whenever you'd like to visit and will come here for a few years as well. But by sharing this with you, we are placing all of our lives in your hands. It's vital for your safety and ours that you never tell anyone about any of this, regardless of how good your intentions are."

"So I have to cancel my appearance on Larry King tonight?" he joked. Raven just rolled her eyes. His face turned serious as he took her hand. "Thank you for trusting me. I get the feeling that isn't something that you're in the habit of doing. Does Brittney know? Where is she?"

"Ruby took her to the hospital," I said. "We told her pretty much everything we just told you. She took it really well."

His face turned all fatherly as he assessed the color of my cheeks. "How are you feeling? You look a lot better."

"I'm fine– I was just run down from getting so cold. I'm anxious to find out how Rae's doing though. Do you think you could run us up to the hospital?"

He flashed me my favorite half smile. "It'd be a lot faster if we took the car."

We all laughed at his god-awful joke. Maybe we really could get through this.

* * * *

As soon as we entered the waiting room, Brittney's parents smothered me in hugs and kisses as they thanked me.

"If my dad hadn't broken into the other shanty as fast as he did, we both would have drowned," I said after reading their minds to find out what story they'd been told. David picked up on it and played along convincingly enough while they thanked him. "How's she doing?"

"She regained consciousness about ten minutes ago," Brittney said. "She's down getting another set of scans to check for swelling on her brain, but so far everything's fine. They let us in to visit with her for a couple of minutes. She was a little groggy, but she hasn't shown any signs of brain damage, and her body temperature is back to normal."

"Thank God!" David blurted out before turning toward her parents. "I'm so sorry that I let this happen. I never should've left them alone in the shanty like that."

"Nonsense, David," her dad replied, patting his shoulder. "Brittney is nineteen years old and knows her way around an ice shanty just fine. It was just a freak accident. If it wasn't for your quick thinking and your daughter's heroic rescue, Rachel would be dead right now. How do I thank both of you for giving me my daughter back? How– " his voice broke off as he choked back tears.

David gave him a hug. "You don't need to thank us, Jerry. Brittney and Rachel are more like Emily's sisters than her friends. The only thanks we need is seeing that beautiful little girl bouncing around our house again."

"You have to know that we feel the same way about Emily," Brittney's mother said. "Her senior picture is on our mantle right between Brittney's and Rachel's. We think of her as our daughter too."

"Thanks, Judy," he said with a gracious smile. "You both have been wonderful to her."

While we'd told Brittney and my dad almost the same story, there was one critical difference that I needed her to know about. "Britt, can we take a walk for a minute?"

She stared at me for a second before she caught on. "Oh, sure."

We headed down the hallway and into an empty family changing room. After locking the door behind us I spun around and sat on the ledge of the sink.

She hopped up on the ledge next to me. "Things must have gone pretty well with your dad."

"Not really. He's not too crazy about me being a vamp. I wasn't as open with him about how I became like this either."

"What did you tell him?"

"I knew it would crush him if he found out that it was my choice, so I kinda led him to believe that I was infected from being bitten during the attack. He knows that Raven saved me from being killed, but he doesn't know anything about the agreement she made to do it."

"All that matters is that he accepts who you are now," Brittney reassured me. "There's no sense making things harder for yourself by sharing unnecessary details. And I know you're stressing about it, but he'll come around– you're his whole world."

"Thanks." I turned my body sideways to face her. "I'm sure you already know this, but you can never mention this stuff to anyone, not even Rachel or your parents. If people found out that vampires existed, we'd all be toast in no time."

She let out a resigned sigh. "I was hoping you might let me tell Rachel when she got older, but I understand. You can trust me– I won't let you down."

"I know that, girl!" I playfully nudged her shoulder, trying to lighten the mood. "Just think, now that you know, I can fly you out to visit me whenever you want. It's been horrible having to hide things from you the last couple months."

"Really? Sienna would let me stay with you guys?"

"Absolutely. All expenses paid."

Her lips opened into a beaming smile. "Sa-weet! So what have you been holding back from me?"

"Let's see… I had to delay my classes until the summer to give me time to get used to the whole vamp thing. We all live in an amazing house on the south end of Boston. I can run like two hundred miles an hour, kick and punch through solid steel plates and jump hundreds of feet with ease. And if that wasn't freaky enough, I have some kind of weird super ninja gift that Sienna doesn't even understand. Oh, and I'm not a virgin anymore."

"Oh my God!" Brittney yelled, throwing her arm around my shoulders. "Details, girl! Who's the guy? How was it?"

I told her all about what led to our little club adventure, how I'd met Daniel, how much fun we'd had dancing, how amazing our night in the hotel was, and the note he had left in the morning.

When I finished she slowly laced her fingers through mine. "But now you can't see him anymore."

"I don't even know if it'd be safe– I might hurt him if I got too excited. Not that I have a choice. Raven made it perfectly clear that it could only be a one-time thing.

"That really sucks, Emme. He sounds like a great guy," Brittney said. "But given what happened today, I understand where Raven's coming from. There's no way you guys could date without him eventually finding out. And not to sound cruel, but if we have to keep your secret from my family, people that both of us love and trust, then you shouldn't be putting yourself in a position where you end up telling someone you barely even know."

I couldn't believe that she was siding with Raven, but I couldn't argue with her logic. Not being able to date Daniel wasn't much of a sacrifice compared to what I was asking her to do. "You're right. How can I sit here and give you and my dad ultimatums about how important it is to protect our secret when I'm the one taking risks that end up exposing us? It's awesome that you guys are a part of my life again, but it was really selfish of me to come here."

She looped her arm around my shoulder and gave me a hug. "I'm glad you did. It would've killed me to never see you again."

"Me too– that's why I cried when I opened your gift."

After a long cuddle, I leaned back and continued. "One more thing. Even though you've been too nice to say anything about it, I'm sure you've noticed that we all have a really strong scent."

"It's not that bad," she insisted. "It's kind of pretty really. I feel like I'm on Mackinac Island when the lilacs are in bloom."

"So you knew it was coming from me?"

She grinned. "Well, I had no idea why you guys all smelled the same before this morning, but I didn't believe Sandy for a second. Men's body sprays aren't even that strong."

Brittney ran her fingers through her chocolate-brown hair, sweeping her bangs away from her gorgeous face. It was the same simple motion I'd seen her do a thousand times before, one that always caught the attention of every guy within sight. My mood darkened when I realized that she'd never blend into a crowd.

"What's wrong?" she finally asked.

"I'm really worried about you getting attacked. Vampires tend to avoid small towns like this, but there are bound to be some in Lansing and the other big cities where you'll be playing tournaments. And with your looks, they'll notice you, regardless of how many people are around. If they ever catch you alone– " I couldn't bear to finish the thought.

"Oh," Brittney muttered. Outwardly she remained calm, but I could tell from her thoughts that she was afraid. "I feel weird asking you this, since you're um…one of them, but is there anything I could do to defend myself?"

I wanted with all my heart to show her how to break our trance. If Kelly's theory was correct, she wouldn't be able to learn, but that was just a theory. And even if I did have some kind of extra genetic ability, that wouldn't necessarily mean that it was what allowed me to break vampire trances as a human. For all we knew, any human could learn to do it if they were given enough time. In the end, whether she could learn or not was irrelevant. Attempting to teach her would break my promise to Sienna and put both of our lives in danger.

All I could do was give her the same advice that I'd given my father.

"Crowds good, alone bad. Check." I appreciated her effort to make me laugh, even though she was only masking her fear.

"If the worst should happen and you're tranced– like you were this morning– don't forget that they can hear your thoughts. Stay calm and tell them that you are close friends with Sienna and her coven in Boston, and that you have already been sworn to secrecy. There's a good chance they'll know her. Even if they don't, they may feel compelled to check with the leader of their coven before they do anything. I'm going to program all of our numbers into your cell phone as well. I wish there was more I could do to keep you safe."

"I'll be fine," she assured me. "I mean, come on, I've got my own built in vamp radar and a coven of kick ass vampires in my corner." We both giggled.

"So what's up with you? Are you and Kyle still together?" I asked, feeling guilty about dominating the conversation.

Britt picked at the frayed thread in her distressed look skinny jeans. "Nope. We broke up before I left for school. We both knew it wasn't going anywhere, so there was no sense trying to do the long distance thing."

"I'm sorry."

"Yeah, right. Like I don't know you want to do back flips right now. Who do you think you're talking to girl? Vamp or not, you still suck at lying."

I snorted. "Okay, I admit I wasn't his biggest fan. But he was still your first, and you guys dated for a really long time. It must have been hard on you."

"Thanks," she said, nudging her body against mine. "I'll never forget him, but it's nice knowing I'm free to date whoever I want without feeling guilty– not that I've met anyone yet."

Suddenly I heard Rachel's name enter my mind from someone other than our parents. I focused on the thoughts of her doctor as he walked down the hall. "Rachel's scans are normal. Dr. Staley is about to tell your parents that they expect her to make a full recovery, but she'll need to stay in the hospital for observation for another two to three days."

Brittney threw her arms around me. "You did it. You saved her."

"Let's go see her."

After the doctor finished giving her parents the update I'd already shared with Britt, he said that Rachel was awake and alert and could have visitors as long as we didn't stay too long. Brittney, her parents, David and I followed him down the hall to her new room. Rachel's face lit up as soon as she saw us. She had about thirty stitches on the left side of her head above her hairline, along with a nasty looking bump. Her long black hair had been cut short above the wound, and almost the entire side of her head had been shaved. At least the scar would be concealed when her hair grew back.

Jerry and Judy spent several minutes smothering Rae in tearful hugs and kisses, not letting up until she pleaded for her sister to save her. Brittney sat down on the bed next to her and took her hand. "I'm so sorry, Rae."

"What happened? What knocked me into the hole?"

"I did. After I turned down the heat, I tripped on the top of my snowmobile suit and fell on top of you. I got up as fast as I could when I heard you scream, but you were already gone. There was blood all over the ice and in the water– I thought I killed you." Brittney buried her head in Rae's lap and began to weep.

"Don't cry, sis. I know you didn't mean to hurt me," Rachel said, squeezing her around the shoulders. "How did I get out from under the ice?"

"Luckily Emme was on her way over to us when it happened. She came barreling into the shanty and dove in after you while I was still frozen in shock. When David spotted her swimming under the ice he broke into the shanty she was headed toward and pulled you both up."

Rachel shot me a wide-eyed look. "Weren't you scared? The water must have been freezing!"

"Oh, it was," I said with a laugh. "I didn't think about it long enough to be scared. I'd never let anything happen to you." I reached out and gave her hand a quick squeeze. "I love you, munchkin."

"I love you more. You're like the coolest girl I've ever known."

Rachel peered past me at my father, her face full of uncertainty. "I'm sorry I almost got her killed. I'll understand if you don't want to take me fishing anymore."

"Oh, honey! You didn't do anything wrong," David said, rushing to her side. "I'm just so happy that you're going to be okay. My little fishing buddy is always welcome."

"You mean it? We can still fish together?"

"Whenever you want, sweetheart," he promised.

She gave him a tight hug then turned eagerly toward her dad. "Have you picked up Emily yet? When do I get to see her?"

Jerry's eyebrows curled up in confusion. "You just talked to her honey. You don't remember?"

"Doctor!" Judy yelled, already half way to the nurse's station.

"It's okay, Mom!" Brittney called after her. "She's talking about her golden retriever puppy. She decided to name it Emily."

Jerry let out a huge sigh of relief. "Geez, pumpkin. You scared us half to death! The doctors are saying you should be able to come home in a couple of days. Once you're back on your feet I'll take you down to pick her up."

"And I think Emily is a perfect name for her," Judy added, flashing me a smile.

Chapter Thirty-Four
Battle Plans

My mind wandered back through the entire trip while I lounged around in bed late into the morning. If I looked at it from Sienna's point of view, the trip was a total disaster. Two humans that she had little choice but to trust found out that vampires existed, and one of her daughters almost froze to death. Going there was definitely not in the best interest of our coven.

Still, Rachel was going to be fine and would be coming home from the hospital today. And while I still had my doubts that things would ever be close to normal between me and my dad, at least he'd agreed to visit in May. My new family had latched onto Britt like she'd joined our coven, inviting her along dancing and snowboarding, and disclosing far more about their personal lives than I ever thought they would. They had almost her entire spring break trip planned before I even found out she was coming. I had no doubt that Britt and my dad would keep things quiet, and I no longer had to live a lie with anyone that was important to me.

But as enjoyable as it was to reminisce, I was too excited to stay in bed any longer. Since my initial lesson, Sienna and I had fought three times without any incidents, and I'd finally convinced her that it was safe for me to fight against the rest of my family. Diligently practicing my Kata routine and fighting with Ironsides had further honed my unique abilities, along with my self-control. Limiting myself to moving at sword fight speed was no harder for me than moving at human speed in public.

I still had a lot to learn in spite of my mysterious gift. While I was great at spotting openings, I had trouble thinking more than one move ahead, which left me at a huge disadvantage if Sienna managed to counter my initial attack. Our last fight was the only time that I'd clearly beaten her. Today was going to be different though. Not only was I going to fight against my sisters for the first time– we'd also be fighting in teams.

After taking a scalding hot shower, I threw on the scrubbiest workout clothes I could find and hurried down the hall. Sienna and Raven were stretching on the floor, patiently waiting for us to join them.

"Sorry I slept so late," I said, sitting down next to Sienna. "It felt so good to be back in my own bed again."

"I hear that," Raven agreed. "I'd still be in bed if Sienna hadn't asked me to help her prepare for this."

I arched my brows at her. "Prepare?"

Sienna glanced up from stretching her groin. "We were trying to determine what the best teams would be."

"Ahh. What did you come up with?"

"If I was going for the most competitive fight, I'd take Sandy and go up against the three of you," Sienna responded. "But I think you and Raven will learn a lot more fighting shorthanded. The whole point of group fighting is to teach you to work together as a team. You'll find that your individual talent levels have very little impact on how effectively you fight together. It's kind of like playing doubles tennis. What typically happens when you try to have the two best singles players who have never played together play a doubles match?"

"They get crushed."

"But why?" she challenged. "If they're the best players and could easily defeat either of their opponents in a singles match, why do they lose when you put them together?"

I grinned, realizing where she was going with this. "Because you need to learn your partner's tendencies, what shots they're capable of making and what their weaknesses are in order to anticipate their moves and play together as a team."

"Exactly," Sienna said with an approving smile. "The same concepts apply here. It will take several months of practice before we all feel comfortable fighting together. Unlike the rest of your training, this is not something you can master on your own– your sisters and I have just as much to learn as you do."

Even though I was eager to go up against Raven, I loved the idea of us being a team. "You and me, sis!" I shouted, raising my hand toward her.

She leaned around Sienna and gave me a high five. "Let's take 'em down, ninja girl!"

"As if," Sandy shot back, strolling into the room behind Ruby. "Well, maybe if we were blindfolded."

"No, we'd still kick their asses," Ruby said. Sandy snorted and the rest of us joined her in laughter.

After we finished stretching, Raven cranked up the music and led us through a short warm up. By the time I put on my fencing gloves and picked up my broadsword, adrenaline was racing through my veins. Raven selected a 36-

inch Katana Samurai sword and led me toward the back of the room.

"Sienna is going to try everything to get us to separate," she whispered. "Whatever they do, we need to stay together— our only chance is to keep the fight two on three. This is a purely defensive exercise. Don't let them draw you into an attack, regardless of how tempting it seems."

"How will we keep track of each other?" There was no way I'd even be able to defend myself if I was looking around all the time.

"We'll fight almost back to back but turned just enough so we're in each other's periphery vision. Since you're faster than I am, I'll have you fight on my left. That will leave you a bit more vulnerable, since more of your back will be exposed to your non-sword hand."

"Sounds good." I paused, my expression becoming much more serious. "I know we're outnumbered, and it's the first time we've fought together, but I'm not big on the whole losing thing— let's kick some ass." She gave me an exuberant smile.

"You guys got your strategy worked out?" Sienna asked.

"Ready when you are," I said, carving a Z through the air with my sword.

She laughed. "Good to hear. Let's go over a couple of things before we get started. First of all, there will be five of us flying around and coming at each other from multiple directions, so we all need to be extra careful. I think this could end up being the most useful training we've ever done, but if anyone does something reckless, I'll stop it immediately."

Sienna focused on me. "Brooke, you've done a tremendous job of controlling your movements in our fights, but in this exercise you're overmatched by design. You can't let your desperation push you beyond what the rest of us are capable of."

"I won't, Mom." I groaned. It appeared that she still had her doubts about my control after all.

"We wouldn't be doing this if I didn't trust you," she assured me, picking up on my snarkiness. "As far as the rules are concerned, each round of fighting will begin in the middle of the room. When someone gets hit, they'll call it out and everyone will stop. After some coaching we'll reset and resume fighting. Once you get hit twice, you're out, and will stand against the back wall until one of the teams wins. Each week we'll switch teams up so that we all have a chance to fight together." Sienna pulled on her gloves and motioned to Sandy. "That's it. Let's kill the music and get started."

Sandy shut off the stereo while Raven and I took our positions next to each other in the center of the room. After they picked up their swords, Sienna headed around to my left while Ruby and Sandy slowly inched toward Raven. Once Sienna had gotten behind me, she stopped circling, trying to force me to turn away from Raven in order to defend myself. I brought my sword around and held it over my left leg, tensing for her attack.

She took another step closer to me, and then inexplicably shifted her attention to Raven. Even though she was still 20 feet away, there was no way she'd be able to react in time if I struck. She'd never been this careless in any of our fights. Smelling a trap, I peeked over my right shoulder just as Ruby launched herself toward Raven's back. After taking a quick step to shield her, I swung my sword downward, catching Ruby's blade and guiding it safely away. As I spun back to my left, Sandy yelled that she was hit.

"Yes!" I gave Raven a celebratory fist bump for scoring the first point. Sandy's black and turquoise sports bra and matching fitness pants were unscathed, so I figured she'd been hit in the stomach.

"Great job, Brooke," Sienna praised. "You honored your responsibility to protect Raven's back and remained disciplined even when I gave you a free shot at me."

"Raven's instructions really helped," I said. She couldn't have predicted their strategy any better.

Sienna turned toward Sandy. "As for the attack, even though you were meant to be the decoy, you always have to be ready to defend yourself. Real fights are extremely volatile situations. You can never assume anything is going to go as planned."

"I know," Sandy said, obviously still pissed with herself for letting Raven get the better of her.

Once Raven and I returned to the middle of the room, Sienna confirmed we were ready, and then bolted toward me in a full-out assault with Ruby trailing close behind. I whipped my sword around to meet hers just before it hit the left side of my neck, and then jumped high enough for Ruby's sword to pass harmlessly beneath my feet. By the time I landed, Sienna had circled around to my right and was already thrusting her sword toward my exposed chest. Since I didn't have time to block her attack, I threw myself backward onto the floor, her sword passing within an inch of my cheek. Before Sienna could finish me off, Raven announced that she was hit.

Sienna reached down and helped me to my feet. "Do you know what you did wrong?"

"Not really," I admitted.

"When you see multiple attackers coming toward you and you know you have to protect your inside, never engage the outside attacker first," she instructed. "You gave Ruby all of the room she needed to separate you from Raven. Instead, move to your inside to avoid the initial attack and engage the most immediate threat to your partner."

"That makes sense."

Sienna placed her hand on Ruby's shoulder. "Great improvisation on your part, Ruby. Rather than getting frustrated when Brooke dodged your attack, you capitalized on the opportunity her mistake presented you." Ruby's face lit up at her compliments.

I walked over to Raven, who'd thrown what was left of her dark blue tank top against the back wall. "Sorry about that."

"Hey, this is a long way from over." She held her sword up in the air, and I struck it with my blade.

When fighting resumed, Sienna approached me from the front while Ruby and Sandy moved in a flanking position toward Raven. I knew she was going to try to tie me up long enough for them to knock Raven out of the fight. Tired of sitting back, I raced straight toward Sienna, making her break down in a defensive stance, and then I lunged to my right and swung my sword sideways across Ruby's back.

"I'm hit!" Ruby shouted in surprise. She quickly wheeled around to find me grinning at her. She laughed, pulled off her now mangled quarter sleeve fitted t-shirt and threw it on top of Raven's.

Sienna angrily shook her head. "That's my fault. I should never have let her get behind you like that. You sold your bluff well, Brooke. Not being predictable is crucial in a fight. You caught me totally off guard."

Raven put her arm around my shoulders. "Score one for ninja girl."

"One more hit on Ruby or Sandy and the teams are even!"

The second the next round began Ruby and Sandy charged straight toward me. Remembering Sienna's earlier advice, I edged even closer to Raven and intercepted Sandy's sword, taking it all the way down to the floor. With her sword trapped under mine, Sandy was helpless, but Ruby was on top of me before I could capitalize, forcing me to pivot away and guard my back. When Sandy recovered, she sprung forward and thrust her sword straight ahead. The speed of her attack was impressive, but her aim was poor, allowing me to easily deflect her blade. As I turned back toward Ruby, I yanked my sword across my body just in time to keep her from striking my left shoulder, and then executed a downward block to guide Sandy's sword away from my right hip.

Out of the corner of my eye I caught a glimpse of Sienna. Her fierce onslaught had Raven frantically backpedaling– there was no way she'd last much long on her own. In a desperate attempt to protect her, I crouched down and prepared to launch myself toward Sienna. Before I could move, Ruby's sword sliced up my chest and across the left side of my neck.

"I'm hit," I shouted, completely disgusted with myself. My purple yoga top was split wide open from the V-neck all the way down to my belly button. I ripped it the rest of the way off and added it to the growing pile in the back of the room.

Sienna pulled Sandy and Ruby into her arms. "Nice work you two. I knew you could get a hit in on her if you worked together."

"We can't take credit for that," Ruby said, looking down at the floor.

Sienna tilted her head. "What do you mean? What happened?"

"Brooke wasn't having any trouble fighting us," Sandy explained. "The only reason Ruby was able to hit her is because she was watching you."

Sienna's eyes darted to mine. "Brooke– "

"I know, that was really stupid of me," I finished for her.

"Yes, it was." She gave me a warm smile. "I know you felt like Raven was in trouble, but if you try to do too much in a fight, you'll just get yourself killed. It's very possible that I would've gotten the better of her, but at least she had a chance. If this had been a real fight, Raven would now be up against three vampires, all but ensuring her death."

"I understand," I muttered. "And I was having plenty of trouble fighting you guys. I doubt I would've lasted more than a couple more seconds anyway."

Sandy giggled. "Nice try, girl."

"I wouldn't have lasted…more than…a couple seconds," Ruby said, acting it out like a scene in a play. Everyone burst into laughter.

After taking a few swigs of Gatorade, I bounded down the hall to my room and grabbed a few tops for everyone. I pulled on a black and pink sport cami and tossed tank tops to Ruby and Raven. It didn't bother me to be topless in front of them, but having my breasts bounce around while I tried to move was distracting– not to mention uncomfortable. Raven and I walked back to the center of the room and prepared for the next round.

As soon as we were underway Sienna launched herself into a forward roll and jumped over me, landing between me and Raven. I slid over to protect

Dangerous Waters

Raven's back and turned to face her. Sienna stepped forward with her left foot and thrust her sword toward my stomach. I snapped my sword downward, pushed her blade aside and countered with an upward slicing attack toward the left side of her chest. She gracefully spun to her left to avoid the hit, and then crouched down and whipped her sword around toward the back of my knees. As I jumped her sword, I pulled myself into a forward flip, swinging at her neck while I was inverted. Only a swift dive to the floor saved her from being hit. She was just getting to her knees when I landed, which left her utterly defenseless. Just before my sword came down across her back, Raven called out that she was hit.

"God damn it!" After taking a couple of deep breaths to calm myself, I reached down and helped Sienna to her feet.

She tilted my chin up with her hand. "That was amazing, sweetheart. Your skills are growing at an exponential rate– I've never seen someone attack while inverted before. If it wasn't for my desperate flop on the floor, you would've taken me down before Raven was hit. I didn't even have my sword anymore."

"Thanks," I said, totally dejected. Even though I knew the odds were against us, I thought that we'd at least be able to knock one of them out before we lost. The only way that would happen now was if I could win fighting one on three.

Sienna glanced at Raven. "So what happened over here?" I could tell by the gash in her sweats that she'd been hit across the right thigh.

"I was actually holding my own against them until Ruby broke off her attack and headed for Brooke," Raven replied. "When I tried to cut her off, Sandy got me in the leg."

"You're doing awesome today, Ruby!" Sienna said, flashing a smile. "When you outnumber your opponent, you should always help out wherever you're needed the most. In this case you definitely made the right call."

After receiving a Rocky'esque pep talk from Raven that would have made Mick proud, my competitiveness was back in full force. So what if it was one on three? I'd already fought against Sienna and Ruby without getting hit. I could do this. Once I was set, Ruby and Sandy slowly circled behind me while Sienna approached from the front. Rather than making myself dizzy trying to spin around in circles, I decided to focus on Sienna and listen intently for even the subtlest of sounds from behind.

From the slight variations in their breathing I could tell that Sandy was on my right and a little closer to me than Ruby– maybe fifteen feet. They were both at about 45 degree angles off of my shoulders. Ruby's breathing was calm and steady. She was shifting her weight back and forth like someone preparing to receive a serve in tennis. Everything about her was passive. She wouldn't be the one to strike first.

I heard Sandy draw in a deep breath as Sienna shifted her weight ever so slightly onto the balls of her feet– it was time. At the sound of Sandy's left foot leaving the floor I spun around to my left and crouched low to the ground. Sandy was almost on top of me, but her target had moved after she'd committed to her attack. Her sword was still up above her head, leaving her entire body exposed. I thrust my sword upward into her stomach, shattering the blade into pieces.

Sandy stopped mid-swing and looked at me in disbelief. "What the hell!"

"How'd you do that?" Sienna asked, putting Sandy's expletive into a more formal question. "How'd you know precisely when to strike?"

"It really wasn't that hard," I said, trying to downplay what I'd done. "I could tell from their breathing that Sandy was going to attack first. When I heard her pick her foot up off the ground I knew it was time to move."

"Being able to paint an accurate picture of everything that is happening behind you utilizing only your hearing is truly extraordinary," Sienna said with a mixture of fascination and pride in her eyes. "I can't wait to get your DNA test results back."

"Me neither." After Sienna told my dad that I had a unique ability that I must have inherited from my ancestors, he was quick to help. In addition to providing all of the information on my grandparents and great grandparents, David allowed her to take hair and cheek swab samples from him. He even gave her one of my mother's brushes, hoping that we could recover her DNA off of it. Sienna now had a small army of genealogists and historians trying to trace my roots back to around 500 AD, over fifty generations. Given the lack of record keeping over the vast majority of that time, the research would take years. Even then the results would be sketchy and incomplete.

While the genealogical DNA testing would give us less conclusive information than their in depth research, it'd be much faster and would help to confirm and guide their work. Supposedly the Autosomal DNA testing that Sienna ordered would tell us the genetic percentages of my ancestry from around the world. My mother and father's DNA would validate my results and provide some clues to help target which side of my family stemmed from Asia. Assuming Kelly's theory was right, and I had roots back to the Far East.

Dangerous Waters

I had to admit, the thought that I might have descended from some ancient warrior clan was kind of cool. I felt like I should be wearing a kimono and have my hair bound up with those chopstick-looking things. I stared down at the broken off handle I was still holding on to. "Crap. I loved that sword."

"Try mine," Raven offered, handing me her Katana Samurai sword. It was about the same length as the one I'd been using, but that was the only similarity. It had a curved, slender, single-edged blade, a decorative circular hand guard and a handle long enough for me to grip with both hands. I rapidly twirled it around my body and executed a couple of attacking maneuvers to get the feel of it. The sword was perfectly balanced. I could see why Raven liked it so much.

"What do ya think?" she wondered.

"This feels great."

She grinned. "I thought you might like it. There are some advantages to fighting two handed, but I wouldn't try to change without practicing first. It's not like the weight of the sword is an issue for us. Oh, and sis," she continued. "That was one of the coolest things I've ever seen."

I leaned forward and pulled her into a hug. "Thanks."

Sandy picked up what was left of my old sword and walked over to stand next to Raven while I made my way back to the center of the room. Sienna wasted no time going on the attack, launching herself behind me to my left. As she brought her sword around toward the small of my back, I turned and pushed it aside, and then swung my sword straight up toward the left side of her neck. She leaned back just as the tip of my sword passed through her reddish blonde hair. Knowing that Ruby was closing in, I wheeled around and executed a downward block, pushing her blade behind me, and then launched myself into a forward roll before springing back to my feet.

Sienna was on me instantly, thrusting her sword toward my stomach. I brought my sword across to meet hers, and then leaped toward Ruby, who was now about fifteen feet behind her. She stumbled backward as she blocked my downward slicing attack, falling onto her back. Sienna could see that Ruby was in trouble and rocketed toward me at astonishing speed, swinging her sword on an upward angle toward my left hip. Knowing the legendary strength of Raven's favorite sword, I wound up and snapped it into Sienna's with force, shearing her blade off just above the handle. I slowly raised my sword to her throat, but decided to give her a pass when I heard Ruby get back to her feet.

Ruby peered at Sienna, unsure of why she was just standing there.

"Just you and me," I said, trying my best to sound intimidating. Ruby just rolled her eyes.

As she circled around to my left, I closely studied her movements. After only a couple steps, I knew I could hit her at will. While she was moving fairly swiftly, she wasn't paying enough attention to how she moved. She was facing sideways with her sword held far out in front of her, leaving her back totally exposed. Even worse, she routinely took her eyes off of me. It appeared that Ruby had picked up some bad habits from years of not having to fight on her own. The next time her focus shifted, I peeked at Sienna. She shook her head knowingly before motioning for me to continue. I realized that feeling sorry for Ruby wouldn't do any good. I had to show her what she was doing wrong. As soon as she looked away again I sprung toward her, bringing my sword down across her back before she even started to react.

"Son of a bitch!" Ruby shrieked. I could hear the shock in her voice.

"Do you want to take this one?" Sienna offered.

I nodded. "Ruby, if you're going to turn away from your opponent, you need to rotate your upper body toward them and keep your sword near your backside. And whatever you do, don't ever take your eyes off of the person you're fighting. A fraction of a second is all it takes for us to cross an entire room."

I was worried about how she'd react to receiving advice from me, but she seemed open to it. She began to circle me again, with her torso turned toward me and her sword on her back hip. "Like this?"

"Perfect! And remember, eyes on me." I picked up my sword and rotated to stay parallel to her. After a couple of seconds I shot behind her and brought my sword down toward her back, but this time she was able to spin around in time and deflect it away.

Her face beamed. "Cool. Thanks, sis!"

"Anytime."

"I think that's probably a good place to stop for today," Sienna announced. "Having the three of you watch me and Brooke fight wouldn't do anything to further your training. Next time we'll see how Brooke and Sandy do together."

"Let's do it, girl," Sandy said, lacing her arm around my waist from behind.

After turning my head to steal a rather salty kiss, I anxiously approached Sienna. I felt like an ass for even considering giving her training advice, but after seeing the flaws in Ruby's technique, I couldn't keep quiet. "I don't mean to be disrespectful, but I think we need to add something back into our training."

"Oh? What do you think is missing?" She seemed a little surprised by my statement but wasn't offended– at least not that I could tell.

"I understand why it's important for us to learn to fight together, but you need to keep working with us individually as well. We may not be lucky enough to have someone with us when we're attacked, and there are some things that are a lot easier to learn one on one."

Sienna gazed into my eyes. "I completely agree, except for who should be doing the teaching."

"No, I didn't– "

She put her finger to my lips to stop me. "Everyone in this family knows that you're already a much stronger fighter than I am. As our most gifted fighter, it's your responsibility to teach the rest of us what you can. Will you do that for me?"

"There's still a ton we can learn from you," I argued. "Especially me. I may have raw physical skills and some kind of gift that lets me learn faster than normal, but you've actually fought vampires. I'd be happy to help you with our training, but I can't do it on my own."

Sienna chewed on her lip for a moment, then gave me a cute little smile. "I'll never get used to your modesty. Nonetheless, you do have a point. I think it'd be best if we worked together."

Chapter Thirty-Five
Paint the Town Red

"So what was your favorite part?" Ruby asked, her focus shifting from the I-90 freeway to me.

"I think you know the answer to that." We'd spent almost two hours meeting with the vice president of research, along with the two top scientists at the New England Aquarium. Given my interest in global warming, they'd spent a lot of time discussing how the various animals that depend on the sea were being impacted by climate change and the steps they were taking to help. For someone not planning to go into the field, it would've probably been pretty dull, but I was captivated the entire time. I couldn't wait to get back to school. "How did you get them to meet with us?"

"We've probably funded about a quarter of their research. All I had to do was make a couple calls."

I ran my fingers through her silky black hair, tucking a chunk of her layered bangs behind her ear. "Thank you. That was so cool. What did you like the most?"

She bit her lip as she thought for a moment. "I'd have to say the harbor seal training– those little guys were so cute."

"And smart," I added. "I couldn't believe some of the tricks they could do."

While Ruby typed the address of the mall into her navigation system I pulled my iPhone out of my purse. I'd heard the familiar de-duh noise earlier but didn't want to interrupt our conversation.

I couldn't keep the corners of my mouth from turning up in a small grin. Britt and I had been texting each other relentlessly since our trip, but this one wasn't from her. "Holy crap. Alex actually texted me."

"How are things down under?" Trying to change lanes so she didn't get stuck behind a semi, Ruby stepped on the gas and her navy blue Escalade shot forward.

After skimming the message to make sure it didn't contain anything too personal, I decided to read it out loud. "Brooke, Stefan and I just returned to Sydney after diving in Baird Bay on the Eyre Peninsula. You would've loved it! There were sea lions and dolphins everywhere. We also dove with great whites in

Dangerous Waters

Port Lincoln. The guide thought we were nuts for going down without a cage. It was quite a rush. How'd your trip home go? I hope it wasn't too eventful, if you know what I mean. Only twelve more days until our first date (not that I'm counting or anything). Write back soon. Miss ya, Alexander."

"What a sweetheart," Ruby said with a smile. "I still remember my first shark dive with Kelly. A tiger shark ripped the leg off his wetsuit after he tried petting it like a dog. I laughed so hard I hyperventilated on the oxygen and had to surface."

"No-way-in-hell. That's all I'm sayin'."

She laughed. "My big, bad ninja warrior sister is scared of a fish?"

"Pretty dumb, huh? I guess those stupid *Jaws* movies have scarred me for life. Vamp or not, sharks still terrify the crap out of me."

"I can't tease ya too much. I slept with my light on for a week after we rented *Friday the 13th* a couple of years ago."

"Ch-ch-ch-ah-ah-ah," I uttered in the most ghoulish voice I could manage, imitating the sound effect that always came before Jason did something horrible.

"Cut that out!" Ruby hollered. I roared with laughter.

"You think that's funny huh? We'll see who's laughing when I trance a great white and chase your ass around on your surfboard."

"You wouldn't!"

Ruby flashed a devilish grin and began to hum the Jaws theme. "Da-da, da-da, da-da-duh-da, da-da-duh-da."

"I give, I give!" I shouted. "Please promise me you won't do that!"

"I don't know, I think Kelly would get a kick out of it." She sounded way too much like she was seriously considering it. When she saw how horrified I was she finally cracked and started to giggle. "I'm just messing with ya. I like sharks way too much to watch you slice one up into sushi."

"Yeah, like that'd happen… I'd croak from a heart attack right after I wet myself."

She smiled and glanced at my face. "You're so gifted that I forget how young you are sometimes."

"You mean that I really am nineteen?" I guess technically I was eighteen, since I was changed before my birthday, but I wasn't going to quibble over a couple weeks.

She nodded. "That's part of it. But also that you've only been a vampire for a month. Right now you still think very human."

"I still feel human. I mean, my body is a lot different, but I still feel like me inside. Will that change?"

"You'll always feel like yourself," she said, giving my hand a squeeze. "What I meant was that your decision-making and thought processes will change as you become more accustomed to your new body. It takes far longer to learn to think like a vampire than it does to learn to move like one."

"I gotcha, like when I went jogging with Sandy for the first time and couldn't make myself jump the river."

"Exactly. When you were human, jumping a river that wide wasn't an option, so your mind balked at what you were attempting to do. Once you forced yourself to do it, you learned how easy it was and your mind adapted. Now I bet you don't hesitate at all when you come to the river."

"Nope, it's my favorite part. I jumped it three times this morning."

Ruby gave me a shrewd smile. "But you still haven't jumped the main river, have you?"

I nervously played with my tights, pulling the nylon away from my skin and letting it snap back into place. "It's so wide– I really don't know if I can jump that far."

She threw me a rather impressive eye roll. "Yes you do. Your mind just refuses to believe it. It seems impossible viewing it through human eyes. Just like jumping the tributary did before you forced yourself to do that."

"I know you're right," I muttered.

"But you still won't believe it until you show yourself you can do it. That's why it takes so long to adjust our thinking after we're changed. It doesn't matter what people tell us. The only way to learn is through experience."

Ruby took the MA-30 exit, heading toward the Natick Mall.

"So what did Kelly say about what happened in Traverse City?"

"Before or after he hung up on me?"

My eyes widened as I looked at her. "So he's mad at me?"

"Not at all," Ruby reassured me. "Kelly and his family are really impressed by what you did. Very few people would risk their lives to save someone else– even someone they love. They're so excited to meet you that they tried to get me to move our trip up to January. I told them we couldn't, since we have Raven and Sandy's birthdays."

I tilted my head. "Then what was Kelly mad about?"

She blew out a breath as she rolled up to a red light. "He was really upset with me for not calling him sooner. At first I didn't understand why, since he couldn't have done anything to help from California anyway. And it wasn't like anyone died or anything. Then he asked me what I'd do if he called up and said 'Oh, by the way, Melanie went to Vegas and got married yesterday.' He didn't have to say anything else. The hardest part of our living arrangement is finding the right balance when it comes to sharing with each other. Sometimes I feel like I'm boring him with inane details about my day, and other times something like this happens, and I realize I didn't share enough with him."

"That must be tough. I've never even tried to date someone long distance before. I go through a little of that with my dad, but I don't share that much day-to-day stuff with him– not like I would with a boyfriend anyway."

"A boyfriend?" Ruby said, raising her eyebrows at me. "So you're not willing to put that title on Alex yet?"

"Not without Raven smothering me with a pillow first," I joked. "I mean, I like him, and we have some chemistry together, but we haven't even gone on a date yet."

"Are you sure there isn't more to it than that?" she prodded.

"What? Sandy? I guess that could be a part of it. She keeps telling me I need to date other people– well, date guys anyway– but it still feels like I'm cheating on her. Not that we've actually went on a date yet, either."

Ruby pulled into a space near the front of the parking garage, and then gazed out the windshield for a few seconds before turning to face me. "That's not what I meant, and you know it. I was hoping you'd really open up to me today."

"I've never talked about my relationship with Sandy with anyone before. You still think I'm holding something back?"

She stared directly into my eyes. "So you don't still have the note from Daniel in your purse."

I angrily reached for my purse. "I can't believe– "

"I didn't snoop," she cut me off, looking a little annoyed by my accusation. "You thought about him constantly while you were human."

"Oh." Except for my brief conversation with Britt, no one had asked me about Daniel since our night in the hotel together. "I just couldn't make myself throw it away. I know I can't ever see him again."

Ruby gently lifted my chin. "But you wish there could."

I nodded. "I love him. I couldn't imagine a more perfect guy for me."

She stroked my hair and kissed me on the forehead. "I wish there was something I could say to help you feel better. Daniel is an incredible guy– we all liked him."

I took a couple of tissues out of my purse and wiped my cheeks. I couldn't say for sure that I'd never feel this way about a guy again, but there was a chance Daniel would be the only one I ever loved. If that was the case, I could live with it, as long as I had Sandy and the rest of my family.

"I didn't mean to make you cry."

I forced a faint smile. "It's okay. It felt good to talk about it."

* * * *

"Don't even think about it," Travis growled, seeing Teresa reach for her door handle. "They're getting out together, and even if they separate inside, we're not attacking her in a mall. We'll have to wait."

"Apparently we're not attacking her anywhere," Teresa snapped back. "She went back to the car on her own at the aquarium, and that gas station they stopped at was abandoned. You're just stalling. I knew you were way too big of a pussy to go through with this."

The muscles in his right arm flexed, curling his fingers into a fist, but he stopped short of backhanding her. There was more than a little truth to her words. While he would never admit it to his crazy ass, unfeeling sister, he was scared. When they'd first moved in with Stefan, he'd challenged Alexander a couple of times– wrestling, shoving– the kind of stuff guys do to feel each other out. It never ended well for him. And while he was confident that Brooke wouldn't put up much of a struggle on her own, if Ruby got involved, all bets were off. The combat training she'd received from Sienna commanded a healthy respect, and he wasn't in any hurry to put it to the test. "Sooner or later they'll separate for more than a couple seconds. Who knows, maybe she'll go somewhere by herself tomorrow. You just need to be patient, sis. This is risky enough without being stupid."

"So that's your big master plan? Bore me into submission? Fuck that." Teresa flung her door open and hopped out before Travis could get a hold of her arm. She was halfway across the parking lot by the time he unclasped his seat belt and took off after her.

* * * *

After entering the lower level of the mall, we angled off to the right and headed down the main corridor toward Neiman Marcus. "So what are you getting Sandy for her birthday?" I asked.

"I'm not sure yet. Any ideas?"

"She doesn't seem to have a necklace that means that much to her, at least not one she wears a lot." I ran my fingers over the dolphin and Celtic cross pendants resting against my chest.

"You're right," Ruby agreed. "Pretty much the only time she wears a necklace is when we're going out, and even then she just picks whatever goes with her outfit the best. What'd you have in mind?"

"I was thinking of something with a separate charm or gem for each of us, maybe our birthstones or something."

"That sounds awesome– I think Sandy would love it. Can I write my name on the tag too?" she teased.

I took her hand and stopped walking. "It can be from you."

Ruby nudged me with her shoulder. "I was just kidding. I'm not going to steal your gift."

"No, really," I insisted. "I already got her a high-end sound system for her Charger. I was also planning on having the picture Britt took of the four of us put into some kind of an engravable 'Sisters' frame. We could shop for the frame and the necklace together."

She grinned. "Sounds like a plan. I think we'll all want one of the pictures though."

"Good call. So where should we start?"

Ruby pointed across the aisle. "There's a Tiffany's up there on the right."

"Perfect!" I was counting on a mall this size having at least one upscale jewelry store.

As we made our way over to the glass case containing necklaces and pendants, the two sales associates gave us scrutinizing, "are they worth the trouble" looks. While we were dressed fairly casually, Ruby's gray-suede Manolo Blahnik booties and my black Prada tote bag quickly caught their attention.

"Can I help you ladies?" the thirty-something blonde asked.

"I hope so," I responded. "We're looking for a very special pendant for our sister's birthday, something with each of our birthstones in it."

She smiled. "How many stones?"

"Four– peridot, alexandrite, aquamarine and citrine." Her assistant grabbed a pen and began to take notes. I briefly listened in on her thoughts to ensure that she had them right.

"May I ask how much you're looking to spend?" the blonde woman asked, trying hard to suppress her enthusiasm.

"Price is not a concern, Catherine," Ruby said, pretending to read her name tag. "But time is. I'm sure this will be a custom order, and our sister's birthday is on Monday."

"I see. Fortunately we have jewelers on staff and an assortment of loose stones to choose from. What type of setting do you have in mind?"

I bent down to study the pendants on the lower shelf. "What would you recommend?"

Catherine unlocked the cabinet and picked up a butterfly pendant off the lower shelf. It had four pear-shaped stones arching outward like wings from a thinner oval body in the center. "I think something like this would look nice."

Ruby turned toward me. "It's a cute design, but a butterfly wouldn't mean anything special to Sandy."

"I agree." I glanced at Catherine. "Do you have anything with an ocean wave or a beach? She's really into surfing."

Catherine disappeared under the counter again and returned holding a circle shaped pendant with a cresting wave inside. "Well, we have this wave pendant, but it's just blue sapphires and some accent diamonds. I'm not sure how we'd incorporate the birthstones into it."

"Now we're getting somewhere," Ruby said, taking it from her. "How big is this?"

"It's an inch in diameter," her assistant chimed in.

"What do ya think?" Ruby wondered. "Could we make something out of this?"

I gnawed on my lower lip as I thought. "I love the shape of the wave, but I think the pendant should be heart shaped. As for the gems, we could use aquamarine for the sky, and then layer the other three in the wave with citrine on the bottom, peridot in the middle and alexandrite on top."

Her face lit up. "I like it! Maybe an inch and a half wide?"

I nodded. "Any bigger and it'd be kinda gaudy."

Ruby peered at Catherine. "So is that doable?"

"Assuming you want single gems for each color we'll have to use much larger gemstones and cut them to fit. You may be charged for any scrap that we can't reuse."

"That's fine," Ruby said. "Do you need any other information from us?"

"Would you prefer silver, white gold or yellow gold for the setting and the necklace?"

Dangerous Waters

"Yellow gold?" I said, making it more of a question.

"That's what I was thinking– twenty-four carat of course."

Catherine reached behind her and took the notepad and the pen from her assistant. "I won't be able to provide you with an estimate for this until I speak with one of our jewelers. Could I get your contact information?"

After providing both of our numbers, Ruby took out her platinum Visa card and handed it to her. "We don't have time to wait for an estimate. I'm sure it'll cost more than two thousand, so go ahead and run that amount now as a deposit. We'll pay the balance when we pick it up. I want you to contact your jewelers immediately and get them working on this. I understand that this is an expedited order. We're willing to pay whatever fees are necessary to ensure such a short turnaround time, but it needs to be available for pick up by the end of the day on Friday."

"I can't promise– "

Ruby cut Catherine off. "If it's completed on time and to our satisfaction, you can add a thirty percent tip onto the bill."

"It will be ready by five p.m. on Friday," she assured us, her mind already calculating her windfall. Catherine was on the phone with the jeweler before we were three steps from the counter. Ruby certainly knew how to motivate people.

Unsure of where to begin searching for the frame, we walked up to the customer service desk just down the aisle in front of Nordstrom's. The sweet, elderly woman behind the counter pointed out where Hallmark and Things Remembered were on the diagram of the second level before launching into a rather lengthy story about her grandson. Only an opportune phone call enabled us to escape and head toward the escalator.

"They should really hire more outgoing people to work in customer service," Ruby said on our way up to the second floor.

"I hear ya! I was about ready to pull up a chair." We both giggled.

When we stepped off the escalator, I noticed that both floors of the mall had identical T shaped layouts, with Macy's and Sears anchoring opposite ends of the top and Neiman Marcus on the bottom. Lord & Taylor was located at the intersection of the T with only a large food court separating it from Sears. Hallmark and Things Remembered were right next to each other, almost directly across from Lord & Taylor. After coming up empty in Hallmark, we continued our search next door.

"What about this one?" Ruby said, holding a shadowbox up in front of her. It was about the size of a laptop, with a white raised wood frame and green ribbons trailing down the left side and across the top. "Sisters" was spelled out on oval pieces of sterling silver woven into the ribbon on the left. Below the opening for the picture was a caption inscribed on another piece of silver that read "Chance made us sisters, love made us friends." The ribbon across the top had another oval shaped silver plate sewn into it that was left blank. The ribbons and metal plates sat on top of the raised surface, casting shadows onto the background.

I couldn't believe how lucky we'd gotten. It was like it had been custom made for our family. "God, that's perfect."

"Sœurs de sang pour l'éternité?" Ruby asked in perfect French, running her finger across the top metal plate.

"Definitely." We picked out four more of them, carefully checking for any flaws.

When we went to pay, the sales clerk explained that they'd have to send the frames out to be engraved, but ensured us that she'd have them ready by noon on Friday. Since we were sure she wouldn't understand French, Ruby asked for a piece of paper and wrote down exactly what the engraving should say. We were both caught off guard when we heard her reading it in her mind. "Sisters in blood for eternity?" she asked.

"It's a sorority thing," I replied calmly. "Each of our new members is being presented with a picture of their fellow sisters at our ceremony Friday night. That's why it's so important that the frames are ready by then."

"I figured it was something like that." She handed my change back to me. "Like I said before, I'll make sure I have them back by noon."

I flashed her a smile. "Thanks, Tammy. I was supposed to do this a week ago— you're a lifesaver."

As soon as we were out of view, Ruby wrapped her arm around my shoulders. "That was pretty smooth, sis. You're getting better at this."

"It's easy to lie when you know what they're thinking."

"True," Ruby agreed. "But knowing what to say wouldn't matter without a convincing delivery. You didn't hesitate at all. Stroking her ego was an especially nice touch."

"Thanks."

She gave me a quick hug and gestured toward the food court. "I'm kinda thirsty. Want to grab something to drink?"

"I need to make a pit stop first." I squeezed my legs together for emphasis.

Ruby snorted. "Nature calls. I'll get ya a Diet Dew and grab us a table."

Dangerous Waters

"Sounds good," I called over my shoulder, already halfway to the restrooms. Once I'd finished, I touched up my makeup and adjusted my black three-quarter sleeve pullover top so that my bra straps weren't showing. It was one of my favorites. It had strips of sheer material going down the sleeves, which made it look pretty sexy for a casual top. It also went well with the multi-color, abstract print skirt I was wearing, which had loop and tie detail going up the left leg. Combined with my black winter tights and black suede pumps, this was one of my cuter outfits.

When I entered the food court, Ruby was still in line. She rolled her eyes impatiently, and then grinned and motioned for me to find us a seat. Shopping during the holidays at one of the most popular malls in Boston had its drawbacks. After circling the table area twice, I walked over to the railing and gazed down at the first floor while I waited for someone to leave.

* * * *

Teresa shook her head in disbelief. "Come on, Trav. Look at her! She's just standing there dead-to-the-world like a fucking zombie! We're never going to get a better chance."

He chuckled, glancing at her. "You mean other than the fact that there are about a million people around, and Ruby's only twenty feet away."

"Just keep her off me for a few seconds— it'll be over before anyone even realizes what they're seeing. Once Brooke's dead, I'll join you back up here by the railing. There's no way Ruby will stick around to fight both of us, not when she's worried about her sister."

Taking his momentary silence as consent, Teresa launched herself off the exposed air vent they'd been perched on, gliding down thirty feet to the floor below. Travis's futile attempt to grab the back of her shirt came up empty, and he swore under his breath as he followed. When he landed, Teresa was inside the food court making a beeline for Brooke.

* * * *

Ruby screamed my name with absolute terror in her voice. Before I could spin around, I felt something smash into my back, causing my head and arms to whip backward as my body broke through the railing and fell toward the floor below. I tried to pull my feet up under me to land, but whoever had hit me was still on my back, riding me toward the ground. It was all I could manage to get my hands out in front of me before we crashed through a crystal sculpture and hit the floor.

As I rolled over, frantically trying to recover from having the wind knocked out of me, I caught my first glimpse of Teresa. She grabbed a fistful of my hair, pulled my head up and smashed my face into the ground. Everything went dark. I lay motionless as she dug her knee into my back and pressed my head against the floor. "You won't be getting your necklace back this time, bitch."

Teresa yanked both chains off my neck and firmly rubbed her hands together, grinding them into dust. She let out a sadistic laugh as she blew the tiny metal fragments into my face. With a great deal of effort, I pulled my arms up underneath my body and pushed hard off the floor, knocking her off of me. I'd just gotten to my knees when I felt my body being hurled through the air, crashing through a glass store front and several racks of clothing before tumbling to a stop near the back of the store.

I tried to get up, but someone had a hold of my shoulders. I could tell by how weakly they were pushing that the person wasn't a vampire. "I'm okay," I mumbled.

"You're in shock, sweetie," a middle-aged woman said, comforting me. "We've already called 911. Just stay still– an ambulance is on the way."

I didn't have time for a debate. Expecting Teresa to pounce on me at any second, I leaped to my feet, knocking the woman to the floor, and removed my shoes and what was left of my skirt. Whether I wanted to fight in a public place in front of hundreds of witnesses was irrelevant– this wasn't going to end until one of us was dead. I anxiously checked for blood and was relieved to see that– in spite of the ass kicking I'd just endured– I'd somehow escaped without injury. It would've been so easy for her to finish me off when I was lying helpless on the floor. Thankfully, she was more worried about destroying my necklace than killing me. Wanting more sure footing for the fight, I spread my big toes out, stuck my nails through my tights and pulled them back over my feet.

When I emerged from the sporting goods store I'd been thrown into, Teresa was slowly crushing the throat of a terrified security guard, his feet dangling in the air beneath him. Bodies were scattered all around her– police officers, security guards and several humans who'd probably just gotten in the way. It was sickening. As soon as she noticed me, she dropped his body to the floor and took a defensive stance.

"I was hoping you weren't dead yet," she said, her words betrayed by the terror on her face.

I gave her a disgusted look. "What the hell are you doing? Trying to get us all killed?"

"Like we have anything to fear from them." She motioned toward the pile of bodies in front of her.

I was tempted to point out what a complete moron she was, but I knew I'd just be wasting my breath. "It didn't have to be this way. I don't blame you guys for trying to feed on me. Alexander is my friend now."

Her eyes filled with rage. "You…don't blame us? Oh, that's rich. We lost everything because of you!"

"You didn't have to– all you had to do was follow Stefan's rules."

She tossed the now lifeless guard like a human missile into the stream of people headed for the exit, his body taking down several of them. "Why should we? Why should any of us? What's the point of having all this power if we never use it? I didn't become immortal so I could live like a fucking coward."

I was through talking. Wherever Ruby had gone, I needed to find her soon so we could get the hell out of here before this place turned into a warzone. After taking a couple deep breaths to settle my mind, I focused entirely on Teresa. She was crouching down in a side stance with her left foot forward, her hands held like a boxer at chin level. While her squatting style gave me a smaller target from the front, it also put her center of gravity far too low.

Spotting my opening, I harnessed all of my strength and darted to her left, getting behind her before she even began to react. As I passed by, I dug the nails of my left hand deep into the left side of her throat, raking them all the way across the back of her right shoulder. She collapsed in a heap, blood spurting several feet into the air from her severed jugular. Teresa pressed her hand against her neck while she flailed around on the floor. After a couple minutes her body went limp.

I had no idea where Ruby had gone, and I wasn't crazy about the idea of leaving my ID in the middle of a gigantic crime scene, so I decided it'd be worth the time to hunt down my bag. I knew that the fastest way to locate it would be to call my phone, but using one of Teresa's victim's phones would eventually lead the police to me. Even if I destroyed the phone afterwards, it wouldn't take much detective work to figure out that they had one and get the records from their cell carrier. An idea came to me as I looked at Teresa's still form. Unless they couldn't identify the body.

I rolled Teresa over and felt the left front pocket of her jeans. *Bingo.* Once

I'd thoroughly checked the rest of her pockets for any form of ID, I stood up and dialed my phone. By the third ring, I'd traced the sound back to the base of the crystal statue we crashed through and pulled my bag out from underneath a large pile of debris. I quickly exchanged phones, selected Ruby's number and waited for the call to connect– busy. Figuring that she was talking with Sienna, I called Raven instead. She picked up on the first ring.

"Where are you?" she asked, sounding more than a little panicked.

"I'm okay, Raven. I'm still in the mall on the first floor. Where's Ruby?"

"She's not with you!?" Her words sent a wave of terror crashing over me. I was speechless. "God damn it! Answer me!"

"N-n-n-o-o," I stuttered, my lower lip trembling. "I haven't seen her since Teresa attacked me. I called her phone, but it's busy."

"She called Sienna about ten minutes ago, before her phone went dead. She was still in the mall. You need to find her, sis. Hurry. We'll be there soon."

Ignoring the dozens of people who were now gawking and pointing at me, I coiled my body and shot back up to the second floor, gracefully landing next to an overturned table. My mouth fell open in shock. Except for three tables in the far corner of the room, the entire seating area had been obliterated. There were pieces of tables, brick, drywall and chairs strewn everywhere, along with several bodies, their cries and moans only adding to my fear.

"Ruby!" I called out after digging through several piles of wreckage. I closed my eyes and took a deep breath, trying to detect her scent– nothing. My own scent was too strong to be able to identify another vampire at a distance, but at least I knew they weren't close by.

After sprinting around the entire second floor without picking up any sign of her, I was starting to panic. Trying to force myself to think clearly, I focused on what I did know. Ruby had been in a fight with a vampire. I didn't have any idea where she was, but it wasn't hard to guess who she'd fought. My heart raced as I took out Teresa's phone, scrolled down to Travis's number and hit the call button. *What if he answers instead of Ruby? What the hell am I going to say?* The noise of people screaming around me was almost deafening, so I was surprised to hear a phone ringing inside Sears on the other side of the food court. I tossed her phone into my bag, still ringing, and sprinted for the door.

Travis's phone was lying in the center aisle not ten feet from the entrance. The smell of fresh blood filled the room, but I could still detect our scent– at least one of them was in here. There was a wide path of destruction through the front half of the store, ending pretty close to where I was picking up our scent. I grabbed his phone and rocketed forward.

In less than a second, I reached the toppled rack of riding lawn mowers that marked the end of the debris and launched myself over them. When I landed, my feet flew up in the air, causing me to come down hard on my back before skidding into a pile of lawn chairs. My entire body was covered in blood, but it wasn't mine.

I scrambled to my feet and rushed to the end of the aisle, emerging in the appliances section. Travis was sitting on the floor about 40 feet away with his back against a dryer, pressing a folded up sweatshirt against his stomach. His white t-shirt was ripped in several places, and his arms were covered in blood. Just as my body started to relax, I caught a glimpse of something off to his right. There, lying on her stomach in a large pool of blood, was my sister. Dead.

"Noooo!" I shrieked. My knees buckled, sending me tumbling to the floor. "Oh God no!"

Hearing me, Travis jumped up, stumbling back awkwardly against the dryer he'd been leaning on. In addition to the large gash across his stomach, he had deep scratches on both arms and down the right side of his face.

"Where's Teresa!" he yelled, wincing from the effort.

It felt like my heart had been torn from my chest. All I wanted to do was curl up in a ball and die, but I knew I had to deal with him first. "She's dead, you fucking bastard."

The disbelief in his eyes soon faded, and he slumped down in despair. I thought he would start crying, but after a few seconds his jaw stiffened and he let out a disturbing chuckle. "I guess that makes us even."

I sprung to my feet and slowly walked toward him, feeling truly evil for the first time in my life. "We're nothing close to even, you worthless piece of shit. You have no idea how much I'm going to make you suffer. I pray that your sorry ass stays conscious long enough for me to enjoy this."

"I'm so scared," he said, mocking me while he inched closer to Ruby's body. "You think a couple of fighting lessons with Sienna is going to make a difference in how this ends? How many years had your sister trained with her– seventy? A lot of good that did." Travis lifted his right foot into her side and rolled her onto her back.

The grisly slash across her throat made me cringe. I turned back to Travis. "Have you looked at yourself lately? Even if I left right now, you'd be dead in a couple hours."

The cockiness instantly left his face– he knew I was right. "Fucking bitch!"

he hollered, kicking Ruby in the side. She moaned.

Before his foot touched the floor I was on top of him, throwing a front kick into his stomach with such force that my foot sunk several inches into his abdomen. His body catapulted backward like he'd been hit by a train, flying through two heavy steel racks of power equipment and a cement wall, where it disappeared out of sight.

When I found him again, he was lying on the floor twitching. One of his legs was missing, and his left arm was broken in several places. His torso was twisted all the way around, his butt facing upward even though he was lying on his back, and most of his intestines trailed out of the gaping hole in his belly. It was gruesome. I bent over and vomited what little fluid was in my stomach, and then raced back to Ruby's side.

"I'm here, Ruby," I said, cradling her in my lap. I pulled off my top and held it against her neck to slow the bleeding.

"I'm so cold," she muttered. Her eyes were still closed, and she was barely breathing.

Suddenly I was holding someone else in my arms. He was a young vampire, maybe sixteen, and had a deep gash across his bare chest. His body was shaking with fear, and blood trickled out of the corner of his mouth. I was back in *her* world again. She was sitting next to a roaring fire in the center of an enormous cave. Moonlight was flowing through a natural skylight in the ceiling, which also vented the smoke from the flames. Three female vampires stood behind the boy, the same ones who'd killed her in one of my previous hallucinations.

"Savitah semuvé," the cat-eyed vampire whispered to him, caressing his cheek. She leaned her head back and opened her mouth. An intense pain ripped through my gums as her canine teeth elongated, protruding at least a half an inch below her raised lip. She bit deep into her wrist and held it over his wound, letting her blood pool and stream down his chest. After only a few seconds, she raised her wrist to her mouth again, reopening the almost completely healed wound. She tilted his head forward and cradled it while he drank. Once he got strong enough, he pressed his teeth into her to keep the blood flowing.

"Carisa," she said in a firm but patient voice. When he kept drinking, she shouted the word again and yanked her arm away. After taking a moment to gather herself, she gazed down at his chest. A layer of skin had already formed over the entire wound. She glanced at the three women behind him, and they stepped forward and hauled him away.

Dangerous Waters

I was back– or at least I thought I was. Ruby was in my arms again, but my gums were still killing me, and I'd lost a good part of my color vision. I slid my right hand out from under her head and touched my mouth. "What the fuck!" I blurted out, feeling my all-too-real fangs.

Ruby peered up at me and let out a blood-muffled gasp.

Tears streamed down my cheeks. "Don't be scared! It's still me."

"Your…eyes."

My eyes? That's what you notice? If seeing them freaked her out more than the daggers sticking out of my mouth, they must be super creepy. Then it hit me. As impossible as it sounded, I'd physically changed to resemble the vampire from my dreams. Maybe that meant I had her abilities as well.

It was a reach. Even if she actually existed and could do the things I'd seen, there was no guarantee that her powers stemmed from a common ancestor. And even if they did, that didn't mean they were still within me, God knows how many thousands of years later. In spite of the odds, I was willing to take the risk. At least I had a chance to save her. I ran my fingers through Ruby's blood-soaked hair. "Do you trust me?"

She nodded her head slightly.

"Savitah semuvé," I repeated. I had no idea what it meant, or if it was even important, but this was a crazy enough idea without me ad-libbing. Knowing that I was in all likelihood committing suicide, I nervously raised my right arm to my mouth. "Please let this work."

Ruby made a futile attempt to stop me, but it was too late. I clamped my jaw shut, burying my teeth into my forearm. My body was so full of adrenaline that I barely felt the pain. When blood entered my mouth I spit it out reflexively, like a swig of rotten milk. It tasted strange– acidic and bitter. Trying my best to copy what I had seen, I held my arm over Ruby's neck until the entire wound was saturated, and then flipped my wrist over to check if the bite had healed. All that was left was a small puncture wound, which was rapidly closing.

I eagerly tore into my flesh again, ripping a five-inch gash below my elbow. "Drink, Ruby. It'll heal you."

Her jaw fell open and soon filled with blood, but when she tried to swallow she choked and spit it up. I pulled her up into a sitting position and tried again. After her third forced swallow, she pressed her lips against my skin and began to feed, stopping every few seconds to move her mouth further up my arm.

I couldn't figure out why until I remembered what the boy had done. "You need to bite into me. It's the only way to keep the blood flowing."

"No," she grumbled. "I won't hurt you."

Hearing the renewed strength in her voice made me smile. "You're not going to hurt me. I've already done it twice– it'll heal in no time." Since the wound had totally closed, I pulled my arm away and bit into it again. Some of the excitement must have worn off, because this time it hurt like hell. "Now please, dig your teeth in and keep it open. I'm not that big on the whole self-mutilation thing."

Realizing that there was no point in fighting me, she sunk her teeth into the fresh wound and resumed feeding. After a couple of minutes I began to feel lightheaded, but I wasn't about to stop her until I knew she was okay.

I leaned forward so I could see her neck. Pale pink skin, like the cheeks of a baby, now covered her entire wound. Within seconds the pigmentation changed, the new skin blending in perfectly with the surrounding tissue. If it wasn't for the somewhat stretched appearance of the more youthful skin, it would've been impossible to tell she'd ever been injured.

"Carisa," I said, recalling the end of the ceremony.

She stopped feeding and gave me a dumbfounded look. "What?"

I burst into laughter. "Never mind. How do you feel?"

"Amazing– I don't think I've ever felt this strong in my life." She inspected her throat with her hand. "What just happened?"

Before I could answer, Raven, Sandy and Sienna stormed in through the back doors. Ruby was still half lying in my lap, and we were both soaked in blood, so it's no wonder they all thought the worst. As soon as she saw us, Sienna crumpled into a pile and burst into tears. We both hurried over to console her.

"It's okay," Ruby said, nestling up to her on the floor. "I'm going to be fine."

"Going to be!" Sienna grabbed Ruby's arms and started checking over every inch of her body. She froze when she reached her neck.

After an awkward silence, Ruby met her gaze. "Brooke healed me."

Judging by their stunned faces, you would've thought she said I snatched a baby out of a stroller for a snack. I quickly covered my mouth in embarrassment, only to find that my elongated canine teeth had retracted back into my gums at some point.

Raven was the first to recover, wrapping her arms around my waist. "You're never going to stop surprising us, are you?" she said, unsure whether she wanted to laugh or cry.

"You think you're surprised? I just turned into some prehistoric Draculette."

Sandy cocked her head to the side. "Prehistoric what? Wait. What happened to your eyes?"

"It's a long story. What do they look like?" I had a pretty good idea what to expect from my visions, but it's not like I'd seen them or anything.

She brushed her lips against mine in a quick, steamy kiss. "I'm not gonna lie to ya, babe. They're kinda freaky."

Babe? That's new. She was so claiming me as her girlfriend, which made me want to do far more than kiss her, but I set that aside and huffed. "Can you be more specific?"

"The irises are a really pale green, and the pupils are, um– "

"Shaped like a cat's," I finished for her. Her expression confirmed my fears.

"I'm sure we all have tons of questions, but now is not the time," Sienna interrupted. "Half the Massachusetts National Guard is probably on their way here by now, not to mention every cop within a hundred miles. There's nothing we can do about what people saw, or the footage that they took, but we can't leave any non-human evidence behind." She paused and glanced around the room. "We need to do what we can to clean this up and get out of here."

I knew it would only be a matter of hours before videos showing some kind of superhuman beings on a mass killing spree spread to every city around the world. Even if we managed to sneak out of the country, we'd be spending the next several decades hiding out in remote villages, completely isolated from society. I wouldn't be able to go to college, get a job or do anything other than rot away with Ruby inside of whatever shack we were living in. By the time we could show our faces again, my father and everyone else I loved would be gone. I had no idea how I was going to prevent that future from becoming a reality, but I only had minutes to do it.

About the Author

CM Michaels grew up in a small town in northern Michigan as the youngest child of a close-knit family of seven. He met his wife, Teresa, while attending Saginaw Valley State University. Together they've provided a loving home for several four-legged "kids," including Sophie, their eternally young at heart, hopelessly spoiled spaniel.

He has always enjoyed writing and still has fond memories of reading his first book, a children's novella, to local grade schools when he was fourteen. CM is currently working on the third book in the *Sisters in Blood* series, along with a fantasy romance called *Kerrigan's Race*.

An avid reader since discovering Jim Kjelgaard novels in early childhood, he has since increased his favorite authors list to include Kelley Armstrong, Peter V. Brett, Richelle Mead, Rachel Caine and Laini Taylor. When he's not writing, CM can be found curled up with a good book, watching movies or hitting the hiking trails with his wife.

CM currently resides in Louisville, Kentucky.

Connect with CM

Official Website:
http://cmmichaels.com/
Facebook:
http://www.facebook.com/UFAuthorCMMichaels
Twitter:
https://twitter.com/UFAuthor

Milton Keynes UK
Ingram Content Group UK Ltd.
UKHW020741180224
437973UK00015B/1611